PAY-PER-HEART

A REVERSE HAREM ROM-COM

GRACE MCGINTY

ALSO BY GRACE MCGINTY

Hell's Redemption Series: The Redeemable/The Unrepentant/The Fallen

Damnation MC Duet: Serendipity/Providence

The Azar Nazemi Trilogy: Smoke and Smolder/Burn and Blaze/Rage and Ruin

Dark River Days Series: Newly Undead In Dark River/Happily Undead In Dark River/Pleasantly Undead in Dark River

Black Mountain Mates: Hunting Isla

Eden Academy Series: The Lost and the Hunted (Prequel)/Heart of the Hounded (Prequel)/ Rebels and Runaways (Book 1)/Sweethearts and Savages (Book 2)

Shadow Bred Series: Manix/Frenzy/Feral/Crave

Stand Alone Novels and Novellas: Bright Lights From A Hurricane/The Last Note/ Inside The Maelstrom Part 1 and 2/Sticks and Stone/Pay-Per-Heart

Omega Lottery: Tryst In The Dark

PAY-PER-HEART

1

BLAKE

I stood in front of the empty lot with two wieners in my hand, like this was amateur night on the Hub. You know which Hub. Don't make me spell it out.

There were large chunks of concrete littering the corner block, with pieces of rebar poking up at odd angles like a spider that suddenly died—the victim of a bigger, meaner spider, probably. I really felt for those eight-legged demons from Hell.

"You know, it's not going to suddenly reappear, no matter how long, or how often, you stare at it. You don't have to come back every day just to check."

I turned to the owner of Heinrich's Wiener, Schnitzel & Pretzel food truck. Heinrich had been here for my first visit to this empty lot, when I'd had nothing but two big suitcases and even bigger dreams. He'd watched on with his sparkling blue eyes as I sank to the ground and cried like a baby, then he'd given me a soft pretzel. It had been hot and salty, just like my tears.

We'd bonded after that, Heinrich and I. At least, I thought we had.

"Are you trying to get rid of me, Hennie?" I asked with a huff, walking back over to the light blue outdoor setting he set out in the shade of his food truck. It was hot, but not like it was in Georgia. In Georgia, I'd always had so much boob sweat, the Georgia Forestry Commission could have declared my under-boob region it's own tributary. I took a bite of one of my wieners and sighed happily. Life had let me down, but these Vienna sausages were consistently the highlight of my day.

Hennie leaned forward on his elbows as I opened my laptop, and I tried not to stare at his bulging fore-arms. He was young, maybe in his late twenties, and he was so fit, it was like he'd never tasted his own pretzels. No one could have unlimited access to such bready goodness and look that hot. "Never, Blake, but stealing my wifi and staring at a building that was demolished over six months ago isn't going to help."

I glared at him, my fake outrage just making him smirk. "I'm not stealing your wifi. I eat two of your pretzels and at least one wiener a day. I'm a paying customer." Granted, that was all I ate every day, since most of my savings were being eaten up by the shitty-ass motel around the corner I'd had to check into while I mulled over my options.

There weren't many, so there wasn't much mulling going on, but I was in denial. This was what happened when I was impulsive. Well, not impulsive.

You see, it started a year ago. I'd dropped out of my Accounting course at college, because I hated it, and started a community college course on Graphic Design and Digital Art. I'd found my passion.

So when I got an invite to the exclusive Baldessari School of Art, for their piloted Digital Art and Design program, I'd jumped on board. I looked at the modern monstrosity of a building on Street View on Maps, had a video conference interview with the Dean of Admissions, paid the exorbitant amount of tuition fees upfront, and packed my bags.

The last month at home with my parents had been filled with fights; it'd been awful. Impulsive I wasn't, but stubborn? That's a whole different question. I was as stubborn as the day was long. So when my parents had said I was foolish to give up my Walmart job to play on my computer all day in LA, I dug in my heels and told them they were wrong.

When my friends had told me I was crazy to break up with Paul, the boyfriend I'd had since senior year, who refused to come to LA with me? I told them that if he couldn't support my dreams, he wasn't the right guy for me.

That decision I stood by. Paul had told me I was being stupid, that I should stay in Dahlonega, Georgia, with him. He'd offered to move in together. Hell, he'd even said we could get engaged. He'd offered everything but support for my dreams.

I wasn't the type of person to settle. Besides, I was twenty-two years old; I wanted to live before I settled down and joined the Real Housewives of Dahlonega.

All completely justifiable, right? I'd done my due diligence.

Except when I arrived at the address on the admission forms, there was nothing. No pretty concrete and glass building. No students. Definitely no Digital Art department. Just rubble and Heinrich's wiener truck.

Cue the tears. And the soft pretzel.

Back to the options. Option one was I returned home and ate humble peach pie in front of everyone. I wasn't overly fond of this option.

Option two was that I tried to find another job in LA and maybe some kind of housing, all before my money ran out. Shouldn't be too hard during a housing crisis, an employment crisis and an absolute abundance of graphic designers, right?

Wrong.

I was determined to succeed despite this obvious first setback, which was why I kept coming back to this spot every day, to stare at the results of my impetuousness and, yeah okay, steal Hennie's wifi.

I glared at the man in question as the lunch rush began, but he just gave me that shiny white smile back. He shouldn't be so handsome *and* sell the world's fluffiest carbs. It was almost unfair.

I flipped open my computer while he was busy, checking out the job guides. Graphic designers turned out hundreds of results, but mostly for people who wanted a decade of experience or wanted me to do it for free as "exposure." Well, guess what? Exposure didn't buy me wieners.

On a whim, I pulled up JeffsMarket, a kind of community noticeboard/platform for crazy people to share their alien abduction experiences. I typed in some general keywords and hoped for the best.

Pulling out my phone, I spent the next hour texting the numbers from job posts. In return, I got three dick pics, one photo of an impressive set of bolt-on boobs, one offer of a glory hole visit, and a legitimate marriage offer from a guy looking for a green card. More disheartening than one guy's shriveled little mole dick, however, was the amount of people replying that the position had already been filled.

I heavy-sighed when Hennie sat down beside me, sliding me a Coke. "The search continues?"

I nodded, chugging the cold soda. "No luck yet."

Hennie leaned back in his chair, making his black tee stretch taut across his chest. "There's always porn.

I've seen the way you handle two Vienna sausages. There's gotta be a market for that."

I punched him in the chesticle. "Real funny, Heinrich. I'll be sure to sign you a copy of *Blake Bangs the Bratwurst*." I clicked on the next advert and perked up.

WANTED: Graphic designer and video editor for a collective of social media influencers. Position is on a commission basis, but does come with room and board for a shared house in Beverly Hills. Please text [login to reveal number].

"HEY, THIS SOUNDS LIKE SOMETHING." I tried to keep the excitement out of my voice as I turned the screen to face Hennie.

He quickly read through the ad, his brows climbing higher and higher, before he laughed. "Blake, that one is definitely porn. Beware the Beverly Hills casting couch, *Liebling*." At my frown, he reached over and squeezed my shoulder. "It'll all work out. You'll see."

He stood, and I sucked in the groan that wanted to escape at the view of his super-toned ass. I was way off dating right now. I'd only just broken up with Paul. I had enough trouble and I certainly didn't need to add "rejected by the only pseudo-friend I had in this angel-forsaken city" to the list.

Still, I scrawled down the number on the ad onto a

napkin, stuffing it in my notebook and continuing my search for a job, then shifted to a search for an apartment. I spent another thirty minutes using Hennie's wifi before I headed over to the public library to read smut and steal their wifi instead.

STUMBLING into my hotel that night, I tried not to wince at the stale smell of old cigarettes and cheetos. Eu De Desperation. The concierge—a grand name for a guy with a greasy comb-over and a beer gut—caught me as I was climbing the battered old stairs to tell me next week's fees were due. I promised him that I'd get it for him tomorrow and tried not to cry.

I ate some ramen out of a mug and watched the only channel on the television, which happened to be Evangelical TV—twenty-four-seven hymns to heal your soul. I sang along, not because I was particularly religious, but damn, some of these songs were as catchy as Chlamydia in Vegas.

Putting my laptop on charge, I tried not to think about how desperate I was. I didn't want to spend another week in this shitty hotel. My mind flicked back to that ad that had seemed like it was the answer to all my problems. Maybe it was legit; maybe it was just a hype house of seventeen-year-olds dancing to twelve-second song snippets without their shirts on. I could do that, right?

It couldn't hurt to at least inquire. Pulling up my notes, I found the number and grabbed my phone, then quickly typed out my enquiry text. What had the world come to that you could text potential employers these days? Anyway, it was succinct and professional, introducing myself and listing my credentials, as well as attaching the link to a couple of examples of my work. Throwing my phone down, I flopped back onto the bed, the only piece of furniture in this shithole.

I was humming along to Jesus being a boat on a river or something like that, while reading a book I'd picked up from the library, when my phone buzzed.

> Probably Porn: Blake, we love your work and would like to meet you tomorrow at ten. Please bring your portfolio and references.

There was an address listed below it, and I used some of my precious phone data to look it up. *Wow.* It was incredible, all glass and modern architecture, and was that a damn pool?

Every disaster-filled scenario of what could happen raced through my mind, my inner voice sounding— unsurprisingly—like my mother. The best worst-case scenario was some kind of sleazy porn producer. I'd pack my pepper spray. The catastrophic worst-case scenario was that they were human traffickers and I'd end up being sold for body parts.

I could always go home, I guess.

I shuddered at the thought of my parents saying "I told you so." Who needed two kidneys anyway?

Me: See you at ten.

Impulsive Blake was back at the wheel, and I was just along for the ride.

2

BLAKE

I t took me over three hours, two buses and one train to get to Beverly Hills by ten. I huffed and puffed from the bus stop to the house. It was a solid twenty-minute walk, hefting my large plastic folio and my backpack with my laptop and everything I didn't want stolen from my hotel room. The LA sun was warm today, and I'd opted for a pair of tailored shorts and a long-sleeved blouse that was now sticking to my arms like it was made of plastic wrap. My shorts had hiked up, and I was getting chub rub on my thighs. My hair was equal parts frizzed and wild.

I was a mess. But at least if it was porn, I looked like such a wreck that they'd probably reject me at the door.

I stood in front of the geometric monstrosity of glass and hard angles. It had probably cost a fortune, but it looked like a kid had designed it all out of white Lego. Shoving my hair off my sticky forehead, I took a deep breath. I had this. I was good at what I did. Talented. Professional. They'd already given me an interview from the sample; all I had to do was bring it home.

I knocked on the door and waited. And waited. It was a big house, so maybe they had to make their way downstairs? I knocked again.

Finally, the door swung open. A guy stood there in a tight black shirt, jeans, and no shoes. Now, I wasn't a foot person. Honestly, they usually kind of looked like pale, ugly sea creatures beached on land. But this dude had nice feet. All tanned and no hairy hobbit toes.

Maybe he was a foot model? Such a thing must exist. Or maybe he was a model-model, because the rest of him was *hot*.

Like call-your-mama-and-tell-her-you've-met-your-future-husband hot.

Like please-bend-me-over-any-available-surface hot.

The guy pasted a pained, yet polite, expression on his face. "Sorry, this is private property. I'm going to have to ask you to leave."

I blinked. "Excuse me?"

"You'll have to leave. We don't accept home visits."

"Listen, buddy, I just dragged my ass three hours to

this ugly house at *your* request. I'm not leaving until I have my interview."

Did I mention the heat made me irritable? Probably should've thought about that before I moved to California.

Now it was the guy's turn to look confused and surprised. "Excuse me?"

Sucking in a calming breath, I pushed down the raging gremlin who wanted to come out. "You organized for me to have an interview at this address at ten. I'm Blake. Blake Wilcox."

The guy slowly blinked. "*You're* Blake Wilcox."

"Yes," I said slowly. He was pretty—it would be unfair of nature to make him smart too. He was just out here, just maintaining the balance, bless his heart.

"You're a woman."

Okay, nice feet, but really, no brains. "Yes?"

He shook his head. "I'm so sorry. There's been a mistake. I'm sorry for wasting your time." The asshole had the audacity to try and shut the front door in my face.

Yeah, over my dead body. I jammed my sneaker in the door. "Um, no. This is not happening." I shoved the door a little, until he was forced to stumble back a step. Remember the heat induced irritability thing? Here we go. "You can't not give me a job just because I'm a woman—that's against the law. I sat on a peak-hour train to be here. Some old dude grabbed my ass repeatedly while we were jammed on like sardines. My boobs are sweaty, and I think I'm getting chub rub on my thighs. There is no way on God's green damn earth that I'm leaving without doing this interview."

Yeah, after that spiel, I doubted they'd even give me the job, but hey, it was the principle of the thing.

The guy just blinked some more. I raised my brows, daring him to disagree. Would I actually report him to… whoever you reported discrimination to? Probably not. But he didn't know that.

Eventually, he shrugged. "Okay. Don't say I didn't warn you." He stood aside and waved a hand, ushering me in. Well, that sounded ominous, but I was committed now. If they buried my body, at least I'd shared my location with my bestie Jeanna. She'd tell the police where to find my dismembered body.

Because apparently, I too was lacking in the brains department, I stepped into the house. The entry foyer was huge, with the main focus some kind of suspension staircase defying gravity as it went up to a landing on the first floor.

"Come on through to the study. The guys are in there."

I mean, I felt like I could overpower one guy, and let's face it, I was just chunky enough that hoisting my unconscious body would be difficult for a man by himself. But two or more guys? Yeah, maybe this hadn't been my best idea.

Still, I followed along like a puppy behind this guy's glorious, well, behind. *Man, what an ass.* Past the stairs, the foyer opened up into an entertainment area with huge glass walls that ran right along the back of the house, drowning the area in light. A long table sat on one side of the room, and a state-of-the-art kitchen on the other. I wasn't much of a cook, but even I knew the appliances were fancy.

He turned left, ushering me through the door into another light-soaked room. Judging by the desk in front of the window and the shelves along the walls filled with books, this was the study. Two guys were lounging on the couch, looking at their phones. Well, until the first guy cleared his throat, and they both looked up.

"Who's the girl?" the first one asked, his voice gruff and low. His dark brown hair was pushed back from his forehead, with tattoos climbing up his arms and his neck, only then to be covered by a well-groomed beard. He was also stupidly handsome, and I had to remind myself they were social media influencers. Being hot was a prerequisite.

The first guy with the nice feet sniffed. "This is Blake."

"Blake has boobs," the third guy stated, kind of obviously, though he had an accent and *boobs* sounded like *bewbs*, which was pretty adorable. He was South American, I thought, judging by the beautiful gold of his skin, those dark brown eyes, and lips so pouty I wanted to take a bite. How did I know all that skin was golden? Because he wasn't wearing a shirt, and he had abs for days and days.

Holy crap.

I cleared my throat and hoped I wasn't blushing. "Yep. I'm Blake. I have boobs. I guess you guys were expecting a man?"

The guy who'd met me at the door had the good grace to blush. "Uh, yeah. No offense, but if we'd known you were female, we wouldn't have even sent you a message." He shook his head. "Let's start over, hey? I'm Harrison. The tattooed guy is Everett, and the one who seems allergic to shirts is Darwin."

Politeness had me automatically replying, "It's nice to meet you." If I was being honest, this was shaping up to be my weirdest interview ever, and I'd once had to do an impromptu break dance to get a job inside a chicken costume.

Everett ran a tattooed hand over his face. It had a black and white rose across it, and oh look, there was also a lion's head and a clock. He had the basic white guy sleeve starter pack.

Apparently, almost being booted to the curb made me bitchy too.

"Blake informs me that we are obligated to interview her because of discrimination laws in the State of California," Harrison told the others as he walked over to the desk chair and flopped down in it. "So, first, let's take a look at your portfolio."

I handed them the mounted examples of my digital art, and they passed them around between themselves. Grabbing my laptop from my backpack, I opened it up to the series of videos that I'd created last night for this moment. Not knowing what platform they used, I'd tried to keep them on trend and edgy. I'd wanted to make it varied, but also showcase my style properly. Placing the laptop on the desk beside Harrison, I made sure everyone could see it, then pressed play.

I cleared my throat, before launching into the spiel I'd created for this moment. "As you can see, I can stylistically match whatever aesthetic you need for your social media package, from bright and fun, to more moody and seductive." The images on the screen shifted to match my words. "I am proficient in a range of photo and video editing tools and suites, and I can also advise on lighting, effects and artistic composition."

I continued on, clicking through the slideshow of images and videos, explaining each one and the elements I'd used to get the overall vibe of each piece. After ten minutes, Darwin's eyes were shiny with interest, and even Everett was leaning forward, elbows on knees, as he listened intently to my pitch.

Finally, I reached the end of the presentation. I looked around at them and shrugged. "My prices are reasonable, especially if accommodation is included in the position. How many accounts would I be doing the artistic direction for?"

Harrison shook himself, like he was in a daze. "Only the three of us."

Three? I could do three.

"And for what platforms?"

Everett gave me a smirk, and something inside me clenched. Probably my ovaries. That shit should be outlawed. "Multiple, including ClockTok, the Gram"— his smirk got wider—"but predominantly ClickHeart."

I choked on my own saliva. "Excuse me?"

Harrison shrugged. "I warned you."

ClickHeart wasn't a social media platform, not really. No, ClickHeart was a subscription service where people paid to see, uh, people get naked. A lot. "You guys do ClickHeart?"

Don't ask their account names. That would be unprofessional.

I swallowed hard, trying to grapple with the remaining threads of my professionalism. "You're fine —uh, I mean that's fine. You're not fine. I mean, you are fine, but that's not what I meant," I babbled, and the professional inside me shriveled up and died. *Fuck me.* Sucking in a deep breath, I nodded. "I mean, I can definitely do video editing for that. Just out of curiosity, how, uh..."

"Naked do we get?" Darwin supplied, his face so

open and sweet. At my nod, he grinned at me. "Very naked."

"Okay. All right. Okay. All right." Fuck, I was stuck in a loop. "No, it's fine. I can work with that. It's okay."

Harrison snorted a laugh. "We'll keep that in mind." He stood, and I knew this shit was almost over. Not only this interview, but my dreams of success outside my small hometown. I couldn't go down without a fight.

"Wait!" I chewed my bottom lip. "I have some questions too." I ignored Everett's raised eyebrows. "Are you guys perverts who prey on women?"

Harrison leaped back, like I'd tried to shock him with a taser. "*What?* No. Of course not. Just because we're on ClickHeart, doesn't mean we are fucking predators. We respect women, obviously."

I nodded. "Good. And rent is included in this job? Like, it's room and board? Are there any other expenses?"

"Uh, no, we get food sent in and Everett cooks—"

"Great. And there'd be contracts and everything would be above board? Are there any benefits? A 401(k)?"

"No. I mean, yes, there'd be an employment contract, and medical, but no 401(k). Look, Blake—"

I was losing them. "Look, I know I wasn't what you expected, but I really need this job and this house. Otherwise, I'll lose *everything* I worked so damn hard for. I'm living out of a hotel that had roaches living in the bathtub, and my only other option is to go home to the people who told me I'd never make it. I promise I won't make it weird, and I mean, we're all mature adults, right? What's a little dick between co-workers? Please don't write me off just because I've got boobs," I joked, winking at Darwin, trying to lighten the mood and erase the desperation that colored my previous embarrassing statement. "I work hard, and I know my skills are exactly what you need. Just think about it, okay?"

With that, I gathered up my laptop and portfolio, and retraced my way back to the front doors. Closing it quietly, I let out the burning oxygen in my lungs.

Fuck. That couldn't have gone worse. I couldn't wait to tell Hennie that he was right. It was porn. But first, I was going to head to the library and look for more jobs, because I was pretty sure I'd never see this part of Beverly Hills ever again.

3

BLAKE

The Evangelical Channel was doing what I liked to call the Christian Golden Oldies. I was humming along to "He's Got The Whole World In His Hand" while reading the smuttiest vampire porn book the Arcadia Branch Library held in its collection. I'd even splurged on an entire bag of Reese's Pieces to make myself feel better.

By six p.m., I'd convinced myself I didn't want that job anyway—who wanted to cobble together video of someone's dick all day? Not me.

But then I got into bed and stared at the mold spot in the center of the larger, sagging water stain, on the worst popcorn plaster ceiling in all of LA, and got sad again. That place had been a mansion. Everything had been so shiny and new, and the granite floors had sparkled so much I knew they had a cleaner. Living there would've felt like I'd made it, even if I really hadn't. It would be better than here, though even here was still better than my childhood bedroom if I had to do the walk of shame back home.

There was no point having a pity party about it, but it was hard to shake. I hadn't even gone and gotten my regular daily pretzel, because I couldn't stand the idea of Hennie thinking I was a failure. Which was dumb, because Hennie was my wiener guy, not my friend.

My phone buzzed, and I sighed. Jeanna had said she'd call to see how my first week of "Art School" was going. I hadn't even told Jeanna it was all a hoax, because no matter how much I loved her, the sad fact was she couldn't keep a secret. If she ran into my mom on Main Street, it would all come tumbling out, whether she wanted it to or not.

Both of my eyebrows raced up my forehead when *Probably Porn* ran across the screen. Calling to tell me I'd been unsuccessful, probably. Could I not answer and hope that it would be like Schrodinger's Job Opportunity?

Sighing, I answered. "Hello?"

"Blake?" a deep voice asked, but I had no idea which one it was. Probably not Darwin, and I'd almost bet not Everett either.

"Speaking."

"Blake, it's Harrison. We, uh, interviewed you today."

I snorted. "I don't think either of us is going to forget that shitshow anytime soon."

He chuckled breathily. "No, probably not."

I sighed heavily, waiting for the inevitable. "Look, I'm sorry for wasti—"

"You got the job."

I gasped so hard, I choked on air. "Excuse me, *what?*"

"You got the job. You can start tomorrow, if you want."

Okay, so I'd just spent the last six hours of my day lamenting the fact I wouldn't get the job, but now that I had it, I was suspicious. Was this a trap? Was I about to be trafficked? Would the cops turn up to find my dismembered corpse and say, "Well, what did she think was going to happen, moving in with a bunch of men she didn't know?"

"That's great. I just have a couple of follow-up questions."

I could feel Harrison's eye roll through the phone. "Of course you do."

He could be snarky all he wanted, but he wasn't a woman. He wouldn't know what it was like to worry about being left alone at a party with your best friend's boyfriend, or walk through a parking lot in the dark, or through the park in broad daylight when a man was walking behind you.

"Do any of you have a criminal record?"

"No. Everett and I grew up in rural Minnesota, and there wasn't anything illegal to do there, other than smoke weed and race cars."

"Have you ever done either of those things?"

"Yes. But I've never been caught."

Well, at least he was honest. "And Darwin?"

"He emigrated here from Ecuador. His dad died when he was twelve, and he was raised by his mother and six sisters. Trust me, he'd rather cut off his own dick than hurt a woman. Hell, pretty sure the women in his family would do it for him."

I hummed a noncommittal sound. "That would be a shame, considering it's his bread and butter." I chewed my lip. Was I really going to do this? "Any drama I should expect? Stalkers? Crazy girlfriends, either past or present?"

"No, ma'am." Yeah, okay, I could hear the Minnesota in him now. "Any other questions?"

I took a deep breath, in and out. "Why? You guys seemed pretty set against it."

He cleared his throat. "A couple of reasons. Most importantly, you were by far the best candidate we've seen so far, and we must have done fifteen or twenty of these fucking interviews. You were professional, and your work was amazing. Secondly, you're right. We are grown damn adults entering a professional relationship. It doesn't need to be weird, and honestly, you were more harmonious than some of the condescending assholes who talked down to us. They clearly thought that showing your dick on the internet must mean you're too stupid to do manual labor or some such shit." There was a slight irritated growl to his voice. It was a nice voice. Not something I should really be thinking about my potential employer.

"Lastly, Darwin kind of went to bat for you. He said he liked your vibe, and if we weren't hiring you because we thought we couldn't keep our hands to ourselves, then we were the problem and not you. Darwin is a feminist. Or loves women. Probably both." There was a long pause. "So, what do you say?"

Remember when I'd said I wasn't spontaneous? I was beginning to think that might've been a lie. "I'm in. I'll start tomorrow." I tried not to think about all the wild what-ifs, and just went with my gut.

My gut said we were going to get some kind of chronic lung disease if we didn't get out of this hotel soon.

"That's great! Grab a rideshare tomorrow morning to haul your stuff over, and we'll pay for it when you get here."

We said our goodbyes, and I hung up. *Holy shit. Holllll-eeeeeyyyy shit.* What had I done?

I climbed out of the bed, pulling my suitcases from the tiny closet, packing so I didn't think. Because if I began to think, my mother's voice would start echoing in my head, and she'd tell me about all the poor girls she'd seen on those after-news exposé shows.

Still, I didn't sleep a wink that night.

BRIGHT AND EARLY, I ordered a rideshare and checked out of the dingy hotel. The front desk receptionist for today had baked beans on his wifebeater, and smelled like sewer rat, but he was really friendly.

"It was nice having you. I hope you enjoyed your stay."

I gave him a tight smile. "I did, thank you. I made a lot of friends." If you included the two mice and forty thousand fleas, that wasn't even a lie. I handed over the key, paid my bill, and tried not to cry at the hole in my savings it made.

Then someone honked from outside the door. "I better go. Thanks again!"

The driver was standing near my bags, looking half-asleep and more than a little disgruntled. He must have been close to sixty, and his hair was messy. "Is this it?"

I clutched my backpack closer. "Yep. My entire life." He hefted them into the back of his newish Honda with a grunt. "Sorry about that. Bodies are heavy, you know?" I joked, and the guy stilled.

"Really?" His eyes narrowed.

"What? No!" The hell was wrong with this guy? I was clearly kidding.

He let out a relieved sigh. "Thank fuck, because I don't think I could have gone through another police investigation." His voice was slightly accented, but I wasn't sure I could detect exactly what accent. I stood outside the car door as he climbed in, looking at me from between the seats expectantly. "Are you getting in or what?"

I got in, despite his words. "Uh, probably don't tell people about transporting bodies," I grumbled, and the guy snorted.

"You joked about it first. Besides, I didn't know she had her husband chopped up in those fucking bags. I thought she just wanted to visit the pier before she flew home."

I held up a hand. "I'm going to stop you there, because that really isn't as reassuring as you think."

Still, I messaged my new employers my ETA.

> In the rideshare. Apparently, this guy accidentally transported body parts for a murderer? Does that make him an accomplice? Just so you know. I should be there in like, 57 minutes exactly. If I don't make it, tell my mom I love her.

There was no response, and I huffed an annoyed breath as the driver pulled into peak-hour morning traffic. *Fuck.* I stared out the window, wondering if this wasn't a sign that it was all a huge mistake. I wasn't cut out for city life. No one had been murdered ever in Dahlonega.

My phone buzzed in my hand. I hadn't had my phone off silent in like five years, because I wasn't a serial killer or your bingo-playing grandma.

> Probably Porn: We've all been there. If you've ever ridden the Red Line downtown, you've probably been an accomplice to transporting a dead body at some point too. We'll see you in another 48 minutes. If it makes you feel better, turn on your location sharing and we'll make sure you don't end up in the Pacific.

I called him some not very polite names under my breath—because how was that reassuring?—but still turned on my location sharing, although it felt a little like jumping from the hot pan into the fire.

Finally, exhaustion, the warmth of the LA sun on my face, and the soulful sounds of Annie Lennox playing from the front seats lulled me to sleep.

Mama never said I was smart. Obviously.

4

BLAKE

"For someone who was worried about being murdered, I don't feel like sleeping in the back of an unknown person's vehicle was the safest move."

The voice startled me awake, and I shot upright. Well, I tried, but the seat belt locked, tugging hard against my neck until I choked a little. I flailed as I fought against the restraints, until a hand leaned over and released the belt.

"Jesus fucking Christ. What have we done?" the voice muttered, and I blinked blearily to look up into the grumpy face of Everett. His whiskey-colored eyes were disapproving, but his lips were twisted into a crooked smirk. "You all good there, Sunshine? You've got a little drool..." He waved a hand at the corner of my mouth, where drool had indeed crusted on the corners.

Eek.

Scrubbing a hand across my face, I crawled from the car. "Sorry. Didn't sleep much last night, and I've always been a bit of a car narcoleptic." I straightened out my tank that had twisted on my body and tugged at the waist of my jeans so no one could see my asscrack. I looked past Everett to Harrison and Darwin, who both looked amused. *Dammit.* This was a great first day impression.

The older driver frowned between me and the guys, then up at the mansion. Then he looked back at the guys. "Is this the right place?" he asked me, despite the fact my bags were already on the driveway.

I nodded. "Yep. These are my new employers."

His frown deepened, and he glared at the guys. "If I see her in my porn videos on the Hub, I am coming back here personally. I was a Soviet soldier in the eighties. I have killed people." Now that he said it, I could hear the staccato rhythm of an Eastern European accent.

The guys all looked at him, wide-eyed. Now I felt kind of bad for thinking he was going to murder me. I gave him a pat on the arm. "Don't worry. It's not porn." *Well, not really.* "I promise I'll be fine."

He didn't seem to believe me, but muttered something under his breath and gave me a stern look. "You're too trusting. Trust no one." With that pessimistic piece of advice, he climbed back in his car and drove away.

I looked over my shoulder at the guys. "What a nice man."

Everett looked at me like I was insane, but grabbed my bags. Harrison was just shaking his head. "You've had me tracking your phone for an hour because you thought he was sketchy."

I shrugged. "Well, obviously I was wrong."

Darwin laughed and clapped his hands. "Welcome. Come on in!" He still wasn't wearing a shirt, which was probably why my Uber Guardian Angel had been so suspicious.

I followed along behind his well-muscled back and tried not to drool. I'd given myself a pep talk last night. No matter how attractive they were, we were just going to be business colleagues and maybe friends; otherwise, this had the potential to get so, so very messy. Like silent-toddler-for-fifteen-minutes level messy.

"Everett will put your things in your room, and I'll give you the grand tour, yes?" Darwin suggested, and Harrison made an amused noise. Darwin was enthusiastic, but with that big, white smile and those dark eyes that seemed to be alight with pure joy, who couldn't get caught up in the moment?

"Sounds wonderful."

In the blink of an eye, Darwin turned into a shirt-less real estate agent. He had a pretty belly button. Was it weird to think of people's belly buttons as attractive?

"So this is the kitchen. It has all the appliances, and if you need help working them, ask Everett."

I raised an eyebrow. "Why Everett?"

"This is his domain. He was a chef," Harrison answered. I thought about the grumpy, tattooed man. Yeah, I could see him barking orders at other chefs. Harrison pointed to a cupboard to the left of me. "We emptied that one out for you. Any foods and things you don't want anyone else to touch goes in there. Just know that Darwin has a sweet tooth and will raid any chocolate he finds *anywhere* that isn't in that cupboard."

Darwin huffed. "It isn't like that. I wouldn't steal it." He folded his arms across his chest, making his fore-arms huge and his chesticles get bulgy. Puffy? Biteable? Whatever.

Harrison shook his head. "No, but you would consider it abandoned and then eat it," he quipped back, and Darwin gave him a guilty smirk.

"True. But enough of that. Come and see the pool."

The tour went on. They showed me the pool, the theater room, and the office once more. The back deck with its cabana loungers basically looked like heaven.

There was a light-filled art studio made from timber on the other side of the pool, and I could see intricate vases drying on a shelf. "Who's the potter?" I asked, and Harrison lifted his chin.

"Me. I sell the vases from my website."

"And do you do it... you know...?"

"Naked? Yeah, I do," he said with a laugh. "You're going to have to get real cool with nakedness real quick, Blake. We've agreed to limit nudity to our work-spaces for your comfort, but Everett works out of the kitchen, and let's face it, your entire job will be to edit the footage."

I frowned. "I know! I'm just adjusting. I promise it won't be a problem."

Darwin chuckled beneath his breath, and Harrison shook his head. "Show her your workroom," he told Darwin, who grinned at me before leading me back into the house, past the office, to another ground floor space. Pushing open the door with a flourish, he ushered me in.

"This is where I do my work. I'll explain about it more later, but please come in."

The room was pretty simple. Noise-canceling panels, a computer monitor on its side attached to the wall, a camera set up and a ring light. All completely legit, if you didn't take into account the wingback chair right in front, the super slutty strip lighting and the sex couch. I knew it was a sex couch because it was S-shaped, and if you looked at it for too long, your brain started conjuring sex positions—it was basically voodoo.

I cleared my throat, keeping my voice as professional as humanly possible. "So, if Harrison's, uh, thing is naked pottery, what's your thing?" I couldn't see any props anywhere, though there was a studded leather trunk in the corner.

In response, Darwin hooked his thumbs in the waistband of his basketball shorts. "Might be easier to just show you."

Then, I swear to all that is holy, he pulled his shorts down to his knees, and sitting between his thighs was the fucking Loch Ness Monster.

"*Holy fuckballs*," I gasped, making someone chuckle, but I couldn't tell who because I was pretty sure Darwin was snake charming me with his giant anaconda. It didn't help that I caught a flash of shiny metal on the underside of his dick. He had piercings. In his dick. I couldn't decide if I was horrified—because that had to have hurt like a bitch—or weirdly turned on. Probably a combination of both.

"Stop feeding his ego," Harrison grumbled. "In answer to your question, he does nothing but stroke his dick and talk dirty, and the viewers love it."

Yeah, I bet they did, because wow. Just. Wow.

"Oh. Okay. Yeah. No, I can see that," I babbled, clearing my throat. "I look forward to seeing you work. Professionally, I mean. Not like I'm going to be creeping. Though I guess it wouldn't be creeping, because I have to see it. Not that—"

"How about we show you to your room upstairs?" Harrison interrupted my word spiral, and I'd never been more grateful for anything in my life. He looked over at Darwin, raising an eyebrow. "Put it away before you fry the brain of our new *employee* in the first hour."

I wasn't sure if the emphasis was for me or Darwin, but it was a timely reminder anyway. "Sure, lead on." I followed him out, then up the grand stairs in the middle of the foyer. My face felt like it was on fire, and I was acutely aware of Darwin climbing the stairs behind me.

At the top of the stairs, Harrison took over the tour duties. "Left side belongs to me and Everett. This one's mine; Everett's is the second door up there. We share an ensuite." He pointed to the right of the landing. "That's Darwin's master bedroom there, and up in the corner is the guest room, which is now your room." He led me up to the door, though the hallway had opened up into a small sitting area filled with plants and comfy couches. I could see myself sitting there, reading in the morning sun. The space led out onto a balcony, and I sighed. So pretty.

Harrison continued. "Your doors all have locks, and that window over there is actually a sliding door which will give you a private entrance onto the balcony if you need it. There's a small ensuite over there, and only built-in closets unfortunately."

Good lord. He was apologizing for built-in closets? I'd had the same hand-me-down, ratty set of drawers in my room back home since I was born. "That'll be fine. I don't have much stuff."

We all turned to look at the two suitcases sitting in the middle of the floor. Everett was nowhere to be seen, but I was okay with that. The room wasn't huge, and having Darwin and Harrison in here was overwhelming enough.

Darwin gave me a broad grin, and I flushed. Every time I looked at him, all I saw was his monster dick. Harrison just rolled his eyes. "We'll let you get settled in. When you're ready, come down and we'll have a team meeting and sign contracts. Everett's cooking." The corner of his lip twitched with what could have been a smile, and his laughing eyes confirmed it. "With his clothes on. So don't worry about finding something to eat for lunch."

I just nodded, and continued nodding like one of those bobble-head statues of Arnold Schwarzenegger that my grandpa used to collect. Finally, they left, and I collapsed facedown onto the softest bed I'd ever felt. It smelled clean and fresh, and nothing bit me on the cheeks while I was buried up to my ears in comforters.

This bed was worth the embarrassment. But first, I had to Google what all those little piercings were on the underside of Darwin's cock.

5

BLAKE

I spent an inordinate amount of time putting away stuff in my tiny little bathroom. Someone had stocked a little basket under the sink with softly scented soap, shampoo and conditioner that was way out of my price range, makeup wipes, plus pads and tampons, which shocked the shit out of me. I doubted they'd had time to do it for me, but it said something about the guys that they'd had these things in the bathroom cabinet for guests. It said something about the type of men they were.

Considerate man-whores.

Seeing all my things lined up in this beautiful bathroom made me feel like I had my shit together, rather than the fact I'd just moved in with a bunch of strangers—who I was avoiding, even though it was probably better to get this over and done with as soon as possible.

Splashing water on my face, then tying my hair back up on the top of my head in a messy bun, I walked out of the ensuite. I'd put everything away in the "unfortunate" built-in closet, still barely taking up any space at all, and now the room looked... well, not mine, but somewhere I'd like to make mine, even temporarily.

Stepping out, I straightened my shoulders and sucked in a fortifying breath. I could do this. I was a mature adult. Retracing my steps back to the staircase, I followed the voices to the back deck. The smell down here was amazing.

I realized Everett was grilling out the back, his Henley pushed up his arms. Man, was it just me, or was that like the sluttiest thing a man could do? Honestly, forearm porn was what this guy should be doing. They were strong and tattooed, and should come with a warning: will cause monsoon season in the lower tropic region.

"You're here!" Darwin said, his smile wide, his nipples out. I never thought I'd be so puritanical about a man's naked chest, but here we were. He came over, hugging me quickly but tightly. "Would you like a drink? We have soda or beer." Before I could answer, he pushed a bottle of Coke into my hand.

I gave him a tight smile, stepping away. "Something smells amazing."

Darwin beamed. "Everett used his special rub. He's very good with his meat."

I choked on my Coke. "I'm sure he is."

Everett just rolled his eyes. "It'll be ten more minutes."

I wandered over to where Harrison was sitting on one of the sun recliners, his iPad propped on his thighs. Plonking down onto the recliner beside him, I looked over at what he was working on. He was cursing beneath his breath as he moved his finger along the contrast controller on a still photograph. It went way too dark, obscuring the details of the photo.

"May I?"

Harrison looked over at me, his eyebrows raised. "Sure. It's what we're paying you for."

I snorted. "Not yet, you haven't." I opened the controls of the basic photo manipulation software—nowhere near as advanced as mine, but it would do for this. Quickly getting a handle on the elements, I highlighted the photo of his hands on a long column of clay. I shifted the focus, so the strong muscles of his fingers wrapped around the clay were the focal point, but if you looked past them, you could see the intense way he was looking down at you, his blue-green eyes shadowed until they were just molten darkness that promised pleasure.

It was a hot photo, and I wondered who took it. "Do you guys have a photographer? This is great."

"Darwin's our photographer, but we all take turns behind the camera," he said, watching me intently. "I'm usually the videographer for Everett's segments, because otherwise, they'd take forever to film."

"Who films Darwin's?"

His face curled into a knowing smirk. "Why? Are you offering?" Before I could spit out some kind of lame denial, he shook his head. "Darwin's clips, as well as mine, are mostly stationary. The tripod works."

Nodding, I put the finishing touches on the photograph. Happy, I hit the Save button and passed the iPad back. He took it and looked it over, zooming in on certain parts and shaking his head slowly. "That's insane. You're really talented."

I waved a hand, like all my training and study meant nothing. "It's pretty simple." It wasn't. "Just takes a little study."

Harrison made an unconvinced noise in the back of his throat. "I think I'll just leave it to you. How about we go over the contract while we eat?" He uploaded the picture to his socials and to his ClickHeart account as I watched.

We all walked over to a large glass table set out on the deck. There was a huge Cobb salad, along with more meat than a dinosaur would eat in a day.

Someone had put on music, and it played softly from speakers attached to the eaves of the house.

"This place is beautiful. Did you have to sell your kidney to get them to rent it to three bachelors in their twenties?"

Darwin shook his head. "No, we bought it. We each own a third."

This place was worth like twelve mil on a good day. *Holy shit.* "So the ClickHeart business must pay well?" I choked out. "Maybe I'm in the wrong profession?"

Everett snorted. "Maybe you are." Despite his words, his tone definitely told me not to quit my day job. Rude. I mean, I was no raging beauty; I got that. My curves were a little too soft to be considered trophy beautiful. My thighs were a little too thick, my face a little too asymmetrical. I was no beauty standard, but I'd had my fair share of admirers, thank you very much.

Darwin, this sweet man, jumped to my defense. "She's very beautiful. She would make good money on the socials. Soft. Womanly. Men want that too, not just the generic model-like pornstars."

Everett pointed his fork at the other man. "No one said *our employee* wasn't attractive. Don't be so fucking sensitive."

Well, this conversation had already spiraled out of control. I raised my hands. "No need to worry; it's not a career path I'm interested in anytime soon." I took a sip of my Coke, so I could hide my embarrassment behind the glass.

Darwin shrugged. "Well, if you ever change your mind, I'm looking for someone to peg me."

Soda burst from my mouth like a fountain. All over my chest, the food in front of me, and a little on Everett's arm. Both Harrison and Everett glared at their friend. He just shrugged, his tiny smirk telling me he knew exactly what he was doing.

"For fuck's sake, Darwin," Everett growled, wiping his arm across his chest to remove my spit.

I was speechless. I could hear Morgan Freeman's voice in my head muttering, *"The woman was too stunned to speak."*

Harrison sighed, going back to his food, despite the fact that there was definitely some of my spit now in his salad. "This might be a good time to go over the conduct clause in the employment contract." He grabbed a manilla folder from where it rested on the lounger behind him. "These are the terms of your employment, including remuneration and rental agreement, that kind of thing. Most of it is pretty standard, except the sexual harassment clause." He glared at Darwin. "If at any point you feel harassed and have proof, we'll pay you out the remainder of your contracted salary for the year.

"If you enter into a romantic relationship with any members of the house, you both have to sign a rela-

tionship agreement, and you'll waive the sexual harassment clause in regards to that person. The relationship
contract gives any of us the right to terminate your
employment immediately, with three months' severance pay. All these amounts are listed in the contract."
He cleared his throat. "However, the harassment clause
goes both ways. If you make unwanted advances on
any of us—"

"Emphasis on *unwanted,*" Darwin said with a wink.

"For fuck's sake, Darwin, stop flirting for five
minutes during the damn sexual harassment speech,
could you?" Harrison huffed, shaking his head. "As I
was saying, if you make any unwanted advances on
the three of us, you will be terminated immediately
with a severance pay of two weeks. How's that all
sound?"

"That all sounds fine." I had a feeling that if I were
a more sensitive person, Darwin would have crossed
the line already. He was flirtatious, but I found it more
amusing than confronting.

Harrison nodded, handing me my contract to read.
And I did read it. I wasn't about to get screwed, just
because I didn't take the time to look through the fine
print. The guys were talking softly in the background
as I went over everything. The amount of money I was
getting paid almost made my eyes fall out of my head.
Honestly, I almost shook as I signed on the dotted line.
With that kind of money, I really didn't care if the fine

print said I had to give them my kidney and my firstborn.

I signed two copies of the agreement, and Harrison put one back in the manilla envelope for me. "No going back now," Everett murmured, his voice dark and ominous, but there was a slight uptick to his lips that made me think he was teasing me.

Turning to the cooling food in front of me, I took a bite and moaned. *Oh my god.* It was divine. The steaks were perfectly done, seasoned to complement the meat rather than overwhelm it. The salad dressing was a revelation, and the grilled corn was juicy, with some kind of spice mixture on the cobs to make them sweet, salty and a little hot. There were little wedges of lime beside them too, so I squeezed one over the top and tried again.

Harrison laughed. "If you keep making noises like that, Everett's going to use you as a backing track to his content."

I flushed pink, but continued to eat. This might be unconventional, but it felt like the start of something good. I was going to ignore everything else but the job. I wasn't going to focus on my failures that had led me here, or my attraction to the guys, or even my embarrassment. I was going to be the best damn designer they'd ever had. In twelve months, I'd have enough money to have options.

Life was looking up.

6

EVERETT

We watched Blake move back into the house with a grin, complimenting me on my food once more with such open-faced honesty that I almost blushed. Me. Blush. For real.

I picked up my beer, downing the rest of the bottle in one go. "Holy shit. Did we just hire Pollyanna to do porn? If I wasn't going to Hell before, I definitely am now."

Darwin laughed, but he was watching her go with literal heart eyes. Harrison was going to have to watch him, or he'd be breaking the harassment clause on the first day. More so than he already had.

"Would you seriously let her peg you?" Harrison asked, his lips pulled tight in a grin that I knew as well as my own.

"Yeah, for sure. She looks like she'd be gentle, right?"

I shook my head, picking at the remainder of the salad with my fingers. My parents had been frugal as hell, and wasted food was a sin. I didn't ascribe to the sinning shit, despite my Hell comment before, but some things were hard to unlearn. I hadn't managed to shake some of the more toxic opinions my parents had indoctrinated me with, so the chances that I'd start leaving food about was pretty slim.

"I don't know, D. It's the sweet ones you have to watch. She might have your balls in a vice and a whip across your thighs before you can say 'Yes, Mistress.'"

Darwin just groaned happily at Harrison's teasing. "Stop. I have to do a video this afternoon, and I don't want to have to rub my dick raw to get a cumshot."

This was the type of dinner conversation you had when you were best friends with people who peddled sexuality for a living. I didn't regret my job, not in the least. I loved that I could combine my passion for cooking and my desires all in one extremely lucrative career.

Except now, that sweet little thing was going to be editing those videos, and I still wasn't sure how I felt about that. She'd be there, watching me get my dick out, probably blushing the whole time. My dick got hard at the very idea of her making those soft little noises she'd made over my food, but instead of corn, it was when she was staring at my cock, imagining me fucking her.

This was why I'd voted against hiring her. She was too sweet and too pretty for this shit to work. When I'd said that, Darwin had cut me down to size, making me feel like a complete piece of shit for not hiring the perfect candidate, just because I didn't think I could control myself.

I'd met Darwin's sisters, and I knew that being the youngest child in a family full of girls had made him a bit of a feminist. I mean, he still swung his dick around on the internet, but at least he was an equal opportunity employer.

Harrison raised both hands. "I know better than to get in the way of a good cumshot."

Darwin sipped his beer with a smirk. "I bet you do." He waggled his eyebrows at us, and I flipped him the bird.

I shrugged. "I give her a month before it's all too much and she leaves. Or Darwin fucks her and she leaves. Or she falls in love with Harrison, and she *has* to leave."

Harrison bumped his knee against mine. "Stop it. I'm giving her the benefit of the doubt, and so should you. This might surprise you, but we aren't fucking irresistable."

"I, for one, find your whole personality grating," Darwin added, but his eyes were full of mirth.

"Asshole. For that, I hope she pegs you with a pineapple."

We all winced at the image. "Too far, man. Too far."

"Whatever happens, she's got pretty good skills, and we should take advantage of that before you guys fuck it up." Harrison stood, gathering up the plates. Darwin helped, but neither of them actually ventured into the kitchen. That was my domain.

Ever since I could remember, I'd loved to cook. First, as an escape from my house, when I'd go over to my grandmother's and she would teach me to cook the French meals from her childhood. Later, when I was a teenager and she'd died, I'd get up in the middle of the night and bake when I couldn't sleep. Quietly, so I didn't wake my parents and have to undertake another lecture from my father about it being a woman's job to cook.

He wasn't a culinary savant, by any stretch of the imagination. His idea of fine dining was when his steak had gravy instead of ketchup. But my mom had won the battle, probably because she liked to eat the foods my grandmother had taught me, and so I was allowed to continue cooking late at night.

When Harrison and I had moved away from that small-ass town to a city that had some of the best chefs in the world, my passion had only grown. I'd worked in some amazing kitchens, but when I found myself working more often than I was living, not even the fact that it was my passion could stop me from leaving.

ClickHeart wasn't easy money, like people thought, but it was easier than construction work like Harrison had been doing, and easier than ten-hour shifts in the kitchen, surviving off of triple espresso and narcotics.

Harrison had dragged me out of that lifestyle kicking and screaming, but he had my thanks and devotion for doing it. Actually, Darwin should probably go on my list of thanks too, because without him, neither Harrison or I would've ever gotten to this point. We would've just continued to struggle instead.

I packaged up the leftovers, putting them in their allocated spot in the fridge. Darwin often teased me that leftovers didn't need a labeled position in the fridge, and he was probably right. But it made me feel better, soothed something inside of me. This area was my domain. It was as orderly as my brain was chaotic.

I was sitting in my tiny office nook in the kitchen, working on creating an easy recipe for next week's content when the girl snuck into the kitchen. I watched quietly as she opened and closed cupboards before startling when she saw me in my nook.

"Oh, I'm sorry. I didn't know you were working." She looked guilty, but then she smiled, and it lit up her entire face.

"My ass is covered, so I'm not *working* exactly. Just planning. Is there something I can do for you?" If she said she wanted to cook in my kitchen, I'd probably lose it.

She flushed a pretty shade of pink. I wondered if her other cheeks would turn that color if I spank– *Fuck. No.* Bad thoughts, especially after Harrison's little speech.

"Uh, I was just wondering if there were any snacks? I work better when I'm chewing, like my hindbrain is distracted from second-guessing everything I've ever done with my life while I'm chewing, and all that's left is the artistic side of my brain." She winced. "That sounds crazy, doesn't it?"

Completely. But given that I needed to put leftovers in a particular spot, who was I to judge?

"Yep. Completely insane. What do you need to snack on?" I asked, uncurling from the stool in case she tried to make a run for the kitchen and messed shit up.

She shook her head, backing away. "Don't worry. I'll grab something when I'm at the grocery store next."

"Stop!" She froze instinctively, and a part of me preened that she'd followed my command. "I asked you a question, Sunshine. What do you need?"

"Uh, cookies?"

My lips curled into an incredulous smirk. "Cookies? Your brain food is cookies?"

She fisted her hands on her hips. "They're the perfect snack food for working, thank you. You can hold it easily in one hand without getting dirty, or between my teeth if I need to use two hands—"

I'm sure she isn't trying to make this explanation sound filthy.

"And it's big enough that I won't accidentally choke if I swallow it wrong."

Okay, maybe she is.

I held up both hands before she got to the part where the cookie would slap her ass and make her call it Daddy. "All right, I'm convinced. I think Harrison has some thin mints around here somewhere..." I searched the butler's pantry for the jar that held what she needed. Finding it on the top shelf, I walked back to find her leaning on the bench as she stared down at her phone, her breasts pressed together, giving her some serious cleavage. I would've thought she'd done it on purpose if she didn't jackknife upright as soon as I re-entered the room.

When I handed her the jar of cookies, she looked like I'd just handed her the finest confection from the world's most masterful pastry chefs. "A whole jar! It's been so long since I've had Girl Scout cookies. I swear, if this was in my house, it wouldn't have survived a week, let alone long enough that you have to search for it." She opened it and held it out toward me. "Do you want one? I only need one." She grabbed one, frowning. "Okay, maybe two."

She tried to hand the jar back, but I shook my

head. "Take them all. Put it beside your desk—you might need it for sustenance."

She grinned again, tucking it under her arm. "Thanks, Everett. I better get to work. You guys aren't paying me to stand around and eat cookies." She gave me a little wave and disappeared further into the house.

I went back to my nook, searching my cookbooks for something that might work. When I stopped on snickerdoodles, then added a caramelized white chocolate stuffing, I told myself it was because oozing white stuff was what my viewers would want, and that the decision had absolutely nothing to do with our new graphic designer.

What a fucking liar.

7

BLAKE

I spent the next couple of days eating the cookies that kept randomly appearing in the glass jar I'd grabbed from the kitchen, and getting to know the guys' individual aesthetics, preferences and their content.

That last part was awkward. I'd signed up to Click-Heart and subscribed to all three of their accounts. There was something supremely illicit about watching Harrison sitting at a pottery wheel, completely naked, his hands smoothing up and down whatever piece he was trying to make with the clay. That piece was the only thing stopping you from seeing his cock, but every now and then, he'd shift to get something and you'd see his dick in all its glory.

I found myself riveted to my seat, watching him create, holding my breath to see a flash of penis. Jesus

H. Christevelt, I was so screwed. But I had to admit, it was compelling viewing. On top of that, he was talented as hell as a potter. His creations were gorgeous, and they were dotted around the house. I was fairly sure I'd eaten my breakfast cereal out of one of his pieces this morning.

Everett's content was equally compelling, yet sexy in an entirely different way. Honestly, he barely spoke in his clips. But when he did, it was to give clear, concise directions so you just *knew*, deep down, that he was like that in the bedroom—telling you what he wanted, what he wanted for you, praising you when you did a good job. His entire body was gorgeous, barely hidden by a tiny little apron, because "The only hot liquids I want around my cock are your juices as you're coming on it." Direct quote. When he'd growled that into the camera, I thought I was going to combust.

But both Everett and Harrison were tame in comparison to Darwin. I hadn't grown the lady balls to look at his content yet. I knew that it would be difficult to meet his eye afterwards without flushing the color of a tomato every single time.

I couldn't put it off for much longer, though, as I knocked on the door to his office.

"Come in," he called, the soft sound of his voice almost musical. Don't get me wrong, he definitely had that West Coast accent, but you could still hear traces of his Ecuadorian upbringing in his words, probably picked up from his relatives.

I pushed open the door to see Darwin in his wing-back chair, a tablet in his hand. He was wearing low-slung gray sweats, his smooth, golden skin looking gorgeous. He was temptation in a hot, six-foot package.

His smile was wide when he looked up and saw me. "Blake! How are you settling in?"

I was already flushing. *Dammit.* "Uh, good. Thank you. I just want to talk to you about your aesthetic."

He raised both eyebrows and pointed to the couch. "Take a seat, if you'd like?"

The couch sat in front of a ring light, but there was no camera attached to the tripod. I sat down hesitantly on the edge, wondering what exactly he did on this couch. And how much bodily fluid might have been wiped from the soft black leather. Purple LEDs cast an ethereal glow over the room.

"I just wanted to talk to you about your aesthetic before I started messing with your videos," I said, trying to keep my tone modulated and professional, and not let on that I could see the long line of his dick through his sweats.

"You've looked at my feed, yes?"

I flushed again. "Uh, not yet. Thought I might just have a conversation with you first, in case you were looking to update, or you know, something."

He shrugged, leaning back a bit, making his abs

ripple. "Well, I know a lot of creators with similar ClickHeart subscriber bases to me have turned to inviting other female creators in to collaborate—"

"By collaboration, you mean..."

"Have sex," he said, his tone amused. "I'm hesitant to take that step just yet, as I'm not sure that it's the right move for this account."

The idea of a beautiful woman riding this equally beautiful man was hot... but also made a stab of jealousy spear my gut, because I was stupid. My vagina, Virginia, wanted to volunteer as tribute. She'd seen this sexy man naked, and was still having wet dreams about her male counterpart. Let's call him Peter. Peter the Python Penis.

"Maybe wait until you feel like it's something your audience wants." *Or until I leave and therefore won't have to feel completely physically inadequate as I edit the video of live porn.* Because while I'd been forced to study the guys' ClickHeart accounts, I'd also scrolled through the app, and some of the women were gorgeous.

When God had been handing out beauty, I'd been finger-painting with boogers at the back of the line.

Darwin hummed his agreement. "Perhaps. Or maybe a regular guest star, but masked. Like Darth Vader. Or Mickey Mouse."

I blinked. "You want to be pegged by Mickey Mouse?"

He threw back his head and laughed. "It would be a story to tell at parties, wouldn't it?"

Well, I couldn't deny that. If someone told me about the time they were taken to the happiest place on earth by a giant mouse over a glass of cheap white wine, I'd be riveted.

"Fair point." I cleared my throat. "Until then, you want your content to continue to be color-coded?" His color-coding trick was actually genius, and I'd worked most of the system out from scrolling through the feed without ever pressing play.

Purple was for those with a praise kink.

Red was for those who were searching for a little degradation.

Blue was for something a little more personal. A bit more of a close confidant and less of a porn scenario. Sometimes they were Q&A's, like, you know that old show Ricki Lake? Except Ricki Lake was a twenty-five year old Ecuadorian guy with a ten-inch dick.

He nodded, his face taking on a more serious, business-like expression. "I think so. Though if you want to make it look more professional while keeping with the color themes, I'm okay with that too. If I was more creative, I wouldn't be doing this." He waved a hand around the room, and I frowned. It was the first moment of self-deprecation I'd heard from any of them since I'd been here, and I wasn't sure I liked it coming from the normally jovial man in front of me.

"You make thousands of people happy. That's a talent."

"Millions."

I blinked. "What?"

"I make millions of people happy. I think my last subscriber count was 2.3 million."

I couldn't help the high-pitched bat-whistle gasp I made. "Holy freaking *shit*, Darwin. You're a bonafide celebrity." His grin was back, and that made me happy —probably an inappropriate amount of happy, given our employment situation.

"Well, my dick is a celebrity, at least. Me, not so much."

I didn't think that was true at all. There was something magnetic about Darwin, which was why he didn't need a gimmick like Harrison or Everett. He had the force of his sunshine personality, and that was enough.

Still, I pulled out my iPad and showed him my thoughts. "I thought we could pull some stills, carefully curated to not show so much that it makes the Gram censors upset, but enough to tantalize and draw people across to your ClickHeart account."

Darwin's eyes never strayed from my face the whole time I spoke, like he was absorbing my suggestions and really listening to what I had to say. It was a heady experience, being the sole focus of this man.

After an hour, he had to prepare for a live video,

and I excused myself. He gave me a smile, squeezing my forearm. "We made the right decision, hiring you. I know the other two had their misgivings, but I had a good feeling. I knew you could do great things if we just gave you the opportunity."

I swallowed a lump in my throat. When was the last time anyone—my parents, my friends, my ex-boyfriend, even—had believed in me blindly like that, without disclaimers and caveats? I couldn't even remember. So I gave him a watery smile. "Thanks, Darwin."

His alarm went off, giving him a ten-minute reminder that it was almost time to go live. "Anytime, *Muñeca.*"

I didn't stop to ask what that meant, but it still made me happy. So when his livestream alert pinged on my phone notifications, I almost joined. My thumb hovered over the notification for longer than I'd like to admit, but in the end, I swiped it away.

I had to look at his content; I knew that. But I didn't want to see him flirting with other people in his comments just yet. So instead, I walked into the nook under the stairs that was currently serving as my office and opened up his profile on my computer.

Putting my headphones on, I clicked on a random purple video. I told myself it was just the first one that caught my attention, but really, I wasn't sure I could start by watching the sweet man I saw in there look down the lens of his camera and call me a dirty little slut.

I mean, maybe the second or third video, though.

Sucking in a deep breath, I pressed play. "Hello, *Amorcito*," his voice purred at me, and goosebumps of pleasure spread across my skin. "Have you been a good girl today?"

My breath stuttered in my chest. I was so screwed.

8

BLAKE

Call me Cleopatra, because apparently I was the Queen of Denial. For instance, I was going to pretend that I hadn't gone up to bed last night and touched myself in the shower, imagining Darwin putting me on my knees and fucking my face while whispering encouragement. Telling me how good I took his cock. Telling me that I was so beautiful on my knees.

I came so hard, yet still felt unfulfilled. So I did what any other sane, red-blooded woman would do. I blew a chunk of my first paycheck on the best vibrator money could buy, with two whisper-quiet motors for added pleasure. There were three things you shouldn't skimp on in life: a new bed, hair appointments, and things that will give you countless years of orgasms. Pretty sure Nostradamus said that.

The following morning, everyone was up early—a meeting with their accountant, apparently. The real type, not the one who was a front for the fact that you're a sex worker.

Before they left, I wanted to give them a quick rundown on my design ideas, especially for stills. I'd taken some of the photos the guys had given me in the shared files, but also some frame shots from the different clips on their feed.

A posed photo was one thing, but Darwin with his head tipped back, his plump lips parted and his shoulders slightly curled as he came was something that couldn't be recreated with a camera and a tripod. It needed to be done in the moment and caught frame by frame. So I'd cropped that still with a dry throat, so you could only see from his elbows up, given it some of our agreed lighting and aesthetic, and printed it out for them to see.

Everett was the only one in the kitchen, dressed in a button-down shirt and perfectly pressed pants, and I swear, you wouldn't know he was essentially a porn star. Instead, he looked like a sexually repressed office worker, but somehow still so fucking delicious, it was distracting.

He handed me a coffee from his special—and apparently insanely expensive—machine. The blend was perfect, of course. I was beginning to realize that when it came to food and coffee, Everett was a bit of a perfectionist. One day, when I grew the lady balls, I'd ask why he hadn't remained a chef and had instead turned to getting naked and doing naughty things with strawberries.

I took a sip and moaned. I'd never be able to go back to instant now. "You've ruined me."

The corners of Everett's lips curled. "Have I?" He purred the words, and heat pooled low in my belly. I was going to have to find Jesus or something, because I wasn't sure I could cope with all the sexual mojo flying around this place. At least my parents would be happy then.

Instead, I played dumb and pretended I didn't know his question was an innuendo. "Yep. I can never drink coffee from anywhere else ever again. Even the cafes aren't this good."

It was the truth, too. I didn't know what he did or where he got his beans from, but it was glorious. I hummed around another sip, as Harrison strode into the room. He looked at his watch—a watch that cost more than most people's cars—then back up at us.

"Stop giving Blake coffee orgasms. I can't go to this meeting with a hard-on again."

Everett snorted, but I was stuck on Harrison's statement. "Again?"

He waved a hand. "Where's Darwin? He needs a new alarm clock. He hasn't replaced the one he stuffed in the toilet last month."

I'd come to discover that Darwin was many things, but a morning person wasn't one of them. As if Harrison had summoned him with the pure grumpiness of his mind, Darwin stumbled, bleary-eyed, into the kitchen. He made grabby hands in Everett's direction, and the ass in question passed him a travel mug. He was watching Darwin with a soft look of affection on his face; both he and Harrison were.

It was then, in that moment, that I realized they weren't just housemates and business partners. They were friends. Family, even.

Darwin let out a relieved sigh as he gulped down the hot liquid, and I gaped. "Fuck, do you have no sensation on your tongue? How are you not burning the inside of your mouth out right now?"

Darwin smirked around the rim of his cup. "I promise you, my tongue works just fine."

Everett huffed. "I cool it for him. He has no patience otherwise. Ulcerated his mouth the first time I made him a coffee."

Harrison shook his head, handing Darwin a muffin. The breakfast food just appeared on the kitchen countertop every morning. I didn't know how, and I didn't know when, but they did. I, for one, was grateful to the baked goods fairy for giving me my carbohydrate delights every morning.

I cleared my throat, setting down my coffee and trying to drag my brain away from images of them whipping off their dress pants like the Chippendales in Vegas. Pulling my folder toward me, I tried to shape my face into something professional. "Before you guys go, I just wanted to get your okay for these mockups, and then I'll start making you content." I slipped out the samples, spreading them out over the breakfast bar. The guys crowded around me, and I tried not to flush at the heat of their skin so close to mine. God, I needed to get laid.

"I think I've covered everything that I brainstormed with you guys, but, uh, women aren't as visual as men, so I added little flavor lines from the clips I pulled some of these images from, and I'll add them in the copy information of each photograph in your respective cloud files. If you use them, it's entirely up to you, but they were the lines that, uh, spoke to me the most."

The guys were far more capable of keeping a professional attitude while looking at naked pictures of each other, or maybe they'd been doing it for long enough that they'd become desensitized, or maybe they just didn't have the same ingrained moral hangups about nudity to overcome.

Everett looked up at me, his fingers tracing over a picture of Harrison with his hand wrapped loosely around a hunk of clay, his lower lip pulled between his teeth. "These are good."

I grinned, like he'd given me a shiny gold star. "Thank you."

"You are very talented, *Muñeca.* I trust your vision," Darwin said, wrapping an arm around my shoulder and kissing the side of my head softly. Was it weird that he was so cuddly when we were all standing around looking at a photograph of him coming on camera? Probably for normal people. I probably should protest the contact and maintain boundaries, but if I was being honest, I was touch-starved. Darwin's strong arm around my shoulder felt nice, his casual affection healing something inside me that I hadn't even known was broken.

And it wasn't like he was just this touchy-feely with me. He hugged the guys just as much, patting them on the back and kissing the tops of their heads. His love language was definitely touch; that was for sure. So every time his lips brushed my cheek, I told my racing heart to calm its tits. Its valves? Its raging aortas? Whatever.

"Thanks, D." I rested my head back against his shoulder and looked at the pictures in front of me. "It's easy enough to make you three look attractive."

Everett shook his head. "Don't do that," he growled.

I moved back into Darwin's body more, and he slipped a hand down to my hip to steady me. "What?"

Harrison came to the rescue, because Everett was still frowning at me. "Short-change your hard work. You're talented. Own it. You don't have to depreciate your skills with us."

I swallowed hard. Had anyone ever said that about me, ever? Especially in relation to my work? I didn't think so. Well, maybe the guy who owned the "Art School," but then he'd screwed me out of a bunch of money, so I wasn't sure his opinion counted.

I cleared my throat, swallowing down the emotion that had suddenly decided to lodge itself there. "Thanks, guys."

Darwin's thumb was rubbing my hip bone unconsciously, and I was suddenly overtly aware of the gesture. My face flushed even redder, and Harrison flicked his eyes down my body to the point of contact with a roll of his eyes. "Let's go." He tugged my emotional support Ecuadorian away, but when he'd shoved him mostly out the door behind Everett, he looked back over his shoulder. "Darwin is right—we all trust your judgment. Do what you like, and we'll use it."

I nodded mutely and watched him go. Why did I feel like I'd been through the wringer every single time I was in the presence of more than one of them? I gathered my mockups back into the folder and did some deep breathing exercises.

Well, I inhaled an apple crumble muffin while I stared at nothing in the distance. Same thing.

My phone buzzed in my pocket, and I frowned, seeing that it was my mom. I needed to call them, maybe give them my new address. Tell them that the art school was a scam, but that I'd still found a good job in graphic design. I was still living the dream; it just looked a little bit different now.

Instead, I let it ring out and go to voicemail. I gave it another two minutes, then typed out a quick message.

> Sorry, Mom. In class. I'll call you tonight.

I had no intention of calling her tonight, or any other night. I was pretty sure interrogators took lessons from her, or maybe I was just incapable of lying to my mother face to face. But if she called me, I'd be spilling my guts in minutes, and then she'd never let up about me returning home.

Instead, I messaged her to remind her I was alive and happy, and I'd be conveniently unavailable until I grew enough backbone to tell her that I *was* happy, even if everything was messed up.

That was all there was to it.

Decision made—or re-validated, as it would be—I returned to my work nook and opened up my files. Harrison had filmed yesterday as well, so I would start on his edits now. By the time he got home, he'd have something he could load immediately.

It might be unorthodox, but for the first time in ages, I felt fulfilled. That meant something.

9

BLAKE

I lay on the floor of the media room, spending my first big paycheck like a real grown-up. The guys sat around the edges of the room, cameras set on tripods and headphones over their ears as they played some war game while streaming the video of them playing, and their game play, on what I had come to know was ClickHeart for nerds. If their ClickHeart content was for the ladies—statistically, their audience data was between sixty-seven and eighty-nine percent female—then their KillSwitch streaming was for the guys. Basically, you paid to watch people play games you also played. It didn't make sense to me, but what did I know?

The guys chatted and joked, like guys do, making crude jokes and generally talking shop about whatever the game was. I didn't need to do anything for this service, though, which was why I was extreme shopping with my headphones on.

I wondered if they'd let me get an axolotl? Nah, I'd kill it and then feel sorry for Arturio the Axolotl. Maybe I'd start with sea monkeys. I typed that in and added it to my cart. This was fun.

I'd been here nearly two weeks, and I was getting more comfortable. I'd walked in on Harrison in the bathroom yesterday and hardly even blushed. I'd also worked out the times Everett liked to film, so I could avoid the kitchen altogether.

If the work was good, then the companionship was even better. Even Everett was warming up to me, albeit slowly. He shared his popcorn on movie night; that was basically a declaration of unimpeachable friendship now.

Darwin threw down his headphones, and I realized they were done. Saving my cart, I sat up. "Did you have a good time conquering and plundering?" I asked, as they all closed down their computers. I really didn't need to be in here with them, but I didn't mind the silent camaraderie and I hated feeling left out. And lonely. Definitely came from being an only child.

Harrison waggled his eyebrows. "Plundering is my favorite sport."

Everett grunted. "Speaking of plundering, I haven't gotten laid in ages. I think we need to hit the club."

My eyes went wide. "It's eleven at night!"

Harrison laughed. "Sweet little country mouse. The club is only just getting good. Haven't you been out in LA yet?"

I shook my head, and Darwin clutched his chest. "This is a tragedy." He stood over me, his feet either side of my hips so if I pushed up just a little with my hands, I'd be nose to cock. "Get dressed, Doll, because we're going to party tonight."

I was already shaking my head. "You guys go. I don't think I even have anything I could wear." That was a lie. I had the standard, necessary, little black dress. But they didn't know that.

Darwin pulled me to my feet, leaving me pressed scandalously close to his chest. Well, it would have been a scandal, if it was anyone but Darwin. "Then put on your sexiest bra and panties, borrow one of Everett's button-downs, and call it an outfit. Because you're coming out with us, *Muñeca*, and I'm not taking no for an answer." He purred the words in my ear, and a shiver went through me.

This man should be illegal.

"I think you're optimistic if you think my ass is going to fit into one of Everett's shirts."

It was the wrong thing to say, because everyone's eyes immediately dropped to my ass. My face flushed hot, and Everett growled. "Your ass will fit fine."

Shaking my head, I pressed a hand against

Darwin's chest, giving me some space to lift my other finger and point it at his face. "Fine. I might have something that works, but only for an hour. Then I'm Ubering my granny ass home, okay?"

He leaned forward and nipped the tip of the finger I was waggling in his face, and I felt the ghost of that bite right down to my clit. "Whatever you say, *Muñeca*. We leave in thirty minutes."

Still shaking my head, I walked out of the room and took the stairs two at a time. Thirty minutes wasn't enough.

IF I WAS WAITING for my teen movie moment where I walked down the stairs and everyone was gobsmacked by my beauty, I was still waiting.

"Dammit, Blake, hurry up! The Uber's here!" Harrison shouted, then grumbled something to Everett. "Fucking hell, Darwin, your hair is *fine*. You're worse than Blake, and she's a damn girl. Let's go." Apparently, when it was time to go anywhere, Harrison turned into a drill sergeant.

I took the stairs one at a time, because I was in platform heels that I hadn't worn in at least a year, and I was teetering around like a gangly lizard making a break for freedom. Everett was waiting at the bottom of the staircase, looking effortlessly handsome. Honestly, it looked like he'd just run wet fingers through his hair and thrown on a clean Henley, yet somehow he'd transformed into a wet dream or some kind of fashion model.

"I might actually hate you," I grumbled as I walked past him, making him laugh.

"Sure you do, Sunshine."

I flushed, tugging at the hem of my skirt. My friends had always told me my thighs were too chunky for a dress this short, but I told myself I didn't care. It was tight, sure, but it sat mid-thigh, not up around my asscheeks.

I chewed my lip and looked back over my shoulder at him. "Is this okay? No, you're right—this is a terrible idea. I don't have anything good to wear. I'll stay home. You guys go and have fun. If you aren't home by this time tomorrow, I'll assume you were murdered and will keep your coffee machine," I joked, heading back toward the stairs.

Everett grunted, stepping in my path. "You look good; you're coming out. Get that sweet ass in the damn Uber, or I'll put you over my shoulder, and we both don't want that."

"We don't?"

He leaned closer, giving me a lopsided smirk that did wild things to my chest. "I'm not sure you're ready for where that ends, Sunshine. Now go." I let out a little squeak of alarm and spun on my heel, hurrying toward the front door.

Harrison stood there, tapping his foot impatiently. His eyes dragged down my body, and if there was a test in his gaze, the arousal that flashed through his eyes was definitely a pass. But it was gone as soon as it arrived, and he waved me toward the Uber, hollering for Darwin. Everett slid into the front, being a few inches taller than both Harrison and Darwin. The Uber driver was looking a little annoyed, but he pretended to be patient, which was more than Harrison was doing.

Finally, Harrison stepped out the door in front of Darwin, and they locked up the house before sliding into the back of the car with me. I tried not to breathe too deeply, wedged between the hard bodies of Darwin and Harrison; I wasn't sure I could cope with how good they smelled. Or worse, how good they felt. I mentally hurried the Uber through the busy streets of LA.

Darwin slung his arm over my shoulders, pulling me into his side and giving me a little more room on my left where Harrison's thigh was pressed right along mine. I cleared my throat. I needed to get out of my head before I spontaneously combusted. It would definitely be messy, and I was pretty sure the guys would have to buy this nice man a new car.

"So, where are we going?"

"Hole," Harrison answered, though he was still

looking out the front windshield like he was mentally giving the driver directions. I was beginning to think that perhaps Harrison might be a little bit of a control freak, though he hid it well.

I might be new to LA, but even I'd heard of Hole. It was where the young and trendy went to get blind drunk and put clips of it on the Gram. I probably couldn't afford the door charge on that place, even with my awesome new job. Plus, I was woefully under-dressed.

"We can't go to Hole! I look like someone's hillbilly cousin. These shoes are from, like, 2006? Nothing I'm wearing is LV. I'm going to be ridiculed in the public bathrooms," I groaned, and Everett just laughed. He actually laughed.

"Don't worry so much, Blake. You'll be fine. You'll have a great time. The place will be so busy, no one will even see your shoes unless you're dancing on the bar. Are you going to dance on the bar?" Harrison raised an eyebrow, and I huffed as I shook my head. "There you go. Stop stressing."

"Yeah, *Amorcito.* We'll go and drink and dance until your knees are weak," Darwin purred in my ear. Hearing him use the same term of endearment that he growled into the camera at the beginning of all his videos had an almost Pavlovian response for my vagina. Actually, Pavlov's dogs and my nether regions had a lot of similarities at that moment; apparently we'd both been conditioned to get a little moist around the lips on command.

I cleared my throat, immensely glad that the back of the rideshare was dark, though he could probably feel the radiant heat coming off my blushing cheeks. "Sounds good."

The guys began to talk about investing in property and creating trusts, and I was happy to sit in the back and collect the remains of my composure from the floor of the car. My skirt had slid up a bit, and I tugged at it, trying to drag it back down my thighs. But no matter how much I wiggled, I couldn't get enough leverage to pull it over the soft curve of my upper thigh. Now that I was focused on it, I felt embarrassed by the way my thighs splayed on the seat. I definitely didn't have a thigh gap, and I could almost guarantee ninety percent of the women at Hole definitely would.

My friends had been right; this dress was far too short. I tugged at it again, until Harrison reached over and grabbed my hand, stilling my restless movements. "Stop wiggling. It's fine," he said mid-sentence, before going back to the conversation he was having with Everett.

But he didn't let go of my fingers. I wouldn't say he was holding my hand romantically—more like you'd hold a child's hand to stop them from putting a month-old French fry they'd found on the floor into their mouth.

Soon enough, the Uber driver was pulling up to the curb and we were all climbing out. I was fairly sure I flashed Darwin as I scrambled from the car, but considering how often I'd seen his dick in the last week, it would make us even.

I let out a long whistle as I took in the line to get in. It went down the street and around the corner. "We might have to go somewhere else. There's no way we're getting in tonight. You guys are hot, but this is LA, and that line looks like a sausage fest already."

Everett rolled his eyes, ushering me toward the door, his body between me and the traffic. "Sure thing, Sunshine. Lucky for us, I know a guy." He pushed me toward the entrance, skipping the line, and I could feel the dirty looks we were getting. Everett stopped in front of a bouncer, who was like six foot seven and built like a ginormous cloud. A thunder-cloud that could pummel you into the earth, but still a cloud.

The guy smiled at Everett. "My brother! I didn't know you were coming tonight." He gave Everett a bro-hug, then Darwin and Harrison too. He looked down at me from a great height. "Look at you. You're barely bite-sized. Hardly a snack."

At this point, I wouldn't be surprised if he consumed small children to achieve his huge stature. "I might be a snack, but I'm a spicy one. I'll definitely give you indigestion," I replied with a grin, and the security guy laughed, pulling me in for a suffocating hug too.

Everett grabbed me and dragged me back to his side, planting me there. "This is Blake. She's our new housemate."

The security guy—who no one had introduced yet —raised both eyebrows. "Like, housemate-house-mate?" His waggling eyebrows left little doubt to what he meant. "What's your page handle, Snack Attack? I'll subscribe."

Jesus fucking Christ. Was this what it was like for the guys? Like, hey, nice to meet you, what's your user handle so I can watch you stroke your dick naked?

"She's not on ClickHeart. She's just a housemate." Harrison's tone was flat, which seemed to just make the big guy laugh.

"Sure thing, friend. Go on now. Have fun." He ticked us off a list, and I could hear the disgruntled groans of people in the line. But only for a second, because the noise inside the club was insane. It was warm enough that none of us had coats to check, and we moved straight through the crowd.

"How'd you get on the list for Hole?" I yelled over the thumping music. Everett was leading us toward the back, where he stepped away briefly to talk to another bouncer, who also hugged him. Stepping back, he rested his hand on my spine as he guided me through the roped-off area to a spot that was a little less busy, but still really loud.

"I'm the owner."

"*What?*" I gasped, coming to a stop and making Harrison run into my back. I could feel his laughter through my shoulders. Pushing me gently, Everett steered us up another set of steps to a small, private area, curtained off from other partygoers.

"He's a silent partner," Harrison yelled. "He bankrolled Jako's vision."

I couldn't get my head around it, not really. This place was an LA institution, and he was doing Click-Heart? Why?

I had a million questions, but just then, a hot male waiter appeared, his white t-shirt so tight that I could see his nipples through the fabric. He put a bucket of ice and a bottle of tequila on the table, and must have caught me staring with my mouth hanging open, because he winked in my direction before heading back to the bar. Yeah, I was definitely giving him a tip.

"Are you done ogling?" Everett asked, his lips pulled tight as he took in the people around us. This might be the upper echelon of the club, but it was far from empty. There were several rowdy groups in outfits that probably cost more than most minimum wage workers would make in a year.

Darwin grabbed the bottle and poured me a drink in a shot glass with the name of the club etched onto it.

Then he did some for the guys too. "Here's to new friends and the good life," he announced, knocking back his shot quickly. He waited until I'd done the same, the expensive tequila smooth until the burn hit my gut. "One more for the road, then let's dance."

I did the second shot he handed me, and stood. I had a feeling tonight was going to be wild.

10

DARWIN

I gripped Blake's hand in mine as we weaved through the crowd. I nodded at Jefferson, the rope guy by the VIP section, and stopped to ask him how his wife was. They'd just gotten married two months ago; the guys and I had attended the wedding.

"She's good. And pregnant! A honeymoon baby, the doctor called it." His face stretched in a wide smile, and I pulled him in for a quick hug, smacking him on the back. I was about four inches shorter than him, but Jefferson was the most gentle security guard I'd ever met. I'd once watched him pluck a girl off the bar, carry her like she was an injured baby bird to the front of the building, then stuff her and her friends in a cab with a driver we all trusted implicitly. He took his job seriously, and he wasn't here for the chance to crack skulls, which I knew Everett and Hole's management appreciated. It was why he had the job of manning the VIP section.

"Congrats, man. I'm so happy for you, you horny bastard. Did you even see any part of Hawaii while you were there, or just the inside of your hotel room?" I teased.

The big guy blushed, but grinned back at me. "Like Ash would've let me get away with just staying in the resort. She had us climbing fucking mountains. It's a wonder I wasn't too exhausted to make a baby."

I laughed, but I believed it. Ash and Jefferson had met at Hole four years ago; she was the first bartender Everett had personally hired. They were a sweet couple, and they truly loved each other. It was one of those once-in-a-lifetime kind of romances—the kind I wanted so bad, it hurt. But instead, I got quick fucks and women who wanted the persona, not the man. It wasn't in the cards yet, but hopefully one day, it would be.

Blake smiled and laughed along with us, though she'd never met neither Ash nor Jefferson before. She struck me as the kind of person who would be elated by other people's happiness.

I said a quick goodbye to my friend, sending my best wishes to Ash, and continued to pull Blake along behind me as we worked our way through the heavy press of bodies to the dancefloor.

It was sunken, with different tiers, until the very bottom was just a writhing mass of people dancing. The bar and DJ booth sat opposite each other, on the highest tier, and watching drunk people climb the steps to get more booze was one of the highlights of my night every time we came here. One day, someone was going to topple down, and they'd try and sue, but Hole's lawyer was a shark, and between liability waivers at the front door and Hole's insurance, I didn't like their odds of succeeding.

I stopped to say hello to a few people who knew me; either because we came to this club a lot, or because they followed me on ClickHeart. It was easy to tell the difference between the two types, but my response to both was the same. They usually wanted something from me, but I wasn't in the mood to pander to them tonight. Tonight, I wanted to dance with the pretty girl holding my hand.

I pulled her onto the dancefloor with me, and she looked around nervously. The tequila obviously hadn't kicked in yet. "Relax, *Muñeca*. It's just you and me and the music." I pulled her closer until I could grab her hips, lifting the hand still holding hers until she threaded her arm around my neck. I swayed a slow two-step for a while, moving her body with mine in a slow rock. She looked up at me with big eyes that shone in the strobing lights, her lips curled in a small smile that might be happiness, or maybe a touch of embarrassment. But I didn't want her to be embarrassed. I wanted her to feel free.

"What does that mean? *Muñeca?*" She butchered the Spanish, but I found it more endearing than I normally would.

"Doll," I murmured into her ear.

She scoffed. "Maybe a Cabbage Patch doll. I'm hardly delicate or breakable." She grinned. "I mean, it doesn't fit very well. Though, I do have a creepy stare if I don't blink for a while." She opened her eyes really wide and gave me a dead-eyed look, which really was kinda creepy—or it would be, if the laughter didn't keep curling her lips when she was trying to be serious.

I didn't even know why I called her Doll, though I think it had something to do with her fragility. Not on the outside, of course; there was nothing frail or breakable about Blake on the outside. But on the inside, she seemed one harsh word away from shattering.

"I think it fits fine. Let's dance, baby girl. I wanna see those hips swing." I pulled her even closer, spinning her until her back was pressed against my front. Her arm reached back to grab hold of my neck again as I swayed her to the music, her body cradled tight to mine. I banded my other arm across her waist, holding her tight.

Our bodies fit together like perfection with her heels on, making her only four or so inches shorter than my five-eleven. I told my dick to settle down. We were just dancing, and it didn't matter if her juicy-as-fuck ass was brushing all up on my cock, we were just friends. Harrison had said it had to be that way so we didn't get the shit sued out of us, though perhaps this dance was already breaking more than a few rules.

If I shimmied her dress up her thighs a little bit, bent her over just a little more, I could slide right inside her. If we weren't in the middle of a crowded club, of course. She shook her ass right against the zipper of my jeans, and I clenched my jaw. Fuck, maybe *even* in a crowded club, if she kept grinding on me like that.

The song changed to something even more upbeat, so for both my sanity and my aching balls, I turned her in my arms and moved a little faster—a little less like we were undertaking foreplay. I could feel eyes on me and I looked up to see Harrison staring down at us, longing written right across his face.

Apparently, our fearless leader was as enamored with our new housemate as I was. Even if she was thoroughly off limits.

I spun her in my arms until we were dancing back to front again, her hips swaying as she fell into the music, her breasts straining against the tight fabric of that little black dress. I turned her slowly until she was presented to Harrison, and he could see the way her head was tipped back against my shoulder, her lips a perfect little O of pleasure that only mindless dancing could bring you.

People encroached on our space, men wanting to dance with Blake, or women wanting to dance with me, but I wasn't ready to share just yet. Not with anyone but Harrison from the level above us. He leaned forward onto his elbows, his eyes burning into us, like he was committing to memory the way she moved for later.

I knew I was.

My phone buzzed in my back pocket, and I pulled it out. I wasn't even surprised to see it was Harrison, giving me shit about having my hands all over our new employee.

> Harrison: Do I have to give you guys
> the sexual harassment speech again?

I snorted, like he wasn't up there having all sorts of impure thoughts about our *employee.* I shoved my phone back in my pocket and gave him the finger from where Blake couldn't see, before dropping my hand back down to cup her hip.

He was probably right, though; I hadn't pushed for her to get this job just so I could get her into bed, and I'd feel awful if I was the reason she left. I needed to ease back a little.

The next woman who came up and tugged on my arm was a pretty little thing, though not really what I wanted tonight. But with Harrison's words still banging around in my head, I raised an eyebrow at Blake in question. She nodded her head, a smile on her face, so maybe I'd read her signals all wrong. Now I was definitely glad that I hadn't done anything embarrassing, like grind my now-hard dick against her ass.

The woman who was gripping my hand danced well, her body moving with the music and mine in a way that suggested she was some kind of professional. Maybe a backup dancer or something. But no matter how good she was, my eyes kept drifting back to Blake, as she danced by herself. She was definitely in the moment, the awkwardness of earlier now gone. I watched as guys came up to her, and she just ignored them until they left.

The girl in front of me wrapped her hands around my neck, pulling my attention back to her as the music devolved into something a little more upbeat, and I was forced to concentrate.

When I turned back around, Blake was gone.

11

BLAKE

There were certain muscles you only worked when you danced, and my thighs might never be the same after dancing with Darwin for what felt like hours. The man could *dance.* I didn't want to make him sound like a cliché, but he moved his body so sinuously against mine, I was pretty convinced that the only thing that stopped this from being straight-up porn was the fact that I was a shitty dancer, and that we were fully clothed.

I watched a woman come up and grip his hand, tugging him toward her, and when he cast me a questioning look, I nodded. He seemed to be asking me permission to dance with the woman, but he didn't need it. We were friends; that was all, and barely that. He could dance with whoever he liked.

I danced by myself as I watched her dance with him in a way I could only wish to move. They were like something straight out of the animal kingdom as they rolled their bodies together to some R'n'B hit from the nineties that had been redone into a dance track.

Trying not to feel awkward, I lifted my hands in the air and just tried not to look like I was a giraffe having a seizure. As much as I wanted to say that I lost myself in the beat, I really couldn't. I was too hyper aware of the couples around me dancing, including Darwin and the girl who were definitely two items of clothing away from fucking on the dancefloor. I was too aware that I was offbeat, that I didn't know what to do with my hands or my feet. I wasn't nearly drunk enough to not care about any of those things.

Putting my hands down, I cleared my throat, suddenly feeling awkward. I should get off the dancefloor, maybe go and find the other guys and see if they'd found friends for the night. If they had, I might just head home. I wasn't used to these late nights. I couldn't afford the expensive drinks. I hated inhaling the hazy mist from the smoke machines. It was too sweaty, and there were too many people. All valid excuses to go home.

In reality, watching Darwin dance with the other girl made something twist in my stomach, and I didn't think it was the tequila.

I was about to step off the dancefloor when two large hands gripped my hips. I spun around too fast—jello-thighs and too-high heels nearly making me face-plant right there in the crowd—just so I could give the handsy bastard a piece of my mind.

"Blake?"

Shock made my whole body go still. "*Hennie?*"

The concerned face of the first LA friend I'd ever made was there, his brows lowered over his pretty eyes. Blame the tequila, or the weird flood of emotions that just came over me, but I threw my arms around his neck and hugged him.

His strong arms banded around my back as he returned the hug. "Fucking hell, Blake. I'm so angry at you."

I froze, stepping away. "Why?"

"Why? Are you kidding me?" His disappointed look was awfully familiar. I'd seen it many times before. From my mom, when I'd chopped off all my hair in freshman year with my dad's buzzcutters. From my art teacher, when I'd painted a six-foot vase of white tulips that kind of looked like a giant dick ejaculating. From Jeanna's mom, when I'd told her that boys didn't look like Ken dolls beneath their pants, back when we were in sixth grade.

Hennie gripped my shoulders. "You answered a fucking ad on some random message board, then disappeared. I thought you were *dead* when you didn't show up the next day. I thought you'd gone to some dude's house and been murdered and sold for parts."

Oh shit. Hennie really did seem mad. "It wasn't like that."

"I was going to go and see the cops to report you missing. Otherwise, who would have known?" He shook his head, and my chest ached at his disappointed look. "I went to your hotel to see you, and the guy at the desk said you'd checked out, but wouldn't give me any of your details. I'd prayed you'd gone home or something, and weren't actually buried in a shallow grave somewhere."

I winced, because I could see his point. "I'm sorry, Hennie. I'm fine."

"I can see that now." He sucked in a deep breath. "For weeks, I've been carrying around this guilt about not reporting you missing. But I don't know anything about you. Not your last name. Your phone number. What was I going to tell the cops? A girl didn't show up at my wiener truck today, and now I think she's been murdered by weirdos she met on the internet?"

I gripped his forearm. "Hennie—"

"Is everything okay here?"

I spun again, and Everett was there, looking huge and menacing. I didn't have to be Spiderman for my senses to tell me that this could spell trouble. "Everything's fine, Everett. This is a friend of mine, Hennie."

Everett reached out to grab my arm, pulling me

closer, but Hennie lunged forward to grab my other hand, like I was about to disappear again before his very eyes. Everett's eyes narrowed at where his fingers were wrapped around my wrist.

"Hennie, this is my new housemate, Everett. And kind of my boss. Funny story, you were right about it being porn."

Hennie's hand fell away as his mouth fell open. "You're doing *porn*? Blake..."

"No! Not me. I wouldn't ever..." I looked at Everett. "Not that there's anything wrong with porn. Whatever brings in those dollar bills, right? Just not for me. Uh, no one would want to see me wobbling around on camera cooking tacos, anyway."

Okay, so now they were both looking at me like I was insane. Desperately searching for backup, I realized I wasn't going to get it from any of our other housemates. Darwin was still doing some kind of Latin dance—that probably should be illegal—further into the crowd, and I could see Harrison on the upper floor, talking to a girl whose asscheeks were visible from here. He leaned toward the girl, and I frowned. Maybe he was about to kiss her? Maybe he was telling her his secret recipe for the perfect slip casting?

Either way, I wasn't getting any backup from those two.

"How about we take this back up to the table and talk it over?" I said hopefully. I'd apologize later for potentially cock-blocking Harrison. I was just getting this weird little testosterone disagreement off the dance floor, that's all. It had nothing to do with the fact Harrison was now palming that girl's perfect asscheeks. Guess it wasn't the secret to slip casting. Pretty sure things were still slippery, though.

Not waiting for the guys, I plowed through the crowd back toward the roped-off VIP area. I looked over my shoulder to make sure Everett let Hennie through, then climbed the stairs. I didn't even care that my dress was riding up my sweat-sticky thighs now. I stomped over to the leather booth we were occupying and slumped down, pouring myself a couple of fingers of tequila and downing it before the guys caught up. I had a feeling I was going to need it.

Hennie took the last few steps faster than Everett and sat down beside me, so I poured another shot of tequila and handed it to him. He took it, but his eyes were back on mine, searching for answers. "Where'd you disappear to, Blake?"

I sucked in a deep breath, my eyes flicking to Everett again. "I got a job that came with room and board. I started the next day. I'm sorry I didn't tell you." And I *was* sorry. You didn't have to be an empath to tell he'd been legitimately worried for my wellbeing.

"What kind of job has you out partying with your boss at two in the morning?" His eyes were narrowed in Everett's direction, but my *boss* just stared back impassively.

As if by some evil divine intervention, Darwin reappeared and flopped down on the bench on my other side, leaning in to kiss my cheek loudly. "*Muñeca,* where'd you disappear to?" He gave Hennie a big smile. "Ah, I see where you disappeared to." He leaned forward. "I'm Darwin, Blake's housemate."

Hennie shook Darwin's hand, his eyes narrowing further. "You were saying?"

"Look, the place was in Beverly Hills, and the graphic design work is... interesting. I saw an opportunity and I took it, okay?"

"You're living in Beverly Hills, with two guys?" Hennie's voice rose an octave.

"Three, actually," Darwin added. "She's a super talented artist. There's only so many ways you can make jacking off look artistic, but Blake manages it."

I wanted to gag Darwin, but I didn't think he'd see it as a punishment.

Hennie blinked slowly. "Jacking off?"

I swallowed hard and pasted a smile on my face. "Yeah, they're creators on ClickHeart."

"ClickHeart," he repeated.

Everett snorted. "It's like the room has an echo."

Hennie's furious gaze snapped to him. "Maybe it can echo this," he growled, giving Everett the finger before turning back to me. "You're doing graphic design for porn stars?"

I nodded. He made it sound way more salacious than it actually was, but I guess when it boiled down to it, that was it in a nutshell.

Hennie's eyes flicked between Everett and Darwin. "And how long until you *suggest* she joins you if she wants to keep her job?"

Darwin grinned harder, happily buzzed from the tequila. "I already asked if she wanted to peg me, but she said no. Gotta respect the no, man." He narrowed his eyes at Hennie. "How do you feel about Mickey Mouse?"

I slapped a hand over Darwin's mouth before he made this whole thing worse. I was rethinking the ball gag. "It's not like that, I promise. We have an ironclad employment contract, complete with a very comprehensive sexual harassment clause. Despite what you might think, I'm not a complete idiot."

Hennie shook his head. "It wouldn't be the first time you've fallen for an offer that's too good to be true."

Ouch. Again, not wrong, but that one stung a little. "You don't even know me, Heinrich." I gritted out his name between my teeth. "I don't owe you any explanations. You can take your pompous attitude and fuck right off."

Everett tensed, like he was ready to help Hennie

along with leaving, but suddenly Harrison appeared next to the table. *Yay, the third Musketeer. Just great.*

"What's going on?"

"Blake's old friend was just leaving," Everett growled, climbing to his feet.

Hennie took a deep breath. Dismissing Everett's aggressive stance, he turned back to me. "Sorry, Blake. I didn't mean to come off like an asshole. I was worried. But I trust you know what you're doing." He gave me that smile that did strange things to my insides. "The truck isn't the same without you."

I melted, despite my annoyance. "Aww, Hennie. Are you saying you miss me?"

He laughed, his face tilting back slightly so I got a good look at the sexy column of his throat. Could throats be attractive? Was I a vampire in a past life? I definitely wanted to suck something, but it wasn't his blood.

That smile threatened to melt my insides again as Hennie reached over and gripped my hand. "Do you want to go on a date with me this Sunday?"

I reared back, like he'd just asked me to buy a small island nation with him. It seemed far more likely than Hennie wanting to date me. I felt like every set of eyes in the club was on me at that moment, especially those of my new housemates. Employers. Untouchables. If that didn't help make my decision, nothing would.

"I'd like that. Let me give you my number."

I ignored the disapproval coming off Everett in waves as I programmed my number into Hennie's phone, then texted myself a message to get his number. This was for the best. Hennie was fucking amazing, and having a crush on any of the guys I lived with was a recipe for disaster.

Problem solved.

12

BLAKE

We left the club not long after that, surprisingly without any extras, even though the guys had come out to get laid. I kind of felt guilty that my drama had ruined the night, but on the other hand, I wasn't really in the mood to listen to the guys bring home women either.

Call it sexual frustration; you wouldn't be wrong.

But even the next morning, everyone was quiet. Everett handed me my coffee as usual, but no one seemed to be making the normal bantering conversation. Maybe they were hungover? I had no idea how much tequila they'd ingested while I was on the dancefloor.

The only one who was his normal, happy self was Darwin. He stumbled out of bed, his hair adorably mussed, his eyelids drooping in a way that seemed to just make him look sensual. He kissed the side of my head and made a beeline for the caffeine. "Tequila. I love the Devil's juice, but it does not love me." Shaking his head gently, he sucked down the whole cup of coffee in one mouthful. That was almost sacrilegious. "So did I dream of the hot guy making eyes at you last night, or are you going on a date with Mr. Tall, Blond, and Germanic? Has he texted?"

I gave Darwin a crooked smile, because Hennie had messaged me already this morning. He'd sent me a *Good morning* text that made me way too ridiculously happy for only two words. "Yep." I gulped my coffee too, but unlike Darwin's, mine was a respectable temperature and burned my tongue. "Motherfucker."

Everett huffed and walked out. I watched him leave with a frown, my gaze flicking to Harrison, who just shrugged. He looked the most hungover of all of us, unlucky bastard.

"What about you? Did you get the phone number of Asscheeks McGee?"

Harrison snorted coffee out of his nose. "Excuse me?"

"The girl you were flirting with on the balcony, with the, you know..." I made butt-squeezing motions with my hands. See, we could be friends. There was no need for jealousy.

Harrison shrugged. "Nah, we didn't have much in common. She'd just seen my page before. I try not to date girls who are chasing me for a clay lay, you know?"

I blinked at him slowly. "Uh, no. I do not know. What the fuck is a clay lay?"

It was Darwin who answered. "Someone who wants the persona and not the man." He seemed sad. "I mean, it was nice at the beginning. Especially when ClickHeart went big for a while and everyone had it. We couldn't go out without getting laid. Once, Everett banged three different girls in the employee bathrooms at Hole in one night."

"Such a fucking hardship," Harrison deadpanned. "But after a while, you don't want an easy lay from someone who's chasing a quick story to tell their friends. You want something more."

I rolled my eyes. "Poor little pornstars. Do you know the last time I got laid? *Six months ago.* My vagina has packed up and moved onto greener pastures. That's why I'm going out with Hennie. Who knows, maybe he'll break my drought."

Darwin laughed. "Maybe, *Amorcito.*" He sighed. "I better get to work. There is no rest for us wicked adult entertainers."

There was a scrunched-up look on Harrison's face —his hangover must be really kicking his ass—but he downed his coffee. "Me too. Don't know if I can face the camera this morning, but I have a backlog of orders I need to deal with."

"Do you need any help?" I asked. The idea of using my computer with tequila brain made me squint in pain.

Harrison gave me a long look, but eventually shrugged. "Sure. I never turn down an extra set of hands. Except for Darwin's. The man doesn't know how to be gentle; I swear he breaks more orders than he packs."

Darwin rolled his eyes. "I only broke one bowl. Don't be so dramatic."

"You'd only packed two orders!"

Darwin looked completely unapologetic. Harrison huffed, stomping out of the room toward the pool house that doubled as his workshop and inventory room. The sun was starting to blaze down on the pool, making it sparkle enticingly. It might've been pretty, if the reflection wasn't like a laser beam to my skull.

Harrison's workshop was not at all what you'd expect from an artist. While there was a healthy smattering of clay on just about every surface, the place was organized within an inch of its life. There were labeled drawers for tools. Labeled totes for each of the different clay mixes. Everything had a label. It was like a seventy-year-old woman had discovered a label maker and gone on a spree.

I looked at the projects he had drying on a shelving unit running along the wall. They were beautiful. Stepping closer, I admired a bowl he'd painted with small, delicate little flowers around the rim. In a soft sage color, Harrison had painted an overgrown bramble moving over the soft curves of the bowl. It was pretty.

In the corner was his big, blue kiln. It looked like a fridge on stilts, but I knew it was running because it had warmed up the room. Careful not to touch anything, I went further back into Harrison's office. This was where he did all his shop orders, and already, I could see a long strip of packing slips flowing across his desk.

"You can pack. The supplies are over there on that bench. Double wrap everything, then fill any void space with soft fill."

"Yes, sir."

Harrison snorted and got to work. He was all business, but after the first few orders, he lost his shirt. His body was beautiful, though he wasn't ridiculously cut, aside from his arms and shoulders. He had great arms. And hands. And lats.

The man would look delicious walking away.

He put on a playlist as he worked, an eclectic mix of rap, pop, rock, and what could only be described as Mongolian Metalcore. I worked diligently, admiring each piece before wrapping it up like a delicate baby, secure in its box on the way to its new home.

The silence was comfortable, but after twenty minutes, it was Harrison who broke the moment.

"What's your deal?" It wasn't accusatory, despite the words. He seemed legitimately interested.

Carefully finishing the bubble-wrapping I was doing, I looked over my shoulder at him. He was watching me closely, like he was waiting for me to drop some kind of bombshell. "What do you mean?"

He shrugged and went back to picking stuff off the shelves. "I just realized that other than your education and work history, we know nothing about you. We talk about work, or ourselves, and you just let us. You're a bit of an enigma." He gave me a crooked smile that made me swallow hard.

"You guys are just more interesting. There's really not much to know."

Harrison walked over, placing a long, thin vase on top of my pile of tissue paper and bubble wrap. Then he boosted himself up onto the bench beside me. He was so tall that I had to look up at him. "I find that hard to believe. You're out here in LA by yourself—that takes some serious balls. I find it hard to believe you were some goody two-shoes Mary Sue before this."

I let out a humorless laugh, because that's exactly what I'd been. "You'd be surprised. I went to school and got half-decent grades, but I wasn't a brainiac. Went to a community college, where I flunked out of Accounting but could still pursue my art. I had three close friends, two of whom haven't even messaged me since I came to LA, plus an ex-boyfriend I met in middle school who just wanted me to get a 'real' job at Walmart and forget about making something of my art. You understand, right?" He was a potter who did porn; he had to understand people not appreciating your art. "Honestly, I wish I had some kind of intriguing backstory, but I don't. Most interesting thing that ever happened to me was when I got arrested."

As soon as I said it, I wanted to take it back. You didn't tell your employers that you'd been arrested.

"Woah. Hold up. That wasn't in your background check."

I frowned up at him. And I meant up. I was literally face to nipple with him. "You did a background check on me?"

He raised an eyebrow. "Of course we did. You were going to live with us. What if you were a murderer?"

Well, I guess. "Makes sense." I went back to wrapping the vase, before placing it in a long, square box.

Harrison nudged me with his foot. "Well?"

Playing dumb was definitely the best play right now. Maybe he'd just forget I said anything?

"Well, what were you arrested for? No, let me guess... Drunk and disorderly?" I shook my head. "Public nudity? You and your beige boyfriend get caught tickling bits behind the Quik-E-Mart?"

I frowned. Paul would never. He didn't even want to have sex fully naked, let alone in public. "No."

Harrison slid from the bench. "Come on, you gotta give me something."

His computer pinged, signaling a new order. "Look, more customers. We should pack it straightaway."

"It can wait. Now, stop deflecting. I want to know why you got in trouble with the law." He was so damn close now as he leaned on the bench. "Jaywalking?"

I shook my head. "We have so many orders to pack. Maybe we can talk about this later?" Harrison was grinning, quickly shaking his head. "Fine. It was for destruction of police property."

His eyes went wide, his mouth dropping open. "*No fucking way.*" His hands wrapped around my shoulders, and he turned me toward him. "You're going to have to explain, because I would never have pegged you as a rioting revolutionary."

I shook my head again. "It wasn't like that. The Chief of Police for my town lived next door, and it involved Turkey Bacon."

"Turkey Bacon? You're fucking with me right now, aren't you?"

God, I wish I was. Maybe I should have just said it was drunk and disorderly. "How much money would I have to give you to forget I said anything?"

He smirked. "Not for all the gold doubloons in all the land. Spill it, Jailbird."

I sighed, putting down the packing tape. "Fine. It's really not that interesting." I looked up at his twinkling blue eyes. *Fuck, why is he so handsome?* Clearing my throat, I looked away. "Like I said, I lived next door to the Police Chief and his family—including his shithead kid, Caleb. They had a whole bunch of pets, including an attack turkey named Turkey Bacon."

"Turkey Bacon, got it. Go on." His grin was so wide now, I was worried it might crack his face.

"Well, Caleb had trained this fucking turkey to attack people when he whistled. You ever seen a full-grown turkey coming at you? It's scary as hell. They have these big claws and beady little eyes."

"Sounds terrifying."

I narrowed my eyes at him. "They *are* fucking terrifying. Anyway, Caleb used to let out Bacon every day after I got off the bus and let him chase me all the way to my front door. I was sixteen and terrified of that damn bird. So this day, I got off the bus, but Caleb hadn't been at school that day so I thought I was safe. I walked home, looking at my phone, oblivious to the horror that was about to befall me.

"Turns out, they were lying in wait for me in his backyard. I don't know if Bacon was just especially angry with me that day, but when Caleb let him out, he went after me like he was possessed by Satan. I swear, he was right on my heels. I could hear his little neck testicles slapping together—that's how close he was."

Harrison was making a choking sound, his lips

pressed tightly together. "No, continue. Sorry, had something in my throat."

I rolled my eyes. "Anyway, on this day, his dad was home for something, and his squad car was parked in the driveway, blocking the path to my front door. His window was down, so I did what any rational person on the run from a fucking velociraptor would do. I dived into the squad car. Except, I forgot that Bacon had wings and a fair amount of speed, and the bastard just flew in after me. I dived out the driver's side, but Bacon got stuck in there. He wasn't very smart, just angry. Anyway, I ran all the way home and locked myself in the house."

I cleared my throat, my cheeks flushing pink with embarrassment. "Turns out, the squad car dash cam caught the whole thing, and Chief Dunsten decided it was my fault. Bacon did like six grand worth of damage to the interior of the squad car." I winced, still remembering how angry he'd been and the look of disappointment on my mom's face. "My dad argued that if it was anyone's fault, it was Caleb and his damn attack turkey, so eventually they dropped the charges after scaring the heck out of me for a couple of hours. The end."

Harrison was laughing so hard now, there were tears streaming down his face. "That was *so* much better than I ever could have imagined. Thank you, Shawshank, for making my day."

I could feel the flush of my cheeks as he stared down at me, his eyes sparkling and his gaze dropping to my lips. "Uh, I'm glad my childhood trauma could entertain you."

His hand came up to cup my cheek, his wide smile still threatening to send me blind. "It really does. You're something else, Blake. You really are." He paused, his eyes intense. I was super aware of the fact his naked chest was so close that I could feel the heat of his skin. I could see the steady rhythm of his pulse in his throat. His subtle cologne was filling my lungs. Was he going to try and kiss me?

Did I *want* him to kiss me?

Well, the answer to that one was easy enough. Hell yes, I did.

Still, after a few seconds—which felt like an age when you weren't drawing in life-giving oxygen—his smile dimmed a little. "Uh, we should get these all loaded up for the shipping company to come and collect. Then we should hit up the pool; we've earned it."

I huffed out a breath and smiled back. "Sure. Let's get these boxed up." My head was relieved he hadn't kissed me. It would have made things weird. Still, I hoped my tone didn't betray the disappointment I felt in my gut.

13

HARRISON

Blake walked out of my studio a little less bright than she normally did, and I felt like a giant fucking asshole. Apparently, Darwin wasn't the only one on struggle street when it came to our effervescent little artist. I pushed the feeling in my chest away and moved around the studio, cleaning it up. I wasn't quite as insane about the need for organization as Everett was, but still, I liked shit to be orderly.

I got lost in the music, in the drudgery of cleaning, when the door to the studio opened again. Everett stepped inside, shutting the door quietly. I frowned over at him. He didn't often come to my workspace.

"You okay?"

He nodded, taking up the stool that Blake had just vacated. "I'm fine. Just wanted to check in on you. It's hard to find a moment to just hang out lately."

I felt like it had been hard for longer than just lately, but still, I smiled and pressed my shoulder closer to his. Everett had been the one steadfast feature in my life for so long, and I loved him more than anyone. But it had been hard.

For so long, it had been hard. When he'd been lost to long nights and drugs, it had felt nearly impossible to drag him out of it. We'd scraped up enough money to send him to rehab, and honestly, it was the best money I'd ever spent. I would do it all over again, because he'd come back out of there no longer the strung-out mess he was before, but the boy who'd been my best friend forever.

We'd never looked back, never devolved back into that world where he needed a little something to get him through the long-ass shifts, and I didn't need to wonder exactly where he was sticking his dick, who he was getting drugs off, or if he'd just be dead on the street one day.

I'd almost taken him home, back to Minnesota—I would have bitten the bullet and done exactly that, if I didn't think it would've made him worse. Unfortunately, a lot of the demons he was running from were caused by our hometown.

Were caused by me.

I looked down at him, giving him a warm smile that I hoped conveyed how proud I was of him every day.

"It's getting busier and busier as the platform takes off, but that's a good thing. Means we're almost at the maintenance plateau, where we have a solid fan base and we don't have to keep pushing content to maintain the algorithms." I'd said all this stuff before, but it was good to remind us both. "As long as you're still feeling good?"

I never used the word relapse, but it was an ever-present problem between us. He squeezed my arm. "I feel good, Harrison. Stop stressing." He chewed his lower lip, a tell he'd had since we were kids. "The girl—"

"Blake," I corrected.

"Yeah, Blake. What do you think about her?"

I froze. Fuck, had something in my dealings with her shown how much I desired her? I mean, in this industry, desire was as common as fucking breathing. You didn't enter an entire platform based around nudity and not feel anything. Though I'd become desensitized, I guess, to the industry's idea of perfection. There were only so many perfectly tanned beauty queens I could take, those girls who'd failed to become Miss America and decided to get their tits out on camera for money. They all looked the same. Fake blonde hair. Fake blue eyes. Fake tits. Smiles that never quite reached their eyes.

I wanted something else. Something different.

Something like Blake.

But I kept all those thoughts inside. "I think she's good at what she does. My feed looks so fucking amazing lately."

He stared up at me, his eyes narrowed. He'd grown out his beard, and there was a red tinge to it that wasn't present in his hair. It made him look more rugged, which probably helped with his numbers, but it was still so freaking weird when I thought about the teenage boy who hadn't been able to grow a mustache until he was seventeen. Not that I would ever tease him about it, because to this day, my mustache and beard wouldn't connect. I had a baby face; it was really fucking annoying.

"That's not what I meant, and you know it. I mean personally. Not how good she is at her job."

This was a minefield, and I wasn't sure how to navigate it. "She's a nice girl. Sweet. Funny. Way too fucking innocent for this town, that's for sure. She's going to be eaten alive." She was also beautiful, though I didn't think she realized it, and that in itself was refreshing. It was that internal kind of beauty which shone through to the external.

"Why? Don't you like her?" I'd call bullshit if he said he didn't, but probably not to his face. Some things he had to work out for himself. I couldn't be his savior all the time. You didn't react like he had the other night at the club if you had no interest in a woman.

I didn't really know how I felt about that—least of all because she was an employee. But people in glass houses, right?

He shrugged, his eyes moving to the drying rack that held some of my latest pieces. "She's nice enough, I guess." He didn't meet my gaze.

I scoffed. "I've known you forever, Everett. Don't bullshit me. You've been making her cookies, for fuck's sake."

He glared at me, but dropped his eyes again quick enough. "They help her productivity. It's just good for business."

I laughed in his face. "Come on, man. We both know that's a load of bullshit. Why are you out here right now? You want my permission or something?"

Everett had dated many, many women since we'd moved to LA. No, that was a lie. He never dated them. He fucked them, usually only once, sometimes for a slightly longer period of time, but never long enough to call it a relationship. Or hell, even a regular booty call. He'd never asked me for permission before, but I knew why he was doing it now. This had a good chance of going so damn badly for us all.

"Kinda, yeah."

"Then my answer is no."

He scowled again. "Are you saying no as a business owner or as my friend?"

I huffed an angry sound. His *friend.* "Because she's our employee. She's our housemate. She isn't someone you can just fuck once or twice and forget about it. Even if she's after something casual, it would ruin the dynamic of the team. Because a large chunk of not just *our* money, but Darwin's too, is tied up in keeping her happy and not being sexually harassed. If you're horny, head back to the club tonight and leave Blake alone."

He growled an angry noise and stood, getting all up in my face. "It's not like that, and you know it. I wouldn't ruin everything to get laid. We both know I can get pussy as easy as I can breathe. That's not what this is about. I'm tired of the chase, Harrison."

His words hurt my chest, that little part of me that wondered if he would ever be happy. "And you decided that proximity was the best option?"

"Jealousy isn't a good look on you. Don't pretend like it's all me fucking this up, and you don't want her too. I saw the look on your face when I walked in. That smile wasn't for me. I see the way you fucking watch her. So you can be as pious about it as you want, but we both know you want to sink between those soft thighs too. At least I'm honest about it."

I choked out a rude noise, standing up and giving him my back as I pretended to tidy the work bench. "Honesty isn't normally your strong suit. It's avoidance and blame. So excuse me if this is a bit of a surprise turn of events."

He stood and stomped out of my workshop, and I deflated. I felt wrung out by the exchange, which was how I usually felt when I had any kind of deep and meaningful conversation with Everett. Neither of us had ever been any good at expressing our feelings. In fact, we tended to avoid it like the plague.

Sighing, I moved back toward my wheel. Maybe I could use some clay therapy and catch up on some back orders. I was just cutting off a piece to put on the wheel when the door slammed back open again. I was surprised to see it was Everett, because I was certain he'd have stomped up to his room and sulked for a little while longer.

He strode toward me. "You're wrong. I'm not a fucked-up kid anymore, Harrison. I'm not running and hiding from anything that might feel like commitment just because I'm a giant screw-up. I'm not interested in Blake because she's conveniently located or any such shit." He huffed. "I think I'm interested in her because she reminds me a little of you."

I melted on the inside, but kept my face impassive.

Everett ate up the steps between us. "I like her because she cares about making things perfect, even though it's fucking subscription porn. I like her because she looks at my cookies as if they're a biblical revelation. I like her because she doesn't look at us differently for getting our dicks out. She reminds me of home, but the *good* parts of home, you know?"

He stepped closer to me, and I breathed him in. "Oh?"

He leaned down, gripping my chin where I sat on my stool. "Just like you."

Then he leaned down and kissed me.

14

BLAKE

My eyes were beginning to sting from staring at the screen for so long, and my nose was hurting from where my glasses sat across the bridge. In short, I needed a break. And chocolate.

My headphones were blasting old-school Nirvana, and I jerkily walked down the hall to the sounds of "Smells like Teen Spirit", my hands flinging around in front of me like I was having an involuntary spasm as I air-guitared through the whining riffs.

HERE WE ARE NOW. IN CONTAINERS. HERE WE ARE NOW. WITH RETAINERS.

I walked through the foyer into the kitchen, humming the tune. Chocolate first. I spun toward the cupboard, and there was Everett, completely naked.

I looked at his dick, currently not being hidden by

his tiny little apron. It was just there, hanging out in the breeze like a salami in a curing cabinet. It was a nice dick, really. Long and thick, but not too thick. Like a good amount of thick. It was pretty, even. A good dick for ClickHeart. Had I mentioned it was thick? It rested against tanned thighs, but they weren't very hairy or anything. Nice manscaped balls.

Fuck, I'd been looking at his dick for too long.

"Blake!"

Oh shit. I pulled out my headphones and looked up into the annoyed face of Everett. He raised a single eyebrow at me. "Are you done staring at my cock?"

I cleared my throat. "Sorry, I forgot you were filming. It's, uh, a very nice penis. A penis made for show business, you know? I was just after the chocolate." I was going to try and eat so much of it that I fell into a sugar coma and hopefully never woke up.

Everett didn't move as I stepped around him and grabbed the chocolate from the top cupboard. The food he was cooking smelled delicious. I walked to the other side of the kitchen island and looked at his camera setup. It was a little too off-center, and if I shifted it just to the left, it'd make his chest look huge while also getting his profile in his shots. And I mean, you could still see the cutting board too, which was apparently important.

"Can I, uh, adjust this?" I pointed to the camera, but waited for permission. I'd be pissed if someone screwed with my composition. He nodded, and I waited for him to finish retying his apron and get back in the shot. I moved the camera around, panning toward his hands before panning back into the position I thought was better for a transition. He picked up where he left off, halving a chicken filet and pressing whipped butter into the flesh, like he was stroking between the folds of a vagina.

Then he spat on it, and I gasped.

His eyes flicked up to me, and I flushed. *Whoops.* But honestly, I couldn't drag my eyes away as he dipped it in buttermilk, then held it up to let the excess run off. Milky-white liquid dripped down the seam of the chicken vagina before he pressed it into a plate of flour, dipped it in the buttermilk again and coated it in crumbs. He turned his back to the camera and turned on the stovetop, showing a toned, muscular ass to the world.

I wanted to sink my teeth into that ass. I wanted to scrape my nails over the skin as it flexed beneath my fingers while he pounded me.

"Press pause. I have to move the camera."

It took me way too long to realize he was talking to me. I hit the pause button quickly, then passed him the tripod, camera still attached. He moved it to a spot on the bench beside him. It got his abs and his frying pan, sure, but he could do better.

"May I?"

Everett nodded, and I extended the tripod right up, so it was almost in line with the cabinet. I angled it down a little so it got his face, the long lines of his body, the pan, and then the slight bulge under his apron. Then I turned the range hood light on, giving shadows and depths to the angles of his body.

"Perfect. Are you ready?"

He nodded, staring right past the camera at me, his eyes hooded, like he was imagining all the ways he wanted to bend me over this countertop and fuck me. Then he shifted that expression right down the lens of the camera, and I could almost hear the fangirls weeping.

"You want your oil sizzling hot, but not smoking. It's all about the long, slow cook. Nothing good ever came from rushing to the end..."

I sat on the bench and watched him work. The soft, firm way he spoke, the way he was methodical about every step, the way he handled a knife, even the way he ate a carrot, was all sensual in a way I couldn't really put my finger on.

Finally, he was done, and I pressed the end button. We stood there in silence for a moment, me sitting on the countertop, his camera clutched in my hands, him in front of me in nothing but a short apron.

"That was, uh, so good. So good. I'm sorry again for barging in, and, uh, looking at your penis. I didn't mean—"

Everett reached out and gripped the back of my head, his fingers threading in my hair as he dragged me into a kiss. It was hard and possessive, and over way too quickly.

When he pulled away, I sat there, dumbfounded. I sucked in oxygen, like he'd just stolen the very air from my lungs. He looked at me, his panic reflecting mine for a long moment. Then he turned and almost sprinted out of the kitchen, leaving me there holding his camera, his kitchen a mess.

What the hell was *happening* this week? Ever since I'd gone to that club with the guys and saw Hennie, they'd been weird. I wasn't self-absorbed enough to think it was because they all fancied me. They were hot as fuck, yet I was a passable six on my best day. Right now, I looked like a goblin from under a bridge —my hair was in a messy knot on my head, there were Cheeto stains on my vintage MTV shirt, and I was wearing my tights that had a hole in the back of the thigh. Not exactly seduction attire.

But that kiss... That had been one hell of a kiss. Demanding, yet so fucking hot that I still felt like I was about to combust. This was going to make it weird, I could just tell.

So I would do what any smart, mature woman would do. I was going to ignore it and pretend it never happened, while secretly thinking about it late at night while I touched myself.

Like a grown-up.

APPARENTLY, avoidance was the way to go. Neither Everett nor I spoke about what had happened in the kitchen, and life went on. I thought for sure he'd have gone to Harrison and confessed, and then we'd need to have an awkward conversation where we'd talk sexual harassment claims and me leaving. Like being sent to the principal's office when you wore a dress with spaghetti straps to school. But surprisingly, it was like it had never happened.

Hennie was picking me up for our date in an hour, and I was still in my workout clothes. Not that I ever worked out in them—they just mopped up the sweat in this damn heat. So far I'd discarded jeans as too hot, and dresses because they'd give me chub-rub unless I wore bike shorts underneath, and I wasn't sure that was first-date sexy.

We were going to a German beer garden in the Hills, and he'd said to dress casually. But it was still a date. I wanted to get laid. No, I *needed* to get laid already. I was like a starving woman in a buffet, and I was going to go straight for that delicious, decadent cake that was so bad for me but kissed like a man possessed, until I couldn't think about anything other than kissing him again. I mean, eating cake again. The metaphors were failing me today.

Finally deciding on a pair of cut-off jeans, an old band tee and my favorite platform Converse, I threw them all on. It would have to do, because I was quickly running out of time. I still needed to do my face so I didn't look like a sweaty swamp troll.

In the end, I kept it simple and had ten minutes to spare. It was moments like these that I missed my friends, though. I wanted to send a picture and ask them if I looked okay, but since I'd arrived in LA, the group chat had been depressingly silent.

Whatever. I'd make new friends. Ones who would accept that not all change was bad and that sometimes, you had to chase your dreams.

With that thought buoying me up, I stuffed my purse and phone in my vintage Coach bag and left my room. Making my way down the stairs, I knocked on Darwin's workroom door. If I had a friend in LA, it was Darwin. He was blissfully free of artifice and he said what he meant, even if it was wildly inappropriate. You always knew where you stood with Darwin, and I appreciated that a lot more than any fake friendship.

He mumbled what I thought may have been "Come in," so I hesitantly opened the door. It was better to reveal the interior of Darwin's room slowly, just in case he was in the middle of setting a scene, entirely naked. Sometimes, he'd even be in the middle of other things—that tended to be embarrassing and had a way of unsettling me for the rest of the day. You only had to watch his face once while he was stroking his huge anaconda dick for it to be indelibly burned into your brain forever.

Opening the door slowly, I huffed out a relieved breath to see he was in sweats and replying to subscribers on his computer. He spun to face me with a grin. "*Muñeca,* you look nice."

"Do you think?" I stepped back and spun in a circle, and Darwin slow-clapped in appreciation.

"Absolutely. Those shorts make your ass look"—he bit his fist—"mmph. Delicious."

I flushed, both at the compliment and with pleasure. I was so gone for this man, but no. *No.* I was keeping my libido, his libido, and that stupid organ that beat inside my chest well and truly under control.

On impulse, I leaned forward and hugged him. "Thanks, Darwin." His chest was warm, his skin smelling like his citrus body wash, and when his arms came up to wrap around my back to return the gesture, a small part of me wanted to fall into his lap and let him embrace me forever.

A small, dangerous part of me.

With way too much effort, I pulled back. He gave me a broad smile. "Anytime, *Amorcito.*" He gave me a soft expression, brushing a wayward curl behind my ear. "Now go, enjoy your date. Maybe get laid for the both of us, because it has been awhile."

I rolled my eyes, finding that hard to believe. Still,

when I walked to the front door, Harrison was there, giving the stink-eye to Hennie. I cleared my throat, and they both turned toward me, dropping their weird macho staring competition.

Hennie smiled, his eyes drifting up and down my body. "You look amazing, Blake. Are you ready?" Nodding, I stepped out onto the front porch with him.

Harrison's hand brushed across my shoulder, stilling my stride down the steps. "You'll message me if you aren't going to come home, right?"

Hennie huffed. "Are you kidding me? What are you, her dad?"

Harrison glared. "I'm her employer, and her house-mate. And you're some random guy she met at a food stand. If you were so concerned about her welfare before, then you should understand my position now," he snapped back.

I held up my hands placatingly. I was really getting tired of being fought over like the last cupcake at a children's birthday party. "It's fine. I promise I'll text if I don't think I'll be home tonight." It was kind of touching, even if they were all being irrational boneheads.

Harrison nodded and released me. I threw him a wink over my shoulder and hopped down the last few steps. I hadn't been able to immerse myself in the big city lifestyle until now, so I intended to make the best of it, even if the date didn't go anywhere.

Hennie opened the door of his car for me. I didn't

know cars, but this one looked nice. The seats were leather, and the interior shone. Sliding in, I watched Hennie walk quickly to the other side and climb in. I buckled up, and he looked over at me, his grin wide. "All set?"

Nodding, I smiled back. "Let's do this."

15

BLAKE

My arm shook as I fought to hold it in place. I couldn't give up, not after I'd come so far. I wouldn't let him beat me. I wasn't sure exactly when he'd turned from a friendly face into my archnemesis, but that was what he was now.

"You're going down, Laurence. I can do this all day." My bravado was false, because anyone could see my hand shaking even as I said the words. It was down to the two of us now—me, relying purely on my hand strength, and Laurence, the guy who looked like he snapped girls in half for fun.

"You got this, Blake. Hold strong," Hennie murmured quietly in my ear, sending a thrill down my spine at the warmth of his breath on my neck. "Think about the glory. Think about your legacy. Think about the free beer." I huffed a laugh. However, even that sounded shaky now.

Bierernst was apparently a very serious competition held on Sunday afternoons at the Bavarian Biergarten. There was a range of games, from the *Schluckspecht*, where everyone had to drink beer from a dick-shaped stein, and the first one to down it, won. Second competition was the *Männerfreundschaft,* where men had to stand over their friends, and one had to pour a stein of beer in the other's mouth without using their hands or arms. Whoever was the driest at the end, won.

Lastly, there was the *Masskrugstemmen*, where you had to hold a stein filled with a liter of beer in front of you with one hand, and the last one to lower their arm was the winner. Somehow, it was down to me and Laurence, mainly because I already had a stein or two of beer under my belt from the last few games, which made my arm feel impervious to the obvious pain it must be in. I didn't think these games were official German games—hell, I wasn't even sure if the words were proper German words—but people were having fun, and I was about to get myself and Hennie free beer for the rest of the night.

I just needed Laurence, the six-five lumberjack with a ginger beard, to quit already before my spindly little arm gave up for good. "Give it up, Laurence. You can only hold that ham hock you call a hand in the air for so long."

"You're cute, little girl, but I could hold this for hours." He didn't even seem even a little shaken. His fist was still holding steady, like he was a surgeon with his scalpel. I was screwed. My hand started to tremble more vigorously, splashing beer over the edges, until finally, I had no choice but to let the stein bang loudly down onto the bar.

"Ooooh, and that's bad luck for our underdog, Blake. Our winner is Laurence!" the DJ crowed from the small stage. "I know who management was rooting for. That guy looks like he could put away a whole keg and then drive his grandma to church, amiright?"

There were more cheers, and Laurence came over, slapping me on the back and propelling me forward a foot or two. "You did good, kid. Why don't you leave the pretty boy to his own devices and let me buy you a beer?"

I laughed, nudging him with my shoulder. "You're getting your beer for free, you cheap ass." Laurence threw back his head and laughed, as did Hennie. "Sorry, my friend—I think we've already discovered I don't have the stamina required to keep up with you. But I wish you luck!"

"Come on, we better get you home before your *boss* calls the cops on me," Hennie yelled as the music started up again. I tipped an imaginary hat at Laurence, following along behind Hennie as he led me from the crowded bar. The afternoon had been the kind of date you only saw in romcoms. It helped that the day was beautiful, and so was Hennie. For once, we'd talked about more than pretzels and how depressing my life was.

I'd learned that the food truck was his grandfather's business, though back in his grandfather's day, it had been just a little pretzel cart on a corner. When his grandfather retired at the age of eighty-three, a fresh-out-of-college Heinrich Jr. took over the business. It was Hennie who'd turned it from a little corner cart into a food truck he took to festivals and concerts, Hennie who'd used his newfound business skills to turn it into a comfortable business.

Hell, I barely knew him and I was proud of his accomplishments.

I told him all about my life before LA. About how art made me feel alive. As the night went on, and as the beer flowed, I told him deeper things. How sad I felt that my parents didn't understand or support my passion. About how my friends had basically abandoned me as soon as I was out of sight. And no matter how it made his jaw tighten, I told him how seen the guys made me feel, even if we only had a professional relationship. How, with them, I could be authentically myself, because there was no subterfuge or disguise when you've had to airbrush someone's testicles.

Now, he wrapped an arm around my shoulders as he led me to the parking lot. I ordered a rideshare as he snuggled close to me, and I leaned into his warm, solid body with a sigh. I was at that glorious level of drunkenness, where my body felt floppy and loose, and everything seemed good in the world. "I had a nice time tonight."

He kissed my temple, holding me a little tighter. "I did too."

"We should go back to your face—place."

He laughed, the sound loud and warm and spreading over my skin, like its own kind of embrace. "I think you've had way too much Bavarian revelry to do anything but go home and sleep it off.

I huffed. "I wanted to break the drought. It's been so long." It sounded like a whine, and indeed, it probably was. But it did elicit a growling sound deep in Hennie's chest.

"Baby girl, I'd be delighted to break the drought for you when you're sober and can feel every single way I'm going to give your body pleasure." He spun, until he was pressing me against the wall of the bar with his body, his arms bracketing my shoulders. "When you can give me proper consent, I promise I will make you scream my name."

I'd like to say I did something sexy like moan. In reality, an awkward giggle came out, sounding like a high-pitched "Heeheehee," and I folded at the knees like a soggy paper bag. Hennie snorted a laugh, wrapping an arm around my waist so I didn't hit the ground completely.

"Fuck, you're cute," he mock-grumbled, spinning me around until I noticed a sedan idling beside us. "Let's get you home."

Putting me in the Uber, he belted me in before climbing in after me. I leaned my head on his shoulder, breathing him in a bit more. "You smell like pretzels."

His chuckle puffed against my cheek. "If I didn't know firsthand how much you love pretzels, I'd probably be offended."

I looked up at him. He was too handsome for me, and when he woke up tomorrow, the beer having worn off, I worried he'd know it too. I wasn't going to waste this moment.

"Can you kiss me, Hennie?"

He didn't answer, just dropped his lips down to mine, kissing me softly. A few brushes of his lips teased mine, and I gripped his shirt, pulling him closer. Or maybe not letting him escape. He buried his hand in my hair and deepened the kiss, his tongue dipping out to stroke along my lips before pushing further into my mouth to stroke against mine. It was lazy and unhurried, like he had all the time in the world to kiss me, and not just the duration of this one car ride.

After giving the driver what must have been a ten-minute show, he pulled away, breathing heavily. I could feel the hard line of his cock under my hand, hear him groan when I squeezed gently, but he stopped me before I could try and dive beneath the waistband of his jeans. Lacing my fingers through his, he placed our joined hands on his thigh and wrapped the other arm around my shoulders, playing with the ends of my now-wild hair.

The sound of the car—and maybe the copious amounts of beer—made my eyes feel heavy. Regardless of my feelings, they drifted closed of their own accord, wrapped in the warmth of a man's arms for the first time in what felt like forever.

Voices dragged me from my sleep, though they were hushed, and I could barely understand more than a few words.

"...beer than a sailor." An amused laugh.

"You better not have..." A growl.

A few more hissed angry words.

I knew I should wake up and diffuse the situation, but I was comfortably pressed against someone's chest, my body held tightly in their arms. I wasn't tiny, so the fact someone was hefting my ass would normally make me feel self-conscious. But not tonight. Tonight, I was giving myself over to that sweet spot between drunk off my ass and fast asleep.

Someone hushed the voices, and I was passed from

one set of arms to another. Gone was the warm smell I associated with Hennie, and in its place was something cool and masculine. I knew I should open my eyes and look at who was carrying me like an invalid, but I didn't want to. I'd just continue to pretend to be asleep instead, because I was a grown-up.

Strong arms clutched me close, and I could vaguely hear Hennie murmuring goodbye.

"Come on, I'll drive you home..."

Then the voices faded, and all that was left was the steady roll of someone climbing the stairs. Damn, if whoever it was tripped and fell, I'd feel like a complete idiot in that moment before I broke my neck and died. My obituary would read something like *He couldn't handle all that junk inside her trunk. RIP.*

I chuckled at my own drunken joke before remembering I was supposed to be asleep. *Shit.* I pressed my lips together and pretended to snore, making the chest I was against shake a little.

"I know you're awake, Sunshine."

"No, I'm not."

"Your sleep talking game is real good, then," Everett grunted, shifting me higher on his chest with an *oof*. Kicking open a door—mine, I assumed—he strode in like he owned it. Which, I guess, he kind of did. But he didn't put me straight down. "Maybe you'll sleep talk and tell me if you had a good date?"

"Mmfwasgood," I agreed, snuggling my face closer to his chest. "You smell nice."

"Did you let him kiss you?" he asked, holding me closer to his face.

I nodded. "Mmhmm."

"Did he kiss you better than I did?"

This time, I peeled one eye open, because I wanted to see his face. Squinting because his face was spinning like he was on a bad LSD trip, I shook my head. "Not better. Different. I liked kissing you both." As I yawned, all my limbs suddenly felt like they weighed a ton. I wiggled, and he slid me onto the bed. I crawled up into the pillows and attempted to bury myself under the blankets, without making any effort to pull them back. "But I can only have one. So unfair."

Then I felt myself drift back to sleep.

16

BLAKE

Despite the absolute bucketload of beer I'd had the night before, I felt kind of good the following morning. The Bavarian Biergarten obviously watered down their booze. Either that, or it wasn't cheap swill, and therefore I didn't feel like I was being poisoned. Whatever the reason, my head only throbbed a little as I stumbled outside into the late morning sun, coffee clutched in my hands like a lifeline. I needed Vitamin D of the sunlight kind, considering I didn't get any of the sexy kind.

I remembered vague bits of the night after the Beer Olympics started, but there were a few blank patches. Most of the car ride home, except for Hennie kissing me. And me confessing that I'd liked Everett kissing me too. I almost wished I'd forgotten that part and could be blissfully ignorant of the embarrassment. I dragged a hand down over my face. I was going to do what I did best right now, and just pretend it never happened.

Today was my day off—because apparently, no one watched porn on a Monday—so I decided to work on some of my own art. Climbing into the round day bed that looked a little like a nest and was fast becoming my favorite place in the house, I grabbed my tablet and pen, and started to sketch.

I'd never been good at freehand drawing, but my art teacher had told me that just because you were naturally good at one thing and not another, it didn't mean that learning the other thing wouldn't make you an artist of more depth. I hadn't agreed at the time, because what was the point of failing at something over and over again, when I could be perfecting the thing I was good at? But now, I could appreciate what she was trying to say. Studying the composition of a face would make me better at my job, even if it was editing social media pictures.

I mindlessly sketched until my tablet flashed, my mother's name appearing with a request for a videochat.

Holy shit. Holy shit.

No, I could do this—just keep it vague and upbeat. I needed to talk to her at some point; now was as good a time as ever. Clicking Accept, I pasted a bright smile on my face.

"Hi, Mom!"

"Blake. You answered very quickly. What are you doing?"

"Uh, nothing?" Fuck, why did I sound guilty? I wasn't even fibbing yet. "Just sketching on my tablet. How are you?"

"Oh, you know. As good as I can be. My sciatica is playing up again, but at least I'm not June Whitman."

"What's wrong with June?" I asked, trying not to sound too relieved and make her suspicious again. Mom liked to gossip, so she would be on a ten-minute tangent about June and then probably come back around to everyone in town and at the church before coming back to me. It'd give me time to scramble for answers.

I kept my questions vague, but definitely requiring more information, so she continued on. I asked about Dad and the garden club, but I avoided so many topics, it was like walking through a mine-field. We didn't talk about my ex, even when she mentioned him in passing, so I knew she was still keeping in touch with him. We didn't talk about my friends. We definitely didn't talk about my art or the course I was supposedly doing—at least, not if I could help it.

She was telling me about the Jacobsons' poodle being split for custody during the divorce, when the patio door opened. "Hey, Shawshank, do you want a juice for your hango—oh, hey. Sorry, you're on the phone."

"Blake, who's that?" My mom's voice was suddenly an octave higher. She was looking to the side, like she could see around the frame of the video call. "Blake? Are you frozen?"

I wish. I was tempted to fake a glitching sound, but I didn't know how authentic it would sound. Maybe if I sat really still and didn't breathe, she'd get confused and wander off. Actually, that might be just bears.

"Blake?"

I cleared my throat. "Oh, just a colleague, Mom."

"Why is he in your dorm?"

"Uh, the accommodation is co-ed. This is a communal space?" Fuck, a lie, but not really. That was the key to lying well, right? Keep it sort of true?

"Why is he calling you Shawshank? Have you been getting in trouble with the police again?"

Jesus H. Christ. She made me sound like a damn master criminal. Or a crackhead. "No, Mom. I just told him about Bacon the turkey. It's a joke. Oh, I have to go to class. I'll call you later, okay? Love you, bye!" I mashed the End Call button like my life depended on it.

Harrison looked at me guiltily. "Sorry about that. I didn't see you were on a call."

I shook my head with a sigh. "Not your fault."

He sat down beside me, handing me a tumbler

filled with something green. I was polite enough not to screw up my nose, but apparently, my thoughts were written all over my face.

"Just give it a try. I promise it tastes good, and your poor liver will thank me later." Taking a sip, I raised both eyebrows. It was earthy tasting, but also surprisingly sweet. I made a happy humming sound, and Harrison laughed. "So, you still haven't told your mom about the academy or getting a new job?"

"Nope." I popped the p for emphasis.

"Do you intend on doing it?"

I sighed. If I was being honest, I'd thought about just waiting out the year, creating a fake certificate to show my parents, and never admitting I'd been scammed like a ninety-year-old war widow. "Maybe."

Harrison shook his head. "That's a no, I think. Well, who am I to judge? Everett and I left Minnesota, rather than be honest with our parents."

"About being influencers, and the ClickHeart stuff?"

He shook his head. "No." Standing, he peeled off his shirt until he was only in a pair of shorts. "Want to swim?"

Shaking my head—because I was struck mute—I just stared like a creeper as he dived into the pool. He swam a few lengths, and I watched his muscles stretch as he glided through the water. The sound of the splashing drew the other guys out too, and Darwin cannonballed into the water with a splash.

Swimming to the edge, he grinned at me. "Get in, *Muñeca*. The temperature is perfect."

It did look amazing, but the glare of the water was starting to give me a headache. I held up the tumbler of green juice. "Soon."

Darwin swam away, finding an inflatable ring to climb into and lounge on the water. Everett was sitting on the edge, casting me looks that I was pointedly ignoring as I sketched mindlessly. Soon enough, Harrison came over to talk to him, dragging half his body out of the water to rest his arms on the ledge. He looked like a merman, and I drew him as such, catching the bunched muscles of his back, the slicked-back waves of his damp hair. The way his face was tipped up to look at Everett as they talked quietly.

I included Everett, adding him topless but with a jaunty little sailor hat, which made me giggle softly to myself. I took my time with his tattoos and the arm muscles that bunched completely differently as he stared down at Harrison with affection. His face was soft, his lips slightly curled, his eyes totally focused on the man beside him.

I studied the image on my tablet in front of me with a frown. There was something there that I was missing. I messed with the shading a little more, but that wasn't it. It was something to do with the eyes. I hadn't recreated the sparkle enough. The look of—

"*Holy shit.*" I looked at the picture, then back at the guys, then back at the sketch. "Holy shit." Tossing my tablet to the side, I stared at Everett and Harrison. "Holy shit, you're *gay.* You're gay, and I kissed your boyfriend." I scrambled off the day lounge. "I'm so sorry. I didn't know. I mean, how could I know? Actually, *you* kissed *me*, you asshole!" I shouted, glaring at Everett. "You two obviously love each other, and you're kissing me? That's so wrong. God, I'm so stupid."

"Blake—"

"It's like that silly meme that goes 'History would say they were just roommates.' But you aren't roommates, are you? You're... You're lovers?" I frowned as everything they'd said and done didn't line up with the people I'd just drawn in that sketch. "You had your hands all over that girl in the club," I said accusingly at Harrison, before snapping my gaze to Everett. "And you *kissed* me."

He raised an eyebrow. "So you've said."

Harrison pushed him, swimming toward me. "Blake, you don't understand. It's complicated."

"Is he your boyfriend?" Harrison hesitated, but then he gave me a single nod. I looked at Darwin. "Did you know?"

Darwin shrugged, still floating in the inflatable ring. "Yeah, of course. It isn't a secret, I didn't think?"

He looked between me and the guys. "I just assumed you knew. You only have to be in the room beside them for a little while before you get a real eye-opening idea that they're more than friends, no?"

I felt like such an idiot. Grabbing up my tablet, I stomped into the house, ignoring their calls for me to come back. I had to come to terms with the fact they'd lied to me. Kinda.

I mean, they'd given me that whole sexual harassment spiel, and this whole time, they were a couple? On the other hand, they were technically my employers, so they didn't really owe me their relationship status, right?

I stomped into my room and shut the door, confused about why this was affecting me so much. The sad truth was I was upset because in my head, I'd built a fantasy around Everett, and Harrison too, for that matter. One where they swept me off my feet, where beautiful men like that could love me.

Or maybe it was PMS. *Yeah, let's blame PMS.*

17

BLAKE

I hid out in my room for the rest of the day, but by the following day, I knew I had to get my shit together and go back downstairs to have a proper discussion. One, because I had a job I was supposed to be doing, and two, because I was an idiot for behaving the way I had yesterday. They didn't owe me anything, and I'd stomped away like a freaking toddler.

So hiding out my room had been partially because of embarrassment, as well as disappointment. A disappointment I wasn't going to overanalyze anymore.

The house was silent again, but I could tell the housekeeper had been through, because the place looked like it was ready for a magazine shoot. Everything had been cleaned and polished until it shone, and there wasn't an ounce of clutter anywhere. They were like a ghost, or a Brownie, just appearing in the early morning before anyone woke, and gone before Everett came down to turn on the coffee machine.

Definitely one of the best parts of living here.

I found Harrison in the office by himself, his headphones in his ears as he stared at a spreadsheet on his laptop. Knocking hard, I sucked in a few fortifying breaths before he turned.

His face instantly folded into a frown. "Blake—"

"I'm sorry."

We both spoke at once, and he shook his head immediately. "No, you have nothing to apologize for— we should have been more upfront regarding our history. Everett told me he kissed you; we should have spoken to you then, at the very least." He stood, walking over to where I remained frozen in the doorway. "My relationship with Everett is complicated. But I promise you, he is free to kiss you, as long as that's something you want too?"

I wasn't sure if he was asking me a question as an employer, as a friend, or as Everett's not-quite-boyfriend.

"I think I need to understand a little better. You guys..."

"Fuck?" he offered helpfully.

"Yeah. And you love each other?"

Harrison's mouth quirked up on one side. "Yeah.

He's my best friend. We've been through a lot together."

"So you're a couple?"

He sighed, dragging me further into the office so we could sit down on the couch in the corner. "Yes and no. Everett is a part of my soul, but we aren't monogamous. We've never been monogamous. At first, it was because we came from a tiny-ass town in Minnesota that was homophobic as hell, so we both had girlfriends and tried to write off the things we did with each other as just teenage exploration. Girlfriends would come and go, but we could never give each other up. Eventually, we came to terms with the fact that we were meant to be with each other. There was no giving him up.

"When we came out to our parents, it didn't go well. For either of us. So we left, came to LA, scraped by on his kitchenhand wage, and I did construction. But there was something missing, something that wasn't right. He was everything, but neither of us were... I don't know, soft? Nurturing? We were best friends, we fucked, we cared about each other. I'd take a bullet for him, but we were both kind of emotionally stunted by the reaction of our families. By those little voices that had been indoctrinated into our brains that what we were doing was... unnatural, I think is how my mother put it."

He huffed a bitter laugh, and I couldn't resist the

overwhelming urge to hug him any longer. Wrapping my arms around his waist, I squeezed him tight to me, trying to infuse him with every ounce of my care and respect so he knew I was on his side. "That's not true at all. It's the most natural thing in the world." I pulled back so I could look up into his face, seeing the sadness that pulled at the corners of his eyes, even though his lips were curled into a small smile. "Besides, I can vouch for the magnetism of Everett firsthand." I waggled my eyebrows, and his laugh was real this time.

"I bet you can. Kinda leads me to the point, really. I wasn't telling you this story for sympathy, I promise. What I'm saying is that both Everett and I are bisexual, though neither of us have ever pursued another relationship with a man. Only with women. So whatever you and Everett have, it's okay."

I chewed my lip, my arms still tight around his waist. Because I had Hennie, I should tell him that it didn't matter, that I would respect the boundaries of our agreement and keep everything strictly platonic.

But then he reached down and cupped my chin, tugging my lower lip from my mouth. "You're making it swell," he said softly, and my lips parted further as I stared up at his face. His blue eyes were dark, and I felt like I was stuck in their hold. He leaned down slowly, and I *knew* he was going to kiss me. He was moving slowly, giving me time to step away before things got weirder. But my hands felt locked against his spine, trapping him to me so he couldn't escape.

His lips brushed mine, and I tried not to think about the amount of different men I'd kissed in the last forty-eight hours, instead focusing on the warm, firm kiss Harrison was brushing over my lips. He tasted minty, like he'd just brushed his teeth, and his teeth scraped over my bottom lip, the way mine had been moments before.

His hands dropped gently to my hips, his fingers pressing tightly into the soft flesh there. He deepened the kiss, his tongue sliding into my mouth. I moaned against his lips, and he jolted away.

He was breathing heavily as he broke out of my arms and took several steps back. "I'm sorry, that was so inappropriate. A mistake."

Ouch. I'd been called a lot of things before, but a mistake was a new one. I gave him a tight smile and a laugh that sounded fake, even to my own ears. "Accidents happen. We've both made mistakes these past few days. How about we forget about it? Oh, look at the time. I should go to work."

With that, I got the fuck out of that office. Kissing one boss was an accident. Kissing two was a problem.

With truly shitty timing, my phone buzzed in my pocket. Pulling it out, I instinctively knew it was going to be Hennie, because Karma really was a petty bitch sometimes.

. . .

> Sausage Peddler: I had an amazing time on Sunday. Can't wait to do it again.

I WINCED. *Fuck me.* I was such a screw-up at this. Maybe I should've stayed back in my tiny-ass town and married Paul, so I'd never know the absolute guilt of leading way too many men on, like some kind of small-town Jezebel.

> Me too. We should set something up for next week. Bring pretzels.

> Sausage Peddler: You only want me for my carbs.

> And your giant cock...tail frankfurts.

> Sausage Peddler: I'll have you know, it's at least as big as a bratwurst.

> I bet you say that to all the girls.

The more we bantered back and forth, the more I found myself smiling as the message notifications appeared on my phone. But also, the more resolute I became. No more fucking around with the guys. I'd concentrate on Hennie and what we had going on. We had something good, maybe even something great, and

I wasn't going to squander it pining over men I couldn't have.

Decision made, I got back to work photoshopping out weird shadows on a portrait of Everett in the kitchen, adding a little shadow around the bulge behind his apron, creating contrast on his tattoos, shifting the lighting until he looked like a moody bad boy who was making you breakfast after fucking you hoarse the night before.

I spent hours on the promotional image until I could feel his gaze like a caress. It meant nothing, except that I'd done my job correctly. That was all.

I could do this. I was a professional.

Losing myself in my music and the art, I repeated that to myself as I edited the video we'd made the other day. Adjusting the lighting, adding a sexy sound-track behind it, slowing it down so every moment of eye contact was prolonged. The heated expressions, the moody scowl—all of it was enhanced.

And if I paused on the moment when he looked past the camera at me, if I zoomed in on the pure lust in his expression, if I let my heart race and my stomach twist at the expression? It was just a natural reaction.

It didn't mean anything.

I needed to get the hell out of this house. Not with Hennie, or with the guys. I needed some serious girl time, and I once again felt the loss of my girl tribe. Still,

LA was a big place, and I needed to find something that involved people with all their clothes on.

Shooting off a quick message to Darwin to say I was going out, I saved my progress and grabbed my purse. I needed to get out of here.

18

BLAKE

laying tourist at the Getty Center that day gave me a much-needed reset, and I found a new rhythm with work. Being among the classic pieces of art had really reinforced why I was here, in LA. In life, even. I wanted to make art, as a career and not just a hobby, like everyone back home had suggested. And if I wanted that, I had to be serious. I was making big bucks with the guys, and to ruin it for dick was a stupid move.

Decision made, I went back to treating the guys like housemates and friends. No more moon eyes. No more stolen kisses. Just an average working relationship. Everett and Harrison seemed to silently understand the shift in our relationship back to professional, and no one made any moves.

The only person who seemed to be struggling with

keeping a professional distance was Darwin, but I didn't think that was anything personal. He was just a hugger. I was going through his art package with him in my office, and he was making all the right noises as he looked at the mockups.

"Beautiful, *Muñeca*. I had no doubt. Maybe adjust the font on this one? It is hard to see with the dark shadows in the background."

I made a note directly on the copy I was showing him. "No worries. I can do that."

"So, Blake. You want to tell me what is going on with you and our other two housemates? It has been slightly frosty here lately."

I shrugged. "It's too confusing, Darwin. I don't want to create a drama just because I'm a woman, and prove their initial hesitation over hiring a woman right, you know?"

Darwin hummed, dragging me back onto the couch. "I see. It's not because of their sexuality?"

I reared back so I was looking at his face, my mouth hanging open in surprise. "You think I'm being cold because I don't like that they're bisexual?"

"No, sweetling. But you wouldn't be the first person to hide their bigotry behind different excuses."

I shook my head violently. "No, of course not. I still think they're amazing men, and even braver than I originally thought. But it's messy getting in the middle of what they have. Even you have to admit that."

He cuddled me back into his side. "Life is messy, with those two especially. But you are an artist. Surely you know things need to get a little messy if you want to create something amazing."

I breathed in the soft scent of him, appreciating the heat of his skin against my cheek. He was wearing black sweats with no shirt again, so his dusky pink nipple sat right beside my cheek. Like, I could've flicked my tongue out and licked it, that's how close it was. I resisted, though, because I'd legit just had an entire meltdown about boundaries.

"You aren't suggesting I pursue them despite the fact they so obviously love each other, right?"

I'd been watching them with different eyes. The soft touches that I'd never noticed were suddenly like beacons. The way that Everett always made Harrison's coffee first, even if he wasn't in the room yet. The way Harrison complimented every dish Everett made. The way they sometimes finished each other's sentences.

I'd been so *blind*. Almost as blind as those two.

Darwin shrugged. "We live an alternative lifestyle already. Why are we being pushed into boring boxes in our private lives, when we have the opportunity to truly love how we please?"

I could feel the frown creasing my brow. My mom would chastise me for giving myself wrinkles, if she could see me now. Hell, she'd chastise me for more than my wrinkles if she could see me curled up next to a half-naked Darwin, despite how innocent the gesture was. I'd go straight to a nunnery for that one.

"What are you suggesting, Darwin?"

He kissed the top of my head. "You'll figure it out, *Amorcito.* And when you do, let me know." He straightened, turning so he bracketed me between his body and the back of the couch. "Now the real important question. Blake?"

There was something about being between a rock and rock-hard abs that kind of broke a girl's brain, but I managed a distracted, "Mmm?"

"Will you come to the AdEx Awards with me?"

My eyes flew up to his. "The what?"

He flopped back down beside me. "It's the Oscars for, like, the sex entertainment industry. It's only the second year they've accepted nominations for the best subscription accounts on ClickHeart and its competitors, and I got nominated."

I bolted up straight, throwing my arms around his neck and giving him a tight squeeze. "Holy shit! Darwin, that's a big deal. Congrats! Of course I'll go with you." I pulled back and dropped my arms. "Are you sure you shouldn't go with someone more... I don't know, glamorous? Or someone from the industry?"

Or someone with an actual sense of style?

He just shook his head. "No, I want to take you. You're important to my brand lately, and that definitely got me more viewers and more attention from the judges. You deserve to be there too."

This man, he was too damn sweet. "Thank you, Darwin."

He kissed the side of my head and dragged me back down to his chest. "You deserve it. Now, show me those still shots again, the ones from the bath."

I pulled my tablet back out and showed him the shots, and the whole time, my brain whirled. Did I want to go to a big event with him? Right now, we lived in this tiny bubble, where hardly anyone knew what I did for a living. But if I attended such a massive event, it would be like admitting this was what had become of my dream.

I wasn't ashamed, but I kind of felt like I should be. And that wasn't fair to any of the guys, least of all to Darwin, who hadn't been anything but amazing this whole time. Giving myself a stern talking-to about being a giant hypocrite, I started making plans.

"When are the awards?" I asked, interrupting the comfortable silence between us.

"This weekend."

I sucked in so much oxygen as I gasped, I choked on it. "This *weekend?*" I screeched. "Darwin, I can't be ready to attend an awards night in three days! I don't have a dress. My hair looks like it's been chewed by a giraffe with no teeth. I can't do it."

"Doll, you stress too much." Said the guy who

probably just had to throw on the tux in his wardrobe and be done. "Besides, I've got you. Give me twenty minutes; I'll fix all your problems." He grabbed his phone and called someone. "Dani? I need your help." He frowned. "No, I'm not in jail. If I was in jail, I would have called Olista." I could hear the sound of a woman's voice down the line, and Darwin rolled his eyes at me. "I know only psychopaths call when they could text, but I didn't want to wait six weeks for you to send a reply. This is urgent."

He switched to rapid Spanish, and they seemed to be negotiating. Darwin's eyes kept flicking back at me, his lips curling into a smile, before he'd roll his eyes again.

"Okay. Okay. Yes, see you then. *Te amo.*" Hanging up, he tossed his phone on the couch beside us. "Dani will meet us on Rodeo Drive tomorrow."

"I can't afford Rodeo Drive, Darwin!"

He waved a hand. "Don't worry about it. Dani knows people."

Great, Dani knew people. But who the hell was Dani?

19

BLAKE

Turned out the guys owned an insane underground garage that was like stepping down into the Batcave. What would you expect a man who owns a mansion in the Hills to drive? Probably not a Prius, yet here we were. Actually, all of the cars were electric or hybrid. Though one of them was a sleek new Tesla, so maybe they weren't all as economically conscientious as Darwin, but still, points to the guys.

When I pointed it out to Darwin, he laughed as he drove up and out of the garage. "Sports cars are nice, but at least I don't have to worry about someone stealing my Toyota every time I step away."

We drove down to Rodeo Drive, and Darwin parked in an underground garage beneath what looked like an open-air mall. But, you know, designer-style, so everything looked like it had been plucked out of Milan. A valet parked us, and Darwin escorted me up the elevator and into the main courtyard.

"Dani said she'd meet us at Chanel."

"Who's Dani again?" I asked casually, because if I was about to meet one of Darwin's exes, I felt like I should be mentally prepared for that.

"I'm his twin," someone said behind me, and when I turned, I'm fairly sure my jaw hit the faux cobblestones. The woman in front of me was *gorgeous*. Absolutely stunning, which made sense if she was Darwin's twin, because he was a handsome guy.

But that wasn't what shocked me. What shocked me was that standing in front of me was Diani Rose. High-end fashion and Victoria's Secret model, notorious socialite, fashion icon and social influencer, Diani Rose.

I didn't take my eyes off the woman in front of me as I reached out and punched Darwin in the arm. "You are in so much trouble, Mister."

Diani—Dani—laughed. "Oh, good. You aren't prone to simpering like his last girlfriend. We'll get along just fine. Hi, my name is Dani." She held out her hand. "You must be Blake. I've heard a lot about you in the group chat."

I blinked slowly, the synapses from my brain to my mouth failing. "Group chat?" I replied dumbly.

"Uh-huh. The family group chat. DeeDee wonders

why we mute him in the messages, but he gossips like an old maid." She hugged her brother, who kissed the top of her head affectionately. "Let's go—we've got an appointment at Chanel, and I only have so much sway. Dee, we'll meet you at Toro's at one. The reservation is under your name. Go buy yourself a new suit; you've been wearing your old one since your prom days." She hooked her arm through mine and dragged me along. "When he told us about the whole Blake misgendering thing, I'm not going to lie, I thought it was hilarious. The boys need some shaking up."

I was wildly out of my depth right now. "You know the guys?"

Dani snorted, coming to a stop outside the glass-fronted door of Chanel. "Of course I do. You know Darwin and I have five older sisters, right?" I nodded. "Well, Everett and Harrison became the brothers poor Darwin always wanted. Which meant they've been folded into the family, like their last name is Zambrano too. Mama even prays for their souls along with Darwin's—given that they are doing the devil's work, you know. Showing off their penises to the world," she said in a heavily accented imitation of her mother, while crossing herself, but she laughed as she did it.

"So your mom knows that Darwin..." Uh, this was a weird conversation to have with a person who'd shared a womb with the man whose dick I saw on a near-daily basis.

"Is a pornstar? Or a social media influencer, as he likes to be known. Honestly, I think it would be less offensive to be called a pornstar these days."

Pushing through the glass doors, I tried not to let my eyes bounce like I'd never stepped foot in a designer store before. Which I hadn't, of course. We had an outlet mall and Cynthia's House of Fashion back home, and let's just say, neither stocked Chanel. I was suddenly extremely aware of the fact I was wearing a simple black wrap dress that I'd bought at a thrift store. It had no label and had been $4.99, but you could tell it was quality. Plus, I looked nice in it.

"Diani!" Someone swanned across the room, tall and elegant, her perfect sunshine-blonde hair piled professionally on top of her head. She reached over and air-kissed Dani on the cheek before smiling softly at me, flicking her eyes up and down my body, then frowning. "Dani," she hissed. "You know we have nothing here that is going to fit this gorgeous creature."

I didn't know if I should be offended or complimented. She was calling me fat, but she'd also called me gorgeous.

Dani waved a hand. "Darwin is not big on details. Besides, aren't you meant to have the full range of sizing?" Her sarcasm was thick, and the assistant rolled her eyes.

"Sure we do. Online." She snorted derisively. "Apparently, only thin women like to shop." Considering both of them had to be a size four or less, their derisive tone made no sense. They fit perfectly into the demographic.

Dani patted my back. "I should introduce you; I'm being rude. Blake, this is my bestie, Celine. Blake is Darwin's new roommate."

The girl's eyebrows shot straight up. "Oh! You're *Blake!* I've heard all about you."

I flushed pink. Who knew the grapevine was this convoluted?

Dani was nodding. "It's a big secret, but Celine and I want to start an accessible high-fashion brand to rival these old white guy fashion houses. Something with a little flavor and flair. Something that will fit both you and me, and look glorious on us both. A runway for all people." She kept her voice low, but there was no shortage of passion.

Celine was nodding along, her eyes shining with pride. "Soon we'll have enough connections that we can poach a few contacts." She slid her eyes around the room. "But you didn't hear that from me."

I mock-zipped my lips.

Celine grinned at me, then turned back to Dani. "I have it on good authority that Lustra just got a new shipment of old Hollywood vintage, and I know there'll be something there for Blake. She has that beautiful Golden Era figure—she's going to look like the sexy lovechild of

Jessica Rabbit and Marilyn." The elderly sales assistant across the room started to give us the stink-eye, though her face transformed when she took in Dani, clearly recognizing her. "I've got a lunch break coming up, and I wanted to check it out as well. Wait for me?"

Dani nodded, linking her arm back with mine. "We'll be checking out the new Volette line." Volette was one of the biggest fashion brands to come out in the last three decades, taking on even the stalwarts of the Italian and French fashion houses.

Celine moved away to help customers who'd just walked in, and Dani swanned around like she owned the store and found it wanting. The price tags on some of these things were giving me heart palpitations. I had no idea what Lustra was, but I hoped the cost was less than an eye-watering six grand for what was essentially a black sack with glitter thread.

Dani dragged me over to Volette to kill some time before Celine's break, and I stood in the background as the assistants fawned over her. She was gracious, but seemed slightly annoyed. She refused to let me fade into the background either, instead getting my opinion on things and actually listening, as if I wasn't the worst-dressed person in the room. Nothing in here would fit me, even if it was my style. When Dani tried on a jacket that looked the color of cat vomit, and the store assistant cooed over how gorgeous she was in it, Dani read the dislike on my face and requested my real opinion.

I shrugged. "The color of that fabric looks like the front garden of a frat house after a rush party."

The store assistant, who'd introduced herself as Sandy with an X—though I couldn't figure out where the X went—screwed up her nose in my direction, like I was the vomit in the room. "You make it work, though, with your figure," she cooed. "We are high fashion, and sometimes that means being daring with your clothing choices, not just going with the Walmart aesthetic."

Well, I knew where that one was aimed.

Dani had wandered back into the racks, tuning out Sandy with an X's fawning, so I did something that would have horrified my well-heeled grandmother. I gave Sandy with an X the finger. "I don't have to work in high fashion to know when something's an eyesore. And that thing is ugly as hell."

She narrowed her eyes at me and lowered her voice. "What would you know? The only thing that will fit you in Beverly Hills is the Cirque du Soleil tent three blocks over. Better hurry, though—I hear they're leaving in two days."

I blinked at the venom in her voice. All because I hated a jacket?

Dani was suddenly between us. "You did not just say that." She stripped out of the jacket and threw it into the face of the girl. "I'd start writing your resume, shop girl, because you're done. No one—and I mean *no one*—speaks to my friends like that." She pulled out her phone, and her fingers flew across the screen. Sandy with an X's face went pale. Dani grabbed my hand. "Enjoy your last day of work, *puta.*"

She dragged me out of the high-end store, muttering in Spanish. We made it down the street and around the corner before she pulled me to a stop, then hugged me. Like, *really* hugged me. I could see the hugging thing was definitely in the DNA. "I am so sorry she treated you like that, Blake. No one should be able to speak to you like that. No one." She went off on another tangent in Spanish again, but I heard the word *puta* a few more times. That word I knew.

"It's really okay, Dani. I'm aware that I'm not a perfect size zero."

She hissed, her eyes fiery. "I don't care if you are a size thirty, Blake. No one gets to put you down, especially not around me. We're friends; I don't care if we only just met. You mean something to Darwin, so you mean something to me. That means I'll call out that bigoted bitch, and she'll get fired. I've got one hundred and twenty million followers—I mean more to that brand than some little assistant with too high an opinion of her own style. If I don't call out the double standards of the fashion industry, who will?"

The fire in her eyes was intense, and I stood a little

bit in awe, and honestly, a little terrified of her. She was defending me like I was flesh and blood, which was more than my mother ever had. I still remembered one particular shopping trip as a child, with Cynthia commenting on my measurements and my mother telling her to give me a bigger size, because I'd gotten my grandmother's thick waist and belly pudge. They'd thought I couldn't hear them, but that shit had affected my self-worth for years.

My own mother wouldn't defend me, yet this random fiery woman was willing to drag down an entire fashion house for me. Looping her arm through mine, Dani smiled over my shoulder at Celine, who was hurrying toward us, her eyes wide.

"Did you just slam Volette? Girl, that post has already hit nearly a hundred thousand likes, and I only just got the notification that you posted."

Dani grinned at me. "No one insults my friends."

I was going to cry. *Gah. Nope. Not me. Not here.*

Celine squeezed my shoulder softly, her eyes knowing, and I knew she'd been on the receiving end of Dani's righteous protection too. "How about we go buy something completely fabulous?" she suggested.

I nodded, clearing my throat. "Let's do it."

20

BLAKE

Lustra turned out to be a consignment store off of Rodeo Drive. Apparently, Celine hadn't been the only person to hear about the new shipment, because the place was swarming when we got there. But Dani stuck out her elbows and forged ahead, and soon enough, I had an arm full of dresses she'd foisted upon me.

In contrast to the previous stores, no one here seemed to give a flying fig newton who Dani was. It was a feeding frenzy, and neither Celine nor Dani seemed scared of getting their hands dirty. It was intense. They even had security to break up fights. Have you ever seen a high-society bitch fight? It was all twelve-carat knuckle-dusters, and Manolo Blahniks to the jugular. It was vicious, and I kind of loved it.

"Move your ass to the counter or the change rooms,

kid, or just get the fuck out of the way. Let the rest of us give those items a new home." Some woman with a short bob and oversized owl glasses jabbed a bony finger at me.

Celine appeared like an avenging golden angel. "Unless you want to lose one of those cheap acrylics, you'll keep your hands off our haul, lady," she hissed, directing me toward the change rooms. There was a little line, but we stepped up just in time to nab the next spot. "Don't even worry about those ones, because I've found you the perfect dress." She looked around the crowded store. "DANI!" she hollered like a fisherwoman. "Okay, in you go. Strip off your clothes. You'll need a hand with this one."

I didn't have time to do more than gape at her as she stuffed me into the change room and waved at me to get undressed. She hung a full-length garment bag on a high hook, unzipping it with the flourish of a magician. As I stood there in just my bra and underwear, she gave me a quick up and down.

"You're going to need proper undergarments for this dress. Dani will know where. Now, hold still." In a wave of silk and velvet, she pulled the dress over my head, letting it settle down my body with a tug until the ends brushed the ground. Not going to lie, it was tight, but it was beautiful. Celine worked silently, adjusting sections and ensuring the lines of the dress fell like shadowed waves. "It needs a little adjusting, but I can make that work. Okay, ready?"

I gazed at myself, a little awed, in the mirror. Fitted at the waist and flaring down in a classic gown shape, the black dress was strapless and made predominantly of silk, except for a panel of abyss-dark velvet on the chest and another flowing in a triangle down the back, into a small train.

Celine pushed me out of the change room, and there was a collective *ooh* from the waiting crowd that made me flush. Celine went to stand beside Dani, and Dani sighed. "That's the one. She looks gorgeous. Do you feel gorgeous, Blake?"

I nodded, still a little stunned to be standing in such an amazing dress.

Celine's smile was almost like that of a proud artist. "It's an obvious replica of an original Christian from the fifties, but it's a good replica. Materials are quality."

"You're sure it's a replica?" Dani asked, her eyes traveling over the dress, like a farmer buying a prize cow.

"Girl, you think I would even contemplate altering a real Christian Dior? You're out of your freaking mind."

Dani stepped forward, rubbing the silk gently between her fingers. "It's good, for a knock-off."

Celine grinned. "You know it. What do you think, Blake? Is this the dress? Don't feel obligated, because even if you don't buy it, we both know it's coming home with Dani anyway."

The supermodel in question waggled her brows. "Nothing I've picked can rival this. You've got good height for this dress too: not too tall, not too short. It's like it was made for you."

Yeah, sure—with a few adjustments, like an entirely new back. Right now, the thing didn't even zip halfway up my spine.

Soon enough, Celine was helping me out of the dress and giving it over to Dani, then I was tying my thrift store wrap dress back on and sliding into my six-year-old Converse. When I emerged, neither Dani nor Celine were anywhere to be seen.

"Blake!"

I finally spotted Dani by the door and dodged my way through the crowd. "Excuse me. Sorry," I muttered, trying not to get in the way of some pushy Beverly Hills Housewives. With a capital H, because it was a serious profession.

Dani had a large shopping bag in her hand, but not nearly big enough to have my dress in it. "Let's go," she said, tilting her head toward the door.

I frowned, looking around for Celine. "But I haven't paid for the dress yet." In fact, I hadn't even looked at the price tag yet, which may have made all the difference as to whether it was coming home with me or not.

Dani waved her hand, stepping out onto the sidewalk. "Celine has it. I've paid for it. Darwin will pay me back, so don't worry about it."

"But—"

"No buts. Celine will do the alterations tonight. You just have to go home and measure across your bust so she can get it perfect." She smiled. "Come on. Darwin is already messaging me and whining he's hungry. Seriously, that man eats like a horse, but never puts on a single ounce, yet I'm out here eating like a bunny and still put on two pounds while I was in Ibiza."

I hurried along behind her, noticing the people around us instinctively moving out of her way. What would it be like to be so in control of your body and your surroundings? She walked right at one man, who looked confused when she didn't naturally move out of his way.

"Watch it, bitch," he growled, and Dani's cheeks flushed red.

"*You* watch it, bitch. I didn't know having a dick gave you automatic right of way," she snapped back, and the guy's face turned an odd puce color. Grabbing her elbow, I dragged her around him. She yelled over her shoulder at the guy in Spanish, and he shouted back until I dragged her back into the high-end mall where we'd left Darwin.

I'd seen the odd paparazzi hanging around outside the stores on Rodeo Drive, but we were off on a side street, so surely they couldn't see her lose her shit, right? I'd feel terrible if someone wrote some shitty gossip article about her while she was literally out doing me a favor.

I couldn't have been more relieved to see Darwin's smiling face as we came up to the restaurant. Dani was still muttering in angry Spanish about the ignorance of people.

"I see my sister is being her usual calm self."

"I think she's hangry?" I said lightly, and Darwin chuckled, throwing an arm around his sister's shoulders.

Dani glared. "Men. Always think you're the center of the universe."

"Even me?" he asked, pouting.

She sighed, still scowling. "Not you, DeeDee. I beat that shit out of you when we were seven."

He threw back his head and laughed. "She ain't lying." He flung his other arm over my shoulder. "Come on. She isn't the only one who gets hangry."

Dani stepped up to the maître d', giving him a friendly smile that had the older man completely smitten in an instant.

"Did you have fun?" Darwin murmured beside my ear.

That was a hard question. It had been frantic and wild, but all in all, I'd enjoyed it. "It was a rollercoaster, but I had fun." I didn't tell him about the shop girl.

Darwin chuckled into my hair. "I know that feeling.

She has always been that way, my twin. She is always giving you one hundred percent of her personality; there's no off switch. I've tried."

Dani waved us on, and I had the feeling of being herded again. "She's intense, but she's lovely."

"Mmm, my mother joked that she got all the go and I got all the stop." He guided me to the table, pulling out the chair for me, which no one had ever done for me, ever. The maître d' did the same for Dani.

"The waiter will be here to tell you today's specials momentarily," he said, giving us a pleasantly professional smile.

I looked at the menu, quickly realizing that none of the items had prices. I had a feeling this was one of those "if you have to ask, you can't afford it" situations. That was okay. I'd get a salad and hope that was the cheapest thing. That's normally how it worked, right?

"Blake got the most beautiful dress. She looks amazing in it. I'll send you the bill, brother dearest."

Darwin nodded happily. "Sure thing. Blake looks amazing in anything."

He said that about *me*, to his supermodel sister. *Gah.* He couldn't be more wrong, but I still flushed pink.

"Get whatever you like, *Muñeca*. My treat." He reached over and put his hand on mine, stroking my fingers gently with his thumb, before picking up his glass of water and taking a sip. I could feel Dani's eyes on me, but I purposefully kept my gaze averted, because if I looked at her now, I knew she'd be able to see just how much I wanted Darwin as more than a friend. She'd see how much I desired being cared for like this all the time. If he was like this for a friend, how much love would he show a woman who had his heart?

My chest ached at the very idea someone would one day be the center of his world, and that person wouldn't be me.

21

BLAKE

The weekend, and therefore the AdEx Awards, loomed on the edge of my consciousness for the next couple of days, which was probably a good thing because it gave me common ground when talking to Harrison and Everett. If we could talk about the awards night, then we wouldn't have to talk about Kiss-Gate.

Whoever would've guessed that a convention of sex workers would be the non-problematic topic of conversation?

Fortunately, both Harrison and Everett were attending as well, so I wouldn't be alone in a sea of strangers. When I'd asked—completely coolly, like the answer didn't matter to me at all—if they were taking dates, the answer had been no. I then realized I was a selfish bitch, since that gave me more satisfaction than I had any right to feel.

I spent hours upon hours stressing about being trussed up in a gown that didn't fit, that I probably wouldn't be able to breathe in, around arguably the biggest sex symbols in the country, both male and female.

As if that wasn't enough, between now and then, I had another date with Hennie, which made me the world's biggest hypocrite. Pushing back from my desk, I uncurled from my chair. I'd spent too long working today, not on the guys' stuff, but on my own art.

It had started with a thought and morphed into something more. Something beautiful, but also sexy. Well, at least I thought it was. I'd taken some of the photographs of the guys and altered them until the guys became almost dream-like. Hazy yet vibrant, like something out of a myth.

I wouldn't show the guys, not yet at least. My fumbling attempts were probably a little creepy really. It was one thing when it was for work—it was an entire other thing when I was doing it on my own time.

Stepping into the hall, I walked toward my room. I was going to get my swimsuit and take a dip, maybe work out some of the tension that was gathering in my shoulders at the thought of the awards night and my relationship woes.

Karma was an asshole. I'd given years to Paul, and

he'd disregarded what I wanted, like my dreams had meant nothing. And now I had Hennie, but I was treating him like he was a consolation prize, when he really wasn't.

I didn't mean to look as I walked down the hall. I really didn't. But I could hear soft murmurs coming from Harrison's room, and the door was cracked just a little. Call me nosey, but I peeked.

Harrison had Everett in his arms, his lips to his cheek, his large hands slipping beneath the waistband of Everett's gym shorts, gripping his ass. I knew the feeling. I wanted to grip that ass too.

Everett was fisting the bottom of Harrison's shirt, moving his mouth to kiss him. It was a hard kiss, void of the gentleness either of them showed me, and I didn't know if that was because I was a woman, or if it was because they knew each other so well and could let out a little of their forcefulness with each other.

Everett's hand slipped down further until he could slide inside Harrison's sweats. Harrison grunted, and while I couldn't see exactly what was going on, I had a pretty good imagination. I willed my feet to move, telling myself that this was a gross invasion of privacy.

I felt like I was sinking in quicksand, like I was Artax, but instead of the swamp of sadness, it was in the sandhole of horniness. The lake of lust. The dung pile of desire. Whatever. You get the point. Right now was not the moment to unpack childhood trauma from a fictional movie.

"Everett," Harrison groaned as he tugged down his sweats, and I saw Everett's hand wrapped tightly around his cock, stroking it roughly until Harrison was gasping and throwing his head back. I gasped, and Everett's eyes met mine.

Shit.

"Either join in or shut the door, Sunshine. This isn't a spectator sport, unless you're naked on the bed playing with that pretty cunt while you watch."

I squeaked out a noise that was nearly inhuman in its embarrassment, and shut the door quickly, hurrying down the hallway, trying to forget what I'd seen. *Impossible.* It was forever imprinted on my brain now.

Almost sprinting the last few feet to my room, I slammed the door shut, breathing heavily. I closed my eyes, but all I could see was Everett's big hand wrapped around Harrison's fat dick. That was it. I needed to put my bikini on and get the hell in the pool to cool off, before I combusted.

And then I'd call Hennie and bring forward our date, because I needed to get laid if I thought that creeping on my employers fucking was a good idea. Pushing down that guilt, I texted Hennie that I wanted to catch up tonight at his place, and that I'd bring wine. Then I pulled on my high-waisted retro bikini and rushed back down the hall.

I kept my gaze averted from Harrison's door, pretending it didn't even exist. I worried that if I slowed down for even a moment, if that door was open again like an invitation, I would invite myself in, consequences be damned. I'd do anything and everything Everett said, and I'd probably enjoy the hell out of it. Then I'd inevitably feel guilty and panic. Then I'd probably call Hennie and confess, and he'd tell me I was a raging ho. Then I'd quit, because I wouldn't be able to stand the embarrassment, until finally, I'd end up living under a bridge, sketching the aliens that had beamed Crazy Pete up in '73 out in Iowa.

"Are you okay?"

I jumped three feet in the air at the sound of Darwin's voice beside my ear. "Fuck me, Darwin. I almost peed my pants."

Darwin tilted his head at me. "Well, not my usual kink, but I'm not against it. I'll try anything once." His lips curled into a smirk as he said it, and I slapped him hard on the chest.

"Uh, that's not my thing either. No shame, though."

Darwin snorted. "No shame. So can I ask why you're just standing on the bottom step of the stairs like you're glitching?" His eyes roamed up and down my body. "In a bikini, at that. Though, no complaints."

I flushed pink, and I worried that maybe you'd be able to see that right across my body. In my frazzled state, I'd forgotten to grab my cover-up.

I shrugged. "I was thinking?"

"Is that a question?"

"No?"

"Was *that* a question?"

I huffed an annoyed breath, but it got me moving. I headed through the front foyer toward the back of the house and the pool, where hopefully I'd sink to the bottom until my lungs exploded.

Darwin followed behind me, looking amused as hell. "Are you going to tell me? You know I love the gossip."

"No gossip. Just needed to cool off." With that, I shallow-dived into the pool and swam all the way to the other end without coming up for air. And then I turned around and came back again. When my lungs finally began to burn, I surfaced. The first thing I saw was Darwin's smiling face as he sat on the pool edge, his feet dipping in the water.

"Confess, *Muñeca*. What made you so hot and bothered?"

"I accidentally saw Harrison and Everett... you know."

Darwin's lips flattened, but his eyes were wild with laughter. "Doing the monthly budget? Packing orders? Trying to make borscht? You're going to have to be more specific here, *Amorcito*."

I narrowed my eyes on him. "I saw Everett giving Harrison a hand job. Are you happy now?"

He was doing a good job of not laughing at me. "Not as happy as Harrison probably was."

I splashed water into his face. "Stop it. I feel terrible. I stared at them like a real creep, and they caught me."

Pushing off the side, I sank to the bottom. I could see the hazy reflection of Darwin above me as he gazed down into the pool. The pressure of the water on my body, along with the sound of the silence, calmed me a little. It would be okay. By this stage, I was queen of the ostriches, and this was no different.

My lungs began to ache with the need to draw breath, so I pushed off the bottom and rocketed to the surface. Then I double-checked my boobs were still in their bikini, because no one ever wants a nip slip.

I floated onto my back as we just existed together in the peaceful silence that had been a hallmark of our friendship, soaking in the sun until my bones were languid. Kicking gently, I moved myself to the edge. Darwin was lying on his side, his head propped up on his elbow.

"What do you think I should do?"

"Put on sunscreen?"

I looked down to realize I was going slightly pink beneath my naturally olive skin. It wouldn't burn, but still, my mother had always taught me that a tan was the first step toward skin cancer. I rolled my eyes at Darwin. "I won't be out here much longer. No, what do

you think I should do about Hennie, and the guys?"
And you, I thought, but kept that bit to myself. "I can't keep dipping between them." I lifted myself up so I was lying on the side of the pool on my arms.

"You know my opinion, *Muñeca*."

I rolled my eyes. "Not choosing isn't really a choice. Besides, it would take a hell of a woman to juggle that many guys, and I don't have the lady balls for that."

"I think your balls are plenty big enough, Blake. What I think isn't big enough is your sense of self-worth. I can see you struggle with your wiener guy already. You make allowances that you normally wouldn't make, because you worry he's out of your league. Like if you voiced what you want, you'll be left with nothing." He leaned forward. "Take what you want, *Amorcito*. Take what you want, and I know that the universe will give you what you *need*, even if you don't know what that is right now."

His face was so close to mine that his breath cooled the water droplets on my cheek. "How do you know?"

He laughed, shaking his head as he rolled over onto his back and looked up at the sky. "I just do."

22

BLAKE

I almost called and canceled on Hennie once I'd cooled down, but I didn't want to be that girl, which was why I was waiting on the front step with a bottle of wine in my hands. Darwin had given me a bottle of Chilean strawberry wine, which sounded freaking delicious. I'd avoided the other guys all afternoon like a ninja, listening for footsteps and running the other direction anytime I heard someone.

Was that a chickenshit thing to do? Yes. I didn't care.

I was clinging to the last days of summer in a soft floral dress that was a couple of inches above my knee, making it flutter prettily in the wind, like I was a movie heroine. I guess we *were* in Hollywood.

Hennie pulled into the horseshoe driveway, and the smile on his face made my own lips curl. Rolling to a stop, he climbed out of the car and grinned at me. "You look gorgeous."

Then he kissed me. Right there on the doorstep. My hands tangled in his shirt as I hung on, his tongue and lips exploring my mouth hesitantly. He pulled back, and I could see how people *might* fall in love at first sight. There was something extremely magnetic about Hennie, a pull I was failing to resist. I didn't want to resist it, not really.

"Hello, *Leibling.*"

"I'm not convinced that doesn't mean 'penis warmer' in German, you know?"

His laughter fanned over my cheek. "I promise it's not." He nipped my earlobe as he leaned in to whisper, "Not yet, anyway."

And just like that, I was once again putty in his hands. The lust I had banked since spying on Harrison and Everett was now back in burning full force. "Let's go," I murmured into his shoulder, stepping away. I felt flushed, my skin tingling with anticipation, despite the butterflies in my stomach doing their best impression of a crash derby.

He led me over to his car, opening the passenger door for me before slipping around the hood and sliding in beside me. As he pulled out of the driveway and into the quiet street, I let the silence of the car, and the irresistible smell of Hennie's cologne, curl around me. He reached across the center console and wrapped his hand on my thigh, giving it a tight squeeze.

"I know—well, I don't know exactly, but I made an educated guess from the tone of your text—that you kind of wanted to skip straight to the dessert portion of the evening."

My face flushed, but I decided to own it. "Not going to lie, I'm kind of, uh, horny right now."

Well done, Blake. Way to sound confident and in control. Not at all like a bumbling virgin.

Hennie slid a brief look at me. "Is that so?" he asked, his voice dropping to a low rumble I could feel across my skin, almost like a purr. I nodded, not trusting my mouth to come out with something that didn't sound completely ridiculous right now. "So if I slid my hand up your thigh..." he whispered, not taking his eyes off the road, but still skimming his fingers along the inside of my thigh. "Would you be wet for me? Would my fingers slip inside you easily, because you're ready for me?"

Holy shit. Well, I would be now. Hennie could talk dirty. "*Yes.*"

His hand skimmed under the skirt of my dress, and I spread my thighs a little more, because no matter how much I'd wished for a thigh gap over every birthday cake in my teen years, they were thick.

Hennie let out a grunt of satisfaction as he squeezed my inner thigh, his pinky finger brushing the fabric of my underwear. I sucked in a breath as he slid the edge of his finger along the seam of my underwear twice more, before withdrawing his hand completely and bringing it back up to grip the steering wheel. "Fuck me, Blake. You're temptation personified. You're making me forget all my good intentions."

"Hennie..." I didn't want a gentleman. I wanted him to pull over and fuck me over the hood of his car.

"Don't worry, baby. I won't make you wait long. The things I want to do to you..." He winked at me, and I let out a shuddering breath. "But you're worth more than a booty call, *Liebling*. I'm going to take you out for dinner first. I'm going to show you how much I value your time and your personality."

"And then you're going to take me home and fuck me silly, right?"

He gave me a crooked grin. "Yeah, *Liebling*. I'm going to fuck you until you're hoarse from screaming my name."

The air in my lungs whooshed out again with relief. "Promise?"

"On my fucking life," he growled, speeding us through the busy streets of LA.

"When you said you were taking me to dinner, this wasn't quite what I imagined." I looked around at the food trucks lining the perimeter of a public park, long poles with strings of lights zigzagging between them lighting up the square. There were tables scattered around, but most people were sitting on picnic blankets under the lights. "It's absolutely beautiful."

Hennie grinned at me, and I felt my heart beat harder. "Not as beautiful as you." He had a picnic blanket dangling from one arm and my hand wrapped in the other. "Come on, let's go claim a good spot. The band will start soon."

There was an absolute melting pot of cuisines from around the world in that one little square. People called out to Hennie as he walked past, and he waved and chatted to a few of them. Some asked after his family, and there were more than a few inquisitive looks in my direction.

Finally, we reached a spot in a slightly darkened corner, on the periphery of the square. "So these are your people?"

Hennie spread the picnic blanket down. "I guess you could say that. I grew up around most of these people, or their families. The old-timers knew me when I was younger, helping my grandfather with his stall, and now I see a lot of them at events like this."

I tried to picture a younger Hennie running through the crowds of people, dodging toddlers and canoodling teenagers. It was easier to imagine him in the food tent, handing out bratwurst. "He started you early then?"

Hennie laughed. "They had me kneading pretzel dough instead of playing with playdoh as soon as I could follow instructions." He kneeled down onto the rug, holding a hand out to me. "Ma'am, your table is ready."

Twisting my fingers in his, I let him pull me down to the ground, tucking my legs beneath me so I didn't accidentally flash the whole park my goodies.

On cue, a folk band started playing a gentle version of "Zombie" by The Cranberries, which was surprisingly good with the fiddle. Hennie tucked his body closer to mine, giving me body warmth and a place to rest. That was what Hennie had been to me in a nutshell, since day one. A safe harbor to rest in. A sun I could bask beneath and know that everything was going to get better. I tilted my head back against his chest and let out a contented sigh.

"Blake?" He said my name softly, ruffling my hair so it flicked across my cheek.

"Mmm?"

"I'm going to kiss you now."

And he did. He hesitated a moment, a fraction from my lips—I guess, to give me an out, except I wanted to kiss this man more than I wanted my next breath. I leaned into the kiss, and his hand came up to cup my cheek as he moved his lips over mine. It was a teasing kiss, just an embrace as he didn't push it further, no matter how much I wanted him to. It was a promise.

Finally, someone wolf-whistled in our direction, and he pulled away with a laugh. "Let me feed you so I can look my father in the eye when he asks if I'm treating you right, and then we can finish what we just started at home."

I raised an eyebrow. "What *you* started. Again."

He brushed his lips across my temple. "Don't worry, baby. I fully intend to make good on all my promises." He stood, pulling me up and into his arms. "Let's go find something to eat."

We walked from stall to stall, Hennie frequently chatting and introducing me to his colleagues. I decided on pupusa, and stood off to the side as the elderly woman cooked it on a flat grill with expert efficiency.

She gave me a smile, a gold tooth glinting in the lighting. "So you and young Heinrich. He is a hand-some one, no?" She was definitely South American, her accent still reasonably thick.

I gave her a self-satisfied smirk back. "Very handsome."

"He ages well. His grandfather was a very hand-some man until the day he died. Good genes. Some men, they age like good wine. Other men weather like donkey hide." She tilted her head at her equally old husband, her face alight with mischief.

"I'm sure you don't mean me, *amor*."

"Of course not." She grinned, handing me my

plate, now with a perfectly cooked flatbread on it. "I'm just saying, that family has good genes. Good for strong, kind babies."

I flushed pink and thanked her for my flatbread. Hennie came up, balancing cheese fries in one hand and wrapping the other around my waist. "Whatever Pearla is saying is a lie, I swear."

"She said you had good genes," I quipped back. "Definitely sounds like a lie."

He kissed my cheek. "On that, she's one hundred percent correct."

Pearla shooed us away to serve the next customer, and we wandered through the crowd back to our quiet spot. "You know, I don't even know how old you are?" I asked as he fed me a cheese fry.

"Twenty-nine."

"Holy shit, robbing the grave much?"

He looked at me, wide-eyed. "How old are you?"

"Twenty-two."

He put a hand to his chest. "Jesus Christ, you scared me! I thought you were going to say eighteen or something. That's only seven years; no need to start calling around retirement villages yet, *Liebling*."

With his blond hair and square jaw, I could almost see what Pearla had meant when she said he'd age well. His hair would go white, but he'd always have that long, straight nose, those sparkling blue eyes, and that jaw.

My phone buzzed suddenly, and I looked down at the screen.

> Grumpy Swedish Chef: We need to talk about our kiss.

I reflexively covered the phone, but it was too late. Hennie had seen the message, and my guilty response. His face shuttered, and the sweet idyllicism of the moment before was gone.

I was going to fucking *murder* Everett.

"Hennie, I..."

He shook his head, lifting his food to his mouth, his face impassive. "It's fine, Blake. We aren't exclusive."

But all the joy from the moment was gone, and I knew that despite his words, it wasn't coming back tonight.

23

BLAKE

Unsurprisingly, Hennie dropped me home after the food trucks, and we sat in the darkened car in front of the house for a long time in silence, until I couldn't take it anymore. "I want to explain."

Hennie shook his head. "There's nothing to explain, Blake. You're a grown woman, and you get to make your own choices about who you kiss."

I huffed, frustration burning in my chest. "I want to kiss *you*." *Fuck.* "I want to do *more* than kiss you."

Still shaking his head softly, he looked away. "You know what? I know enough about you now to know that you should have this opportunity to explore what life has to offer you. There's a whole city"—he looked past me to the glowing windows of the mansion—"a whole house, even, full of people to help you discover what you want. But I can't be a booty call, Blake. I know that's the stereotype for LA guys. Players. I don't have time for that shallow stuff. I want to know that if I'm spending time with a girl, then it's for something meaningful."

It sounded like he was breaking up with me, and we'd only been on two dates. He wasn't even giving me the generic "It's not you, it's me" speech, because we both knew it was me. I was the problem.

I let out a shuddering breath. "It isn't like that. I really like you, Hennie. This isn't something casual for me, I promise. You make me feel..." Wanted. Desired. Safe. None of those words felt right. "You make me feel like I matter. I feel so fucking happy when I'm with you."

"But?"

I wanted to huff out there was no but; however, that would be a lie. Because the but was *there,* in your face, like it had just been on a one-way trip to a cheap Brazilian lipo clinic for implants.

"I don't know what it is. Maybe you're right— maybe it's because I've just made my way to the big city from Bumpkinville, and I'm mistaking every ounce of desire I possess as something more meaningful. But those guys in that house took me in without any experience whatsoever, because they believed in my art. In my vision. So few people have *ever* believed in me like that. And kissing Everett"—and Harrison, and kinda

Darwin, but I was leaving those bits out—"creates more problems for us then any random sex could ever warrant. I mean, for fuck's sake, he's gay."

Hennie's mouth dropped open. "He's *gay?*"

Oops. Probably should have kept that to myself, although no one had said it was a secret. "Well, not gay-gay. Like, a little gay. He and Harrison are a couple. Kinda. But not really. Apparently, it's complicated."

He raised his eyebrows at me. "Apparently."

"I just mean, there's nothing stopping me—us— from investigating what we have, this attraction I think we both feel toward each other? That weird, instant connection?" I held my breath as I looked to him for an answer. This was the real make-or-break moment, because if he didn't feel this same pull, then this whole thing was for nothing.

When he gave a short nod, air rushed from my lungs. *Thank goodness.*

"I don't want to give you up, and then in twelve months, finish my contract and always have regrets."

His whole body went rigid. "So... I'm a consolation prize?"

"What? Fuck. No. You are the *main* prize. I mean, you aren't a prize at all; this isn't a damn race." I leaned across the seats, gripping his face until he was forced to look at me. "You are sexy, and kind, and funny, and I love spending time with you. I want to spend *more* time with you." I brushed my lips over his and sighed happily when he let me. "However, I'd be doing exactly what I swore I'd never do if I abandoned this opportunity, and these guys who are now my friends, for a man. Don't ask me to do that."

Hennie shook his head, but not vigorously enough to shake my grip on his cheek. "I'm not asking you to quit your job, Blake. I'm just asking you not to kiss other men. There's a difference." He peeled my fingers from his cheek. "This is my fault. I was a fool to believe that I could have the girl *and* my dream. Having a girlfriend means giving time that I just don't have anyway. So maybe it's better this way." He climbed out of the car, coming around and opening my door.

Why did this feel so heartbreaking? I'd been on two dates with this guy; I barely knew him. However, as I climbed out the passenger side of the car, my eyes filled with tears.

"You deserve someone who treats you like you're their whole world, *Liebling*, and so do I." Kissing me softly on the lips, Hennie moved away and back to his car, climbing in without looking back and gently pulling away, back out onto the dark streets.

I had no idea how long I stood there, watching his taillights fade. Even after they were long gone, I just stood there in shock. I'd been dumped by the first decent guy I'd ever dated, and it had been my fault.

"Blake? Are you okay?"

I spun at the sound of Harrison's soft voice. "Why wouldn't I be?"

"You've been standing out here for twenty minutes, and you look like you've been crying."

I swiped my face with the back of my hand. It came away damp. *Huh.* But you know what? This hadn't been my fault—well, at least not much. It was Everett's fault.

"I'm going to murder that... fucking asshole!"

I barged past Harrison and into the house. I stormed into the kitchen first, but it was empty, and I ignored the sound of Harrison calling me back.

"Everett!" I screeched, taking the stairs to his bedroom. It was late. Where else would he be ruining my happiness than in his bedroom? Anger was white-hot across my skin, and I didn't think about what I was doing. I burst into the bathroom, making the door slam against the wall.

"Hey!" I could see the foggy outline of Everett behind the shower screen.

"You... You... You complete and utter *asshole*. How could you do that?"

"Do what, Sunshine?"

"You know what you did, you fucking prick." I slapped my palm on the glass. "You sent that message, knowing I was out with Hennie. You *knew* there was a chance he would see it. You knew how he'd react." I was incandescent with anger. "Why the fuck would you do that?"

He growled low. "Get the hell out of here, Blake."

Ripping the shower door open, I stood there. "You get the hell out here and tell me why you'd ruin my chance at being happy." I choked on the words, but I pushed down the angry tears that threatened to burst from my eyes. "He was a good man, a kind man, and he wanted me. I know you don't fucking understand, but he was my chance."

Everett wrenched the taps off and burst out of the shower, making me stumble back. He stood there in front of me, naked, dripping, and furious. "Your chance at what? Settling for the first pretty boy who showed you any interest?" He prowled forward, and I edged backwards, my ass hitting the vanity. My heart was pounding, his stare intense as he held my eyes. "You deserve better. More."

My heart was pounding, but it wasn't fear. No, it was rage, regret, and yeah, a whole lot of primal lust. "You barely fucking know me. How could you *possibly* know what I deserve? You're just a petty asshole who's mad at me for watching you fuck your boyfriend. I'm sorry that I walked past your open door. I'm sorry I stopped. I didn't mean it, okay?"

He stepped close to me now, his hand coming up to grip my chin, his large hand curving around to my throat. "Barely know you? I've watched you every fucking day since you moved in here. I know what coffee you like. I know if you see a dragonfly over the pool, you'll stop what you're doing to watch it, every time. I know you look at Harrison with desire in your eyes, your cheeks flushing as he speaks to you. I know you stroke your wet little pussy thinking about me, late at night." I tried to tear my eyes away from his mesmerizing golden ones, but he held me fast, so I squeezed them shut. His face dropped toward mine, so the low thrum of his voice felt like it was spreading over my closed eyes. "He might have been a choice, but he wasn't your only choice."

My eyes flew open, and he was there, inches away. "Please." It was a whimpered plea.

"Please, *what*, Sunshine?"

I let out an angry, humiliated huff. He wanted me to surrender. To capitulate. My mind wanted me to storm out of there, but it was in a battle with my body, which was already curving toward him.

Just once. We could do this just once. "Fuck me, you pompous asshole."

He chuckled as he dived forward, capturing my lips with his. And it was a capture—I had no doubt, as his tongue pushed toward mine, stroking it, coaxing it, and ultimately conquering it. And me. His hands slid under my ass, and he lifted me onto the top of the vanity.

My knees parted for him of their own accord, and

he slid between them like he belonged there. I was suddenly extremely aware that he was naked, as the hard length of his cock pressed against my thigh.

He wrapped one arm around my waist, the other hand propped up against the mirror so he could pull away from my body slightly. "Is this what you want, Sunshine? Want me to fuck this glorious damn body? Sink into these curves?" He slid the straps of my dress from my shoulders, tugging them down until my lace-covered breasts came into view. "Black lace. Fucking beautiful, even if you are wearing this for another man."

He leaned forward and bit my nipple gently through the lace, a soft punishment. Then he sucked the tender flesh into his mouth, and I arched into his body, the sensation rocketing straight to my core. He moved onto the other nipple until I was moaning his name softly, gripping his head to my breast, right where I wanted him. He was just rough enough to make my body sing, like he already knew me intimately.

"Do your panties match?" he growled around my nipple, making my heels press into the backs of his thighs. His hand slid up my hip, dragging my dress with it, and I wiggled my ass until my dress was free and bunched up around my waist. Everett's lips moved from my breast as he used his free hand to push my legs apart. "Mmm, they do," he purred, dropping to his knees in front of me. "I wonder how they taste."

I collapsed back against the mirror like I was boneless as he licked and stroked me through the lace. He looked up at me, his eyes sparkling with satisfaction. I wondered if I'd survive this.

I wondered if I even wanted to.

24

EVERETT

With my face buried between her thighs and her staring down at me defiantly, I knew I was a goner. Hell, I'd known it before, but now it felt almost inevitable. This woman had taken control of my thoughts, and I couldn't escape them.

I didn't even want to struggle.

When Darwin had told me she was going on a date with that fucking sausage seller, jealousy reared its ugly, fat head, and I'd gambled. What a fucking gamble it was. Harrison was going to murder me, but right here, right now, I didn't give a damn.

"Are you going to come on my face, baby? Are you going to coat my cheeks?" I sucked her clit between my teeth and growled. Her thighs snapped around my head, and I turned my face to bite the thick part of her thigh. She squeaked a protest, loosening her grip, and I went back to licking and stroking her. Then I tore off the fragile lace, wanting to taste her properly.

"Everett!" she hissed, and I smirked.

"I'll buy you new ones. A dozen, if you want." Then I wrapped my lips around her clit, sliding two fingers inside her tight pussy. She gasped, jackknifing in half.

"Oh god," she whispered, her legs trembling, which was always a good sign. "*Please.*"

A caveman-like sense of satisfaction flowed through my veins at the sound of her begging. "Come for me, Sunshine." She scowled down at me, like she'd just remembered she was mad at me, so I scraped my teeth lightly over her clit.

"Mmmph, oh my *fuck*, Everett. You're still an asshole," she moaned, and I curled my fingers inside her, tapping that good spot, until she came on a scream. Her body fluttered around my fingers, her juices soaked my face, and I grinned as I rode out her orgasm with her.

Pulling back, I wiped my cheek on her bare thigh. "Mmm, that's my good girl."

I pushed up off my knees and curled my body over hers. I gave her a sloppy kiss that probably tasted of her juices, plunging my tongue into her mouth so she could revel in the glorious taste of herself.

"Tell me I can fuck you, Sunshine." My dick was aching, it was so hard. If I didn't get inside her right now, I might actually burst. "Tell me I can slide inside that tight, wet cunt and make you mine properly." I kissed down her cheek, over her jaw, until I could take her earlobe between my teeth. "Let me show you how desirable you really are."

"Yes," she breathed, her voice a thin whisper of need.

God, this woman. She fucking wrecked me every single day, and she had no idea. Wrenching open the vanity door, I grabbed the condom I knew was floating around in there. We didn't invite girls over here often, but we all knew that keeping it wrapped was the only way to prevent accidents.

I pulled her off the counter and bent her over it, that glorious round ass just screaming to let me fuck it. Not today, though. I ground my dick against those perfect globes. "Look at you. Fuck, you ruin me, Sunshine." I worked fast, ripping open the condom wrapper and sliding it on. "Are you ready?" I paused, because I wanted—no, *needed* to know she wanted this too. I looked at her reflection in the mirror, holding her gaze. She nodded, but I wanted the words. "Tell me again, baby girl. Tell me you want me to fuck you."

"Yes, Everett. Fuck me already, you goddamn tease," she snapped, but her eyes were flooded with lust.

I slapped her ass hard, then I slid in while she was squeaking with outrage, and it turned into a long, low moan that matched mine. I soothed the red mark on her cheek with my hand as I settled into her, breathing through the need to move, just wanting to prolong this fucking bliss.

I met her eyes in the mirror. "Watch me fuck you." And she did. Those pretty green eyes met mine as I pulled back and slammed home again. I watched her face as her eyes rolled up with pleasure, her lids closing in bliss. I slid out and in a couple more times, a slave to the need to feel that sweet friction.

"Eyes up," I barked, and her eyes flew back to mine. I curled my body over hers, kissing up the curve of her shoulder until I could press my lips to the skin of her neck and suck hard. She moaned my name again, but it wasn't enough.

I wanted to hear it more. Over and over.

Gripping her wrists, I moved them up until her palms were on the mirror. "Hold on tight," I murmured into her ear, then I pulled back and thrust in. Each time, I pulled out almost all the way and slid home, faster and faster, until we were both panting and grunting. I watched her head tipped back in the mirror, her full breasts bouncing with every thrust like a buoy in rough seas. I was transfixed. This woman had me under her spell; I never wanted to escape.

My balls started to pull tight, and I gritted my teeth. "Everett! *Fuck,* I'm going to come... Don't stop. Don't stop," she moaned, like even wild horses could make me stop right now. I didn't change pace, didn't speed up, didn't slow down. I just rode this fucking hindbrain rhythm until she was clenching hard around my cock, screaming my name so loudly, it echoed off the tiled walls.

My rhythm got wild, and I gripped her hips, fucking her harder. I fucked every forbidden feeling, every ounce of jealousy I'd felt, everything I felt for her when I knew I shouldn't, into those thrusts. My fingertips would probably leave bruises, but I'd kiss each and every one.

She was still whimpering her moans, and I knew by the way she clenched around me, she was going to come again. I could hold out.

"Come for me once more, beautiful. Let me feel you one more time." I grunted as she clenched down around me. I reached around and flicked her sensitive clit. That was all it took for her shaky arms to collapse as she came once more, and I came right along with her.

I collapsed over her, sliding my arms beneath her body and protecting her face from the cold, hard marble of the vanity. We lay there like that, lights flashing in my vision, breathing like I'd run a marathon, for god knows how long.

Finally, I peeled my sweaty chest from her back, sliding my softening cock from her body. I peeled the condom off and threw it in the trash, then I stood there like an idiot with a thumb up my ass. What the fuck did I do now?

"Do you want a shower?"

She straightened, her cheeks flushed pink. I could see the bliss receding away as what we'd just done settled in, and I almost wanted to fuck her again, just to chase away the reality of the night.

"No. I should, uh, just go back to my room." She looked around for her dress, and instead, I picked up my shirt and passed it to her.

"Wear this. I'll put your dress in the laundry." I was messing this up. I could tell. "Sunshine... Blake. This was..."

She dragged my shirt over her head. "A mistake? No shit." Her eyes were blank, and I knew I'd fucked up from the beginning. She turned toward the door.

I couldn't repeat my stupid mistakes again. I reached for her hand, stilling her. "No, Blake. Not a mistake. Inevitable. This meant something to me. I know I've screwed up, more than once." She snorted out a rude noise, and I resisted the urge to laugh. "I won't make that mistake again. I want this—whatever this is."

She looked at me, her lips parted, her eyes conflicted. She was shaking her head softly, and my heart clenched. "What about Harrison?"

What about Harrison? That was a million-dollar question, because that man was my soulmate in every way that counted. If I wasn't such a fuck-up, that would've been enough.

But it wasn't enough. It never had been. Not for either of us.

"We'll figure it out. I want a chance to figure it out."

She looked at me for a long time, then she just turned and left. My shirt stretched down tight over her ass, she just walked out, like we hadn't just had amazing sex in my bathroom. I watched her go, my heartbeat pounding in my ears. The door shutting softly may as well have been a slam.

What the hell just happened?

I didn't even bother with clothes, just walking over to my bed and falling facedown on it. My head whirled with thoughts and regrets. I didn't regret having sex with Sunshine. It was... everything I could have dreamed of and more. But I hated how we'd gotten to this point, and I was fairly sure she'd never forgive me.

A knock on my door made me groan into my pillow. Speaking of not forgiving me. "One second." Pretty sure it was Harrison, and I was doubly sure I shouldn't greet him with my dick still out from fucking someone else.

I threw on some sweats and walked over to the door. As expected, Harrison was there, one eyebrow raised. I stood back, and he walked into my room like he'd done a thousand times before. "Smells like sex in here."

"Harrison…"

He held up a hand. "I'm sure I'm not the only one in this house wondering what the hell just happened. And I don't mean the sex. That one was pretty evident from one floor and two doors away. Actually, I'm pretty sure the Janders next door heard that one too." I slumped down onto the floor, and he followed me down. He looked at me intently, his blue-green eyes filled with concern. "She was on the driveway crying, then suddenly she was storming up here like she was ready to fight the very devil. What did you do, Everett?"

I let out a shuddering breath, gripping his shirt so he was lying down on the floor next to me, rather than looming above me. "I ruined her date. I want to tell myself that it wasn't on purpose, but that's a fucking lie. I knew she was on her date when I sent her that message."

Harrison let out a disappointed grunt. "What did the message say exactly?"

I shrugged, like I couldn't remember the exact fucking words of the message. "It was about the kiss."

"Everett," he huffed, his exasperation clear. We didn't keep secrets, so Harrison knew I'd kissed her. I also knew he'd kissed her. We were both in agreement that no matter how amazing she felt in our arms, it was too fucking complicated. There was no other way this could go than badly.

"I know, I know. But D said she was out with that

other guy, and it was like every reasonable thought just left me. There was a caveman in the back of my head yelling that some other man was going to be touching my girl. Kissing my girl. And if Darwin is to be believed, fucking my girl." I implored him to understand with my eyes. "I just couldn't do nothing. I know —" I cleared my throat, because this was the awkward bit. "I know we said that we weren't going to do anything about this thing between us all, but... she's under my skin, and I can't get her out. I don't *want* to get her out."

Harrison was still shaking his head, disappointment etched onto his beautiful face. "There are better ways to do that than making her hate you enough to fuck you, Everett. I shouldn't have to tell you that." He stroked a hand over my cheek. "If this is what you want, I'm happy for you. I'll support you. I promise I won't make waves, as long as she doesn't want to sue us for fucking sexual harrassment."

For the second time that night, I realized I was breaking someone's heart. "No. Harrison, no! That's not what I meant at all. I don't want *just* Blake. I want you too." I dragged him into my arms. "For fuck's sake, Harrison. You're the fucking love of my life. I love you. Any future I have has you in it."

He pulled back, crinkling his nose incredulously. "Then what are you playing at? You can't claim I'm the love of your life and then pursue something serious with Blake. That's not fair to either of us. Eventually, you'll have to choose, and I'm giving you permission to choose her."

I buried my fingers in his hair, tilting his head back to look at me. "I choose you every time. I feel like I've proven that."

"Then you're stringing her along? Time has shown we can't make each other one hundred percent happy, Everett."

"Why do I *have* to choose? Why can't I have you both? Why can't we all have each other? I know you like her, Harrison. Otherwise, you wouldn't be up here giving me the disappointed parent speech. I know you're attracted to her too. Why can't we have it all?"

My heart raced at the idea. I hadn't thought the whole thing through when I'd sent that message, purely operating on a jealous instinct. But the more I thought about it, the more I wondered if Blake had come into our lives like Fate's gift.

"You want us to be polyamorous? Or like, an open relationship?"

My gut rebelled at the idea of either of them sleeping with anyone else. We could have everything we wanted right now. "Definitely poly." We'd seen it in the industry, of course. Polycules with their own Click-Heart accounts. It was almost like a surprise who you'd be seeing on their channel at any time, and in what combination. They were popular as hell, but there was no way I could open up something as intimate as making love to Harrison to public viewing. And there was no way I wanted anyone to see my Sunshine but Harrison.

Harrison tilted his head, and I could see him thinking it through. Then he shook his head. "Fool's dream, Everett. Blake's a good girl. She isn't going to enter into an alternative relationship just because you want her as well." He poked me in the chest. "I don't think she'll enter any relationship with you at all. I saw the look in her eyes; I'm pretty sure she wanted to castrate you."

"It's a fine line, babe. She might hate me right now, but she wants me as much as I want her. The sex was..." I blew out a breath, getting hard again just at the memory of her, curled against me as my hips snapped toward that ass.

Harrison looked down at my dick, then back up to my eyes in amusement. He slid down my body with a smirk. "I see. Well, waste not, want not. Let's see if I can taste her on your cock." Then he tugged down my sweats and wrapped those tempting lips around my cock.

Fuck, if I could make this work, I'd be the luckiest man alive.

25

BLAKE

I hid in my room the following day. I'd dragged my laptop upstairs so I could still work, but I didn't want to see anyone. I ignored the knocks on my door, the texts on my phone. I ignored it all, because I was mad and embarrassed. The very idea of running into either Everett or Harrison in the hallway gave me hives. So I blasted music through my headphones and just avoided the world. If it wasn't for the pleasant ache in my body, and the small fingerprint-sized bruises on my hips, I could almost pretend it hadn't happened.

Someone had been leaving food outside my door, and I knew it was Everett. As much as I wanted to leave it untouched out of principle, I hadn't. I wasn't a person to waste food, and on top of that, as much as I wanted to blame him for everything that had happened, I'd kissed Everett just as hard as he'd kissed me. I'd fucked him just the same as he'd fucked me.

Well, maybe not quite the same way. He'd been almost feral with his need, and I'd loved every single moment of it. Which also made me feel guilty.

The following morning, I knew I'd have to emerge from my room, if for no other reason than it was the AdEx Awards that night, and I'd promised Darwin I would go with him. I showered and primped myself until I was smoother than a baby's ass. Darwin had messaged me earlier to say Dani would arrive at one to steal me away to finish getting ready, and that he'd collect me from her apartment when it was time to go. I kind of felt bad for ignoring him the previous day, but I'd needed the space. If anyone would understand, it was Darwin.

I was just throwing on some sweats when there was a knock at the door again. Probably Darwin telling me Dani was here. "I'm coming," I answered, grabbing my phone and jamming it into my back pocket. Dani had insisted I wouldn't need anything else.

Pulling open the door, I was surprised, and a little chagrined, to find Harrison there. *Shit.* That was what I got for assuming. "Uh, hi."

His lips curled up at the corners. "Don't seem so excited to see me, Blake. I'm gonna get a big head."

My cheeks flushed. "No, it's not like that. Come in."

My room had kinda been trashed, and my bed was

a mess. "I'm not normally this messy..." Well, that was a lie too. "Most of the time, anyway."

Harrison just gave me a lopsided smirk. "It's your room, Blake. Do with it what you want, and if that includes a floordrobe, so be it."

It wouldn't matter soon, because I was pretty sure he was here to fire me. I pointed to the occasional chair. "Take a seat." I sat on the bed, my knee bouncing as I waited for him to speak.

"Blake... I'd be remiss if I didn't ask whether you wanted to enact the sexual harassment clause of your contract. What's going on between you and Everett is outside a professional relationship, and if you feel trapped—"

"Trapped?"

"Trapped into a relationship with him. Or in this house. If you feel uncomfortable, I promise there'll be no hard feelings when you leave."

"You're firing me?" Despite the fact I'd been waiting for it, it still kinda hurt. A lot.

"No! No. We want you to stay on, of course, but we can get you somewhere else to live. We'd pay for—"

I frowned. "I don't want to live anywhere else." It was an impulsive statement that directly contradicted the fact that I'd been hiding in my room for the last day and a half. But I couldn't go back to living alone in an echoey room, with only myself for company. Even if I didn't want to see them, it was reassuring to know there were other bodies in the house. That if I died in my sleep, my body wouldn't be decomposing before anyone thought to come and see if I was okay.

Harrison's eyes roamed over my face, like he was trying to work out what was going on in my mind. "Let's backtrack to you and Everett." My face flushed an unhealthy shade of red; I could feel it. "He told me what happened with you two, and what happened between you and Heinrich. I'll tell you what I told him —that bullshit was not cool. Everett is better than that, I promise you."

Better than what? I mean, was he talking about the sex? Because that had been pretty damn good.

He must have seen the confusion on my face, because he laughed. "No, not the fucking part. That bastard is notoriously good at it—trust me, I know. I mean the manipulative bullshit of texting you on your date. He knew what could happen, and he did it anyway." He shook his head. "He knows better, but I think you have him all turned inside out, and he's not used to it. He's used to being the one being chased, so you've thrown him for a loop." He gave me a grin. "That's good. He needs a shake-up."

"Harrison. I, uh, god, I didn't mean to... No, I did. Fuck, I didn't think we'd have to have the 'Hey, I kissed your boyfriend' conversation again so soon."

He stood quickly from the chair, coming over to kneel in front of me. "What I said before still stands.

You're free to pursue something with Everett if you wish." His hands bracketed my hips. "But remember that Everett and I, we're a package deal until he says otherwise. I like you, Blake, and I'm not going to lie and say I don't wonder what it would be like to kiss you anytime I like." My breath caught in my throat at his words, and the way his blue eyes were swimming with desire. "But until Everett says otherwise, he holds my heart in his hands. I can't—no, *won't* give him up for you, not unless he tells me that he's fallen in love with you and doesn't need me anymore. Because I'll always need him."

I frowned, barely breathing. "So you're saying that if I want a relationship with Everett, I have to have one with you too?"

He shook his head, falling back on his heels, the flash of rejection on his face disappearing so quickly, I wasn't sure if I'd misread it. "No. Just that you have to be comfortable with the idea of me and Everett together, and it would help if we were on good terms. We don't have to do anything—"

I grabbed his cheeks and kissed him. Hard. I kissed him with thought-shattering intensity, because I didn't want to overthink this. I didn't want to moralize it, or have second thoughts about what this would make me in the eyes of society. I kissed him so he knew I wanted him too, no matter how perilous this all might seem.

Harrison met my kiss with his own intensity, until

he was crawling onto the bed between my thighs to deepen the embrace, his long, toned body pressing heavily against mine and making me moan. *Fuck.* He could kiss. Different to Everett, but you could tell they'd grown up kissing each other. They had similar moves.

I buried my hands in his hair and curled my body up into his, chasing friction to relieve the growing pressure of my core. He kissed down my cheeks and my throat, making me chuckle.

He lifted himself on his arms and looked down at me with a cocked eyebrow. "Fuck, Blake. This isn't what I came in here for, I swear."

I laughed. "I know. I kissed you, remember?"

"What's so amusing? I'm going to have to up my game if I'm making you laugh instead of moan."

I stroked my fingers through his soft hair. "No, it's not that. It's just that you kinda kiss like Everett."

Harrison rolled onto his side, propping himself up on his elbow. "That's because I taught him everything he knows. You're welcome."

I flopped back on the bed, my chuckles dying off. "This is a bit of a mess, isn't it? Like, what, the three of us?" That didn't really resonate with me, but not because I had a problem with Harrison. I didn't want to delve into exactly why the thought unsettled me. That was between my subconscious and my therapist.

"I mean, we aren't exactly following the socially accepted path."

"Babe, we're pornstars. We leapt off the socially acceptable path and straight into the river of sin a long time ago." He gave me a sardonic grin. "But to answer your question, yeah, it would be the three of us, for as long as that worked."

We both fell into silence, and into our own thoughts. Could I do this? Have a boyfriend who had a boyfriend? Or would it be more a triangle rather than a straight line? Harrison had definitely seemed interested in *more* when he was kissing me a minute ago. Would I finally get a threeway?

My body felt hot even thinking about being pressed between Harrison and Everett, their lips on my body and on each other. Hands everywhere. Cocks... also everywhere. I mean, it was a pretty tempting picture.

I cleared my throat and had a stern talk to Virginia the Vagina. This was serious. She'd just gotten laid. She needed to let the brains speak now, instead of being a horny bitch.

I looked up at Harrison, stroking away the creases marring his brow. "Just in case me kissing you wasn't enough evidence, I'm totally okay with you and Everett, and I'd never try to come between you two. Anyone with eyes can see how much you love each other. I was just a little blind before."

"Or not peeking through the right doors, hmm?"

I flushed hot again, chewing my lip as the memory of them together made its way along the well-worn path to the front of my mind. "Sorry about that. You just looked..." There wasn't a good adjective really. It had been *hot*, but that was way too basic-bitch of an adjective to describe what I'd felt seeing Everett wrap his hand around Harrison's cock. "Perfect."

Another burst of laughter rumbled from his chest. "We are so far from perfect, we'd be in the thesaurus as an antonym."

I rolled on my side and really looked at Harrison. Past the pretty veneer, although sometimes it was hard to get past the physical attraction. But he was also so damn earnest, and maybe that was why I'd fought the attraction I felt to Everett so hard. I hated the idea of disappointing Harrison. I hated the idea of proving his first impression right, that me being a woman would cause drama in the house.

Yet here we were.

There was a knock at the door, and both Harrison and I lifted up onto our elbows. Darwin was standing in the doorway. "I don't mean to interrupt, but Dani is here to collect you." His eyes wandered over our rather compromising position, his smile crooked. Almost longing. Maybe I was just seeing desire everywhere now, wanting to taste every guy who even showed me a little bit of interest.

It was like I was hoarding men. I was basically a dick dragon.

I cleared my throat, thankful that mind-reading wasn't a thing. "Thanks, D. I'll be right down." I watched him walk away, the sinuous muscles of his back mouthwatering.

"Hmm, maybe four."

I turned back to Harrison. "What?"

He just kissed me, crawling off the bed. "You better get down there. Dani isn't known for being patient. I'm pretty sure only Darwin got the ability to play the long game." He winked at me and left.

I was still shaking my head as I grabbed my purse and wandered downstairs and out the front door. Dani snorted when she saw me. "Girl, you look like you've just been fucked." I climbed into her sporty car, the top down. "Was it my brother?"

My head snapped toward her. "What? No."

She sighed with relief. "Thank fuck, because I'm going to need all the goss, and no one wants to hear about their twin's sex life. Spill, baby girl, because I am dying to know."

Somehow, by the magic of Dani, I was spilling my guts before we even reached the first intersection.

26

BLAKE

To say Everett's dick was the hot topic of conversation for the next six hours was a woeful understatement.

Happily, I met one of Darwin's other sisters, Olista, who was a hair stylist. So convenient. Celine was also there, doing last-minute things to the dress, but refusing to let me see it. Actually, everyone was refusing to let me see anything. Dani insisted that you only got the Cinderella experience once in your life, and she wanted to be someone's fairy godmother. I mean, if your fairy godmother was a five-nine, rail-thin model who vaped like a chimney and started drinking champagne in the middle of the afternoon.

"I refuse to follow the guys on ClickHeart, because *ew*... but Letitia told me that Everett has a cock so big, he has to tuck it down the leg of his pants."

I'd been told that Olista was the eldest of the siblings, and when she made a disapproving noise, I believed it. That noise of unimpressed bemusement came with years of frowning at your younger siblings. "Why are you talking about your brother's roommates, and more specifically their dicks, Daniella?"

I'd also learned that Dani's full name was Daniella, not her runway name of Diani. The things you discovered while holding deathly still as a fiery Latina woman waved around scissors. Though, I didn't even think it was her ethnicity that made Olista bicker with Dani. It was just that they were siblings, so they had that close camaraderie, but also the ability to argue about anything. I'd missed out on that, being an only child.

Dani waved a hand, pouring another mimosa that was ninety-eight percent champagne. "It's an inevitable thing, really. I say I'm a twin. They ask what he does. I tell them. I throw Everett and Harrison under the bus as a decoy when they ask for DeeDee's username." She screwed up her nose in my direction. "Sorry about that."

I waved a hand. "It's their career. I'm not that petty."

Celine looked up from her sewing machine. "It really doesn't bother you, other women ogling men you are, uh, sleeping with?" she asked, but honestly, I wasn't sure of the correct terminology of what we were doing either.

I shrugged. "It's not like I didn't already know. I was hired to help with that very purpose. It would be pretty hypocritical for me to be bothered by it now." Maybe one day, I might feel territorial, but not right now.

Though, if I was honest with myself, the idea of Darwin expanding his repertoire to sexcapades with other ClickHeart artists made me more irrationally jealous, but I wasn't looking into that too much either.

Olista sucked air in through her teeth. "That's very mature of you. Now, tilt your head down."

"Mature or not, I wanna know if his dick is pierced. You owe me that, *Doll,*" Dani cooed, and I flushed at Darwin's nickname for me.

I didn't know how to tell her that it was her twin with the pierced cock—that would lead to more awkward questions—so I just shook my head. "Nope. Everett is *au naturale.*"

"This is very unsatisfactory, Blake. I need details, girl. I've been in a cock drought for so long, they're about to dub it an international disaster."

Celine tutted, pins tucked between her teeth. "Don't joke about climate change. It's a real problem."

Dani leaned forward conspiratorially. "Celine watched a documentary about starving polar bears and now she's an eco warrior."

Olista snorted. "Says the girl who went vegan after learning that male baby chickens were euthanized." She tugged my hair to the side. "Dani talks some serious shit, but she and Celine will achieve big things one day, because they have dreams and morals."

Dani flushed under her older sister's praise, and straightened. "All the more reason I need to get laid. If you see any cute guys at these awards tonight, give them my number. People think models have men lining up to take us out, but it's only men with egos so big, they need a team of people around them just to keep it propped up." She sounded bitter, and Celine cast her a sympathetic look as she wandered back over to the champagne.

"Bad breakup," Olista murmured, and I seemed to remember Dani had been dating a hockey player.

I gave her a cocky grin. "I got it. One guy, pierced D. I'll keep an eye out. I've, uh, done my ClickHeart research, so I can think of, like, three off the top of my head already."

"Why stop at one, Blakey-Baby?" Dani purred, and I flushed pink. "You should take that advice to heart, by the way." She picked up the bottle, forgoing the glass this time. "When it comes to love, why limit yourself? You should have the guys, and your taco truck guy—"

"German food," Celine interjected, snipping a thread.

"And my brother too, so we can be sisters-in-law, because you're sweet and my mama is going to *love* you."

I opened my mouth, but nothing came out. Olista

just waved a hand at Dani. "Stop, Daniella, you're embarrassing her." She tugged and fluffed a little more. "Done. Eat some more *llapingachos*—these awards nights are notorious for terrible food—then I'll start on your makeup."

Llapingachos were small fried potato and cheese patties that were way, way too good. When Olista had turned up with them, Dani had sworn, bitching about fitting into a bathing suit for a shoot tomorrow, while Celine had straight-up moaned. And I got it. Even luke-warm, they were still freaking amazing. Celine had eaten three in a row before stuffing me in my dress, pinning it in a few places and busting out the sewing machine.

I ate another one in two bites, but no matter how delicious they were, nerves were killing my appetite. Olista had pulled in a giant suitcase filled with the tools of her trade when she'd arrived, so I knew my makeup was going to be a long undertaking. I probably wouldn't be able to eat again without ruining it, so I forced myself. Then when Dani thrust a bottle of champagne in my direction, I had that too. God knows, I was going to need some liquid courage.

Dani's loft apartment was in an amazing Art Deco building, complete with a doorman. The windows were large and arched, and she'd styled it like it was ready to be shown in some interior design magazine. Warm neutral tones, with the odd touch of gold to offset the brass windows and fixtures, and the inlaid floors. It was gorgeous and gave me extreme apartment envy.

By now, Olista had laid out all the brushes and tools she'd need on Dani's kitchen table. She clicked her fingers to get my attention, waving at the bar stool that was doubling as her work station. She went to work on priming my face, and for the next forty minutes, no one asked me to speak. I was almost glad to be lost in the silence.

I WAS BASICALLY in a makeup-induced trance when my phone vibrated a little while later, and I picked it up, looking down at a message from Darwin. It was a picture message, and when I opened it, it was a mirror selfie. He was in a tux that fit him to perfection, enhancing the width of his shoulders and then tapering down to the lean line of his waist. He had a bow tie around his neck, and his hair was pushed back in a manner that looked effortless, yet somehow fell perfectly. Clean shaven, one hand thrust in his pocket, and a crooked grin on his face.

He looked like a wet dream.

All About the D: All dressed up, just waiting for our chariot to arrive and the belle of the ball to be on my arm. I hope my sisters aren't giving you too much shit. Well, Dani at least. Olista is a saint—she would never.

I showed Olista the message as she contoured my face. She snorted a laugh. "He's always been so smooth, that one. Got him in trouble as a teen. I spent so much time bailing him and Dani out of crap so Mama didn't find out."

Dani scoffed. "Like what?"

"Like the time you almost got banned from the movie theater for buying one ticket, dressing Darwin up as you, then trying to sneak yourselves both in on that same ticket." She looked down at me, like she still couldn't believe their stupidity. "Right down to the same shirt. I had to go pay Mr. Nguyen three bucks for the apples you used for boobs so he didn't charge you for shoplifting fake breasts. Imagine explaining that to Mama." She muttered a prayer in Spanish.

My shoulders started to shake. I tried to keep my face still, but the laughter was bubbling up inside of me until my body was quaking and my cheeks were pulled tight.

Olista sighed and lifted her brush from my face. "Go on, let it out."

Laughter wracked my body as I cackled. "Apples? Really?"

Dani grinned, not seeming at all remorseful. "You'd be amazed how similar we looked at twelve. I'm pretty sure he liked wearing my skirt too. He said it let his balls breathe." She shook her head with a laugh. "Anyway, he managed to talk the manager out of calling the cops and banning them for life, then they called me instead and made me pretend to be their guardian. Pretty sure the manager felt sorry for them, being raised by their obviously incapable older sister, and let them off with a warning. He could talk anyone into anything, but how he managed it is still a mystery to me."

Celine chuckled. "It's the big brown eyes. Dani uses them to get her way, even now."

"Pfft, never worked on you," the brown-eyed girl in question shot back.

Celine waved a needle around, like a tiny scepter. "I'm impervious to your charms." She made a humming noise. "I think I'm done. What do you think?" she asked Dani, who went over and examined her craftsmanship, cooing over the alterations Celine had made. They talked shop, dropping names that could be either people or stitches, and I could tell this was more than a job for both of them. It was a passion; they were in their element right now.

"We are going subtle tonight," Olista murmured.

"You're beautiful, so we are enhancing your natural beauty. A classic Hollywood starlet from yesteryear. Pretty nude lip, nice clean eye, accentuate those gorgeous cheekbones you have."

She worked like an artist with a canvas, and I went back to being silent. I wished I could have a mirror to see what she was doing, but I had to trust the process. I messaged Darwin back a selfie of my face, with Olista's hands artfully highlighting my cheekbones. She shooed my phone out of the way, but the small glimpse I got made me look like I'd been playing in the mud.

I'd never really gotten the hang of makeup, because I'd been dating Paul since junior year of high school, and he hadn't liked girls who wore too much of it. I'd almost made it a crusade to avoid it after that, like it would somehow endear me to him.

I was regretting it now, though, since the extent of my skills was just tinted moisturizer, blush, eyeliner and lipgloss. Contouring was basically a whole other language that I didn't understand. But I'd make an effort to learn, I decided. *Fuck Paul.*

I managed to sit still for the entire time, even as Olista came at my eyeball with a mascara wand, tweezers and fake lashes. Finally, she stepped away and stood back to view the whole package. I wasn't in my dress yet. It had to be the last thing so nothing got dirty with makeup.

Dani came to join her sister, both of them staring at

me like I was a Picasso on the wall. Dani wrapped an arm around Olista's waist. "You did good. You sure you don't want to go back to being my personal makeup artist?"

"Who'd look after the twins, hmm? I have better things to do than travel around the world with you, eating celery sticks and talking trash with models." Her words were harsh, but she rested her head affectionately on Dani's shoulder.

Her younger sister shrugged. "I mean, the twins like eating celery and talking trash, so really, how different could it be?"

"Touché, Daniella," Olista said with a laugh. "Speaking of which, I best be getting back before Allegra loses control of Daryl and Alex." Allegra was Olista's five-year-old daughter. Daryl was her husband, but Dani had fondly told me that he was a giant child at heart. Want to build a tree fort in the backyard? Daryl was on it. Want to turn the house into the world's longest matchbox car track? Daryl was here for it. Star Wars marathon? Hell yeah. Ice cream for breakfast? Why not—it was basically the same as milk and Lucky Charms.

On the flip side, Allegra was apparently a miniature Olista. Not solemn, but very responsible. She'd be the voice of reason, but she'd still eat the ice cream and build the fort too, if she was outvoted.

I wondered if I'd get to meet them one day. On

impulse, I leaned forward and hugged Olista. "Thank you for your help. I know you didn't have to give up your day off to beautify a stranger, so I appreciate it."

"A stranger? I've heard so much about you on the group chat, I could probably write your unofficial biography by now. From both Darwin and Dani." She patted my cheek softly so she didn't shake loose any makeup, though she'd set it with so much setting spray, I wondered if my face would crack if I smiled. "You look beautiful. I'm glad I could help. You deserve to be spoiled, so let them."

I didn't know if she meant Darwin and Dani, or Harrison and Everett, but I didn't ask. She packed away her stuff, kissed us all on the temple in a way that was more maternal than a thirty-five-year-old had any right to be, and left.

Celine clapped her hands together once. "Let's get you in this dress. It's almost time."

27

DARWIN

For once, we were all on time, so when the limo pulled up out the front of the house, we'd been ready to climb straight into it. We'd swing by Dani's on the way to the awards, then we'd walk the Blue Carpet.

Everyone had been oddly solemn over the last couple of days, and you'd have to be both deaf and stupid to wonder why. Everett and Blake had fucked, and now it was weird. We had to get past it, or the house would come unliveable.

I hated my home being a space for festering feelings. All those sisters, and all those synced PMS symptoms, had meant that for two weeks in every month, our house had been a battle zone. There was bloodshed—literally—and snapped words, then they'd always make up in a way only sisters could.

At least, for another two weeks.

When I moved out, I'd told myself that my home would be tranquil, filled with good communication. Which it had been, until Everett stuck his big foot in it. Well, his big dick, but same thing.

"Do you want to talk about it?"

"No."

"Nope."

Their responses weren't exactly surprising. "I'll kick you both in the balls if you do anything to make her sad."

Harrison raised an eyebrow at me, but Everett's eyes caught mine and held them as he did that disconcerting thing where he brooded in your general direction. Then he nodded. "Fair." He opened the little mini fridge and pulled out three beers, passing me one and cracking the lid off Harrison's.

When he did that shit, it always made me smile. It was unintentionally sweet, the kind of affection you developed over years of being someone else's everything.

"Aw, who said chivalry was dead?"

Harrison gave me the finger, but looked lovingly at Everett. I still couldn't believe that Blake hadn't noticed they were together. Sure, it wasn't in the traditional sense—they both had way too much baggage for that. But in every way that mattered, they were a couple. Bound together, heart and soul.

I'd be interested to see how Blake fit into their dynamic. My knee bounced as the limo cruised through the streets to Dani's upscale apartment, and I realized I was actually nervous. Not about the awards; I couldn't give a shit about that. Would it be nice for our work to be recognized? Sure. Did I actually care if I came home with a phallic-shaped trophy? No. Not even a little.

No, for some insane reason, tonight felt important. Like it was prom night or something, and I wanted to impress the girl I'd been pining over from afar. Dani had been texting me updates, but they were more teases than anything else, and they'd gotten significantly less coherent as the day went on. I was pretty sure my twin had dived into her champagne collection. I hoped to God she didn't tell Blake that each one cost several hundred bucks a pop.

I was worried about Dani, which was partly why I'd asked her for help in the first place. She wasn't bouncing back after her break-up, and that was unlike her. She loved hard, but she healed quickly too. Not from this last meathead, though. She needed a project to keep her mind off things, to remind her what her real passions in life were all about, and that's where Blake came in.

Dani's love language had always been giving gifts. She would give and give and give, even if she got nothing back. On the other hand, Blake was fiercely independent, and she found it hard to accept anything: gifts, praise, opportunities. They both needed this for different reasons. Dani would learn that her shit ex was really just an emotional leech, and that true gratitude and love didn't come wrapped in a toga of red flags. Hopefully, Blake would realize she deserved the world, and not everything came with emotional strings attached. Some people just wanted you to be happy.

We got off the freeway, and I messaged Dani to tell her we were almost there. She hadn't messaged me in a while, so either she'd passed out from her third bottle of champagne, or they were busy.

Finally, we pulled up in front of the covered entrance of Dani's swanky apartment, idling out the front for a moment. I contemplated texting Dani again when the doorman opened the doors wide, and out walked Blake.

She looked so freaking beautiful.

"Wow," Harrison breathed, and I could hear Everett's soft grunt of agreement. Dani had made me buy a Saint Laurent suit that cost an insane amount of money—I could see why now. It was made of soft black velvet with wide, black silk lapels that created a sharp V down the double-breasted tux jacket.

Like the inverse of me, Blake's long, black silk dress skimmed down her body to her waist, then pooled like a midnight waterfall around her body. A black velvet inlay in the bodice complemented me, or I complemented her. Her hair was down, but pinned back on the sides and curled softly. She looked... gorgeous.

I opened the door and climbed out, like I was walking toward a dream. "*Muñeca*, you look spectacular."

She flushed a beautiful shade of pink that couldn't be hidden by makeup. "You look fantastic too," she murmured.

Celine, Dani's best friend and basically my adopted sibling, rolled her eyes. "Now remember, the zipper is hidden in the back velvet panel. You'll have to get one of the guys to help you out." She looked over at me. "Dani took one look at her all beautiful, burst into tears and refused to come down, in case the paps see her looking like a swamp rat. She's also drunk off her ass. She heads off to St Tropez tomorrow, so that's going to be a fun flight for her." She gave me a hard look, and I knew we were on the same page about Dani.

I lifted my chin, acknowledging her unsaid words, and then turned my smile to Blake. "Your chariot awaits."

She grinned at me, while Celine handed me the train of her dress so it didn't get dirty on the street. As she climbed into the car, my view of the guys' faces was blocked, which was disappointing. I bet they looked like they'd been sucker-punched. I know I had.

Finally, she was in the rear-facing seat, her dress tucked neatly behind her feet, and I had space to climb in after her. Sitting beside her, she stole my breath. Her skin glowed in the muted light of the setting sun through the tinted windows. I wanted to taste the sunshine off her bare shoulders. She looked like a queen.

Both Everett and Harrison looked like someone had smacked them, but Harrison recovered first. "Blake, you look..."

"Ethereal," Everett finished.

Harrison huffed an amused sound. "Exactly. Though, I didn't think you even knew that word," he teased his lover before turning back to Blake. "You look absolutely spectacular."

She smiled, but her cheeks remained flushed. "Thank you. It's all Olista, Celine and Dani's hard work. We all know I don't look like this normally."

Everett frowned. "You're beautiful all the time. They had a good canvas to work with."

She mumbled out an embarrassed, "Thank you," and if this wasn't so cute, I'd roll my eyes. She turned to me, the smile back on her face. "You look so handsome, Darwin. And look, you match my dress." She rubbed the velvet of my sleeve, and I resisted the urge to purr in her direction.

"Dani gave me very strict instructions on what kind of tux to get." Right down to the shoes and socks I had to purchase. My sister did not fuck around when it came to fashion.

"She knows what she's talking about, obviously." Blake waved a hand down her body, indicating her dress. She looked past me at the guys, who were the very picture of debonair. Harrison had a dark blue tux on, along with a waistcoat, white shirt and a burgundy bow tie. All of that seemed to compliment his blond, blue-eyed good looks to perfection.

Everett, on the other hand, was all in black: black tux, black shirt, black skinny tie. He had his hair slicked back, his short beard professionally barbered to within an inch of its life. He looked like a mob boss, or a bad boy, definitely not like a chef who got his dick out for likes. In a town full of glittering beautiful people, those two belonged more than any of us.

"Do you want a drink? I think we have beer and champagne," Harrison suggested, and Blake shook her head.

"No, thanks. Olista said no destroying her work until after the event photographs have been taken, and then I have permission to get white-girl wasted. Direct quote, by the way," she said to me. I could imagine Olista saying that. She was always like a second mother to Dani and me, because we were the babies and she'd taken over a lot of the parenting responsibilities while Mama had worked, after our father died.

I laughed. "I'd listen. She'll be watching, because she has eyes in the back of her head, that one. You'll feel the wave of her disapproval all the way from Glendale."

Everett was still just staring at her, and I couldn't get over how little game he had. *Jesus, make a move already.* Jump over the hurdle that was so obviously coming between them and making this shit awkward for everyone. But he just stared and stayed silent, though Harrison filled the conversational black hole, like normal. They were definitely a package deal, those two.

Finally, we pulled up to the event center holding the awards, and there was a small line of town cars and limos. We'd have to wait, and I took the time to center myself. Once we were outside, it would be all Deemon, my handle—all smoldering hot guy, social media influencer and ClickHeart sensation. There was no time for Darwin, an awkward joker with a giant crush on his graphic designer.

"Have I said how thankful I am that you agreed to come with me, *Amorcito*?" I asked softly in her ear, my palm capturing hers so I could twine my fingers between them and use her to hold me steady. Her palms were clammy and kind of sweaty as well, and I could see the nerves written all over her face. "You'll be my rock. My anchor. The person I'll picture naked while I'm giving my acceptance speech." Blake giggled, and Everett huffed a peeved sound. "Don't worry, Ev. I'll picture you naked too, if you want."

Finally, our turn had come, and we pulled up to the Blue Carpet. The car slowed to a stop, and two attendants rushed over to open the doors, like this was the Oscars and not the porn awards. Harrison got out first, giving Blake a wink, and I could hear the yells. The flashes from the cameras outside were only slightly muted by the tinted windows.

Everett went to climb out next, but stopped. "Can I kiss you once before I go, Sunshine?" he asked, and I managed to hold in my "*Awwwww,*" but it was hard.

Blake looked at him, wide-eyed, but nodded. He leaned forward and placed a reasonably chaste kiss on her lips. "You're already the most beautiful woman here," he murmured softly, and then he climbed out too.

I turned to Blake, giving her a wide, reassuring smile. "Are you ready?" She nodded, but her eyes looked panicked. "It's just me and you going for a short walk, *Muñeca*. It'll all be fine."

I slid out of the car, putting my hand back through the door to help her out. She slid out delicately, her high heels gorgeous but impractical for anything except brief stints of walking.

"Let's go win some awards," I murmured, and pulled her to my side.

What I didn't tell her—or the crowd around us—was that I had the greatest prize of all on my arm, although I hadn't won her just yet. But I was working on it.

28

BLAKE

This was all very surreal. As soon as I stepped from the limo, a woman was there, fluffing out my skirt for me, which was totally bizarre. Then she disappeared back to wherever she'd come from, and I darted my eyes around at the people lining the plush blue carpet.

Darwin held out his elbow for me, which I took gratefully. I'd been skeptical about these heels, but Celine had suggested I just use Darwin like a sexy walking stick. Up ahead, I could see Harrison posing in front of a branded screen as people snapped pictures, before moving along and talking to some other "celebrities."

In my brain, I'd thought it would be less LA glitz and glamor, and something more seedy, but I was wrong. There were fans out behind the roped-off carpet, yelling for selfies from their favorite artists. There was a general bustle of people under the bright lights, gorgeous people with handlers—and armed security personnel, if I judged by the very obvious bulge beneath one guy's jacket.

"Deemon, right this way, please." A harried-looking woman with a clipboard appeared, ushering us through the crowd, referring to Darwin by his handle and not his name. "If you could just take your promotional photographs, I'll have an usher escort you to your table." She looked back toward the line of cars, pressing the button for her earpiece and muttering to whoever was on the other end. I stood back as Darwin took his photos, smoldering into the camera in a way that made my skin feel hot. The clipboard lady nudged me forward. "Now one with your date as well."

I opened my mouth to protest, but she wasn't listening, and Darwin reached a hand toward me. At least I didn't have to worry about my mother seeing these promotional pictures. Putting my hand in his, I let him pull me into his body while Clipboard Lady fluffed my dress. I'd totally underestimated the amount of dress fluffing that needed to be done.

Darwin looked down at me, his arm around my back and his fingers curled over my hip. "Don't look so panicked, *Amorcito*. These photos rarely ever see the light of day." His eyes sparkled, and I was transfixed for a moment. Darwin's beauty—not the physical kind—

was something that encompassed you whenever he was near. You never needed to guess how he was feeling, because it was written all over his body language. Sometimes, I just had to ignore what it was saying, for my own sanity. At least for now.

"Smile for the camera, *Amorcito*."

I turned, hoping I didn't look as dazed as I felt. Finally, an usher appeared and moved us along the carpet. I'd lost sight of Harrison and Everett, so I clung onto Darwin's arm for dear life. Eventually, we were through the doors, mingling in a large foyer.

"Darwin!" someone shouted, and I turned to see the literal personification of Aphrodite the goddess moving toward us. "Sugar, it's so good to see you."

She looked like the definition of a sex kitten: pouty pink lips, cat-eye makeup, and big blonde hair that fell like silk down her back and invited thoughts about how it would feel wrapped around your fist. If I were a guy, I'd even pop a boner around this woman.

Darwin gave her a bright smile. "Penny. It's good to see you too." He leaned in to kiss her cheek, and I pushed down the insecurity that washed over me. Darwin ushered me forward. "This is Blake, my date." He didn't say for the night, or that I was his housemate. He just said *date*. Maybe I was clutching at straws, but he made it sound almost possessive.

"This is why you haven't emailed me back about a collab?" She tsked, her shiny white teeth almost blinding. "Can't say I blame you, honey. Your girl is gorgeous. You look like sex on a stick, Sweetness. I'm Penny. Or Peaches, if you want to use our super secret online code names. We don't usually do that at these events, if you're among friends. You can't have a conversation with a man called DongLoverForever about his chihuahua breeding program, and keep a straight face during a conversation, you know what I mean?" she joked with a wink before thrusting out a hand, long pink nails flashing in the overhead light. She didn't look like she was being catty, and her words seemed genuine. The part of me that had been conditioned to see all women as competition flailed a little, lost for what to do in this situation.

So, I gave her an equally authentic smile. "It's nice to meet you. You look absolutely beautiful."

Penny waved a hand. "Thank you, Sweetness. Sometimes it's hard to find designers that will accommodate the girls"—she waved a hand at her boobs, which were indeed bigger than average, though not ostentatiously large—"but I convinced one of them eventually, and now he does all my dresses." She winked at me, and I swear, I flushed. "But look at *you*. You look like Marilyn Monroe with those curves in that dress. Makin' my mouth water. If I didn't like Darwin so much, I might try and persuade you to be my date for the night."

It was official. My cheeks were now so pink, I probably matched Penny's dress. My mouth opened and closed a few times, because there was clearly desire in her eyes. She was definitely propositioning me right now.

A pornstar was propositioning *me* at the biggest beauty buffet in the country.

Darwin came to my rescue. "Sorry, Penny, but this one is all mine. Well, mostly," he purred, winking at me. "I'm not looking to collab anytime soon, but email Harrison and maybe we can get you over to do some less sweaty collabs. How do you feel about baking?"

Penny waved her hands at him, like he was being outrageous. "Sugar, I do not *sweat*," she chastised him, as if the very thought of her perspiring was preposterous. "But I do bake. I'll get my people to reach out to your people." Someone called out to her from across the room. "Well, I best go. Good luck tonight. I'm rootin' for you." She grabbed my forearm. "Blake, it was a delight to meet you. You let me know if this one isn't treating you right, okay?"

I couldn't help but smile. "He's amazing, but if he wasn't, I'm friends with his sister. She'd definitely kick his ass." Penny tipped her head back and laughed, and it was a deep, throaty, seductive thing. Heads turned in her direction, and desire was rife. *Oh, to have that kind of draw.*

"Solidarity. That's what our society needs. Well, I'll

see you lovebirds soon." She sashayed off, and even I looked at her butt.

"I think I might be gay," I whispered to Darwin, who just pulled me into his side, his hand possessively on my hip.

"Penny has that effect on just about everyone. She's sweet, and beautiful, and definitely would have stolen you away if you'd even remotely shown you were interested," he murmured with a chuckle. Suddenly, his body stilled, and he groaned. "Uh-oh."

I looked over my shoulder at the direction he was facing. Harrison stood toe to toe with a guy, his lips curled in a sneer that could almost be construed as a smile if you didn't know him. Everett had a hand on Harrison's arm, like he was just waiting to hold him back.

"Fuck, if they actually throw a punch, we'll all be blacklisted. Wait here, Blake." Darwin let me go and strode over to where Harrison and the other guy looked like they were going to brawl. Everyone was milling around, waiting to see if it happened, but pretending they weren't looking.

I walked hesitantly over too, despite Darwin's command, just in time to catch Darwin's overly saccharine greeting. "Eric. Good to see you, as always." The note of genuineness that had been there for his interactions with Penny was gone. "Harrison, we should probably get to our seats."

I looked over at Eric. He was handsome. Movie-star handsome, even. But there was something smarmy as hell about him that immediately put me offside, maybe his super-white fuckboy smile. His girlfriend was definitely some kind of model, or maybe an actress herself. She was rail-thin, with dark hair slicked back into a high ponytail and a dress that clung to her body in ways I could only dream of. She was glaring at us all, her lips pressed tightly closed but her disdain at the whole scene obvious.

"Run along, Harry." Eric's eyes slid past Harrison, over to me. "This is your date, Deemon?" He chuckled maliciously. "Two fags and a fatty. That should be your channel right there."

I gasped, audibly gasped, like he'd struck me. Everett let go of Harrison's arms and launched himself toward Eric instead, and only Darwin holding him back stopped him from landing a punch.

I wanted to cry. I wanted to rage. I wanted to leave. But I was never the girl who shied away from confrontation; I'd just never really put myself in a position to encounter it.

I knew I couldn't let this piece of shit have the last word, though. "If you're a homophobe with a tiny dick, just say you're a homophobe with a tiny dick. There's no need for all these dramatics." I rolled my eyes in his direction, like he was dirt. "Let's go, Everett," I murmured, reaching out to grab his hand and drag him to my side. It might be the wrong thing to do, but this could only end badly.

Penny appeared, giving me a grin. She looked over at Eric's date. "Aria, girl, I just got endorsed by a great dildo company. I'll send one your way so you can finish yourself off later on, when Eric pumps three times with his lil gherkin and finishes."

Eric snarled at her. "Fuck you, Penny."

"Naw, baby. Not for all the dollars your agent keeps offering mine. No amount of zeros can save you from being a fuckboy." She leaned up and kissed my cheek, probably leaving a pink lipstick stain on my cheek that I'd wear for the rest of the night. "You on the other hand, Sweetness? Just say the word."

She swanned off again, and I didn't stick around. Dragging Everett away, although he was now protectively at my back, I headed for the large double doors. Darwin brought up the rear behind Harrison, like he thought he might double back and take a swing.

"Who was that asshole?" I grumbled as the usher led us to our table.

"Eric, or Prince Eric, as he's known on ClickHeart. He's one of our direct competitors, and he hates that I get more subscribers than him with his cosplay. Plus, he competes against us on KillSwitch, and he's mad because he's shit. All he has is a pretty face—he thinks that should be enough. Homophobic asshole."

We were on a large table with four other attendees,

all ClickHeart creators apparently, but on a lot better terms than the guys had been with Eric. Canapés were placed in the center of the table, and I was between Everett and Darwin. Darwin wrapped his arm around my shoulders, along the back of my chair, and when Everett put his hand on my thigh underneath the table, giving it a squeeze, I didn't push him away. We both needed the anchoring moment as the awards presentation started and the speeches began.

In fact, I covered his hand with mine and twined our fingers. He'd come to my defense—or maybe it was Harrison's—but either way, a part of me had softened toward him. I just hoped it wouldn't be the first step in getting my heart broken.

29

BLAKE

Darwin didn't win his award, but a guy at the table in front of us did, and Darwin seemed content with that. I'd had more champagne than I intended, and was fairly unsteady on my feet by the time we all climbed back into the limo. Darwin, on the other hand, was drunk as a skunk. After he didn't win his award, we'd shared a bottle or three of champagne, which made the world feel like a better place. A fancy cognac company was sponsoring the event, so we'd then moved onto shots of that, and shit got wild.

"God, you're beautiful. Isn't she beautiful?" he asked Harrison for the thirtieth time since we got in the limo.

"She's gorgeous, D. Now, sit back and put your seatbelt on."

I giggled as Everett belted me in, resting my head on his when he leaned over. "You're handsome too, Eferett. And you have a big dick. Not Darwin-big, but like, so big and I actually orgrism—I mean, orgasm—with you and I don't think I've ever orgasmed with a man before. I have with my hand, like, seven times this week. But never a guy. I don't know if I like it."

He sat up and looked at me, his face blurry but his eyes wide.

Harrison was laughing. "Why don't you like it, Blake?"

"It gives me the feels, and I don't *want* the feels. I want to be a ho. Like a mega-slut. I want to live and sleep with you, and Everett, and Hennie, and Darwin. And then all of you at once." A tiny, sober part of my brain was screaming at me to stop. "But I want to take my shoes off more. My feet hurt."

Harrison reached down and lifted my foot into his lap. "I got you, baby." His fingers brushed over the skin of my ankle as he pried my shoe from my foot. If I felt like my feet were still attached to my body, I would have thought him running his thumbs over my arches was hot. Instead, it felt nice, but like, nice for someone else. Placing my sore foot on the floor, he grabbed the other one and flicked off that heel too.

I moaned with bliss. "So good." I leaned my head on Everett's shoulder, and he stroked my hair.

"You're going to have such a hangover tomorrow, Sunshine."

I snorted. "That's tomorrow Blake's problem." I sat upright, head butting Everett in the chin. "We should go out and party. Go back to the club you own, where we totally had to leave because you went all caveman on Hennie." I slumped back in the seat. "I feel sad about that."

Man, they should call expensive cognac truth serum, because my tongue was going wild.

Everett leaned forward. "Why's that, Sunshine?"

"He was a good guy, and I hurt him. If I hadn't been in my ho-era, we could have had something special, you know. But you were hot, and I couldn't help myself."

Harrison was all out laughing now. "I hope you don't remember this tomorrow, Sweetheart. Because you're going to be mortified."

Everett cuddled me closer. "Leave her alone. We aren't going out, Sunshine, because you're drunk off your ass. The only place you're going is home to bed."

"Are you coming?" I purred, though maybe slurred was the right word.

"Nope. You're going to drink a gallon of water and take a Tylenol, and then you're going to sleep away tomorrow."

I pouted, but I already felt sleepy.

. . .

"Wake up, Sunshine." I peeled open a bleary eyelid. "We gotta stop meeting like this."

I shoved at his chest. "Five more minutes."

"Come on. Let's go. Darwin is already in the house in bed."

I stretched and climbed out of the car, wobbling slightly, and hissing as I stood on a rock. "*Fucker.*"

I blinked, and suddenly, we were in my room. "How you can sleep and walk at the same time is amazing," Everett mumbled, fumbling with the back of my gown. "Darwin said there's a hidden zip here somewhere —ah!"

My dress fell to the floor around my ankles. I sighed with relief, launching myself in the direction of the bed. My eyes were closed before my head even hit the pillow. I vaguely felt the blankets pool over my legs and the sound of rustling before darkness stole me away for good.

Pain. Almighty *pain* in my head.

"Fuccccckkkk," I breathed, trying to roll softly to my side. I was in my underwear—no idea how I'd gotten that way—but I was glad someone had gotten me out of that dress, because Dani and Celine would never have forgiven me if I destroyed it.

Shuffling to the bathroom, I groaned as I saw my

makeup smeared all over my face. I looked like a depressed clown. I went to work cleaning off my face, until it shone the unhealthy gray pallor of the walking dead. From depressed clown to zombie. What a step up in the world.

I stumbled back toward my bed, spying the bottle of painkillers and a sealed bottle of water on the nightstand. For some reason, the thoughtfulness made tears well in my eyes. I got weepy when I had a hangover.

I looked at my phone to see I had a message from Dani, and one from Jeanna who was gushing over the photo I'd sent of my dress. I hadn't told her what it was for, of course, just mentioning that I was going to an event for my job.

She didn't ask any more questions than that, instead changing the subject to something that had happened between her and her boyfriend. I wasn't sure if it was because we'd grown apart with the distance, or if she'd always been that generally disinterested in my life, but it kind of hurt a little. Not as much as when she said, "That looks so flattering—you can't even tell you carry a little extra weight around your stomach and hips." I didn't even think she'd intended to be mean; it was almost like reminding me I was fat was a reflex.

I threw my phone onto the bed and snuggled back under the blankets. I needed more sleep. I'd just closed my eyes when there was a knock at the door. I covered my head with a pillow, so the sound wouldn't pound through my head like a sledgehammer.

"Go away. I'm dying."

"We're gonna cure that, Sunshine. Put some clothes on. We're going out for pancakes."

"No, let me stroll into the underworld in peace."

A huffed laugh came from outside the door. "No can do, Sunshine. Ten minutes or I'm taking you in your ducky pajamas."

I cursed him under my breath as I heaved myself back out of bed, sifting through my drawers and searching for whatever would take the least amount of effort to put on. I settled on a pair of sweats and a tank top that had small buttons down the front. I grabbed my sunglasses and pulled my hair up into a messy bun on my head. I couldn't even fathom trying to brush out the bobby pins and hairspray just yet.

I stumbled down the stairs, sunglasses on inside, and I wondered if this was it. The beginning of the end. Had I reached the stage where my liver no longer could cope with an influx of alcohol?

"There she is!" Harrison crowed, and I winced. "Not made for mixing your spirits there, Sweetheart?"

"Shhh," I growled at him. "Take it down three notches in volume, Foghorn, or I will dick punch you." He laughed harder and didn't seem at all offended. I flipped him the bird. "I think I hate you."

He grinned wider, his eyes crinkling at the corners in a way that seemed mischievous. "Is that how you really feel, baby?"

I narrowed my eyes at him, but he was saved by a mussed-looking Darwin stumbling from his room. He looked exactly how I felt. "I'm never drinking champagne again," he groaned. "I'm pretty sure that's what they baptized Satan in." He crossed himself, like he legitimately thought it had come from Diablo himself.

Everett appeared with car keys hooked around his finger. "Come on, D. Stodgy carbohydrates will make you feel better and soak up the devil juice still sloshing around in your guts." They were definitely laughing at us.

Glaring at Everett too, I walked over and hooked my arm through Darwin's. "Let's go. I need to drown in pancakes." I leaned closer. "Do you remember anything about last night?" I whispered, and he shook his head.

"Nothing after Carnal Sausage Factory won best cinematography of the year."

I snorted a laugh. Last night had been surreal until it had been blank. I did remember brief flashes of things. Stumbling down the stairs, Everett's arm wrapped tightly around me. Stepping on a rock. Laughing as I did shots with Darwin and Lolli, one half of a two-person team that did cumshots. Lolli had been nice and down-to-earth, and her partner,

Connell, had been a sweet guy who looked at Lolli like he wanted more than a professional relationship.

I still wasn't sure how you stuck your dick in someone everyday and didn't get attached, but Connell was proof that it wasn't just women who caught the feels.

We took Harrison's Mercedes, and I climbed in the back with Darwin. He buckled me into the center seat so he could cuddle me close. It should be weird, but we were bonding over our mutual pain, and honestly, I wanted the snuggle. It definitely eased my pain.

There was a sudden whirring noise, and I let out a surprised gasp as the roof came down and I realized it was a convertible. So fancy.

As we pulled out onto the road, Darwin held me closer, the wind whipping his hair around, and I saw he'd already gone back to sleep. Smiling, I turned my face into his chest and looked out over the hills of Hollywood. The sun shone down, soaking into my skin, and despite the turmoil, and the emotional roller-coaster I'd been on, this was nice. I felt happy.

Not as happy as I'd feel when I dived into a stack of pancakes, though.

I caught Everett watching me in the side mirror, his face soft. When I held his eyes, he gave me a crooked little grin that made my heart beat faster. I needed to figure this shit out with Everett, and soon, because despite what my brain was screaming, my heart had other ideas. She was a traitorous wench. She'd catch feelings faster than you can say multiple orgasms.

30

HARRISON

Blake had made a habit of coming out to help me pack my orders every week, and I wasn't going to stop her. Not only did I like the extra set of hands, but it was nice to have her to myself, even if it was just for an hour every Sunday.

She bustled around while we listened to the Red Hot Chili Peppers, and she sang along, off-key. Sometimes she'd dance too, and I couldn't take my eyes from her. She wasn't an amazing dancer, but she did it with abandon, her whole body swaying in time with the music.

I was so smitten that last week I'd actually tried my hand at sculpting her, mid-movement. It was okay —I wasn't a great sculptor—but the memory attached to it was more important than the skill shown in its creation. Blake reminded me of a Greek goddess, her body made to be molded by the hands of an artist.

She dragged out the end note of a song before falling into some epic air guitar, and I couldn't help but laugh. I did that a lot lately, just falling into fits of chuckles when she was around. She was amazing. All I wanted to do was bundle her up in my bed and spend hours with her, making love to her body, then talking to her until I knew her all dreams and desires, her hopes and fears. I wanted to know her inside and out.

She picked up a vase and raised an eyebrow. "No offense, Harrison, but this one seems very…"

"Tall?" I offered, trying to keep a straight face.

"Phallic," she shot back, stroking her hand up the thin stem like it was indeed a cock.

I groaned internally at the action. "Hey, whatever" —I looked down at the packing slip for the name of the customer—"BabsOfWhorealon decides to do with her vase is entirely up to her. Actually, you better throw in a 'not for internal use' sticker on the bottom of that one to cover us from liability."

The fact I'd even had to get those stickers made at all still shocked me, but when my public liability insurer had insisted on it, who was I to argue?

She giggled, and her laughter made me happy. She'd been here for just over a month now, and I wasn't quite sure how she'd managed to insert herself into our lives like she was always meant to be here, but she had. She gently wrapped the dick vase and placed it in the appropriate box, chuckling as she repeated the customer name.

Finally, we were done, and I sat down on the stool. It was cooler today, so the warmth of the kiln made the inside of the workshop pleasant. She came over and stood next to me, leaning on the counter beside my head.

"So, what's the go with you and that douchebag from the awards? Prince Eric? What a fucking stupid name. He was my least favorite cartoon prince before this. But now I think even Simba is hotter than that asshole."

I blinked at her. I hadn't thought about that altercation in the two weeks since the event. I tried not to think of Eric at all, actually. "Well, there's a lot to unpack there, but Eric and us kind of fight for the same subscribers. He's just mad that we all have more than he has—Darwin actually has about triple the amount. Plus, we game on the same server on Kill-Switch, and he doesn't know when to turn off the competitive nature."

She frowned. "He doesn't realize it's just a game?"

I laughed, resisting the urge to pull her closer. "You've never played an online game, I'm guessing. The whole server is full of people with rage issues who never get laid and hate us just because we get our dick out on the internet, yet still beat them. For some people, gaming is a way of life." I tried not to sound like a know-it-all, but online gaming was an interesting experience. It was a weird community, filled with amazing people, but more than a few assholes who hid behind their keyboards and mic in their momma's basement.

She hummed a disapproving noise beneath her breath. "Well, I still hate him. Want me to start a throwaway ClickHeart account and post gherkin emojis on all his videos?"

"More than anything," I agreed solemnly, but I couldn't hold back my smirk. "You're something, Blake."

She straightened, her cheeks flushing pink, and I almost wanted to take the compliment back so we didn't tip the careful balance between us right now. I wanted her to be relaxed and happy in my presence. But I also didn't want to hide the fact that I was becoming increasingly more attracted to her.

She chewed her lip as she changed the subject. "What's the plan for the rest of the weekend?"

I shrugged, standing up to gather the box of packages that I'd get collected tomorrow. "*Wastelands* is having an online tournament this weekend, and it should go for the next twenty-four hours. The winner gets a new Mustang or the cash equivalent, so there'll be a lot of people out and a good chance to get more subscribers. We're all signed up, so depending on if we get knocked out or not kind of determines the rest of our weekend. What about you? Any plans?"

She looked out the window, her lips turning down a little. I watched her push the heavy thoughts off, but they were still there, resting at her feet, waiting to climb back into her brain once again. I wanted to know what they were so I could make them disappear completely.

"A quiet one, I think. Maybe I'll do some art while I listen to you guys yell at each other in the name of fun."

I smiled back at her, but it was tight. I had to do something about the Heinrich situation, because I hated to see her so depressed about it. Maybe I'd go out to wherever he was, just get a pretzel and talk to the guy. Explain what he was missing out on. But not this weekend, because I had a Mustang to win.

I led her back into the house, where Everett was cooking up a storm in the kitchen. He'd make enough ready meals that we could eat between rounds, and also enough for Blake, because he was pretty convinced she'd just die without his food, like she hadn't lived twenty-two years without him playing mother hen. But food was also how Everett showed affection, so no matter how much I teased him about it, I knew it was significant.

The afternoon unraveled slowly, all of us set up in the gaming room, Blake reclining on the sectional in the corner, her tablet propped on her knees as she worked. It was rare to see her without the piece of technology in her hands. Either she was working or doing art, and sometimes she even read on that thing. Her blue-light filtering glasses were perched on the end of her nose, and she looked so fucking cute I wanted to kiss her.

Everett snapped his fingers in front of my face. "Are you going to play or are you going to moon about? I need you to watch my back as we raid this warehouse."

I dragged my eyes from her, giving Everett the finger when he shot me a knowing look. *Asshole.*

The day disappeared into the night, and I was vaguely aware of Blake coming and going, my body almost as tuned into her as a sunflower to the sun. But as the night drifted on, she curled up on the couch, her headphones covering her ears, and her eyelids drooping. I knew I should tell her to head up to bed, but I liked her here with us.

My eyes started to burn, and I was about to tell the guys I was done, when Blake screamed. The sound was so jarring—so not Blake—that I froze for a second, but it was long enough to see the reflection of guns in my monitor. I wrenched my headphones off my head as I spun in my chair.

"Get on the fucking ground!" a man in a mask shouted. "On the ground. Your hands above your head."

My hands went automatically to my head as I moved to my knees, but not fast enough. A guy in a bulletproof SWAT vest shoved his boot into my back, and I was slammed onto my gut, my head turned toward Everett. He was yelling back at the SWAT guys, telling them there'd been a mistake, but they weren't listening as they shoved him down onto the floor. I lifted my head so I could look for Blake.

"Blake!" I shouted, but a man with a gun pointed at my face told me to shut the fuck up. I saw her, her eyes wide and filled with fear, lying on her stomach in her fucking duckie pjs, a man with a gun pointed at her head standing over her while another patted her down for weapons. Blake with fucking weapons, in her duck pajamas, was a completely surreal idea.

As terror receded back to fear, my brain started refiring, trying to make sense of what was happening. And there was only one explanation.

We'd been fucking *swatted*.

I met Blake's eyes, and tried to tell her with my own that everything was going to be okay. That this was a mistake, one that someone was going to pay for, even if it took all my time and money to accomplish it.

I looked over at Everett, who was still struggling and protesting. "Everett, shut the fuck up until you have a lawyer," I snapped. I was losing it. I couldn't even see Darwin, and that worried me.

"You're being detained under suspicion of domestic

terrorism activities. You have the right to remain silent..."

I tuned him out, because all I could see were Blake's terrified tears as a cop cuffed her and dragged her to her feet, frog-marching her out the door. The cops patted me down, and soon enough, I went too, losing sight of Everett, though I did manage to catch a glimpse of a terrified-looking Darwin in the corner.

Police lights flashed in our neighborhood, creating eerie blue and red shadows, and there were at least ten cop cars blocking up the road. My neighbors were all out in their robes, looking at us like we were criminals.

They stuffed me in a squad car, and I watched as Everett, Darwin, and a tear-stained Blake were all placed in separate cars. I had no idea how long I sat there, watching cops pour into my house; it could have been minutes or an hour. Finally, two cops climbed into the front and drove us away, the lights still flashing.

I wanted to throw up. I wanted to throw punches. I wanted to *hurt* whoever the little fuck was who thought this was okay. But first, I wanted my lawyer.

31

BLAKE

They kept us in separate holding cells. Well, at least I was kept separate. Maybe the guys were together; I couldn't know. Tears welled in my eyes, and I brushed them away with the back of my hand. I didn't know what was going on. Didn't know why I was here.

They'd told me that someone had accused us of running a domestic terrorist cell from the mansion, which was insane. But when Harrison had snapped at Everett to stop talking and wait for the lawyer, I figured that applied to me too. Not that I could afford a lawyer.

I sat in that holding cell for hours, long into the night. My eyes burned with exhaustion and the tears that I was holding back, and my head pounded from clenching my jaw so tight. Fear still made my blood run cold, making me shiver in the cell.

Eventually, the cell door opened, and a police officer stood there. "Miss Wilcox, follow me." I stood, taught early that the police were there to help me. That I should do what they said. But one had pointed a huge fucking gun in my face earlier tonight, and I hadn't done anything wrong.

I was still in my duck pajamas, and I was freezing. The police officer led me down through the halls, into a small room with a metal table in the center. I'd watched enough crime shows that I knew this was an interrogation room.

I looked over at the police officer. He was an average-looking guy and didn't seem overly perturbed about me one way or another. "I think I'm supposed to have a lawyer? Can you call me one?" My voice was timid, though I'd always thought in this type of situation, I would be tougher. All I wanted to do right now was go home and go to sleep, maybe try to convince myself this was all a terrible dream.

"Your lawyer is coming right now, Miss. They shouldn't be much longer."

Like the cop promised, a man in a suit walked through the door a moment later. "I'd like a minute with my client, if I may?" he asked the officer, who only looked mildly annoyed as he stood and left, shutting the door firmly behind him.

"You must be the famous Blake. I'm Harvey DeLuca. Don't worry, this is a bullshit charge. A messed-up case of swatting. Do you know what that is?" I shook my head, and he sighed heavily. "The plague of the internet. Well, one of them; there's an argument that the whole thing is a plague. Swatting is when someone gets your address and files a fake threat or tip-off that the local police force—in your case, the FBI as well—have to respond to. They'll take statements and evidence, and then they'll have to release you." He looked me up and down, smiling softly at my outfit. "You inspire about as much terror as a kitten. Is there anything I need to know? Anything you should disclose now? We're protected by attorney-client privilege."

I shook my head vigorously. I wasn't a terrorist.

He patted my hand, giving me a reassuring look. "Answer their questions, follow my lead, and we'll be out of here by dawn."

I nodded, something about the confident older man making me feel safer. "Okay."

"Thatta girl." Harvey must have been in his early forties, but he was handsome. He had a light tan that said he liked to holiday somewhere warm, and a ring on his finger that implied there was a Mrs. DeLuca somewhere. "I have a daughter your age, in college. Had her when I was eighteen. To think of the things you guys have to navigate now makes me long for the days when teenage pregnancy was the scariest thing that could happen to you."

The interrogation room door reopened, and two men in suits walked in. Definitely detectives, or maybe federal agents. They were both average height. Both had boring brown hair. One had a thick pair of glasses, but that was the only thing that differentiated them at all.

"We're going to record this, if that's okay?" Glasses asked.

I looked at Harvey, who nodded. "That'll be fine." He heaved a sigh. "Let's keep this short and sweet, yes? We both know this is bullshit, and we still have to do three more of these interviews."

The fed shrugged, and they started with their questions. At first, the answers were easy: my name, where I was from, what I was doing in LA. They got on to more and more personal questions, like my relationship with the guys, what they did, what I did for them. By the time they were done, I'd told them my entire life story, right up until this afternoon. Harvey was mostly silent, pulling up the detectives if he thought the questions were out of line, like whether I was sleeping with all the guys.

"It says here you've been arrested, but never charged?"

Harvey looked at me like I'd lied to him when I said there was nothing to disclose. "It was a turkey incident when I was sixteen."

"An international incident in Turkey?"

I shook my head quickly. "No, the bird. It destroyed a police cruiser. It wasn't my fault. It chased me in there, then got mad when it couldn't get back out. Its name was Bacon." Fuck, if I went to jail because of that fucking feathery velociraptor, I was going home to track down Caleb Dursten and kick him so hard in the balls, he'd have to cough to swallow.

The agents gave nothing away, though the one with the glasses raised an eyebrow at my story of Turkey Bacon.

Finally, they finished their notes and stood as one. Glasses inclined his head. "Thank you for your time, Miss Wilcox. I'll have an officer take you back to your holding cell."

Harvey frowned. "I don't think so. We both know you have nothing to hold her on, and that this whole charge is a waste of your time and my client's. Release her now; she'll promise not to leave the state while you finish your investigation—which will show absolutely nothing. Let her go home."

The Feds looked at each other for a moment before the quiet one nodded. "Someone will come to take you out the front, Miss. They'll have some paperwork for you to fill out, then you're free to go."

They left, and I looked at Harvey, my eyes filling with tears again. "Thank you."

He patted my back. "Don't thank me, Miss Wilcox. I'm getting paid very well to be here. Off you go. By tomorrow, this will all be a story you can tell at dinner parties." He sighed. "Now, I have to go and make sure Everett doesn't take a swing and get stuck in here for a whole different set of charges." He patted me on the arm reassuringly and disappeared out into the hall.

I sat alone in the room for a little longer, but before I could come up with every terrible scenario possible, another police officer appeared. "Let's go."

I followed them up to the front counter, where another officer gave me a whole stack of paperwork I had to sign. They'd seized all of our electronics, apparently, and according to the paperwork, the place had been searched for explosives and signs of terrorist activity.

This was surreal, but I signed everything I needed to. I looked at the officer behind the desk. "You don't think they're going to tell my parents about this, do you?" I whispered, and the guy grimaced.

"You aren't a minor, but if it's necessary to the investigation, they might."

Fucking great. I wanted to cry all over again at the injustice of it all.

The guy handed me my copy of the paperwork and smiled tightly. "You're free to go."

Go where? I didn't have my phone or my purse. I had no money and no way to get home. *Fuck.* Tears spilled over my eyelids. Who did I even call? Not my parents, that's for sure. Dani was in Saint-Tropez. I didn't know Celine's number. Who the hell could I call?

"I'm sorry to bother you, but please could you look up the number for Heinrich's Wiener, Schnitzel & Pretzel Truck?" At least Hennie should have a number listed somewhere on the internet, right?

"Feeling peckish?" the officer asked, his brows raised. But he must have felt a little sorry for me, because he did the search, writing out the number and handing it to me.

"Can I...?" I waved a hand at the phone.

"The public phone is in the entryway. It's free."

I chewed my lip and nodded. "Thank you."

Whatever station this was, it was busy. The general air of desperation in the room was cloying, making my skin break out in goosebumps. Maybe I should wait for the guys, but I was going to take Harvey's advice and get the hell out of here.

I waited for a woman in a skirt so short that I could see the bottoms of her asscheeks to be done with the phone. She didn't look at all nervous to be here, just aggravated and inconvenienced. I guess she probably hadn't been dragged from her home at gunpoint.

With a lot of cussing, she finally arranged for her ride and slammed down the phone. Turning, she glared at me. I averted my gaze. I didn't want to offend her, didn't want to start a fight.

She took a look at my pajamas and my bare skin,

and probably the terrified expression on my face, and her eyes softened. She pulled out a wet wipe from her oversized handbag. "Here. You're gonna want to wipe that down if you're gonna use it. Nothing more disgusting than a public phone in a cop station."

I took the wet wipe and tried not to cry again at the small act of kindness. "Thank you."

She let out a low noise of disapproval and left. I took her advice, wiping the headset down thoroughly. Then I dialed the number on the piece of paper. I listened to the prompts, telling it my name when it asked. I guess they reversed-charged it—just one more thing I was going to have to pay back.

Hennie's voice was suddenly on the line, and it sounded muffled. "Blake? Hello? Are you okay?"

I choked back the emotion that welled in my throat, despite the burn. *Not here. Not yet.* "Hennie?"

"*Liebling,* are you okay? It said you're calling me from the police station?"

The concern in his voice had me blinking rapidly. "I'm okay. I'm sorry to wake you." I sucked in a shaky breath. "I didn't know who else to call. The guys..." I cut off, because if I got into that, I'd be here forever. "I'm really sorry to ask, but would you come and get me?"

There was silence at the other end, then vague rustling. I was an idiot. We weren't a couple. We hadn't ever *been* a couple. We were barely friends. Why would he do this?

Finally, his breathing came back over the phone, with the gentle jingle of keys in the background. "I'm on my way. Which station?"

Relief washed over me like a physical wave, and I told him the precinct and the street address, which was helpfully taped to the payphone.

"Wait there, inside. That's a pretty crappy side of town. I'll come in and grab you." I could hear his car starting. "I won't be long. Twenty minutes, Blake, and I'll be there." The phone ran out of time and hung up, but I still listened to the silence on the other end for a moment.

"Hey, lady. You done or what?"

I looked over my shoulder at a young woman, her hair scruffy and her jaw set in an angry tilt. I put the handset back into the cradle, mumbling an apology as I went over and sat in a hard plastic seat near the door. Cold air blew in every time the door opened, but I didn't move, despite the fact that I was freezing. I wanted Hennie to be able to find me.

Finally, about twenty minutes later, the door slid open, and he was there. He looked mussed, like he'd been asleep, but his eyes were wide with concern. When they fell on me, the wave of adrenaline that had kept me going for this long dissipated, and tears fell down my cheeks.

He strode toward me, his legs eating up the distance between us quickly. He pulled me into his arms, and I clung to him. "I've got you now. Come on, let's get out of here," he whispered into my hair as I breathed him in.

Guilt and relief warred with each other, but I still followed him out into the darkness.

32

HENNIE

I'd never been more scared than that moment my phone rang in the middle of the night, the voice telling me it was the LAPD. My heart had raced, thinking of all the worst-case scenarios that could be at the other end of that call. My parents, my siblings.

I hadn't expected Blake, but that hadn't made the panic subside. She'd sounded so lost, so traumatized, over the phone, and my brain went straight into panic mode. I'd been up and dressing before she'd even asked me to collect her.

Blake had been haunting me, even as I threw myself into work. She'd gotten under my skin in such a short time, and I didn't want to sound like a cliché, but she'd been refreshingly different to the other women on the LA dating scene. She was so freaking funny, and sweet, even if she was also a bit naive. The perfect person to be taken advantage of by the sharks in this town.

As I drove to the station she'd told me, my brain made up scenarios of why she was there, and they got progressively darker, increasing my rage and fear tenfold.

But nothing could have prepared me for seeing her in that clinical plastic chair, dressed in cute little duck pajamas like a child, her eyes big and watery, as if she was trying to be brave and not break down completely.

I hadn't even made the conscious decision to pull her into my arms, to shield her from the world, but she'd come willingly, and I'd murmured soft, reassuring things into her hair as I led her from the building, dodging prostitutes and drunks. Her skin was icy cold, though I didn't know if it was from shock or the fact she was wearing basically nothing.

I'd double-parked out the front of the police station, but I'd take the fine if there was one. I opened the passenger door, gently guiding her in. With her safe inside my car, a part of me relaxed. She was okay. That was all that mattered.

I climbed in and pumped the heater, trying to give her some warmth. She turned to me, giving me a watery smile. "Thank you. I didn't know who else to call," she said quietly.

I was already shaking my head. "You can always call me, Blake. We're friends." Were we, though? It hadn't ended well, and I'd wanted her to be so much more. But I put the thought aside, as she looked out the passenger window.

"Can you take me home? The guys are still at the station, and they can't contact me, so I want them to know where I am."

The betrayal that flared in my chest at the mention of her housemates was a gut reaction, but if she wanted to go home, surely that meant that her house-mates hadn't hurt her in any way. I found that oddly reassuring. I might want her for myself, but it didn't mean I wanted her to be wrong about her housemates. I didn't want someone to steal that sweetness and replace it with something dark and haunting.

I nodded, indicating to get onto the freeway. "Of course I can."

We drove in silence some more, and I desperately wanted to ask her what had happened, but I held my tongue. She'd tell me when she was ready, or I'd ask when she felt more secure at home.

Finally, we pulled into her neighborhood, and I noticed her hands starting to shake. Pulling up into her driveway, I walked around to her side and opened the door for her, my hand hovering close to her lower back as she got out. I walked her up to the front door, where she frowned.

"I don't have my keys, but there's a hide-a-key around the back."

We moved down along the side of the house, into a large backyard, complete with massive stone deck and pool. She found a rock in the garden, carrying it over to me with shaky hands, and I unscrewed the lid. Morning light was just breaching the horizon, casting the backyard in a gray light as I moved toward the back door.

As I looked through the large windows, I blinked. The place was trashed. Every drawer in the kitchen was open, with stuff scattered all across the dining table. Things were strewn across the floor carelessly, as if someone had been searching for something.

Blake moved up silently beside me, looking at the mess with a blankness that was more worrying than her tear-filled gaze at the station. "They must have had a search warrant." Her voice was soft, and I got the impression she'd forgotten I was there.

"A search warrant for what?"

She turned to look at me, her eyes losing their blankness as it was replaced by anger, her jaw tightening so much, it was a wonder I couldn't hear her teeth grinding. Fuck, maybe she didn't want me here, asking questions.

"I should go. I hope..." What did I hope? That whatever she was involved in didn't ruin her life? She was still looking at me, and I would kill for even a glimpse of what was going on inside her head. Instead,

I reached out and gripped her hand. "Stay safe, *Liebling.*"

I turned to walk away, but her hand clung to mine, not letting go. I tugged softly, just in case she'd forgotten she was holding it, but she held fast.

She swallowed hard. "Will you stay? Just for a little bit?"

My heart thudded loudly in my chest, but I stopped pulling away, gathering her close and holding her in my arms. "Of course. Let's go inside."

Even trashed, the house was amazing. Blake moved ahead of me, clearly flustered as she closed drawers and put things away, her feet dragging along the floor with exhaustion.

"Why don't you get some sleep? This will be all here later when you're less wrung out."

She nodded silently and grabbed my hand, dragging me upstairs. Her room—well, at least I assumed it was her room—was also messy. Clothes had been removed from their drawers and dumped on the bed. Everything had been ripped out of her closet, all her toiletries scattered across the bathroom counter.

She walked in and flopped down on the unmade bed, her shoulders shaking with sobs. I crawled behind her, pulling her close to my chest. "What could they have possibly been looking for in your underwear drawer?" I muttered, and she let out a choked laugh that had no humor in it at all.

"Explosives."

"*What?*"

She sucked in another shuddering breath. "Someone called the cops on the guys. Accused us of being a terrorist group. We got swatted."

"The fuck?" I couldn't help the incredulous tone. "No offense, but you don't look like you could hurt a fly."

She shook her head as she buried her face in my chest. "Didn't matter. Someone called the cops and told them that we were building... building bombs. Maybe one of the other gamers on the guys' *Wastelands* tournament? I don't know. So they raided the house, and they pointed a gun—" She sobbed harder, and I held her tightly, like I could keep her together. "It didn't matter that we were completely innocent. They put us in cop cars and left us in cells for hours. They confiscated everything. They're going to call my parents, and they'll make me go home..."

I let her cry it out against my chest until she fell asleep from exhaustion. Wiggling my phone out from my pocket, I Googled swatting over her shoulder. People had died from that bullshit—it was a federal offense, for fuck's sake—and someone was doing it over a videogame? I didn't understand people anymore.

A door opened and closed downstairs, and I heard someone yell Blake's name. Untangling myself from her arms, I walked downstairs to find her housemates. I wanted to know what the actual fuck was going on. Plus, I didn't want them to catch me in Blake's bed, in their house, and make all this shit worse.

I stood on the stairs until they noticed me, which took longer than usual as they surveyed the chaos left behind from the search warrant. It was Everett—the mean, tattooed one—who spotted me first.

"What the fuck are you doing in my house?" he yelled, and I winced.

"Shh, you'll wake up Blake, asshole," I whisper-shouted back. I descended the rest of the stairs as they all watched me warily. "She called me from the station to get a ride home. She didn't have her wallet, a phone, nothing."

The blond one—Harrison, I remembered from the brief introductions at the club—narrowed his eyes. "How'd she get your number if she didn't have a phone?"

So suspicious, but given what they'd all probably just been through, I didn't blame them. "She called my work cell. It's on my website. Your lawyer told her to go home, but I don't think she was prepared for all this." I waved a hand around at the disheveled house. "She's pretty shaken up."

Harrison slumped onto the couch. "We all are. Fuck!" He threw a couch pillow across the room. "Fucking pieces of shit. *Fuck!*"

I had to agree, because doing that to someone was just messed up. They all looked devastated, which dulled the anger that was burning in my chest at them. The rational part of my brain acknowledged that they couldn't have protected themselves against this.

Darwin made a pained noise in his throat. "It gets worse. We've been doxxed."

I looked at him blankly. What the fuck was that? "For those of us in the room who aren't social media influencers?" I asked, and he gave me a sad smile.

"It means someone released our real names and addresses. We're going to have to leave."

They looked wrecked, but I was still confused. "Why?" I mean, a lot of people knew your real name and address, right? The pizza delivery man, the electricity company, people who randomly just walked past your house and saw you in the driveway. What was the big deal?

It was Everett who elaborated for me, though he seemed to be talking more to himself than the rest of us. "We work in an industry selling fantasy to people. A few build up the fantasy until it's something scary and toxic, and they turn into stalkers. Most are harmless..."

But some were not. It didn't need to be said.

"Is Blake in danger?"

Everett growled. "Yes. This is a fucking mess." He tugged at his hair, frustration written in every line of his body. "Maybe they haven't released the information yet? They might be keeping it as blackmail material later." When blackmail was the hopeful option, you knew shit had gone pear-shaped.

Darwin stood. "We need new phones. I need to call my mom. Sometimes my sisters watch my KillSwitch channel, and even if they haven't, they follow my socials. There's no way the swatting isn't all over the Gram by now."

I pulled out my cell. "You can call your mom from mine, if you want."

Giving me a thankful smile, he punched in a number he'd obviously learned by heart and lifted the phone to his ear. "Mama? It's Dee. No, I'm fine. I'd hoped to catch you before you found out. We're all fine. It was completely fake." He slumped back on the couch as a steady stream of Spanish poured from his mouth, the tone calming.

Everett was pacing backwards and forwards, and Harrison had his head tipped back on the headrest of the couch, his eyes closed, but I knew he wasn't asleep. Tension thrummed through every inch of his body. "We can get a hotel suite for now, I think," he murmured. "At least until this isn't in the news any longer. I don't like the lack of security around it, especially with our real names being out there, but we don't have a lot of choice now."

I almost felt bad for them. "Blake can stay with me, while you guys figure this out."

Everett stopped pacing, turning to glare at me. "Over my fucking dead body, pretty boy. You don't get to swoop in here like a white knight and cast the rest of us as villains."

I rolled my eyes. "This isn't about you."

"It's not about you either, and no offense, but we still barely know you. We aren't going to let Blake go and stay at your place like a prisoner."

These guys were insane. The fame had definitely melted their brains. I rolled my eyes. "Fine, you can all come and stay with me temporarily. At least until you get this shit figured out."

They eyed me warily, all except Darwin, who gave me back my phone with a soft, "Thank you." He looked at the others. "Mama said we can come and stay with her in Pasadena if we want, but my aunts are up from Ecuador so we'd all have to sleep in the living room."

Harrison and Everett were having a silent conversation, and after a moment, Harrison sighed. He met my eyes, giving me a weak smile. "Thank you. We'll only stay a week, just to judge the fallout."

I nodded, wondering what the fuck I was doing right now. I was just going with my gut, and my gut said that Blake should stay with me. The idea of her being in any kind of danger made me want to vomit, so if I had to bring them all home to keep her safe, I would.

"Why don't you guys go and pack some stuff, and I'll try putting things back where they belong? At least until Blake wakes up."

Everett nodded, turning to climb the stairs. I had a feeling I knew where he'd be going first.

Darwin patted me on the back. "We appreciate this," he said softly, before climbing the stairs too, though I noticed his feet dragged a little. I'd bet good money that he'd fall asleep before he packed a single thing.

Harrison was the only one left. He looked at me silently, his head tilted to the side, as if he was trying to discover my angle. "Why?"

I shrugged, because I didn't know either. "Seems like the right thing to do."

He watched me a little longer, then nodded. "We appreciate it." With that, he too climbed the stairs, while I went about rearranging the house into something that didn't look like it had been run through by a bulldozer.

33

BLAKE

I woke up bleary-eyed, to the sound of soft snores beside me. Maybe Hennie had stayed, like he'd promised? Rolling softly so I didn't wake him, I was surprised and relieved to see it was Darwin in bed with me.

It was probably a testament to how exhausted I'd been that I hadn't even heard or felt him come in. He was lying on his front, his cheek smooshed into the mattress as he breathed heavily. I wanted to wake him up, see how everything had gone with his interview, no matter how confident Harvey had sounded.

Instead, I let him sleep. I still felt the heavy weight of last night pressing down on my chest, so he would be equally as wrung out. I climbed out of bed, changing out of my pajamas and into some sweats. I needed to clean up, get things back in order before the guys had a chance to fully comprehend the level of chaos the house had become.

When I made it downstairs, it was like the whole night had been a bad dream. The house was back in order, everything in its place. I walked further down the stairs, through into the living room. Hennie lay on the couch, an arm thrown over his eyes and a dish towel over his shoulder, snoring softly.

Had Hennie done this?

I went in search of the other guys, feeling restless until I knew for certain they were here and safe. I looked in the office, a room that Hennie hadn't touched, and I immediately understood why. It was a mess, with paperwork strewn across the desks, drawers open, and huge chunks of paper files missing. I didn't want to touch anything either, so I softly shut the door and went in search of the other two.

As if he knew I was looking for him, when I turned around, Harrison was behind me. By the look on his face, he'd been there for a while, looking over my shoulder at the tossed remains of his office.

I wrapped my arms tightly around his waist. "You're okay." He was stiff in my arms, his hand patting my back almost hesitantly. I looked up at his face; all I could see was guilt. His face was awash with it, and my heart broke. I continued to hug him. "You're okay, right? Because I'm fine, Harrison. I promise."

He stepped out of my arms. "How could you be okay? You were dragged to the police station in your pajamas. Someone pointed a gun at your face, Blake. You were interrogated like a criminal, and it's all my fault. *Our* fault."

He couldn't blame himself for this. "Did you call the cops and make a false report?"

"No, but—"

"Are you a terrorist, and I've been completely wrong about you this whole time?"

He reared back, like I'd struck him. "Of course not."

I gathered him back into my arms. "Then I don't see how this could possibly be your fault, Harrison. You didn't do anything wrong. I didn't do anything wrong. Some little fucker on the internet was an asshole and caused us both a hell of a lot of trauma, and wasted thousands of taxpayer dollars. None of that falls on your head, or Everett's, or Darwin's." I scowled at the thought. "I hope they find the asshole who did it and throw him in a federal prison."

Harrison snorted, his body relaxing beneath my hands. "Unlikely. The guys who do this shit, they're good at covering their tracks. So unless it's some sixteen-year-old kid in his basement who's a total amateur, it's unlikely they'll find the guy."

I melted into his arms more, taking the comfort he was giving me in return like a greedy sponge. Judging by his wet hair and his soft, spicy scent, he'd just showered, and I wanted to bury my face into his chest and not move for days. His hand stroked up and down my back slowly, and the tension that had been constraining my muscles for hours loosened a little.

"Where's Everett? Is he okay?"

"He's up in my bed. None of us wanted to sleep alone last night. Darwin crawled into your bed before either of us could get in there first." His lips twisted in what might have been a smile on any other day, but there was an edge of worry to it that hadn't quite disappeared.

I ran my hands up and down his spine, taking my turn to soothe him. We stood there in silence in the hallway, and I realized he was gently rocking me from side to side as my eyes got heavy. I gently pushed away from his chest. As tired as my body was, my brain needed answers.

"Will they do it again?" I didn't know much about the shitheads who did this kind of thing, but according to Harvey the lawyer, it was a regular occurrence. Did we just let it go and hope the Feds found him?

"We were doxxed as well." At my confused expression, the guilt crawled back over his face. "It's where they release our real names and residential address. Sometimes other crap too."

I shook my head, because it made no sense. "How could they even know that kind of information? You guys are tight-lipped on the internet. I've seen it myself. There's no way to trace your accounts back to here."

Sadness and anxiety dragged at his features like dual lead weights. "I honestly don't know. But I'll contact someone to increase our cyber security. Until this all dies down, though, we're going to have to leave. Maybe sell the house."

I pulled out of his arms. "We have to move?" He nodded. "When?"

"Now. Today. It's not safe. I love my fans, but some of them... Well, I wouldn't want them to know where we live. Heinrich looked at the Gram for us, and the address has already been posted everywhere." He straightened his spine, stepping away, though his fingertips still rested on my upper arms. "Go and pack what you can. I have to go in there and pack up most of my paperwork to send to the lawyers. We're going to stay with your boyfriend for a couple of days, until the real estate broker can find us somewhere else, even if it's temporary."

My brain whirled. This had to be a joke. Yesterday morning, life had been idyllic. Now we were all going to stay with my ex-love interest in his house until the guys bought another mansion. What was happening right now?

.   .   .

Turns out, it wasn't a joke. By lunchtime, everyone was awake, so we headed to an electronics store to make someone's day by buying an exorbitant amount of technology to replace the stuff that had been confiscated. Darwin had joked that it was time for an upgrade anyway and that it would keep his accountant happy, but Everett scowled through the whole process, hovering close to me like he was expecting the SWAT team to reappear.

The guys ended up buying me a new phone, laptop and tablet, no matter how much I protested that I could just wait until it all came back from the cops.

"It could be weeks. Months, even, if wrapping the case up gets pushed down the queue. We need you working, because if we stop, so does the money," Harrison argued, stuffing a state-of-the-art tablet, miles better than my current one, into his cart. "Darwin is correct. It's a business expense, and it makes the accountants happy."

So I just let them buy it, telling myself that I'd give it back if I ever stopped working for them. It was company equipment. All businesses had company equipment, right?

Hennie stood at the back, shaking his head at the sheer insanity of the money they were dropping like it was nothing. It was intimidating, but also a little exciting. Living in the mansion had definitely spoiled me.

I drifted back toward him, an awkward amount of

space between us. He'd come to my rescue—our rescue—but that didn't mean he wanted things to go back to the way they were. Probably the opposite. I was obviously a lot more trouble than he wanted or needed in his life right now.

"Is this weird?" I whispered to him, and he looked down at me, a single eyebrow lifted.

"What, exactly, do you think is weird? That these guys just dropped enough money to buy a car without blinking?" He wrapped an arm around my shoulders, pulling me closer to his chest. "Or that you're moving in with me after only two dates?" He let out a huffed laugh. "Maybe the fact that your harem of boyfriends is moving in too?"

I winced. "Yeah. All of the above."

"Nope, not weird at all, *Liebling*." The sarcasm was thick, but he didn't look mad about it. Man, I'd be so fucking mad if I was in his position. If he'd moved into my house with three girls he was interested in, I'd probably have drowned him in the pool.

"You're a good man, Hennie. I don't deserve your friendship."

He snorted. "Agree to disagree. Do you think The Plastics might hurry along their shopping spree or what?"

I chuckled at the *Mean Girls* reference and gave him a wink. "I'll go tell them I'm tired."

It worked like a charm. From the moment I told

Everett I was still exhausted, to the time we were back in the car, was less than fifteen minutes. The teenage sales clerk had been smiling so wide, I could see his back teeth. Apparently, he worked on commission and was going to use his bonus to buy a guitar. It was a very sweet silver lining to the shitshow of the last twenty-four hours.

We piled back into our cars, with Harrison on the phone, giving the final go-ahead to the security firm to lock down the house and put in new tech to keep it secure. Apparently, there was a branch of the company that would shore up our cyber security too.

I sat in the front seat of Hennie's car as he drove us out of the Hills and into the suburbs, the houses getting less mansion-like and more suburban. The neighborhoods were populated with single-story bungalows, and by the time we pulled into Hennie's home in La Puente, it was like we'd stepped into an entirely different world.

He pressed a button on his dash to open his front gate. His food truck sat in the driveway, making me smile. I had fond memories of that truck. The other guys pulled into the wide driveway behind us in Everett's car.

"Home sweet home," Hennie murmured to me as he opened my car door. "Might not be what you're used to, but it's safe and warm."

I reached up and ran my hand across his arm gently. "Thank you."

He didn't say anything else, just wrapped an arm around my waist and led me to the front door, safe in the comfort of his closeness.

34

When we'd finally gotten back online, it was so much worse than we'd thought. Our information was spreading from post to post, platform to platform, like wildfire. People we'd once known from home were coming out of the woodwork, sharing personal anecdotes about us and our lives, and the rumor mill about Harrison and I had started up all over again, throwing me into a time warp like it was ten years ago and we were still dumb kids in small-town Minnesota.

We all decided that we would release a short written statement, then follow that up with a clip of us explaining what happened and the very real world effects it would have on us, our lives, and our ability to make content. We'd have to rely on some saved content, maybe do some reposts, because there was no way I was getting naked in Wiener Boy's kitchen and making new content.

His house was nice, the kind of place I'd grown up in. He'd said he'd inherited it from his grandfather along with the truck, and I could see it. The neighborhood hadn't quite been gentrified yet, and there were still old dudes in their front yards mowing their square of grass with push mowers. Your average middle-class neighborhood. Four bedrooms, though one was an office with a fold-out couch that Darwin was currently occupying. Blake got her own room, and I was happy enough to bunk with Harrison.

I wouldn't admit this to the guys, but I kind of liked the simplicity of it. His kitchen was nice too—not quite industrial, but quality appliances and fittings. He was definitely in the food industry, and I wouldn't be surprised if he did some prep here.

We'd ordered food for breakfast, because there was no way Heinrich had enough here to feed five people, but we could remedy that later. Hopefully, Harrison's real estate broker could find us something ASAP. Though I might pitch them the idea of a single floor, because I was enjoying not climbing the stairs every day.

Sunshine was still in bed, and I wanted to climb in there with her, but I wasn't a complete dick, despite what people tended to believe. Even I wouldn't rub it in the face of Wiener Boy—especially because it was kind of my fault they'd broken up. He was a better man than me. I would have taken Sunshine home with me and left the rest of us to rot.

The silence in the kitchen was awkward. Darwin would normally smooth this shit over for us, but he was still sleeping too.

"Thanks for having us... again," Harrison murmured around his coffee.

Heinrich shrugged, leaning against the kitchen bench, eyeing us both like we were about to jump up and steal his prized worldly possessions or some shit. "Blake is a friend. It's the least I could do."

Harrison nodded curtly. "We still appreciate it." He cleared his throat. "Blake tells us that you own a food truck. Knowing her love of carbs and meat products, no wonder you guys became friends."

Wiener raised a single eyebrow. "We became friends because she's smart and funny, not to mention beautiful. Her love of carbs is just a bonus." He held my gaze as he said it, a challenge in there to refute any single word he'd just said.

Too bad that on the topic of how amazing Blake was, I agreed completely.

He finished his coffee and grabbed out a large plastic bin of flour, getting to work making some kind of dough. My bet was pretzel dough. There was something soothing about the process of making bread, which spoke to a more basic part of me. Mixing, kneading, proofing. It was a science and an art, one that had evolved over thousands of years to what it was today.

My fingers itched to help. I loved to cook—not just because it was my career, but because it had always been a kind of therapy. If we'd been at home, I would have baked my way through this whole thing.

Harrison watched us, like he was waiting for the blows to begin and he was ready to intervene. "Do you enjoy it?"

Heinrich dragged his eyes from mine to look at Harrison. "It's work. But yeah, I enjoy it. Who doesn't want to be their own boss?"

"I bet it makes for a good place to pick up pretty girls too," I snarked back, and the guy bristled. Harrison's groan reverberated around the room as Heinrich straightened. He was a tall guy, but he only had an inch or two on me, and I had the bulk. I could definitely take him if I had to. I'd been brawling for as long as I could remember, and he looked way too pretty to be much of a fighter.

"Fuck you. She wasn't some random booty call I was chasing. She meant something to me, you jealous fuck. If anyone's an opportunistic asshole, then you need to go check yourself out in the mirror—you'll see the poster boy for someone who takes advantage of women, despite their wishes."

The fuck? "Are you calling me a fucking rapist?"

Harrison stepped between us both. "Woah, woah. Keep your fucking voices down before you wake Blake. She's been through enough in the last forty-eight hours without having to put up with you two acting like mangy dogs fighting over a bone," he hissed. He turned toward me. "Get your shit together, Ev. We've fucked up her life enough for one week; you can control yourself." He turned toward Hennie, his jaw tensing as he tried to give our current host an apologetic look. "He's an asshole, but he cares about Blake too. We all do. Which is why we're here. I promise we'll be out of your hair as soon as possible. I'll go make some calls now."

Harrison hustled me out of the kitchen and back toward the spare bedroom we were currently sharing. I knew he was about to give me a lecture, and honestly, I didn't want to hear it. I knew I was being a dick; I just couldn't help it. So I stepped around him and knocked on the door to Sunshine's room.

He huffed, but instead of continuing to our room, he stopped behind me. Clearly, I wasn't the only one who wanted to check on our girl.

"Come in."

I pushed the door open to see Sunshine sitting up in bed, her brand new tablet propped on her knees. She had the stylus pen between her teeth, and her hair looked like a rat's nest on her head from where she'd slept roughly on it.

I wanted to replace the pen with my dick, and then maybe afterwards, give her some more just-fucked hair. She smiled at us, and my heart thudded in my chest. It was crazy that just a simple expression could do that to me. It wasn't natural. People didn't catch feelings this fast.

I moved toward the bed, climbing beneath the covers beside her. I kissed her temple softly, breathing in the scent of her hair. "Good morning, Sunshine."

"Good morning. Have you guys been awake for long?"

Harrison cleared his throat. "Not long."

Big fat liar. But Sunshine just smiled at him, moving over in the bed so he could climb in on her other side. She passed me her tablet, and I put it on the nightstand. The room was pretty beige, mostly just shades of brown, but I guess Wiener Boy couldn't bake *and* be an interior designer, right? Had to pick a talent, and I knew which one I'd choose.

She snuggled further down between us, and the sense of rightness I felt almost stole my breath. These two in bed with me was basically heaven, and when Harrison curled his body around hers, pressing a soft kiss to her cheek, I knew he thought so too. We just lay there together for a while, none of us speaking, just breathing in the comfort of being together until something loosened in my chest with a crack.

I could imagine waking up with them both, Blake

pressed between us as we had languid, lazy morning sex. Pleasuring Blake between us until she was a wet, sweat-soaked mess and screaming our names for the whole house to hear. Hell, so the whole neighborhood could hear.

My cock hardened in my sweats, bumping against her thigh. I was desperate to make love to her again. I dreamed of the way her hot core felt around my dick every single night. I'd fucked her like a savage once, and I would again, but first, I wanted to show her she was more than just an angry fuck to me. Before I took her like that again, I wanted to make love to her slowly, sweetly, edging her until her whole body shook with the need for release.

Once the thought had entered my brain, I couldn't think of anything else. I gripped her chin and turned her face toward me, kissing her lips firmly as my fingers caressed the soft curves of her side.

She kissed me back on a sigh, her body softening, and she drew back as her hand covered mine. I expected her to stop this, to move my hand away, but instead, she turned her face to Harrison. Her lips parted, the invitation clear, but Harrison was a gentle-man. Even with me, he was kind and respectful—the polar opposite of me.

"Can I kiss you?" he asked, propped up on one elbow. His eyes were devouring her lips, like he was planning all the ways he wanted to kiss her, and it made my own heart beat faster. Would he kiss her differently than the way he kissed me? Would he fuck her more gently? I was suddenly desperate to know the answer.

Instead of answering him, she leaned up and closed the distance between them. I was transfixed as his lips brushed across hers like a whisper, moving slowly like he was tasting her. He sucked in her lower lip, and I was no longer breathing as she collapsed back down onto the pillow, with him quickly following her. He moved across her body, bracketing her ribs with his arms as he pressed her further into the mattress. Her hands came up to dig into his golden hair, and I don't know what he did, but she moaned a little.

That soft sound was going to end me, I knew it. My dick grew even harder, and I nudged my hard cock against her thigh, just for a little friction. Her hand reached between us, her fingers flexing to take in the tensed muscles of my stomach. I rolled a little until she had better access, and her hand traveled down, down, until she was brushing the waistband of my sweats and I was holding my breath.

Harrison's phone ringing broke the spell, and he cursed as Blake pulled back. "Ignore it." He chased her lips again, but she laughed, slapping at his shoulder.

"Answer it. It might be the lawyer. Or the Feds. We don't need more SWAT teams busting in." Her words were light, framed as a joke, but I could see the anxiety she was trying to hide in her eyes.

Harrison rolled to the side, digging his phone out of his pocket as he went. "Hello?" A pause. "Oh, hey. Yeah, thanks for getting back to me. Today? I mean, sure. I think we can." Another pause. "Yeah, eleven. No worries. See you then." He hung up and flopped onto his back. "Get dressed, lovers. We're going to look at houses, and we've got an hour to get across town."

I couldn't help the frustrated huff that ruffled Sunshine's hair. "I *hate* house shopping."

Blake, on the other hand, looked positively gleeful as she bounced out of bed. "Let's go, let's go! Someone wake up Darwin!"

She disappeared into the ensuite, and I rolled over to face Harrison. Leaning forward, he kissed me softly. I felt like I could still taste her on his lips. When he pulled back, my feelings were reflected in his eyes. The rightness of us and her.

35

BLAKE

Rich people real estate agents were a world away from the average real estate agent. They gave you artisanal coffees as you walked through the door, or mimosas, because that was a breakfast drink, of course. You sat in a comfortable office where they regaled you with the wonders of houses that cost more than I would ever make in my lifetime.

It was surreal.

I didn't know what Mark, the agent, had been thinking when we all poured in, but he took it in his stride. He'd automatically dismissed Darwin, though, which put my teeth on edge. Darwin had more money than Harrison or Everett combined; he just wasn't as flashy about it. He wore designer jeans and a shirt he'd picked up from Walmart, simply because he liked the feel of the material.

I sat beside him and held his hand while Mark the Real Estate Bro waffled on about mansions near this celebrity, and that celebrity, and this luxury gym. I could see Everett getting more and more riled as Mark went on, until he snapped.

"Look, we aren't interested in you gouging us for the highest commission, or fucking rubbing shoulders with celebrities. If you want to sell our place out in Beverly Hills, then fucking show us what we want. Single story with lots of square footage. Easy to secure. Lots of land and space, because we don't want any fucking nosy neighbors. Not too far from the city. Go back to your office and find us something we want, because if I have to look at one more house that's a sculpture rather than a home, I'm going to lose my shit and take my business elsewhere."

I suspected I might've given Everett a case of the angry blue balls.

Mark spluttered a little, but soon enough, the smarmy salesman look was back on his face. "Of course. I know the perfect homes."

The places he listed were at least five million dollars cheaper, which was clearly why we didn't hear about them the first time. From those ten, we narrowed it down to three we actually wanted to look at. I mean, that the guys wanted to look at. It was their home, after all. My opinion really didn't matter.

The first place was... horrendous. It was like the architect had traveled the world, and tried to jam influences from every continent into one house. Harrison vetoed that one pretty quickly, despite the good-sized lot and the excellent security fence.

The second place was nice, though it was set into a hill, so it wasn't single story like Everett had requested, but I understood why Mark still showed us. It was warm and light, with a beautiful view over the city. A long flight of steep steps led down to an oasis, with a pool and entertaining areas. Lovely, but still not right.

The last one was perfection. I could tell as soon as Everett walked into the kitchen that this was the one they'd choose. It was wood, concrete, steel and glass, but it was nestled inside a grove of California redwoods. It already had an atelier—which I'd learned was a fancy word for artist workshop—and a guest house, all centered around a plunge pool. It was perfect, and I couldn't help whispering that to the guys as Mark showed us around.

Darwin looked over at me, grinning at my wide eyes and open mouth. I probably looked like a goldfish or a country bumpkin to Mark, who worked exclusively with millionaires. "We'll take it. Tell the seller we'll pay an extra 500k if he helps expedite the paperwork and gets us in here within two weeks."

Mark looked at Darwin, confused, especially when Harrison and Everett merely shrugged in agreement. "I'll, uh, see what I can do. Give me a second."

He disappeared out the front door, and I continued wandering around the house. It was somehow earthy and elegant, and I kind of liked it way more than their old place, not that I'd ever say that to them.

Harrison eyed the boundary fence that was carefully hidden by hedges. "I'll get the security guys out here to check it out and start ordering things, to make sure it's completely locked down."

Everett had gone back to the kitchen to eye the appliances with the same intense scrutiny someone might eye a horse they were thinking of buying. Only Darwin stayed beside me as I moved out into the large enclosed courtyard. It was beautiful, bracketed on all sides by the double-gabled buildings, the huge wall-to-ceiling windows making it feel more like an atrium than a backyard. The trees hung over it, old and established. I never wanted to leave.

"It's nice, isn't it?" Darwin's voice was close to my ear, and I found myself leaning into him for comfort. It felt so natural that I didn't even question it. There was something about him that was like a warm fire in an open hearth, drawing you in to warm your weary bones. "We should christen that pool, underneath the redwoods. Very back-to-nature."

Laughing, I nudged him with my shoulder. "We can't swim in a pool that doesn't belong to us."

He raised an eyebrow, his fingers on my hips tightening. "Who said anything about swimming?"

I laughed again, but when I looked over my shoulder at him, his eyes were burning. "Darwin..."

"Blake," he answered, but didn't say anything more than my name.

"The guys and me—"

He shook his head. "They wouldn't care. They like sharing."

I frowned, but still didn't move away. No matter how much my head said this was a problem, my body had no such qualms, that traitorous hussy. "They share with each other. I don't know what they would say about sharing with you too."

With a sigh, he buried his nose in the crook of my neck, a warm puff of breath sending shivers of pleasure skittering across my skin. "I've let this go on too long." He straightened, stepping away. "We'll talk about it tonight. As a group. But you should know, *Amorcito*, that I'm not one to give up easily. Unless you aren't interested and I've completely misread your cues? Do you want me too?" There was a fragility to his normally flirtatious smile.

"I do, but D, it's not that easy."

"Passion is never easy, *Muñeca*. It's a wild, burning need that has brought men and cities to their knees.

Don't worry about what's easy." He kissed the side of my head. "We'll wait until we get back to your German beau, then we'll talk. I want you to be happy, because you deserve happiness. Everett is inherently greedy for a man with two lovers, but if anyone can get him to look past himself, it's you."

Harrison called us from inside the house, and we moved toward the glass doors, Darwin's hand possessively on my spine. We followed the others to the front of the house, and I climbed into the back seat of Everett's car.

"The owner agreed to the expedited occupancy while the house settles. We can move in next week," Harrison told us as he climbed into the passenger seat of the car.

I nodded, my mind still caught up in Darwin's words, some kind of hopeful trepidation swirling around my gut as I thought about what he'd said. Would they agree? Did I want them to agree? Fuck, I didn't even know if I could handle one of them, let alone three. But I was a lot like Everett in that way—I was greedy. I wanted them all. And Hennie.

There was no way he would agree, but if I didn't ask, I'd always wonder. How many opportunities had I missed throughout my life by just not asking for what I wanted? The questions without answers rolled around and around in my head, Darwin's watchful eyes brushing over me even as he chatted along with the guys.

We stopped and picked up some groceries, Everett putting my favorite creamer in the basket, as well as my favorite chocolate. I realized he'd been paying attention, even when I hadn't thought he even liked me. Even when I'd been dating Hennie, he'd been paying attention to the things I loved. This just made me more confused.

Everyone in the grocery store watched them as they shopped together, and I wasn't sure if it was because their swatting was all over social media, or if it was because they attracted that kind of attention by just existing. They were hot as hell individually, but together, it was a lot. You couldn't help but watch them walk by. They should have one of those warning stickers: *Beware. Radiant Heat.*

Or maybe it was because Harrison held my hand as we walked through the aisles, and everyone was wondering if I lactated beer or had a golden vagina to snag him. There was a definite attractiveness disparity; I could acknowledge that. I wasn't trying to think about it too hard. I was just going to enjoy this while I could.

The whole time we were in the grocery store, my eyes kept wandering to Darwin. By the time we made it back to Hennie's house, I was a fucking mess.

As I helped the guys unload, I noticed the food truck was being loaded up. I had a feeling Hennie had

taken time off to deal with my drama, but I didn't ask—
I couldn't take the guilt of the idea he was losing
money just because my life was a mess.

Luckily, Hennie's house came with an impressive
amount of fridge space, so we didn't take up too much
room as we unloaded the groceries. I couldn't see the
man himself anywhere, but I knew he must be here, if
both the truck and his car were still in the drive. I
wandered into the small backyard to find him cutting
herbs, kneeling in the grass. The sun shone on his
head, turning his blond hair to gold. He was so fucking
handsome that it almost physically hurt.

He looked up at the sound of my approaching footsteps. "You're back." Uncurling himself from the
ground to his full height, he stretched, showing a little
peek of the flesh of his hip. "Did you find anything
good?"

I nodded, walking toward him to sit on the side of
the garden bed. "The most perfect house. They put in
an offer, which the seller accepted. We can move in
next week, so you won't have to put up with us for
much longer."

Hennie shook his head. "The power of having
money, right?"

I shrugged, pretty impressed at how smoothly they
could throw money at any obstacle. "It makes life
easier, that's for sure." I looked at the bowl of herbs at
his feet. "Do you have to take the truck out tonight?"

He sat down beside me. We looked out over the small backyard, just big enough for a grill and his garden beds. "No, I decided I deserved a couple of days off. I have a festival event tomorrow, though, so at least it gave me time to prepare." He nudged me with his shoulder. "Silver lining."

I dragged my eyes to his and was immediately captured by his gaze. There was a world of what-ifs in that look, and I wanted to chase each of them down and find out what we could be. My eyes dropped to his lips. The silence drew out longer and longer, and it was like the world was holding its breath.

The back door opened. Darwin stepped out onto the back deck, his eyebrow raised as he looked between us. His lips curled into a smug smile. "Ah, you found your German beau. If it's okay with you both, I thought we could all have a chat?"

Hennie tensed. "About what?"

"Oh, you know. Us staying here. What we can do to pay you back. Blake's safety. Normal stuff."

Yeah, that sounded suss to me too.

36

BLAKE

When we walked in, Everett handed me a bottle of hard apple cider and Hennie a beer. He shrugged at my questioning look. "Darwin has that look in his eye. I think we'll need it."

"What look?" I sat on Hennie's tiny couch beside Everett, while Hennie took the recliner.

Harrison was sitting on the carpet, his long legs stretched out in front of him, like he was posing for an interior design magazine. "The same one he had when he convinced us to join ClickHeart." Both of Hennie's eyebrows rose, and he leaned back into the plush cushioning of his chair.

Darwin stood in the middle of the living room. "Dearly beloved, we are gathered here today—"

"Cut the crap, D," Everett grumbled.

If I'd learned anything about Darwin in the last two months, it was that he never let anyone else's mood sway him, least of all Everett's grumpy nature. He just rolled his eyes at Everett. "Fine. Skip the foreplay. How you've had so many lovers is beyond me. What we are gathered here today to discuss is what I like to call: Polyamory, or 'Why Blake should get all the sausage in her *Brötchen*.' That's German for bread roll. A shout out to you there, Hennie." He clicked a button on his laptop, and appearing on Hennie's television screen was an honest-to-god slideshow.

I was... flabbergasted. There was no other word for it. It would almost be funny, if it wasn't so shocking.

The first slide was just me, but it wasn't a photo I'd ever seen. I was sitting by the pool on one of the covered loungers, my stylus in my mouth as I stared intently at the screen of my tablet. I was in my swimsuit, one leg stretched out, and honestly, I looked kinda pretty.

"Blake. She's funny, sweet, smart and gorgeous. I think we can all agree, she deserves everything she desires. Am I right?"

My mouth was hanging open. "Are... we doing a presentation on why I should have more than one boyfriend?"

Darwin grinned. "Correct. Next slide. Polyamory. What is it, and why do I think it would work for us?"

The image was a meme of a girl with a half a dozen

hot dogs in her mouth. Harrison laughed, but shut up immediately when I glared at him. Turning back to Darwin, I frowned. "Really?"

His mischievous smile kind of put a damper on my outrage. "Come on, it's funny. Plus, it fits the theme." His first point appeared on the screen. "I think the most important point is that Blake wouldn't have to choose. I know we've all seen her struggling with this over the last few weeks." Everyone looked at Everett, who stared directly at the screen with a tight jaw. "First, when things progressed with Everett, after she'd found out that Everett and Harrison were a couple, which caused conflict. Then with Heinrich and Text-gate."

Hennie's face whipped toward Everett. "You already had a partner and you *still* fucking stole her?"

"It's more complicated than that," Everett growled back, and I was kind of glad I was sitting between them. I threw an imploring look at Darwin, who cleared his throat.

"If we could get back on track. Then there's me. I was going to wait around for all you fuck-ups to eventually disqualify yourselves, but I don't like seeing my *Muñeca* distressed." He met my eyes and held them. "I knew I wanted Blake from the moment I saw her, back when she walked into a house full of strangers—she knew what she wanted and wasn't going to take no for an answer... which leads me to my next slide."

The next slide was labeled 'Blake walked into a

house full of strangers without any fear for her personal safety. Many hands make lighter work: Keeping Blake happy and safe.'

I huffed, crossing my arms over my chest. "It was fine."

Harrison bumped my foot with his. "You didn't even have pepper spray. If we'd been any other kind of men..." A visible shudder ran across his skin.

Darwin raised his hand again. "Exactly. Blake is a strong, confident woman, but she lacks a support system here in LA. As Harrison suggested, what might have happened if she'd answered any other ad keeps me up at night. But between us, we can meet all of Blake's needs, both in regards to her happiness and her safety." He looked at Hennie. "This is all very presumptuous, but for the sake of argument, how many hours a week do you work?"

Hennie scowled. "I don't know. Maybe sixty?"

"And do you think a sixty-hour work week is compatible with a healthy and fulfilling relationship?"

Hennie stood. "Who the fuck are you, my therapist? Look, I've already stopped seeing Blake. I don't really need to be in this conversation."

My chest ached at his words, but I tried to hide it. Darwin looked mildly alarmed and stepped toward him. "Stay until the end. Then if you still want nothing to do with it, we won't push." He stepped closer, murmuring something to Hennie I couldn't hear, but both of their eyes were on me.

Eventually, Hennie sat back down. He didn't look impressed, but I dragged my eyes back to Darwin. He seemed a little desperate now. "I have a whole list of reasons why Blake deserves happiness, but let's skip to how it will benefit you as well." He looked at Harrison. "It splits the mental load of each partner's needs amongst us all. If you're struggling, you can lean on any of us. You don't have to shoulder all your problems on your own.

"Also, there's the feeling of compersion—which I had to Google—which is like the opposite of jealousy, I guess. It's the joy you feel seeing someone you love receiving love and satisfaction from another person. Harrison, I know you've seen how happy Everett has been the last few weeks, with Blake. Does that make you happy or jealous?"

Harrison chewed his lower lip. "Happy, I guess."

Darwin turned to Everett. "There's always been an element of diverse needs between you two, for as long as I've known you. It's why you would go out and pick up women, but always come home to each other. You needed something that you couldn't get from one another, and I wouldn't even try to guess what that is—"

"Why stop amateur psychology hour now?" Everett retorted.

Darwin ignored him. "But you both obviously fulfill that missing need with Blake, am I right?"

Why did this feel so tense? When they both nodded, relief washed over me. This was ridiculous, but I felt like I was on an emotional rollercoaster.

He turned to Hennie. "We are primal beings, born with the innate need for human contact and touch. It doesn't matter how strong you are, how tough, smart or resourceful you are, humans *need* to be hugged and held. It's better for your health, for stress, it helps you sleep. Keeps away depression. You need, like, eight hugs a day just to be okay. Twelve to actually be healthy. Do you get twelve hugs a day, Hennie?"

The man in question raised an eyebrow. "Uh, no. But I don't see how that is a glowing recommendation for sharing a woman with three other men."

Darwin grinned, like he was playing chess and Hennie had just moved himself into checkmate. "How long was your last relationship? For science."

Hennie scowled. At first, I didn't think he'd answer. But eventually, he grumbled, "Two months."

"You're a busy man, Hennie. You have a business that you're passionate about. It's hard work and long hours. It's nice to come home to someone who will hold you in their arms and shower you with love, no?" Darwin waited until Hennie nodded. "But that small piece of your time that she can scrape up every week is never going to be enough for any woman to feel fulfilled. That's where we come in. We can all support each other *and* Blake. You know she's special. She's worth it."

Harrison shook his head. "What's your proposal, D? I know you're coming up to the climax—stop edging us already."

Darwin skipped to the end slide. "The Experiment: A week of living polyamorously."

"The fuck..." Everett breathed.

I swear, Darwin did jazz hands. I read the bullet points underneath. A one-week trial until we moved out. Open communication was a must. We had to throw everything into a relationship. If anyone felt uncomfortable after giving it a go, then they could drop out with no hard feelings.

That all seemed easier said than done.

Darwin came and squatted down in front of me. "No pressure, Doll. This is all up to you. If it's not what you want, we'll drink more beer and forget it ever happened. If you want to give it a go, we can have a week of testing the lifestyle before committing. And if you hate it in the end, then no hard feelings, truly. I'll go back to being your friend. We all will. Are you in?"

Holy shit... Holy shit, holy shit. Did I want to try this? I mean, it was a really impressive slideshow, despite the questionable memes. What was the worst that could happen? I lose Hennie forever? I'd already lost him. Everett would get jealous of Darwin and Hennie?

I didn't see that happening either. He'd already kind of hinted about Darwin, and I knew deep down, beneath that macho bravado, he felt a little bad about the fact he'd fucked with Hennie's and my relationship.

Would it ruin everything with Harrison? I didn't know if he even wanted something that committed with me. I looked at him, where he watched me from the floor.

He must have seen the question in my eyes. "I'm in."

Darwin grinned. "Me too, obviously." He looked at the man next to me. At some point during the presentation, Everett had crept closer to me, his body now right alongside mine, his arm possessively around my shoulders.

He looked between us all, a frown on his face. "I'll give it a try."

I looked at Hennie, his face pensive as he stared at the screen. His eyes slid to mine, and there were too many emotions racing across his face for me to pick one out. Finally, he sighed. "What the hell. If Blake is in—and I mean one hundred percent in and not feeling pressured by you fuckers—then I'm in too."

All eyes turned to me. I held my breath until my lungs burned, then let it out slowly. "I'm in. I don't know why you would all do this, but I'm not going to turn down the chance. And if it ends up just being a week, then so be it, best freaking week of my life. I won't have any regrets."

Harrison flopped down onto the carpet. "Well, there goes the sexual harassment clause. I better call the lawyer."

37

DARWIN

Pretty sure it was part of the human condition that when shit got emotionally vulnerable, people turned to booze. It would explain how we'd all ended up six beers deep in Hennie's living room, flipping a coin about whose bed Blake would sleep in tonight.

Every time anyone said anything remotely suggestive, her cheeks pinkened. I honestly hadn't believed they'd all go for my idea. At worst, Blake could have stormed off and seriously wrecked our relationship, and only marginally better would have been Hennie stomping away like a giant man-child who was incapable of sharing.

The fact that they'd all agreed—even if it was somewhat begrudgingly—was a small miracle, or maybe a testament to how much they all desired Blake.

It sounded completely cheesy, but I really had known she was the one as soon as she barged into the house and gave that presentation on why we should choose her. The more she'd spoken, the more enamored I'd become. By the end of the presentation, I'd been halfway in love with her already.

I'd mentioned her in the family group chat that evening, and Dani wasn't wrong—she was all I could talk about ever since. I'd also recognised that she needed time. She was fierce and a little defensive, and I'd been able to wait. I'd intended to wait, even when she picked up with Hennie. Even when she'd had sex with Everett. I knew I could wait them all out, because even with them, she'd find a way back to my arms. She found solace in me, comfort, and I'd have taken that relationship, even if it never amounted to anything more than friendship.

Harrison sat next to me as Hennie and Everett went through the first round of the flip-off. "You have some serious brass balls, D."

I shrugged, nudging him with my knee. Unlike Everett, who was rigid in his masculinity, Harrison was used to my love language. I told him he was my friend by hugging him. If he sat in front of me, I'd play with his hair. There wasn't anything inherently sexual in the contact, but Harrison, more than any of them, screamed out for the human contact. And Harrison, more than anyone, would benefit from this because he'd been shouldering so much alone for so long.

I'd only met them after Everett had been clean and sober for a while, but there was always this coiled tension in Harrison, like if he let down his guard just a little, Everett might slip. I'd tried to take some of that weight over the last couple of years, but it had always been Everett and Harrison against the world.

He just needed to know that we were all in too. It could be all of us supporting each other.

"It's what's best, not just for Blake, but for all of us. I was just tired of waiting for you all to reach the same conclusion."

Harrison laughed. "The presentation was inspiring. You'll have to send me the whole thing so I can study it." He looked over at the other guys. "Do you actually think this can work?"

That was a loaded question. I *knew* it could work, but only if we all wanted it to. But there were a lot of guys in this equation, with egos and societal expectation bullshit in our brains. So would it actually work?

I wasn't sure.

I wasn't about to tell Harrison that, though. "Absolutely. If we want it to work, it will. If we enter into it like it's some kind of competition, then it's gonna fail."

As Everett lost the coin toss and pouted, Harrison sighed. "I don't know how you think it's going to be anything but a competition, D. We all have something to prove."

I slapped him on the back, chugging back my beer to stand up and take the coin from Hennie. "Teamwork makes the dream work, Harrison. Nothing good ever came from being in competition with each other, rather than making sure our girl is so happy she never wants to leave."

I flipped the coin and wasn't even mad when I lost. In fact, when Hennie won, I took it as a sign from whoever was the Patron Saint of Horny People. Blake was blushing but smiling, and I'd been watching her responses like a hawk all night. When Hennie won, her cheeks darkened to a whole other shade of pink, and her eyes hooded. They had some seriously unresolved sexual tension.

With the question of where Blake would sleep tonight now resolved, we settled back into the slightly awkward getting-to-know-you stage. Because while Everett, Harrison and I knew basically all there was to know about each other—right down to the amount of piercings I had on my dick—Hennie was an outsider.

Harrison, bless his heart, stepped up. "So, has the food truck thing been in your family for a long time? Blake told us your grandfather had a cart, but did your folks also work in the industry?"

Hennie snorted. "Unlikely. My mom hates it. My dad's an accountant and my sister's a dental hygienist.

When my grandfather retired, my mom didn't talk to me for a month after I said I was going to take over his cart and turn it into a food truck business, rather than go to law school. She still hasn't forgiven me."

Everett raised his beer bottle. "To parental disappointment. We can all relate." He looked at me. "Except Darwin. His mother is a saint."

Harrison laughed. "Can you imagine explaining this situation to our parents? They were horrified at the idea that we liked guys. Can you imagine the coronary they'd have if they found out we ended up in a polyamorous relationship with two other guys and one girl?"

The noise that came from Everett could only be construed as rude. "Hopefully, it would give them all a coronary and they can rot in Hell, like they deserve."

Hennie winced. "So, no visits to... where are you guys from again?"

"Minnesota," Harrison answered. "And no. We haven't been back. I don't ever intend on going back either. LA is home now." There was a deep sadness in his tone. I didn't know much about what had happened when they left home. It wasn't something they liked to talk about. But Harrison had explained a little bit to my mom when we went home for Christmas one year, and she'd held him to her chest like he was a little boy and swore in Spanish a lot. So obviously, it was bad. They definitely needed therapy.

Hennie turned to me. "What about your parents?"

I gave him a tight smile. "My father is dead, and my mother... Well, she'll probably light a candle and pray for our immortal souls, but she'll be happy as long as I'm happy. As long as *we* are happy. She loves Harrison and Everett like they're two more sons she never had. Dani says she always wanted more boys and just adopted them into the family to balance out all the estrogen."

She probably wasn't wrong. Growing up in my house during synchronized Shark Week had been a lot like a multi-day hostage negotiation. No sudden moves. I'd wanted brothers more than anything, especially when everything in my house was girly and I'd been forced to carve out space to explore my masculinity.

But I wouldn't change it for the world. I'd known unconditional love like no one else. Every single one of the strong women in my life would step in front of a bullet for me, and you didn't know devotion until you'd been in the center of a group of angry Latinas.

Once, when I was eight, a high school kid had pushed me over and kicked me in the ribs. When Dani told my sisters, they'd found out who the kid was, who his sisters were, who his mama was, then gone over and beaten the shit out of that boy with their math books in the high school hallway. Olista had also poured sugar in his gas tank.

Luckily, Olista had been dating a bad guy at the time, so there was no blowback, but seriously, I wasn't sure there even would've been. No one was stepping up to defend a guy who'd kicked an eight-year-old kid, even if I had been a bit mouthy.

I was brought back to the present by Hennie asking the same question of Blake. Her face paled at the thought, and she shook her head. "They definitely wouldn't approve, or understand. But what's new? Nothing I've ever done has been right, or what they wanted, so why start now? I'd rather chase my happiness where I can than worry about their approval."

No matter how tough she was pretending to be, I could see the hurt in her eyes, and so could Hennie. He dragged her closer until she was snuggled into his side, and in that moment I knew I'd made the right decision, dragging him into this craziness. He gave her something she needed. I hoped we would all give her something she needed.

Hennie kissed the top of her head. "Their loss, *Liebling*. If they can't appreciate how brightly you shine, that's on them. You don't need to dim yourself so they can see you properly."

Yep. Definitely the right choice.

I yawned and stretched. "Well, today has been a rollercoaster. I'm going to bed." I walked over and stared down at Blake. I wanted to kiss her, but now wasn't the right moment. I didn't want our first kiss to be a spectacle to make a point. Tomorrow, I'd kiss her over and over again until I memorized the very shape of her lips.

For tonight, I leaned in and kissed her temple. "Don't overthink it, *Amorcito*. Give yourself permission to just do what feels right. What feels good." With that, I kissed her cheek and waved goodnight to everyone else.

I'd set the stage, but I couldn't make them dance. They had to work out their own individual relationships.

38

BLAKE

Eventually, everyone began drifting off to bed, though I wasn't surprised when it was just Everett, Hennie and I left in the end. If anyone was going to struggle with Darwin's idea, it was going to be these two.

"This is crazy," Hennie muttered, shaking his head, but his arms remained banded around my waist.

Everett's jaw flexed. "Yeah. But no one ever achieved something great by doing what's normal."

Hennie rolled his eyes, pulling me further into his lap. "Very philosophical."

I was almost entirely on top of him when Everett stood and walked toward us. "I'm going to bed. I'll see you in the morning." He put his hands on the couch's backrest, one on either side of our heads. "Have fun,

Sunshine." He brushed his lips over mine. "But not too much fun."

I blinked up at him, alcohol making me brave, and maybe a little saucy. "No promises."

He kissed me harder, pressing me back into Hennie's body, his tongue plunging between my lips. He was laying his claim, and I couldn't help but imagine what it would be like to be pressed between them, making love to both of them. Having both of their mouths on me.

I squirmed, making Hennie groan. "Stop wiggling."

Everett straightened, a shit-eating grin on his face. "On that note, goodnight." He walked stiffly out of the room, and I watched him go.

And then there were two.

The silence got progressively more awkward until Hennie sighed heavily. "Nothing has to happen right now, Blake. Or at all. If this isn't what you want—"

I turned on his lap and kissed him. Hard. This *was* what I wanted. Asking for what I wanted hadn't ever been something encouraged while I was growing up, and now, as an adult, it was even harder.

But I wanted this so bad, I ached.

Hennie gripped the back of my head and took control of the kiss. I shifted around more until I was straddling his hips, and when he ground up against my core, I moaned and tore my mouth away. "I want this, Hennie. I've wanted you for so damn long."

That was all the permission he needed as he stood from the couch, his arms under my ass as I wrapped my legs around him. Holy shit, he was strong. He moved me down the hall, to the other end of the house where the master bedroom was. Propping me against the wall as he fiddled with the doorknob, he finally threw the door open, then kicked it shut behind him. Throwing me down onto the bed, he stood over me, his eyes hungry.

"I've imagined what you'd look like in my bed for so damn long. Ever since you came back to the truck the day after you arrived in LA, looking all forlorn, I wanted to be your knight in shining armor. But I wanted to fuck you just as badly, spread over my bed just like this." He tugged at the hem of my dress. "Well, maybe not quite like this. You're wearing way too many clothes."

I sat up and helped him drag my dress over my head, and when I was just in my underwear, he crawled on top of me, dragging his nose up over my stomach and between my breasts with a happy sigh.

"You're so perfect. A goddess." He turned his face and pulled the soft flesh of my breast into his mouth, sucking hard. Then he pulled down the cup of my bra until my nipple was exposed to the cool night air. He took it between his teeth, scraping the hard bud softly, and I gasped.

"Hennie!"

"Say my name again, *Liebling*. I'm going to make you scream it before we're done."

Wrapping my legs around his thighs, I pulled him closer. Pleasure was building deep in my belly, and I already wanted to beg for relief. He moved up and kissed me again, his lips devouring mine, like he couldn't get enough of the taste of me. It was heady and erotic, and when his jean zipper dragged across my clit, I hissed out my pleasure.

"Naked. Now," I begged. I didn't know if I meant me or him, but I was desperate. A part of my brain wondered if this was the only time I'd get to be with Hennie this way, and I wanted it to be perfect. But I also wanted to do all the things, all the time, right now.

Luckily, Hennie seemed as desperate for me as I was for him, because he was already on his feet, shedding the last of his clothes and tugging at my underwear. I lifted my ass so he could work them down my legs, while simultaneously reaching behind me to unclip my bra, flinging it over his shoulder. He stared down at me, and I was suddenly incredibly aware of how exposed I was right now. His hand slid up my calf to my knee as he kneeled on the bed. Pushing my legs apart, he looked at me hungrily.

"Such a pretty little pussy you have there, *Liebling*. Just need a quick taste."

I breathed heavily as he slid beneath my knees, curling me in half, and flicked his tongue along my slit before settling over my clit. He gave it a few tentative licks, as if he was gauging what I liked, then wrapped his lips around me and sucked.

"Hennie!" The noise I made sounded like an opossum stuck in a trash can, which was probably not a sexy noise, but totally appropriate when someone sucked out your soul through the happy button.

He relented on my clit, sliding one finger inside me, and I clenched around him. "So wet for me, *Liebling*. So warm. I want to climb between your thighs and never leave."

"Please, please, *please*." I wasn't above begging right now.

He slipped another finger inside me, and then his lips were back on my clit. He stroked and sucked, and I arched off the bed as if I were being levitated like in that classic nineties movie. Light as a feather, stiff as a board. They should have tried cunnilingus instead of chanting.

He found that perfect rhythm, and soon enough, I was coming apart beneath his clever, clever hands, his coaxing words bouncing around the room. Wiping his face on my thigh, he crawled back up my body and kissed me. Like a magic trick where you'd pull a rabbit out of a hat, he'd somehow pulled a condom out of nowhere and put it on, all while making me come so hard that I saw more stars than the Hubble telescope.

I bit my lip as my eyes roamed over his body. "I find your ability to multitask very attractive."

"Mmm, really? Want to see me fuck you from behind and play with your clit in perfect synchronization?"

"More than I want my next breath," I laughed, and was suddenly flipped onto my stomach, my ass propped in the air as he stuffed pillows under my hips. Then he was sliding into me. We both groaned, the sound like a release of so much tension that had been building inside of us. Hennie's hand ran up and down my spine as he settled inside me, just the perfect length and width for fucking. Hitting all the good spots, but unlike Darwin, I wouldn't have to pray to the Saint of Vaginal Elasticity to look down on me kindly.

"Brace yourself on the headboard baby. I'm going to need both my hands for this," Hennie commanded, though his voice sounded strained. Then, like he'd promised, he grabbed my hip with one hand and snaked the other one around to find my clit with unerring accuracy. Hell, it might've taken longer for me to find my clit than him.

Applying the smallest amount of pressure, he ground me down into his hand. *Holy shit.* I did as I was told and held on tight as he pounded into me, hitting the good spots over and over again until I was coming way too quickly. But I wasn't done. I wanted more.

I should have known Hennie wasn't finished with me. He fucked me through my climax, making my moans turn into screams, and I chanted his name like a prayer as he shifted my hips, finding all new spots to grind into.

His movements became more erratic, grinding harder and deeper, and I knew he was going to come. His hand stilled as he buried himself inside of me over and over, before pinching my clit as he came. If I'd been a bull, he would have won the championship for riding me for the orgasmically wild eight seconds as pleasure washed over me in wave after wave. He collapsed on top of me, his warmth pressed tightly against my back, though he was definitely holding himself up a little.

After a moment, he pulled out of me, rolling to the side and gathering me back against his body. "That was better than I could have imagined," he whispered into my ear. All I could do was nod. Sex endorphins had rendered me mute.

I lay there until my brain came back online, and when Hennie got up to dispose of the condom, I shuffled over to his ensuite to pee. Gotta get those jello legs to work. UTIs were serious business.

I swapped with Hennie and grabbed one of his t-shirts off the floor, pulling it over my head and crawling into bed. It strained across my hips and boobs, but it was modest enough that if the house caught on fire, I wouldn't be showing my hooha to any sexy firemen that arrived on the scene.

Hennie slipped on some boxers and crawled in beside me, wrapping me back up in his arms. I knew we should talk about this crazy arrangement, or where we went from here, or the fact that me and the guys would be moving out soon, but I didn't want to ruin the moment. Instead, I snuggled back into his body, resting my arm on his where it gripped around my waist. It felt nice, to just lie in bed with a man who wanted me, without expectations or angst. That weird after-sex awkwardness. This was a temporary thing until it wasn't, and there was some freedom in that.

He kissed the back of my neck, despite it being a little sticky from sweat, and I sighed happily. Nope, I was going to take this moment right here and cherish it. Whatever happened next, happened. But nothing would ever alter this night.

39

BLAKE

When I woke up the next morning, I fully expected it to be awkward. You know what's more weird than the walk of shame? The cowboy swagger of someone who got twisted into a pretzel and then soundly fucked for six hours the night before.

But Hennie had brought me coffee at daylight, before heading outside to set up the truck for a festival he was attending. I'd sipped my coffee, napped a little more, and finally dragged myself out to face the music.

Harrison was sitting at the kitchen table, sipping coffee and scrolling through his phone. When he heard me enter, he looked up and smiled. "Good morning. How did you sleep?"

My cheeks flushed, and I could tell from the smirk

on his face and the shine in his blue eyes that he was teasing me. "It was very rejuvenating, thank you."

He tilted his face toward me as I walked past, and it took me two steps to realize he wanted me to kiss him good morning. I hadn't thought about the casual intimacy that we'd show each other during the day, my perverted brain going straight to the night-time shenanigans. Feeling like this was some kind of test, I leaned over and kissed his upturned lips softly. A brief, intimate gesture that still made my heart race in my chest.

When I pulled away, there was a small smile on his face. I walked over to get another coffee, because this seemed like a double-caffeination kind of day already. "Where is everyone?"

"Hennie's in the food truck, finishing up the final loading of stock, I think. Everett is out helping him, which might mean his body ends up in the next lot of bratwurst... I mean, maybe he's on his best behavior out there. The food truck industry is one he's always been interested in, so he's probably grilling Heinrich for answers. Darwin's still asleep because it's not yet eleven, which is when the birds fly in the window and wake him up like Sleeping Beauty."

Harrison's phone rang, and he frowned as he swiped to answer. "Harrison speaking." There was a long pause. "Oh. Sure, I mean, yeah. We'll come down and pick up our gear today. We appreciate it." He stood, still listening intently on the other end of the phone. "I don't know his real name, Agent. We all try to keep our legal names secret, so this kind of thing doesn't happen. He's just gone by Prince Eric for as long as I've known him."

Holy shit. It was Prince Eric who swatted the guys?

"I mean, we've always been competitors, and he's a bit of a dick, but I didn't think he'd go this far. Healthy competition is a long way from a federal offense, you know? Sure. Absolutely. Thanks again, Agent Fletcher. We'll be there today to collect our possessions." He hung up and looked at me with wide eyes. "They're looking into Prince Eric—"

"Such a shitty name."

"Agreed. But yeah, they reckon that he made some kind of threats on his Tweeter against us a while ago and he's their number one suspect in the swatting."

I shook my head, because that was literally insane. The guy was a mega-creep with a huge ego, but honestly, he still made insane amounts of money. I knew the rough market share-follower algorithm and the royalties that came from that, and he definitely didn't need to swat the guys to win a shitty car. He could buy one of those every month with the money he made.

However, he was clearly a petty fuck, and his ego was huge. Plus, the guys had definitely escalated with him during the awards, and what did I know about their history? There was obviously some serious anger between them, if the confrontation that night was anything to go by.

Harrison came over and wrapped his arms around my body, pulling me back against his chest until I could melt into him. Darwin was onto something with the eight hugs a day thing. I already felt lighter, and I was only two hugs into my day.

"They're releasing our equipment and paperwork, and we're allowed to go pick it up from the station. Do you want to come with me today and collect it?"

I took a long sip of my coffee. "Sure. What are we going to do with it, though, now we've replaced all the tech?" Maybe we should have rented the new stuff, but no one wants their nudes on a rented device, right?

"You can keep yours, if you like. I'm sure you're enjoying the better power in the upgrades?" I flushed, but nodded. I'd been saving for a system half as good as the one they got me. I wasn't sure I could go back if I tried. "As for the rest, we can probably wipe them and donate them to one of the local schools. They're basically brand new."

Hennie and Everett came back inside, both of them with serious expressions. *Shit.* Had they had an argument?

But when Everett saw me, his face lit up. "Good morning, Sunshine." He strode over and kissed me, not pulling me from Harrison's arms. "I'm going out to give Heinrich a hand today, so I won't be back until later. I have to get changed, though. He's insisting I wear pants." He winked and gave Harrison a swift kiss over my shoulder before disappearing from the room.

I looked up at Harrison, my eyes wide. "Has he been body-snatched?"

Harrison looked as shocked as I did. "Not that I'm aware of. I think maybe he was going through kitchen withdrawals and is taking what he can get."

Hennie snorted. "He kept making backhanded comments about how I couldn't possibly cope on my own with a festival full of people, until I finally said I didn't have anyone else to help. He jumped at the chance to offer up his services, even if he did sigh a lot as he said it." He walked toward me, pulling me gently from Harrison's arms and into his. "Good morning, *Liebling*. How are you?"

He kissed me as well, and I was beginning to learn the different flavors of their kisses. The way their lips felt, the way they kissed—it was all as unique as the men themselves.

"Even better now," I murmured against his lips. "How long until you have to go and set up?"

He looked at his watch. "About an hour, but it's at least forty minutes to the ground. Don't tell Everett, but I'm glad for the help. It's my biggest event to date, and I'm not sure I could have handled it as a one-man show," he whispered in my ear. "I'll be home late tonight. Don't wait up for us, okay?"

Harrison felt tense behind me. "It's a music festival, right?" At Hennie's nod, he sighed. "He'd hate for me to say this, like I have no faith in him, but can you just keep an eye on Everett? He's in recovery, but things have been a little crazy the past couple of days and I wouldn't want him to relapse."

Hennie frowned, but nodded again. "I'll watch him. Honestly, I hope we're so busy that we sell out early and come home. No time for mischief."

Everett reappeared with a small bag, dressed in a clean black t-shirt and jeans. He looked like a bad boy, tall and handsome as hell. I kissed them both once more and waved them off.

When they'd disappeared from view, I followed Harrison back into the house. "Are you really worried?"

Harrison shrugged. "Not really. But Hennie is a savior, and Everett sometimes needs saving. If they work out they can be symbiotic, then Darwin's little experiment can only go smoother." He bundled me back into his arms and held me close. "And I have a vested interest in everything going as smoothly as possible." Brushing kisses across both my cheeks, he spun me and sent me back further into the house. "Now go get dressed, because we have a date with some government-released evidence."

. . .

DARWIN STILL HADN'T WOKEN by the time we went to collect our stuff, so we left him a note on the table. We took the car across town to the police station where we'd been interviewed, and walking back in here kind of made my skin crawl. Harrison wrapped an arm around my shoulders as we stepped up to the customer service desk.

The uniformed officer behind the counter gave us a tight smile as he finished typing his email, and about two minutes later, gave us his attention. "How can I help you?"

"We were called to say some of our property has been released from evidence and can be collected."

The cop's eyes narrowed, like we'd gone from being victims to potential criminals. "Case number?"

Harrison read out the case number, while I looked around the room. It wasn't as cold here today, and a lot quieter, like the darkness of night brought out everyone's worst fears.

The cop tapped away on his computer, then pointed to the waiting area. "Take a seat over there, and I'll get someone to bring it up."

Harrison sat down beside me, grabbing my hand and linking them together on my thigh. "You okay? I didn't even think that this might be traumatic for you. Sorry." He lifted my knuckles to his lips to kiss them.

He'd fallen into affection so easily; now I wondered just how long he'd been holding himself back.

An uneven smile pulled at my face. "It's okay. It's easier to see this place during the day. Not as scary."

The evidence department didn't seem to be in a hurry, so we sat together in companionable silence, playing games on Harrison's phone and making up stories about the people we saw. A grizzled old cop walked by, his belly bulging slightly over his gun belt, but he didn't seem hard. He just seemed tired. "That guy is close to retirement age. His wife Margie wants to start doing cruises as soon as he retires, and he just wants to build a rollercoaster in the backyard for his grandkids."

Harrison screwed up his nose. "I don't know about that. He's been around awhile. I bet they've given him a female rookie partner who annoys the hell out of him, but he protects her like she was his kid. He's seen how the force can burn out its cops, especially the female ones, and he feels oddly protective of her, even when he's giving her a hard time."

Another set of cops walked through the front door, with two struggling teenagers. "We didn't do anything!"

The cop rolled her eyes. "Jaime-Lee, we literally found two bottles of vodka in your cleavage. There's a time to maintain your innocence, but this isn't it." I snorted a laugh, but covered it quickly before I could get on the bad side of some wannabe gangsters.

Finally, a pen-pusher from Evidence arrived with a hand cart of our crap. There were boxes of stuff, as well as all the computer gear. "You guys really cleaned us out," Harrison grumbled.

The tech shrugged. "Gotta be serious about these things." A smile twitched at his lips. "Though, I think some of our techs enjoyed perusing the hard drives more than others." He laughed at his own joke, like our privacy hadn't been violently violated, all the while being oblivious to Harrison's scowl. We grabbed the hand cart off him and took it out to the parking lot, where we loaded the whole lot into the back of Everett's car.

I loaded in boxes of paperwork with a huff. "What an asshole."

Harrison shook his head. "I'm used to it now. You pull down one hard boundary, and people feel entitled to throw away all social niceties." The trunk and back seat ended up jam-packed. "I'm going to take this hand cart back, and then I say we get the hell out of here and get some ice cream. It's already been a day."

I never said no to ice cream.

40

EVERETT

I'd missed the challenge of being a short-order cook. I had to admire the way Bratwurst Boy had his truck set out; it was orderly and professional. I also had to respect his drive to grow his business, and the professionalism with which he undertook the process. The truck was cleaner than a lot of commercial kitchens I'd cooked in.

There was a steady line seven people deep, and I was busy cooking sausages. I'd tasted one earlier, and it'd almost pained me how good they were. They were that old-world kind of flavorful, not too fussy or filled with complex flavor combinations. They were simple. Hearty. It was a fucking sausage on a stick and pretzels dipped in butter. Honestly, it would be hard to go wrong with food like this.

But still, Wiener Wagon stretched himself. He had

"Heinrich's special sauce," which made me laugh but was damn tasty. Deep-fried dough bites instead of fries. There were several other small things that made him stand out and told me he wasn't just going to coast on the coattails of his grandfather's recipes. I respected that.

"Order seventy-two," I yelled over the sound of some truly heinous electropop, a girl warbling hook lines over and over until I wanted to gouge out my eardrums. I pulled up two wienerschnitzel combos and put them on the counter. "Seventy-three!"

I didn't think we'd ever get to the end of the line, but this rush, this pressure, made my heart race. I definitely didn't miss the long hours of being a chef, but I did miss the complex nature of undertaking so many tasks at once.

An hour later, the headlining act came on, and everyone gravitated to the main stage, giving Hennie and I a break. He slapped me on the shoulder, a burn on his hand from spitting oil. "I really appreciate you coming today. You're right. I wouldn't have been able to handle this."

I lifted my chin. I didn't need his thanks. "Don't mention it. Once word about the garlic butter parmesan pretzels got around, the munchies crowd descended like vultures. Can't predict that." I wiped down the surfaces and restocked the containers, in case we got another wave of dinner customers.

"It's the nature of the business, I guess. Kind of glad you guys had that brush with the cops, so I could give myself the day off and prepare for this properly. I would have run out by lunchtime if I hadn't had the opportunity to make three more batches of pretzel dough." He threw more of the pre-boiled bread goods into the oven, before they'd go into the warmer to wait for orders.

I smirked at him. "You've got a good set-up for a one-man show. You would have survived."

Kneeling down, he restocked the drinks fridges below the counter. "Well, if you ever want to keep your dick in your pants for a week, you're always welcome to come and help me out at one of these events. We work well together."

He wasn't wrong, and no one was more surprised than me. I begrudgingly respected the fucker; I'd thought it would've taken us longer to get to that point. But we moved around each other in the truck like we'd been cooking together for years, and he didn't try to dominate me to show me who was the boss. He'd just given me a quick rundown of the ropes, then trusted me to get shit done.

"I'll keep that in mind. No offense, though, getting my dick out is way more lucrative."

A girl loitering in front of the trucks turned to stare at us. "*Oh my god.* Jenny, I told you it was him! Are you MountMe Everett?"

Hennie trying to hold back his laughter made him sound like he was choking on a dick. If he didn't shut up, I might make it happen. I scowled down at the girl. "Not today, I'm not."

She squealed so loud, I winced. "Holy shit, it *is* you. Can you spit on my pretzel?"

"No!" Hennie and I yelled at the same time.

The girl didn't even have the good grace to be ashamed. "Fine, but can I get a picture? My friends and I all subscribe to your channel. It really sucks about that person doxxing you. What a shitty thing to do."

I sighed heavily, but looked at Hennie. He waved a hand. "Go ahead. Gotta give the fans what they want, as long as it doesn't involve bodily fluids in my food."

I flipped him the bird. "Fine. Wait there." Last thing I needed was a bunch of drunken girls fucking around at the back of the food vans. Untying my apron, I climbed down the stairs at the back of the truck.

The girls were literally tee-heeing as I stopped in front of them. In full rave wear, they were barely covered by more than six inches of clothing, and honestly, it made me feel gross. The first girl handed off her phone to her friend—who I assumed must be Jenny—and I stood by dutifully, keeping my hands as far from her body as possible.

The girl posed for a bunch of photos, and I went to step away. "One more," she squealed and turned to me, grabbing my cheeks and kissing me hard. My lips parted in shock, and when she stuck her tongue in my mouth, I felt a hard, round object left behind.

Wrenching myself out of her grasp, I stumbled away. The pill sat on my tongue for the space of a heartbeat, and in that time, a hundred different excuses I could tell Harrison as to why I swallowed it crossed my brain.

I spat out the pill onto the grass at her feet. "What the actual *fuck* is wrong with you?!" I roared, and suddenly, Hennie was beside me. He must have jumped across the food truck counter.

The girl just giggled. She was truly off her fucking face. "Just sharing the love."

I spat at her feet again, trying to get the taste of her out of my mouth.

"Get the hell out of here, before we call the cops with sniffer dogs over and you get thrown out—or better yet, put in jail." Hennie muttered something else under his breath in German, and I didn't need to be bilingual to know it wasn't complimentary.

Jenny proved she was the smart one, dragging the girl away as fast as she could until they disappeared completely into the crowd.

"You okay?" Hennie asked quietly, herding me back toward the truck like he expected more partially dressed women to jump out and stick their tongue— and other stuff—down my throat.

I waved him off. "I'm fine. I should have expected it.

Though the pill was something new." I inhaled a shuddering breath. "I was an addict. Shit still gets to me sometimes." I didn't want to look up at Hennie, but I wasn't a coward. I was kind of shocked to see that he didn't look at all surprised.

"I know. Harrison told me to watch out for you."

I gave a mirthless laugh. "Well, up until five minutes ago, I might have been mad at him for spreading around my shit without my permission. I mean, either he trusts me or he doesn't. It wasn't like pills were going to accidentally fall into my mouth, right?"

Hennie laughed, then covered his mouth. "Shit. Sorry. Not funny."

I grinned. "It's a little funny now." The smile slid off my face. "And for a split second, I was tempted."

Hennie sat down beside me on the step. "Temptation is everywhere, man. It's the courage to stand up and say no that makes you well again." He nudged my shoulder with his. "Besides, we're co-boyfriends now. Looking out for you is apparently in the job description."

I groaned. "Stop with the sappy shit or I'm going to find that pill before the ants carry it off and build a nest like the catacombs of Paris." The crowd roared at whatever the artist on the stage said, and I slumped back against the door. "Thanks for racing to the rescue, though. I probably could have handled a couple of hundred-pound girls, but it's nice to know you've got my back."

He shook his head, resting his elbows on his knees. "I thought your boy was crazy yesterday. The four of us sharing one woman? It's a fairytale they tell bored housewives. But last night, with Blake... It was something else. *She's* something else. She fucks with complete abandon, like her body is yours to bend and stretch in any position until you both feel good. That's a fucking heady motivator to be nice to your grumpy ass." He huffed a laugh. "I even appreciated you here today. And knowing that she isn't going to be sitting around, wondering if she's made a mistake with me, because I'm out here at a rave all day instead of with her kinda makes me feel less like shit too. Maybe Darwin was right. Maybe I was lonely."

I grunted my agreement. "The fucker is annoyingly empathetic like that. It's why we love him, but kind of also why I want to strangle him from time to time. There's something to be said for being blissfully unaware of your emotional baggage." I stood and stretched, the adrenaline of the moment slowly leaving me. "The person I worry about the most is Blake. Balancing the four of us would be exhausting. Can one woman really have the emotional capacity to want us all—and to need us all—equally? I think, eventually, there might be a hierarchy, and I'm such a grumpy fucker that I'm always going to be at the bottom of it."

Hennie shook his head, watching people break off from the crowd and head back toward us. "I think she'll surprise you. She couldn't even pick a favorite type of hot dog, let alone a favorite guy. I think she'll handle us all just fine, as long as we help her and don't make her feel bad for shit."

I didn't know if that last part was for me or for himself, but I nodded either way. Maybe we could make this work, and if it was what Blake wanted, I would try my fucking hardest to give it to her.

As I slipped my apron back on, I wondered if Hennie and I hadn't just overcome one of the biggest hurdles, all because of some strung-out bitch in three pieces of dental floss forcing herself on me. Fate had a funny sense of humor, that was for sure.

41

BLAKE

I woke up groggily the next morning, right across from the adorable sleeping face of Darwin. I didn't even remember going to bed. The last thing I remembered was watching a movie on the couch between Harrison and Darwin as we waited for the others to return home from the festival.

I kind of felt bad that it had been my first night with Darwin, and we'd done nothing but sleep. But I wasn't a vending machine. You couldn't wait your turn, stick in your dick, and out popped an orgasm and a stick of gum, you know?

"You're thinking very loudly over there." Darwin's voice was slurred as he reached over to tuck me tighter against his body. "Go back to sleep."

Unable to resist, I kissed the tip of his nose. "This

might change your mind about this whole poly thing, but guess what? I'm an early riser."

He snuggled further under the blankets and pushed his face between my boobs. "That's a tragedy," he murmured, his voice muffled. "But this is nice." I laughed as he buried his face further into my cleavage. I had good-sized tatas, and he seemed to be taking advantage of every square inch of real estate.

"You're going to suffocate in there."

His happy sigh tickled across my skin. "I can only hope. Put it on my headstone and don't forget to tell my mom I loved her."

I laughed again, tugging at his hair gently. "Don't say that." But he was already snoring softly. I lay still, smoothing my fingers through his dark, wavy hair until I was sure he was in a deep sleep. I enjoyed the feeling for a little longer, until my bladder decided it had more than enough of waiting for me to get out of bed. Shifting slowly until I could stuff a pillow under his face, I managed to slip away from Darwin.

When I was fully off the bed, I took a moment to appreciate the sexy, rumpled way he slept, arms and legs flung out, lips slightly parted. I had no idea how someone could be attractive all the time, but Darwin managed it. I was lucky he'd looked my way, and I'd enjoy being the focus of his desire for as long as I could.

Grabbing my phone, I realized that despite

Darwin's protests, it wasn't early at all. It was nearly ten. Throwing my robe on, I crept out of the room, into the bathroom, looking at myself closely as I brushed my teeth and hair. I felt like I'd changed from the wide-eyed sucker who'd moved out here—though I guess opinions on if it was for better or worse would depend on who you spoke to.

The other guys were all in the kitchen around the table, looking at their phones, though Hennie was also reading the physical newspaper like an old man. They were still slightly disheveled from sleep, and Everett and Harrison were close enough that their knees were touching.

I took a mental snapshot of the moment, because on this peaceful Sunday morning, I was getting a taste of what life could be like. Dragging myself from the arms of one lover, into the warmth of the rest. I doubted I'd been good enough in any of my past lives to get this lucky, but I was going to cherish it while I could.

Everett spotted me first. "Good morning, Sunshine." He stood, pushing my cup under his fancy coffee machine and playing with the settings. It had definitely made the move from the old house to Hennie's with us. No one wanted a badly caffeinated Everett in the mornings.

That task done, he moved toward me like a missile, wrapping me up in his arms and kissing me like he'd missed me. "Mmm, I've wanted to do that since we pulled out of the driveway yesterday."

I dragged my nails through his soft beard. "How was the festival?" I wanted to ask if he and Hennie had gotten along okay, but they were both in the same room and no one seemed to be sporting a black eye, so I was taking that as a positive.

Guilt flashed across his face before he had time to lock it down. "Everett?"

He looked a little like a deer in the headlights, so I looked past him at Hennie. He chewed his lip, but set down his coffee. "The day was good. We made a lot of profit and had just the right amount of product to sell without waste."

"But?" I could feel the hesitance between them.

"But there was a bit of an incident. Nothing major," Hennie quickly added.

I tried to calm the churning in my gut. "What kind of incident?"

Everett looked down at me, his eyes swirling with worry. "I was recognized by one of the festival-goers. She wanted a picture, and I said sure. Then she kissed me and pushed drugs into my mouth."

My whole body seized, like I'd been electrocuted. I could almost picture some pretty little manic pixie rave girl kissing him. Jealousy was like hot acid in my veins, but I tried to keep my face calm. "And what happened next?" I looked between him and Hennie. Hennie didn't have any loyalty to Everett—he'd tell me if he was lying, right?

Everett's lip curled, in what could have been a smile or disgust, I wasn't sure. "I pushed her away and spat out the pill, obviously, and Hennie jumped the counter of the Wiener Wagon like a superhero, telling her to fuck off while I had a small, tiny, minor breakdown about the whole thing."

I let out a relieved breath—not because he'd had been obviously assaulted and nearly drugged, but because he hadn't, I don't know, picked up the invitation. I shot a look at Harrison, like I could gauge what I was supposed to feel from his response. But he was just looking between us, his own face creased with concern, though he didn't seem angry or jealous.

Everett was staring down at me, like he was trying to read every thought that passed through my brain. "Say something?"

"What would you like me to say? I'm not going to be mad at you because some bitch assaulted you, Everett. I'm not a monster." I stroked my thumb over his cheekbone. "Are you okay?"

He waved a hand, clearing his throat. "I'm fine. More worried about disappointing you and Harrison in one fell swoop, but I'm fine. Not the first shitty person to think they can take what they want just because I'm on ClickHeart."

My coffee was done, and he leaned back to grab it

from the machine and hand it to me. "Thank you." I held the mug between my hands. "And thank you for telling me."

He kissed my forehead. "Darwin's presentation said open communication was important for this to work, and I didn't want to start our trial run with secrets and lies." He sat back down in his chair, dragging me with him.

Harrison's phone rang, which wasn't a rare thing— I'd realized pretty quickly that Harrison dealt with all the business side of things. He invested his and Everett's money, employed the financial planners and accountants and lawyers. He liaised with the PR teams for certain events, got them tickets to networking conferences, did a little bit of everything. He was an impressively organized man, which was so different to the loose artist who made phallic vases.

He answered the phone, and I dragged my attention away from his conversation. I didn't want to eavesdrop. "Did you and Hennie bond while you were listening to synth music?" I whispered in Everett's ear, and he laughed.

"He's all right, I guess." His own lips moved along the sensitive line of my neck. "And hot. I can see why he made you so horny. That man in an apron is a wet dream. Think I could convince him to guest star on my channel? Maybe we could kiss. I don't think he'd be as adverse to it as you'd think."

My whole body clenched with pleasure, my eyes darting to Hennie, though he was back to reading the newspaper and didn't see my flushed cheeks. "The kissing or the naked cooking?" I whispered back.

Everett just winked, but I was distracted from replying as Harrison rose to his feet. "What, right now? Are you sending someone out?"

Everyone around the room tensed at his words. Or maybe it was the way he said them.

"Tell him we'll be there in twenty minutes." Harrison hung up the phone. "That was the security company. Someone just breached the house, and when they sent people out to check, he said he was Blake's fiancé."

What the actual fuck?

42

BLAKE

We dragged Darwin out of bed, and I grabbed my clothes, quickly changing in the bathroom. Everett had wanted to leave me here, just in case it was some whackjob, because who else could it be, right?

But when Harrison had pulled up the front door feed, it had been worse than a whackjob. It'd been Paul, my ex-boyfriend. The guys had still wanted me to stay behind, but honestly, it would be better if I went by myself. That argument had been shut down quickly. So, as a compromise, we were all going, including Darwin, who got a very rushed explanation about why we were all rolling out to the old house to see one man.

Hell, even Hennie was coming. When I'd thrown up my hands in exasperation, he'd just grinned, pulling me into his arms. "I'm just curious about the man who was dumb enough to let you go, *Liebling*. I kind of want to rub it a little in his face too."

And that's what I was worried about. Paul had always had his nose way too far up the butts of my parents, and I was worried. Worried how he knew where I lived. Worried that he'd report back what he saw.

Just... worried.

Maybe the guys were right. Maybe I should just stay home, and they could pretend they didn't know me. I had a feeling it was probably too late for that, though. You didn't just randomly turn up to a stranger's house and ask for a person, unless you were sure they'd be there.

Curiosity killed the cat, and Hennie wasn't the only one who was curious.

It was a tight squeeze in one car, but we all piled into Everett's convertible. Darwin and Hennie were in the back on either side of me, and instead of feeling anxious, trying to keep from touching them so I didn't encroach on their space, I relaxed into the comforting press of their bodies.

This was an unexpected benefit.

Everett pulled into traffic, while Harrison looked at me over his shoulder. "So, tell us about your ex? Is he as idiotic as he sounds?"

I screwed up my nose, thinking about the man I'd been with for so damn long. I'd committed years of my life to Paul, and at the time, I'd thought what we had was brilliant. We'd grown together, and what we had was a comfort more than a passionate affair. But in the end, when I needed him to support me and my dreams, he'd folded like a wet paper bag.

And if I was being brutally honest with myself, we'd never had that sexual connection we should have had. Our sex life had definitely been... mundane. I think I'd only gotten off maybe a third of the time, and that was usually when I'd put in the real effort to get myself there.

"He's the manager of a car yard back home. He was... not exactly popular, but well liked in high school. Firmly in the middle. Invited to parties, but he didn't make the party. And I was the nerd." I huffed out a laugh. "When he asked me out, everyone had been surprised, because they definitely thought he was too good for me. I was a fat kid. Nerdy, like I said. Artistic, too. Not even the middle-of-the-road popularity he had. I thought Paul had seen past that, but now, I don't think he did. He just wanted to be the attractive one in our relationship. Have that upper hand, maybe. I know everyone thought I was crazy when I left him, like I was throwing away the best I'd ever get."

That made Darwin growl, his hand wrapping around my thigh. "That's not true at all. There is no one to match you, *Amorcito*. We can only try."

I gave him a smile, resting my head on his shoulder. He took the opportunity to kiss me softly, and I was never going to say no to that. "LA is an entire world away from Dahlonega. And I think you guys are an entirely different species from the men there."

Hennie snorted. "Obviously." He stroked my other thigh. "Do your parents like him?"

I sighed. "Yes. Loved him like a son. Sometimes, I wondered if they loved him more than me, honestly. He was doing everything that they expected of me. A business-related community college degree, working his way up from the bottom of a local car dealership. He bought his first house when we were nineteen, though his parents co-signed. He was a good town boy, and I was this wild disappointment. Too creative. Not happy with the seemingly perfect life I had."

Hennie's hands stroked up and down my thigh. "Their loss, babe. But what do you think he wants?"

I shrugged. It had been a while since we broke up now, months even. He hadn't called, or texted—hell, he'd even removed me from social media. So what the hell he was doing in LA at the front door of my house?

I sat in silence as I thought of a million different reasons why he'd be here. At first, I'd panicked that perhaps there was something wrong with my parents, but why they would've sent him didn't make any sense.

"He was never my fiancé, though. Never. Even when other kids in our class were getting engaged and having stupid teen weddings, Paul never even hinted he wanted to get married. Thank fuck. If he'd asked me back when we'd first left high school, I might have caved to pressure from my parents and friends, and said yes."

The very idea made me want to shudder.

Everett looked at me in the rearview mirror. "It's okay, Sunshine. We'll figure it out."

The rest of the trip was silent, and soon enough, we were pulling up in front of the old house. I hadn't been back since Hennie had driven me home from the police station. I still hated that someone had stolen our sense of security like that, and I really didn't want to be back here.

Especially not with Paul sitting on the front porch.

I'd often wondered what I'd feel when I saw anyone from home. I hadn't been gone long, but I'd definitely changed. That disappointment straightaway had altered me; it had killed something naive and trusting inside me. Obviously, not quite enough, because somehow I'd still gotten this job, but I realized that I could be as vigilant as I wanted—life would still screw me over.

So when I looked at Paul, it was with a slightly more cynical eye. The guys might have also altered my brain chemistry a little, because he looked way more vanilla than I remembered. Like he'd been dulled by my time in the bright lights of the City of Angels.

We all sat there and watched him for a few

seconds. "He looks like unseasoned chicken," Darwin muttered, and I slapped a hand over my mouth to hold in the snort threatening to bubble out.

"He's not a bad man. He's just not the right one." I still defended him.

"Apparently, it's the *one* in that sentence that was the problem, *Muñeca*."

Rolling my eyes at Darwin, I nudged Hennie with my knee. "Come on. We better see what he wants."

Hennie unfolded from the car, and I saw Paul size him up. The other guys got out too, and his eyes flicked between them all like a prey animal. Finally, I climbed out, Hennie holding the door open for me. Paul didn't seem overly surprised to see the guys. What the hell was going on?

"What are you doing here, Paul?"

He pasted his customer service smile on his face, the one he used when he was trying to sell a shitbox car to a little old lady. So fake. "Blake. I've been worried about you."

I frowned at him, coming to a stop a few feet away on the gravel drive. I stood stiffly as he kissed my cheek in greeting. "Why would you be worried about me? Even if there was anything wrong—which there isn't— you're my *ex*. I'm not your problem anymore, and definitely not your fiancé, or whatever crap you told the security company."

As if I'd summoned them, a guy in a black uniform

appeared, and Harrison peeled off to go and talk to him. Good to know the security company hadn't just accepted Paul at his word.

"Cole saw your picture on a porn site. I wanted to come down and check you were okay before your parents found out."

I reared back like he'd struck me. "On a porn site? Are you kidding me? Cole is one hit on the pipe away from being medically classified as a zucchini, and you just accepted that he saw me in a porno?"

Paul narrowed his eyes on me. "Of course I didn't. I asked to see the site, obviously. And there you were, dressed like a whore next to that guy." He nodded his head toward Darwin, whose lip was peeled back, like he was going to physically tear into Paul with his teeth.

But it was Everett who marched forward, though he only got a few steps before Hennie grabbed his arm. Paul was a pussy. He wouldn't fight back, but he'd definitely get him charged with assault.

I looked over at Everett, and gave him a look that I hoped said *be cool*. "Firstly, Paul, that dress was a replica of a haute couture gown from the 1950s, so I'm pretty sure I didn't look anything like a whore. There's more coverage on that dress than your mama's muumuu on washing day." I stepped closer. "Secondly, that was an entertainment industry gala that I was attending with my friend. So watch your fucking mouth. Lastly, it's none of your fucking business. Go home, Paul. You aren't welcome here."

Paul gave me a feral look. "What will your parents say when I tell them?"

I shrugged, stepping away from him like he was distasteful, which he very much was right now. "I don't actually care, Paul. I don't care what they think. And I don't care what *you* think. So, I'll tell you one more time, go home. I don't need you or want you here."

Something mean flashed in his eyes, and I knew by the end of the day, my parents would have seen that magazine picture of me and Darwin, and would have heard all about how their little girl had turned to drugs and debauchery and whatever else Paul could make up to make him look like a savior and me to look like a fallen Jezebel.

"You've changed, Blake. I bet you're fucking them all, aren't you? Are you spreading your legs for all four of these guys? Is that why they're standing around you, slavering like dogs? It has to be because you're easy, because you're an ugly, fat whale with no education and no job."

"You fucking son of a bitch!" Everett growled, lurching toward him, but in a flash, Harrison was there, holding him back. Barely.

He sneered at Paul. "Get the hell off of my property before I have you thrown off and then charged with trespass."

The big security guy stepped between us and herded Paul toward the road. I lifted my chin, and Darwin stepped forward, unlocking the front door. When I stepped into the cool air of the house, Hennie had me up in his arms. The confrontation had made me feel sick to my stomach, despite the fact that I'd meant every word I said. Deep down inside, though, there was still the girl I once was, horrified by the very idea I might disappoint my parents.

Hennie held me to his chest, and I breathed in his comforting scent. "Are you okay, *Liebling*?" he whispered into my hair. I nodded, but didn't move from his chest.

"What a fucking piece of shit. I should go and beat his teeth in for saying that shit to you," Everett growled. "Get out of the fucking road, Harrison. No one says that shit to our girl. No one." Hennie made a noise of agreement, and I wasn't sure I could deal with two hot-headed boyfriends.

"Don't, Everett. You'll just give him ammunition for the stupid tale he's probably spinning already," I said, more than a little impressed with how steady my voice sounded. Pulling back from Hennie, I looked between the four of them. "If you don't have anywhere to be, we may as well pack some stuff while we're here, do you think?"

Harrison spun me from Hennie's arms, kissing me softly. "Absolutely, baby." He rested his forehead on mine. "I'm sorry you had to listen to that ugliness. None of it was true—you know that, right?"

I gave him a tight smile, but in all honesty, Paul knew me well. He knew exactly where to fire his barbs to hurt the most. "Of course not. He's just a petty little man with a sore ego."

Yet he could still hurt my feelings like no one else. That was the power of bad memories.

43

HARRISON

We spent several hours boxing up the main things from the house that we didn't want the moving company sifting through, including everything in the office and my studio. I was sad to leave this place; it had been our first big purchase, a testament to the fact that we'd made it. It had its share of good memories. We could make new memories at the next house with Blake, though, and I was excited to set up my new studio.

We'd worked well together, even with Hennie in the mix. By the time Blake had worked out all her demons, we were all exhausted and ready to get the hell out of there, back to Hennie's house.

I watched as Blake loaded a box into the back of the car. Although she was smiling and laughing with us, her eyes never lit up with happiness the way they had hours earlier. She was pretending she was okay, but that fucker had hurt her. I regretted not letting Everett pound that motherfucker into the gravel earlier. I could see the doubts creeping into her mind as she looked at us, those words cutting her down, no matter how many times we contradicted them throughout the day.

He'd preyed on her self-esteem, and if I ever saw that fuck in a dark alleyway, he wouldn't be the prettiest fucking redneck on the prairie any longer.

Walking up behind her, I wrapped my arms around her waist, gritting my teeth when she sucked in her stomach beneath my hands. "Let's go home, baby. We'll grab some pizza, watch a movie, and forget that today ever happened."

She gave me a lopsided smile. "That sounds good."

Darwin looked over at her with a frown. He was the most sensitive of us, and he'd hovered around her all day. She climbed into the back seat, and he shut the door behind her softly. As I met his gaze, I could see the rage bubbling in his eyes. "That fucker hurt her feelings."

"Yep."

"You and Everett have to fix it tonight. Show her how beautiful we think she is. How special. If you can't, let me have her again tonight so I can worship her like the goddess she is, until she's too drunk on orgasms to let that asshole's words affect her any longer."

He looked fierce, and it was an odd look on his normally happy face. Not much got to Darwin—not trolls on the internet, or people in the street, or Prince fucking Eric. But someone coming for Blake had set him to rage.

I thumped him on the shoulder. "We'll fix it, D. Don't worry. Between Everett and me, she'll be so filled with endorphins and happiness, she'll forget that cock-stain even existed."

Darwin nodded as he slid into the car beside Blake. I could see him pulling her into his arms and settling her against his chest as he whispered to her, but I couldn't hear what they were saying.

Everett strolled over to me. "The place is all locked up tight, according to the security company's instructions. Felt like mission impossible getting out of there before the alarm was armed, but I think it should be all good."

I stepped closer to him. I liked that the new house wasn't directly on the street, instead hidden away down a treed driveway. I'd be free to hold both Everett and Blake however I liked, without worrying about Mrs. Lehmern next door judging me from her front window.

"I have plans for us and Blake tonight. Better rest up and bring your A-game," I murmured, and he raised an eyebrow.

"Oh?"

"Yeah," I murmured, and bit his earlobe.

Hennie finally got off his phone, so we could leave. He and Darwin were in the back again, and I noticed they had Blake tucked protectively between them. However, instead of the easy way she'd been beside them on the way over, she now sat stiffly, her head back against the headrest as she stared up at the roof of the car, a faraway look in her eye.

I hated it, but that was okay. Tonight, Everett and I would fix it. She'd know how gorgeous she was—or I'd make her come so many times, she wouldn't care any longer.

ONE OF THE most challenging parts of loving Everett was the fact he was such a damn food snob. On top of that, pizza was his favorite food, meaning he was so, *so* picky about his pizza delivery. But the one Hennie had recommended actually made him moan, which was basically a small miracle.

"Holy hell. I need the number for the guy who invented this sauce. It's fucking amazing." He was munching away, staring down at the pizza like it would tell him its secrets.

Hennie laughed. "I don't think you can, because the inventor died about three decades ago. He was friends with my grandfather. He got the recipe from his grandfather, and brought it with him when he moved to America."

Everett grunted. "Lucky. I might have tried to kiss him otherwise."

We all laughed. I looked around at the people in the living room with me. I could see what Darwin was trying to do now, past the sex and girlfriend-sharing. He was trying to create a family, and that scared me a little more than I'd like to admit.

For so long, it had been just me and Everett. The only person who had any effect on my happiness had been as devoted to me as I was to him. We'd faced more trials together than we deserved, but it had made our commitment to each other stronger. Then Darwin came along, but we were friends. Best friends, but still friends.

Now, I was opening myself up to more people, who would all have the ability to break my heart. That was terrifying. Love didn't happen overnight, but it grew. What if we got serious and had kids? Would having four dads badly affect them? What if one of us left?

I shook my head. This was a trial week, and I should just focus on whether the logistics would even work. There was time to worry about the other stuff later, if we decided to pursue this long-term.

"How long until you guys move?" Hennie asked cautiously around his pizza.

Everett grinned. "Sick of us already?"

"Only of the way you moan, like the pizza's sucking your dick. It's weird," Hennie teased back. They'd definitely gotten closer after working in close confines for a day. Clearly, there wasn't a lot of room for big egos in a food truck.

I tried not to feel jealous of their easy camaraderie. While Everett had fucked many women since we'd been together, he'd never fucked another man. It wasn't as if LA had a shortage of attractive gay men either; this was Hollywood.

He wasn't flirting with Hennie, exactly, but I could see that he liked him. I wondered if Hennie was bisexual too, would Everett want to extend our relationship to include him? I got it—he was a handsome guy: tall, well-built, with pretty blond hair and a jawline like a razor blade. I found him attractive as well, because I wasn't blind. But sharing Everett with another man felt infinitely harder than sharing Blake.

I shook my head. I don't know why I was trying to hurt my own feelings tonight.

"Harrison?" Everett called.

"Sorry, what?" I focused on the conversation that was obviously happening around me.

"When do we move in?" Blake asked softly.

I gripped her hand and lifted it to my lips. "The moving company will pick up the keys tomorrow and begin to move our furniture over to the new place next week. So we should be out of your hair in no time. Are you going to miss us?" I teased Hennie.

He grinned, but it didn't quite meet his eyes. "A little. It's been nice having other people here. Not so quiet all the time."

Darwin had been right, though I didn't know why I was surprised anymore. The guy had shown he was far more intuitive about people's feelings than the rest of us. Hennie was lonely.

I patted him on the back. "The new place is less than twenty minutes away. You're always welcome. If this works, we'll have to figure out a way to make you feel as included as the rest of us. Family dinners, maybe?"

Blake nodded, crawling into Hennie's lap. "Yeah. And date nights. Maybe sleepovers?" She wiggled her eyebrows at him, and he kissed her with a laugh.

"Sounds good, *Liebling*."

I uncurled from the couch. "Speaking of which, I'm exhausted. Come on, Sweetheart, it's time for bed." I wasn't sure what she saw on my face, but her lips parted a little. I held out a hand, and she placed her delicate one in mine. I pulled her off Hennie's lap, into my arms. "Say goodnight, little one," I murmured beside her ear. "Tell them they might need to put in their earplugs, because I have plans for you tonight."

Her little gasp was like a starting gun, and I scooped her up into my arms.

"Say goodnight, Blake," I repeated, my voice firmer.

"Uh, goodnight?"

I looked over at Everett. "You're with me."

Everett laughed, but it was short and filled with promise. "Yes, sir."

He was teasing me, because he was the dom in the bedroom. His eyes were already hooded as he followed me out of the room. I'd been thinking about this for hours, and I had a laundry list of things I was going to do to the beautiful woman in my arms—they all began and ended with her pleasure.

By the time I was done, she wouldn't ever doubt how desirable she was to us ever again.

44

BLAKE

My heart was thundering in my chest, and I wiggled to get out of Harrison's arms. "I'm too heavy. Put me down before you hurt yourself," I said jokingly, but it wasn't really a joke. I didn't want him slipping a disc or something.

"Be quiet, Blake. You aren't too heavy, and if you keep up with those self-deprecating thoughts that have been rolling around in your head all day, I'm going to spank you."

My thighs clenched, and I looked down at my vagina with a surprised look. *Is that something I'm into?* I mean, I didn't think so, but here we were. Time to fuck around and find out.

I sighed dramatically, flinging myself backwards. "But I'm like Shamu."

Harrison growled, eating up the distance to the bed

in the room he was sharing with Everett. He threw me down so hard, I bounced.

"On your hands and knees, Blake." It wasn't Harrison's voice that rolled across my skin like a visible caress. That was one hundred percent Everett. "You tested Harrison, and now he gets the joy of turning that pretty ass pink."

I did as I was told immediately, not even thinking to say no to Everett. I slipped onto my knees, my ass pointed in the air.

"Mmph," Harrison grunted, dragging my PJ shorts over my ass and down my thighs.

"Don't move, Sunshine," Everett commanded. "Do you see that, Harrison?"

"That pretty pink pussy glistening at me? You bet your fucking ass I do. I can't wait to bury my face in those pretty folds." Harrison was behind me, and when I felt the puffs of his breath on my damp core, I bit my lip to hold in my moans. "But first, your punishment, bad girl. Six spanks should make you think twice before degrading yourself, I think."

There was a weighty silence before a hard crack left a stinging sensation on my asscheek. It was quickly followed by a gentle caress, but I could still feel the burn.

"Are you ready for number two, baby girl? Do you want to count them for me?"

My whole body vibrated with tension as I waited for the next blow. "Yes," I breathed.

A firm smack on the other cheek, the sting barely registering before he was already soothing it with gentle hands. It meant I wasn't prepared for the third and fourth in such quick succession, and the noise I made was between a squeal and a moan.

"Harrison," I groaned. Why did this feel so good?

"Mmm, good girl. You're taking your punishment so well. What are we up to?"

I was panting with anticipation as I mumbled, "Four." I thrashed my head around until I found Everett. He looked like a sex god, standing naked beside the bed, his tattoos a stark contrast to his pale skin. He looked like a work of art.

Slap. "Five." *Slap.* "Six," I breathed, relief warring with disappointment in my tone. I dropped my face back into the comforter as the bed shifted behind me, and my squeals were muffled as a tongue smoothed over the stinging skin of my ass. One lick, a cool breath trailing over the damp skin. Then the other side. Finally, he buried his face in my pussy, and any control I had evaporated like stripes of his saliva on my hot asscheeks.

"So wet for him, Sunshine. Do you like the way he's eating you?" Everett asked, but I was too lost in the sensation of Harrison's tongue spearing me. A fist wrapped in my hair, tugging gently until I was forced to look up into Everett's face. "I asked you a question, Sunshine. Do you like the way our man is tongue-fucking you?"

"Yes," I hissed as my body clenched.

Everett kneeled on the bed. "Next time, we'll have a good conversation about dynamics and safewords before we play. The idea of having both you and Harrison at my mercy makes my cock weep, Sunshine." His thumb swiped along my bottom lip. "Would you like that? You and Harrison on your knees in front of me, pleasuring me, and pleasuring each other when I allow it?"

I moaned again, and an animalistic noise rumbled from Harrison's lips, making them vibrate against my core. "*Yes,*" I moaned.

"I bet you would, baby. I just bet. Come on, sweet girl. Suck my cock while Harrison finishes you off. I want to be coating your tongue before he's had his fill."

I dived on his cock, like this was a hot-dog-eating contest at the county fair. I didn't have many super-powers in life, but a nearly non-existent gag reflex was one of them. As Everett pushed deep into my throat, his thighs shook, and I felt like the most powerful woman in the universe.

"Holy fucking *shit,* Sunshine. Your throat feels like heaven," he groaned, thrusting gently. I was distracted, though, because Harrison's fingers had come up to strum my clit, and I was weaving on that knife-edge of pleasure. When he slapped his hand against my clit, that was all it took.

My screaming orgasm was muffled by Everett's cock—at least, until he pulled out of me. "I don't want to come in your mouth, baby. I want to come inside your tight little cunt. Are you ready?"

Hard muscles brushed against the back of my thighs, and I looked over my shoulder to see a condom-clad Harrison poised behind me. Fuck, he had a beautiful dick, straining long and hard in his palm. "Ready, Sweetheart? I can't wait to be inside you."

"Please," I whined, despite the fact my body was still shaking from my release. He didn't need to be asked twice as he lined himself up and thrust in hard. My head flopped forward again, dragging along the comforter as Harrison pulled out and slammed back in again.

"Do you like that, Sunshine? Like how our boy feels inside that tight pussy?" I made an unintelligible noise. Everett gripped my chin and must have made some kind of sign to Harrison, who stopped. I protested, but Everett just smirked. "I asked you a question. Do you like how Harrison's dick feels, deep in that hot little pussy? I bet you're gripping him like a vice."

"She is," Harrison said tightly, like it was physically paining him not to move. "Let her go, Everett. I want to show her just how fucking precious she is. How bad she drives me wild."

God, their words were like electric shots straight to the ovaries.

Everett just grinned. "You've made him mouthy, Sunshine. He thinks because we haven't talked about the dynamic yet, it doesn't apply." He raised an eyebrow at Harrison. "I think I'll show him who's in charge right now. I might fuck him as he fucks you. It'll be me fucking the both of you."

Holy shit.

"Do you think you'd like that, Blake?"

"Yes!" I moaned. Okay, so I might have shouted it, and Everett's chuckle set something inside me on fire.

"I bet you would." He stepped off the bed and put his cock back at my lips. "Make my cock wet for him, baby. Use a lot of spit—he's going to need it."

I bobbed enthusiastically over his cock, while he stroked my hair. "Good girl." He looked past me at Harrison. "Move again. Get her back to where she's writhing. I don't think I'm going to last long inside you," he told Harrison, who let out a relieved groan and started hammering into me again, dragging me back up to the precipice.

I couldn't see what was going on behind me, but Harrison's hips jerked a few times, pounding harder until I was sure I was going to feel him in my cervix tomorrow. I could tell the moment that Everett slipped inside him. Firstly, because his whole body shuddered. But mostly, because his movements changed. It was like he was possessed, and I guess, in a way, he was.

"*Fuck,*" Harrison breathed. It was definitely a feeling I could relate to. I was squashed flat on the bed, my thighs pushed wide, Harrison curled over the top of me. I could feel the brush of Everett's knuckles on my hips as he rolled Harrison's hips into mine.

I clenched around Harrison again, making him groan. "Holy shit, *fuck.* I'm not going to last. It feels... It feels..." He made another pained noise, and the sound of it drove me closer to the edge.

"Feel that, Sunshine? Can you feel how wild you make us? This is all for you. We've never done this with anyone else," Everett moaned, his breathing labored. "Special. Both of you are special." His groan almost sounded pained. "Now come for me. Both of you." He fucked Harrison into me at an alarming pace, making the bed quake.

I was helpless to do anything but what he commanded. My orgasm made me see stars, whole galaxies of pleasure bursting behind my eyelids. The chain reaction of my release made me feel powerful as Harrison followed me, his whole body turning to rubber as he collapsed, only Everett's arm banded around his chest keeping him from crushing me.

Everett wasn't done, but he was no longer in tight control of himself either. He was shifting us all around the bed as he pounded into Harrison, finally growling out his own release. We all collapsed into a heap of limbs and sweat, though Everett gently pulled out of Harrison, who in turn gently rolled off of me, his fingers tugging off the condom and tossing it in the direction of the trash can before falling on the other side of me.

"No one told me sex could be like that," I panted, my whole body still being wracked by aftershocks.

Harrison dragged me into his arms, plastering me against his sweaty chest, his heavy breathing displacing my already wild hair. "It's not normally like that," he murmured, planting his lips on my forehead, then my cheeks, then my lips. "It's only like that when it means something."

"And when you're fucking two guys in a wild three-some," Everett added, the hair of his chest tickling my arm.

"Maybe I should have more of this."

Harrison raised an eyebrow. "Meaningful sex or wild threeways?"

I grinned, snuggling between them. "Do I have to choose just one?"

The noise Everett made was almost a purr. "Not while I'm around. Now come here so I can make you come on my fingers again, Sunshine."

45

BLAKE

The next couple of days were slow, and quite frankly, pleasant as hell, with one small exception: Darwin wasn't here. Dani had called him up in a panic after her date to some gala had broken his leg playing beer pong. Like the good twin that he was, Darwin got on the first plane to the East Coast.

I missed him. I felt like I just kept missing him and our moment. He seemed happy to take it slow, and honestly, his giant armored dick was intimidating as hell, so maybe I was dragging my feet a little too. But there was no doubt in my mind that I wanted to climb aboard that giant nope rope between his legs and give it the good old college try.

However, taking that step with Darwin would mean there was no going back. I liked to pretend that at the end of this trial week, if we all decided this situation didn't suit us, we could go back to how we were. Hennie could go back to ignoring me, Harrison and Everett could go back to having each other.

But if I took the next logical step and made love to Darwin, there was no going back. He was an all-or-nothing kind of guy, and I knew being his focus would be a heady and addictive thing.

These were all great excuses for why I was a coward.

As if he knew I was thinking of him, a photo of him in his tux flashed up in a message on my phone. I opened it and sighed. How could a man be so fucking handsome *and* so kind? He was an anomaly of life.

"Darwin again?" Harrison asked from where he was writing content for his posts.

I flipped my phone around, showing him the picture. "He looks so freaking sexy."

Harrison just laughed. "He is an easy man to dress, but if you like the suit, I think all the kudos goes to Dani. No one's naive enough to think he had any say in what he was wearing."

Probably not. Dani also looked beautiful in a short, gauzy gown that I could never wear, and diamond-studded platform shoes.

I zoomed in on the carpet they were standing on. "Wait. Are they at the freaking *Met Gala?*" Sure enough, if I Googled, up came Dani in her Met Gala outfit.

"Holy shit. The gala she needed a date for was the Met?" My brain exploded as five or six press photos of her on the red carpet appeared. She looked gorgeous, though there were no press photos of Darwin.

I sent him a bunch of exclamation points with the words *MET GALA* in capitals, and he had the audacity to send me back a laughing emoji.

"I'm so jealous, it hurts." I wasn't a big fashion girlie, but even I could appreciate how cool that was. No wonder he'd gone when she called.

Harrison laughed, dragging me onto his lap. "Want me to take your mind off it?"

It was like once he'd had a taste, Harrison couldn't get enough. I'd had so much sex in the last few days, my vagina was going to need a reconstruction. My neck and chest were covered in tiny love bites and beard rash. But I always wanted more. I'd never felt so desired, so wanted. It was all-consuming; I couldn't get enough. Hennie, Everett and Harrison all took turns at sharing me, and so far, it was working well.

I leaned forward, brushing my lips over his in a teasing kiss. "And what about the others?" Just because it was working, that didn't mean I wanted to rub it in their faces.

"They're in the drying room, making sausage," Harrison murmured against my skin as he sucked his way down my throat.

"Sounds dirty," I joked, and he hummed his agreement.

"So dirty. Just like the things I'm about to do to you, Sweetheart." He dragged my shirt over my head until I sat before him in just my bra. Pulling down the cups, he sucked one of my nipples between his lips, and I moaned as I pressed further into his body.

Then someone knocked at the front door.

Fuck.

Pulling away, Harrison groaned. "Do we answer it?"

I grimaced. What if it was Hennie's mom or something? "No way. I'll go get Hennie." The knock sounded again, more insistently this time. Climbing off Harrison's lap and throwing my shirt back on, I'd just made it to the drying room when Hennie appeared with a frown. He kissed the side of my head and walked to the front door, throwing it open.

What I didn't expect were cops. My breathing picked up, panic setting in around the edges. I looked for their guns, their kevlar vests and helmets. But they just seemed like normal cops. Not SWAT. We weren't being swatted again. It was okay.

I told myself this over and over again, but the panic didn't subside.

Harrison came up beside me and wrapped an arm around my waist, dragging me close until I was encased in the scent of him and the warmth of his embrace.

Hennie's big body blocked the doorway. "Can I help you, officers?"

There was one big cop, easily standing eye to eye with Hennie. The other was a smaller, slightly more grizzled-looking man. He was the one who spoke. "We have a report of a woman being held against her will at these premises. There have also been accusations of sexual misconduct. Is there a Blake Wilcox here?"

My whole body felt frozen in disbelief. My brain tried to make sense of what the cop was saying, but was failing because nothing he said was actually making sense.

Harrison nudged me a little, and I stepped forward. "I'm Blake. There's been a mistake."

The cops took in the love bites on my neck and chest, and gave me disbelieving looks. "If you could come outside, ma'am, that would be appreciated," the big cop said, and I looked at Hennie. He moved to the side so I could get past, but hovered close behind me, ready to snatch me back into the house.

"Ma'am, are you safe? Your parents have expressed a serious concern that you are being held against your will. That these men lured you to LA with promises of a scholarship, and you're now being held here."

I had no idea how my parents had found out that the scholarship was a lie. The truth of what had happened was all twisted up in falsehoods. "No, officer. I'm definitely here of my own volition. I was lured to

LA with a scam scholarship, but that was way before I met these guys. If you want to investigate a fraud, however, I'll definitely give you the email of that fuck-er." I hadn't reported it because I was embarrassed, but as time went on, I felt more and more guilty about that. What if he was scamming some other poor girl with a big dream and no common sense? "But as for the rest, that's total bullshit. These are my boyfriends."

"Boyfriends?" the grizzled cop repeated.

"Yeah. Plural," Hennie growled, as if daring him to have a problem with it.

A voice yelling from the street sent fear skittering down my spine. "She's been brainwashed, officer! I demand you arrest those men!" My mother shuffled quickly up Hennie's driveway, and it was like all my worst nightmares come to life. She was slightly out of breath by the time she made it to us, her face red and my father behind her like a silent shield. "They've taken my sweet baby girl and turned her into a whore for them. She is obviously a victim. Look at her! She looks like she's been gnawed on by dogs!"

The cops looked down at my lovebites, and I moved closer to Hennie. He didn't hesitate to wrap an arm around me. I felt warmth at my back, so I knew the other guys had also closed ranks around me.

I looked at my parents behind the cops. "Hey, Mom. Hey, Dad. What the fuck are you doing here?"

My mother snarled at me. "Saving you from becoming another victim of the Los Angeles sex trade."

"Are you kidding me right now?" Everett grumbled behind me, drawing the eyes of the cops.

Fuck. I needed the police to leave before they believed my parents' insanity. "Look, officers, I promise I am here voluntarily and of my own free will. I'm in a committed relationship with these men. We are polyamorists. We aren't hurting anyone, and it's all consensual. My parents have wasted your time, so I apologize for that."

Grizzled Cop looked annoyed. "So you won't mind us dropping in to see you again at a later date, just to check in?"

I shrugged. "Sure, if you have nothing better to do. I'll make you coffee. We've got nothing to hide."

Big Cop looked me over once more, then nodded to himself. "We'll take you up on that. I just need some details from all of you, and we'll be on our way."

"On your way? You need to do something about this! Polygamy is illegal!" My mother looked past the cops at me, disgust written right across her face. "You need to come home right now, Blake. Go inside and pack your bags."

"I'm not going anywhere with you, Mom."

My father shook his head. "I didn't want to believe what Paul was saying, but he was right. LA has turned you into a whore. You've made yourself worthless, used. Who would ever want to marry you now?"

I gasped, like he'd struck me. I understood that vitriol from my mother, because she tended to get worked up. But how could they look at me, their daughter, and say such awful things?

Hennie was looking like he wanted to close the distance and beat the crap out of my father. Unfortunately—or fortunately—there were two cops in the way.

My whole body went cold as my gaze ran over my parents. "Go home. Don't come back. If you love Paul so much, he can be your surrogate child now, because you are dead to me. I don't have parents anymore."

Hennie was vibrating with anger. "Get the hell off my property before I get these officers to arrest you for trespassing, as well as filing a false police report. That's illegal, right?"

Big Cop just looked like he was over this shit. "It is." He sighed, handing me his card. "I think we've seen all we needed." He looked at me, his gaze flat and no nonsense. "If you need help, call me, but either way, we'll be in touch."

"Officers, my daughter's obviously had a mental breakdown! I demand you take her to the hospital where she can be properly evaluated for mental illness."

My eyes were now so wide, their corners burned. Was she trying to get me committed?

Everett growled. "Listen here, you old bag. The only person who is unstable right now is you. Get the fuck off the property, like Heinrich asked, or I'll make you leave."

"Are you threatening my wife?" My father took an angry step toward us, and the grizzled cop blocked his way.

"They are within their rights to have you removed from their property, sir. Now, I suggest you both leave."

With one last look at my parents, I turned and walked back in the house. I walked through the living room, ignoring the sounds of shouting and cursing. I walked into the bedroom I was currently occupying and crawled right under the blankets. My hands were shaking with adrenaline, and I tucked them between my thighs. My whole body felt wired, my eyes burning. I wasn't sad; I was so fucking *angry*.

How dare they do this?

How dare they say those things to me?

The more I thought about it, the hotter the rage in my chest grew, until it burst into angry, sad tears. I could never see them again. There was no forgiving them for this.

The guys knocked on the door, but I ignored it, and they were polite enough to give me space. I was a fool to believe that people would accept our relationship.

Most people would be like my parents and Paul. I should break it off before my heart got invested and my feelings for them developed into something more.

But even as I made the decision, a tiny voice in the back of my head was reminding me that I was too late.

46

HENNIE

I felt useless. Blake was breaking down in the bedroom, and I couldn't do anything to help. She'd locked the door last night, not answering our knocks. I was trying to give her space, but I hated that she was hurting. The guys had called Darwin immediately, and he was catching the red-eye back to the West Coast.

I had to go to work, but for the first time in so long, I really didn't want to. I wanted to be here for her, in case she needed me. Though, maybe this was what Darwin had meant by teamwork making the dream work, because even if I was at work, she wouldn't be alone. Harrison and Everett would still be here if she needed anything.

Still, I couldn't go anywhere until I'd checked she was okay. I knocked on the door once more, but it was silent on the other side. "*Liebling*? Blake? Can I come in?" Silence. "I'm going to work, but I just want to check if you're okay. Please?"

I heard movement, then felt the gentle vibration of her padding across the floor. Her features were heart-breakingly puffy as she peeked out through a gap in the door. "I'm okay."

I gently pushed the door open further and stepped into the room, gathering her up into my arms and holding her tightly to my chest. How would I feel to be so betrayed by the people who were supposed to love me unconditionally? I'd be just as much of a mess as Blake.

"It's okay not to be okay, *Liebling*. It's okay to be sad and rage and anything else you want to feel." I kissed the salty streaks of her cheeks. "We're here for you. All of us."

She let out a choked noise and buried her face into my chest. I stroked her back and held her, trying to share my strength with her. She held me just as tightly, and I realized in that moment that this wasn't a trial run anymore. I would give anything for this girl. It mightn't be love yet, but I'd never felt anything like this utter devotion before. I was all in, even if I had to share her with three other men. I'd learn to share, learn to appreciate the benefits of sharing my life with four other adults, both in the good times and the bad.

She pulled back, scrubbing at the tears on her face. "I'm sorry. You should go before you're late."

I sighed, because I wanted to put her to bed, climb in behind her, and hold her through her feelings. But the truck had been closed more than it had been open this week, and I'd worked hard to keep my grandfather's legacy alive. "I don't want to leave."

She looked up at me, her eyes still shiny, despite the swollen pink of her eyelids. "I know."

I leaned down and kissed her lips. "Let the guys in. Let us comfort you." She nodded and looked at the floor, letting her forehead rest against my cheek. I squeezed her once more, then stepped away. "I... I'll see you tonight."

The weight of the words that belonged in the silence was heavy. Finally, she gave me a watery smile. "See you tonight." I watched as she went back to bed, crawling beneath the blankets, but thankfully, leaving the door open.

As I walked into the living room, I found the guys arguing softly. "What's wrong?"

Harrison was frowning down at his phone, and I could see the security feed of his old place on the screen. "It doesn't make any sense."

"What doesn't?"

He leaned back in the dining chair. "How did they know she was here? We're only here temporarily, so none of us made this our forwarding address, or changed our details or anything like that. How did they know she was *here?*"

I shrugged. I honestly had no idea. I just assumed the police knew shit, because the DMV always knew shit. Hell, maybe she'd changed her Amazon shipping address to here, or something. There were ways people could find out information if you really wanted to know, even old people like her parents.

"Maybe Blake told them?" I mean, if I'd moved house, I'd tell my parents, mostly because I'd get their disappointed spiel every day for the rest of my life if I didn't.

Everett shook his head. "No, she was still keeping the fact that the art school was a scam from her parents. She was maintaining the lie that she was staying in dorm housing at the art school. No way would she have given them this temporary address—if she had, she would've had to explain us and all of this."

"Maybe she did, and that's why they showed up?" Harrison offered, still staring down at the security feed.

That wasn't right. I'd seen her face when she saw her parents. She'd been shocked and horrified that they were here. "She's a smart girl. If she told them her address and her living situation, she would have known there was a small chance they'd turn up. But she looked blindsided."

Everett cussed under his breath. "How can a parent treat their child like that?" Harrison snorted but didn't say anything. Obviously, they would know; their story wasn't a happy one either. "Okay, scratch that. How could any *person* who's ever met Blake treat her that way? The girl is pure goodness."

I shrugged. I didn't have any answers. "I don't know. But her door is open, and I told her you guys would be in to lie with her over the next little while. She needs to know we're here for her." I paused, looking between them. "I'm in, for this whole thing. She needs us, and the things I feel for her..." It was hard to explain it to them, that the things I felt for Blake were a burning force in my chest. "She needs to know she isn't alone in the world, and I intend to be a foundation for her for as long as she'll let me. This isn't a trial run for me anymore. Are you guys in?"

Everett grinned. "Welcome to co-boyfriendhood. I'm in too." Harrison cleared his throat, and Everett smiled even wider, if that was possible. "*We're* in." He slapped me on the back, then moved past me. "I'll take first shift with our girl."

He disappeared down the hallway, and I watched him go. It was a weird feeling, but I realized it made me feel relieved he was holding the woman I lov—cared for. I didn't feel jealous at all. I was just happy she was getting someone to lean on while I was at work.

Harrison shook his head, an amused smile on his face. "He's so smitten. Has been all in from the beginning."

"And you?"

"I'm all in too. She's special."

"But you're right. It doesn't make sense." If she hadn't told her parents, how did they know about the school?

"What?" He frowned at me. "What doesn't make sense? You know she's special, just as much as I do."

I shook my head. "No, not that." I flapped a hand at him. "How did they know the art school was a scam? If her parents didn't know, then how did Paul know where to find her at your house? None of this makes any sense."

He ran a hand through his hair. "I don't know."

There was something about her ex that didn't sit right with me, and it wasn't just that he was a raging asshole. He looked just a little too smug for a guy who was chasing his ex, and I wanted to punch him in the face. I mean, the guys had been doxxed, so maybe he'd found it in an internet search, but something was still off there. It was niggling at my brain.

Harrison pulled up the footage from the other day, and we watched Paul snoop around, like he knew we weren't there, until the security dude rolled up. "That's suspicious as fuck. I'll get security to look into him. I don't want him to devolve into a stalker that Blake has to worry about."

I gathered up the stuff I needed to go to work, but

still, I hesitated. It felt wrong leaving her when she was so upset.

Harrison grabbed one of the large tote tubs from the ground and helped me move it out to the truck. "It's okay—we'll take care of her. Plus, Darwin should be home any minute. If anyone can make her feel better, it's him."

Yeah, Darwin had that effect, for sure. One minute, you were angry at the world, and the next minute, you were agreeing to be Ringo Starr in Blake's personal boy band.

Harrison helped me load the rest of the stuff into the truck before going back inside. I wanted to run back in, say goodbye one more time, but I held myself back. I'd just made it onto the freeway when my phone rang, and panic washed over me before I realized it was my mom.

"Hey, Mom."

"Do not 'hey' me, Heinrich Oskar."

Whoops. What had I done this time? "Sorry?"

"Do you even know what you are apologizing for?" My mom's German accent got really pronounced when she was mad. My dad had met her when he went back to the Old Country in his twenties, and sometimes I wondered if it was an arranged thing between them or if my dad really had just fallen in love with my austere mother, like he said.

I sighed heavily. "Um, no. But I assume you're going to tell me?"

She made a rude noise. "Some *man* contacted me on that Face app and told me that my son is engaging in sexual relations with three other men and a single woman, in some kind of den of hedonistic shame. And that the men are pornstars!" She let out a litany of angry German that I didn't even try to follow. I wasn't as fluent in German as my parents.

"The actual *fuck?*" I breathed.

"Do not swear at me, Heinrich!"

I winced as her voice echoed around the truck. "I wasn't swearing at you, Mom. I was swearing at the situation. Who was telling you these lies?"

"A nice boy named Paul. He said you were a good man, a business owner, and didn't need to be dragged down into disrepute."

Fucking. Paul. If I saw that asshole again, I was going to smash his face into a wall until his nose was an innie and not an outie anymore.

I did what damage control I could with my mother, but the fear that I'd be in the same boat as Blake with her parents was a very real possibility. I didn't want that, though I wouldn't hesitate to freeze my parents out for as long as it took them to get their shit together.

And then I'd track down Paul and run the fucker over with my Wiener Wagon.

47

DARWIN

The Uber dropped me off at Hennie's house, and I was out the door before it had even completely rolled to a stop. I'd skipped out on the Met Gala after-parties last night, though I wasn't too sad about that. Eventually, the champagne had flowed a little too freely, and some celebrities began to admit they knew who I was, then got a little more handsy than I would have liked.

Plus, Dani had run into her baseball-playing ex and decided to make some mistakes she'd regret today, but she was a big girl. We all made mistakes, and some you had to make for yourself.

I thumped on the door, and Everett opened it, looking tired and stressed. "You're back. Thank fuck. Come on." He led me into the kitchen, where Harrison was watching a waffle iron like it was about to grow legs and ninja-kick Blake across the room.

When I saw her, I understood why. She looked terrible. Pale, with her eyes puffy, like she'd been crying too much. I moved toward her without conscious thought, driven to hold her in my arms. I dragged her to the couch, pulling us both down onto the overstuffed cushions.

"Ah, *Amorcito*. I'm sorry your parents are cunts."

She let out a short bark of laughter. "I don't think that's in the current rotation of Hallmark cards, but I feel like it should be."

Everett chuckled. "Agreed."

I gathered her on my lap and held her tightly. "Do you need to talk about it? I hate that they hurt you and I wasn't here to do anything about it."

She laid her head on my shoulder. "I keep seeing the absolute disgust in my dad's eyes as he looked at me. As he called me a whore." She gave a shuddering breath. "I feel like the parents who should have loved me unconditionally are dead, and now I'm mourning them."

I murmured soft reassurances, while on the inside, I was livid. How *dare* they hurt her? "They don't matter to your story now. They are the past, and you've got so much life left to be written."

Everett tried to hand-feed her waffles with strawberries and melted chocolate, but she took the fork off him and nibbled at it herself. He huffed, but I was proud of her.

"The moving company emailed this morning. The new house is ready for us to move in," Harrison informed us all.

Good. The sooner I could get Blake behind locked gates where no one could hurt her, the better.

She finished her breakfast slowly as we all made surface-level conversation. I regaled them with the story of seeing an A-list celebrity's nipple when they bent a little too far down and the Hollywood tape failed. I told her about the pretty dresses and the red carpet and the fact that Dani had been sucking face with her ex. I gave her all the useless gossip, in the hope that it would drag her mind away from the bullshit of her life right now.

"Vacation is almost over, baby girl. New house means new content," Harrison teased. "I, for one, am anxious to get back behind the wheel. Hopefully, the whole swatting bullshit has died off and they've moved onto something more interesting."

I hadn't heard much chatter about us being swatted, and the fact was, most of our audience had a short attention span. As soon as people stopped talking about something, it was gone from the public consciousness forever.

As soon as Blake was done eating, I shifted her to her feet. "Come on, *Muñeca*. I need a shower to wash off all the humanity from LAX, and you need to reset. We can wash each other's backs," I teased, giving her a saucy wink that made her giggle softly.

I led her from the room into her bedroom. She had an ensuite; though it was barely big enough to move around, it was plenty big enough for the two of us. I stripped quickly out of my clothes, leaving Blake to decide if she wanted to watch or actually join me. I wouldn't pressure her into anything.

Because I'd realized something on the race home from New York. I'd realized that I actually loved her. It was quick and sudden, and I wouldn't say anything to her just yet, because she needed time to come to terms with the insanity of her life... but I did. I would do anything for her, if she'd let me.

I could feel her eyes on me as I leaned in and set the water a little warmer than I'd normally have it—I knew women liked the water to be set to the same temperature as a lava pit. I threw an inviting look at her over my shoulder, which she almost missed because her eyes were studying my ass like she was going to write a thesis on it.

Soaping up my hands, I ran them over my body like I was in a cheesy porn movie. No one washed their body like this really; it was all rough hands and quick strokes, not these long, slow glides. All that was missing was the bad saxophone music.

I let my hand slide down my abs until I could grip

my dick. She needed to get out of her head, and there was one surefire way to ensure she didn't think about anything but her own happiness.

By making her body sing with pleasure.

She huffed, and then the clothes were flying. Finally, she stepped into the tiny shower cubicle with me, her body pressed tightly to my back.

"Mine," she grumbled, her hands following the path mine had just taken, tracing the indentations of my abs. I tensed so they were even more pronounced, propping my hand on the tiles. Her nails scraped gently over my skin, making me hiss with pleasure before she went down further. I held my breath as her fingers ran over my hardening cock, her fingers stroking my Jacob's ladder piercings. "Did this hurt?"

I covered her hand with mine, tightening her grip a little as water poured over us both. "It did a little, but it also felt good."

"Is pain something you're into?"

I shook my head. "Not normally. I'm much more interested in pleasure. But getting your dick pierced is a weird sensation."

"And how does it feel when you fuck?"

I groaned as her hand started to stroke me, getting harder and harder beneath her small hands. "It feels really good for me. And for you."

She pressed her lips between my shoulder blades.

"Show me. Help me forget how crappy today has been."

I turned in her arms, bundling her up close to my body. "This means more to me than just forgetting a shitty day, *Muñeca*. I've been dreaming of this moment for weeks. Tell me you have too?"

She tilted her head up, so she could meet my eyes. "I've been thinking about this moment since the first day you unleashed that monster in my presence. But it isn't your huge cock that I dream about... well, not *just* your giant dick. It's also because you're the sweetest man I've ever met. Because you show me every day you care. Because I know this will be more than a quickie in the shower. You're going to make love to me, and it scares the hell out of me, but I've never wanted anything more."

I dropped to my knees, pushing her back against the tiled wall. "I'm going to taste you, *Amorcito*. I'm going to suck your clit until you come all over my face, and then I'm going to slide inside you and never leave." I lifted her leg over my shoulder, baring her beautiful pussy to my eyes.

"Sounds like an unhealthily close relationship," she teased, and then I made good on my promise as I wrapped my lips around her clit and sucked. As her knees went weak, I pushed against her stomach, pinning her to the wall to give her support. I sucked that sensitive little bud until she was panting hard, grinding up into my mouth, her fingers buried deep in my hair. Fucking heaven.

"Please, *please,* Darwin. I need you inside me."

How could I say no to that? But I wanted her slick and ready. She needed at least one orgasm before I'd bury my cock inside her. "Come for me, Doll. Come all over my face." The sound of her release echoed around the room, and I tasted her on my tongue as I speared it inside her, the water from the shower washing over me in waves.

I climbed to my feet, gripping the same leg that had been over my shoulder and slinging it over my hip. I needed to be inside her. Needed to feel the way she clenched around me. Notching against her core, I slid the head of my dick in slowly. I was thicker than most, I knew that, and the last thing I wanted to do was hurt her.

But I should have known my Doll wouldn't go gently. Her foot hooked around my ass, she used the leverage to pull me tightly to her, sliding me deep inside in one long stroke.

"Holy fuck," she breathed, and if I could have spoken, I would have agreed. She felt like *everything.* My brain felt like white noise as I dragged myself out, feeling every one of my piercings, then slid back in again. "Oh god... How can this feel so good?" she mewled. "Move, D. Fuck me like you can't live without me."

That was going to be all too easy, because she consumed me now. My thoughts. My body. Every part of me. Pressing her tightly into the wall, I fucked her like she wanted. Smooth, deep strokes that made me see lights around the edges of my vision, her moans the only sound I could hear. Even the sound of the water disappeared beneath the way she was chanting my name, like I was a god.

"I'm coming, Darwin... I'm *coming*," she gasped, her whole body clenching around me, her nails scraping stripes in my back that stung beneath the water. I kept my pace, chased her into bliss as she came around my cock like a dream. I dragged my body from hers in time to come all over the wall.

I'd broken my rule about no unsafe sex, but it was perfect. I'd remember how hot she felt forever now, and it would be burned into my brain for the rest of my life.

48

BLAKE

Darwin dried me off before we got dressed, and the whole time, he was attentive. He kissed every piece of skin he dried, made happy noises as he bit the inside of my thigh. "I've wanted to get my teeth in these thighs since I saw you by the pool that first time."

He sucked the skin, leaving a big hickey, and I slapped playfully at his head. "Stop it! I'm covered in enough bites. I look like I've been mauled by a vampire."

"Mmm, but none of them are mine. Except this beauty." He kissed the mark he'd just placed on my thigh.

I stroked his hair, the dampness making it curl. His back was a mess of scratches, and I wanted to apologize, but I also kind of liked my marks on him. We slowly dressed, and my body unfurled from the sadness that had made me draw in on myself over the last twelve hours. There was something about Darwin's devotion that made me feel like the world would be okay. Though if someone had ever asked me if I'd be yelling out the name Darwin during climax, I'd have told them they were insane.

"Why did your parents name you Darwin?"

He grinned up at me, but there was sadness at the corners of his eyes. "My parents had an agreement. My mother would get to name the girls, and my father would name the boys. My parents were polar opposites of each other in some ways. My mama, she is a woman of blind faith. But my papa? He was a scientist. He believed in evolution and natural selection. My grandfather, on my mother's side, hated him. Thought he was a blasphemous man and forbade my mother to marry him, but they did anyway. Papa said he'd name his first son after the father of modern evolutionary studies, just to spite his father-in-law. And he did."

I laughed as he buried his face in my neck and rained kisses down my throat. "I can appreciate the spitefulness."

When we emerged from the bedroom, Everett and Harrison were sitting around a laptop at the kitchen table. I could hear yelling, but I didn't recognize the voice.

"You're fucking crazy! I hate you, but I'd never

stoop that low." I walked around to the very edge of the screen and realized it was Prince Eric.

"I didn't suggest it was you, Eric. Frankly, I'd be surprised if you had the brain cells to pull such a thing off. But you had our address, and we're your direct competition. I can see why the Feds thought it could be you. I bet your view numbers are looking up this week while we've been out of commission," Harrison sneered.

"*Fuck you.* I don't need to fucking break the law to beat you fuckers. You're old news now, and I'm not about to jeopardize my career just to get a little bit of payback. You've got the wrong guy. You have to tell them that."

Everett curled his lip at the screen. "We don't tell the Feds anything. They're the ones investigating."

Eric looked pale, though it was hard to focus when his room was so gauche. The guy seriously had a mural of a castle on his wall. If it wasn't so weird, it would be... no, it was still weird, no matter which way you looked at it.

"Well, get them to investigate someone else, because I didn't do anything fucking wrong. Just because you're mad you lost out on the best anal shot award—"

"None of us were even nominated for that. He just wanted to bring it up," Darwin whispered.

"—doesn't mean you have to send the Federal Bureau of Investigation to my damn doorstep."

Harrison pinched his nose, looking over at Everett. "I can hang up now, right?"

Everett slammed the screen down in answer. "What an absolute douchenozzle. All balls, no brains."

"And even his balls aren't that impressive," I added, though that made them all frown in my direction. I smirked as I sat down at the table across from them.

Everett pointed a finger at me. "No looking at Eric's balls. Actually, no looking at anyone's balls but ours." I rolled my eyes, but secretly preened at his possessiveness.

Harrison reached over and gripped my fingers. "You seem better. Go for a ride on D's magical disco stick?"

"Certainly made her hit the high notes," Everett added, a shit-eating grin on his face. "I had to jerk myself off in my bedroom to the sound."

Darwin slapped the back of his head. "Stop it, you're embarrassing her. I know you're jealous because you want it to be you."

"Just the thought of your giant python cock makes my asshole snap shut like a Venus fly trap."

Darwin grabbed me a glass of water, without me even asking, kissing the top of my head again. My heart melted into a pool of molten feels, and I wanted to drag him back to my bedroom and make love to him all over again.

Harrison snapped his fingers in my direction. "I know that look. Stop being cock-drunk right now, because we have a house to go see. But first, let's go see your boy. I feel like a wiener."

We rolled up to the lot where I'd first met Hennie. "See that mass of concrete and rebar? That's the Baldessari School of Art." Who would have thought that a few months later, I'd be standing here with my boyfriends?

Harrison wrapped an arm around my shoulder as we looked at the emptiness. "I can't believe you fell for the old Exclusive School of Arts scam. It's the oldest trick in the book."

"Shut up. The guy was really convincing, may he rot in artistic mediocrity."

We were waiting for the lunch rush to calm down, and I sat at the fold-up table that I'd once used as a desk while I got my life in order, all while fantasizing about Hennie. How the turns had tabled.

Every now and then, he looked over the customers and met my eyes, and my heart did a weird little flip-flop in my chest. Finally, the last of the lunch crowd drifted away, mostly because Everett had climbed into the truck with him and started serving.

"He's incapable of letting a lunch service pass without being elbow-deep in it too," Harrison said fondly, his eyes watching his lover as he moved around the food truck. "I think he'd give up ClickHeart in an instant to have what Hennie does. His own little slice of paradise."

Darwin just dragged me into his lap. Consummating our relationship had dialed up his natural touch hungriness to eleven.

Hennie appeared with a plate of hot dogs and a pile of my favorite pretzels, putting them down in front of us before pulling out a seat and tugging me from Darwin's arms into his own. "Missed you today. How can I be this codependent in a week?"

I shrugged and kissed him softly, chasing the taste of garlicky butter on his lips. He pressed closer, his tongue stroking along mine, and I moaned a little into his mouth.

He groaned and dragged his mouth away. "Don't make those noises, baby, otherwise I'll bend you over this table and fuck you, and that'd be bad for business."

The guys told Hennie about Prince Eric and his epic douchebaggery, while I relaxed into his arms. "We have to go check out the new place," Harrison told us both.

Hennie went tense underneath my legs. "It's ready?"

Unaware of the tension in his body, Harrison nodded, a contented smile on his face. "Uh-huh. Everything is moved in—all that's missing is us."

"You'll come and visit, right? And I'll come and visit you."

Hennie brushed his lips across my temple. "Of course I will."

Despite his words, it still felt like something was ending. We couldn't stay in Hennie's tiny house, though. There wasn't enough room for the five of us. Darwin was still sleeping on a fold-out couch. I didn't have a solution, so I just held Hennie close.

Darwin rubbed my back. "Don't panic, *Amorcito*. We'll wait until Hennie is done for the day and he can come with us. Help you christen your room." He gave me a wink.

Someone walked up to the food truck, and Hennie shifted me from his lap, giving me a quick kiss on the head before leaving to serve. I ate some of the food on the table, but the shine of the day had been muted. The only thing that could save it now was a bratwurst on a stick.

"Am I meant to find Blake eating a sausage this attractive?" Harrison stage-whispered to Everett, and just to fuck with them, I ran my tongue up the side, making them all groan.

"Christ, don't do that in public, Sunshine."

We sat around talking and joking until about three,

which was the normal time that Hennie closed his windows and rolled home. Instead, he followed us back to the new house. I was nervous, which was weird, because this wasn't my house any more than their previous one was.

Still, Darwin dragged me out of the car and stood beside me. The other guys came up and stood close to me as well. "Welcome home, Blake," Harrison murmured softly. I gave him a soft, watery smile. I didn't really have a home other than this one now, and I was so fucking thankful for them. He pointed to a long driveway that sat beside the double garage. "I thought that would be a good place for Hennie to put his truck."

The man in question appeared, and Everett went over to direct him into the spot. Finally, we were all together, and Harrison held the key in the door. "Ready for the future?" he whispered dramatically, then threw open the doors.

Whoever our movers had been, they were efficient and must have been as expensive as hell because everything was in its place, not a stray box in sight.

"Wow. This place is amazing," Hennie breathed, and I followed him around as he viewed it for the first time. I'd adored it, and that magic took my breath away all over again. He walked through to the big windows that led out to the courtyard.

Everett pointed to the guest house. "That's yours,

when you're ready, Heinrich. If you ever want to move in. No pressure, of course. If you want to maintain a degree of separation, that's okay. But it'll wait until you're ready to make that step."

Hennie whirled around to face him. "You're giving me a guest house?"

Harrison shrugged. "You said you were all in, right? That means this house is our house. Our family home, if that's what you and Blake want. We aren't there yet, I know, but one day we might have kids, maybe, if that's something Blake wants. Maybe a dog. Things and responsibilities that need to be shared among the house." He must have seen my stunned look, because he quickly grabbed my hands and lifted them to his lips. "We are just forward planning, baby. No rush. Or not ever, if you don't want. It's something we'll discuss way, *way* later."

Everett was just smirking, like he was imagining breeding me big and full of his children, and I flushed red. *Well, hello new kink I didn't know I had. Nice to meet you.*

49

BLAKE

We stayed the night at the new house, and I woke up pressed between Darwin and Hennie. My phone was blaring, and the sound was like an icepick in my ear hole. We'd definitely had too much celebratory champagne. I leaned over Hennie, who took the opportunity to clutch my boobs around his face and sigh happily. Man, I loved these guys.

I froze, my hand poised over my phone. *Shit.* Where the hell had that even come from? It was too soon to love anyone. Love grew over time; it was seeing someone's light, their happiness, and wanting to share it with them. It was seeing their fears and weaknesses, and wanting to stand between them and the things that scared them.

But it was also a moment of recognition in a crowd.

It was an instant connection. It was a flash of lightning that seared your soul forever too. I wasn't sure I was ready to love four very different men, but apparently, my heart didn't care.

"Are you going to answer that?" Hennie's voice was muffled, because he was ear-deep in my cleavage.

I picked up my phone and shoved it to my ear, not even looking at the number. "'Lo?"

"Oh my god, Blake, you'll never guess what happened!"

Why the hell was Jeanna calling me at—I looked down at my phone—6:50 in the morning? "What's wrong?"

"Were you asleep? Fuck, sorry, I always forget about the time difference with y'all." She sucked in a huge breath. "But it won't matter, because you'd definitely wanna know this, and it won't matter what time it is, I promise."

Hennie pulled back. "Who is it?"

"Is that a man? Blake Louise Wilcox, are you in bed with a guy right now? Oh my god, is what he was saying true? Are you really sleeping with a bunch of guys out there in LA? No judgment, girl—I say get you some—but boy, he said you'd been shacked up like a whorehouse."

"Who said?" I asked, though I already knew the answer.

"Paul."

Fucking Paul. I hated that I'd ever once been in love with that raging elephant haemorrhoid.

"But that's why I'm calling. You'll never guess what happened? I was over having brunch with Tracy, because her and Ron just broke up, poor thing. I mean, she was fucking their lawn guy, but we all know Ron has one of those innie penises, so can you really blame her? I was telling her that she could get it on with Shaun—that's the lawn guy—because you know what they say about landscapers. Good in the bush means they're good with the bush, right? I mean, she deserves—"

"Jeanna, you've gotten off topic." She'd always been like this. She was such a sweet person, but she had so little brain-to-mouth filter, sometimes you ended up down a rabbit hole with no idea how you'd got there, and the point she was trying to make was lost to time. It was better to stop and redirect before she got too far away from her point.

"Of course I have. Sorry, Blake. Well, you know how Ron and Tracy live across from Paul? Well, at nine a.m. exactly, this black sedan and Chief Dunsten's squad car rolled up in front of Paul's house. Ten minutes later, they're taking Paul off in the back of their car, handcuffed, and then a whole bunch of other squad cars show up and the officers start removing evidence from his house."

Paul had been arrested? "Why?"

"Well, Tracy called Christina, and Christina called Charlie down at the station, and he apparently said that Paul had been taken in by the FBI for cyberterrorism charges, extortion and like, a whole bunch of other federal charges. They said he was sending SWAT teams to people's houses by making false reports. How scary would that be?"

Holy fuck. Paul was the swatter. He was the one who'd doxxed us and had armed police personnel sent to the house to arrest us.

I rocked back on my heels, falling back into the bed. "Holy shit. It was Paul."

I was shaking my head, because despite him turning up on the doorstep of our old place, and despite my parents knowing where Hennie lived, I'd never thought it would be Paul. He didn't even like computers. He'd always said he kept his around so he could do his invoicing, but in all the time I'd been with him, I'd never seen him use it for anything but spreadsheets and stuff. Now he was a cyberterrorist?

"Did you know he did that stuff?" I'd forgotten Jeanna was still at the other end of the line.

I shook my head, though she wouldn't see it. "I had no idea."

Jeanna was off on another tangent about one of our other friends, but I wasn't even listening anymore. At some point, I must have told her I had to go and just hung up, because both Darwin and Hennie were hovering over me.

"It was Paul. Paul was the one who told the Feds we were terrorists."

Darwin blinked sleepily. "Your ex-boyfriend Paul? With the pudge and the receding hairline—that Paul?" I nodded. "Huh. Didn't see that coming." He snuggled back down beneath the covers, his eyes already closing again. "You going to tell the other guys?"

I leaned over and kissed him, his full lips like soft pillows beneath mine. "Yeah, I am, Sleeping Beauty. I'll see you at lunch."

"Beauty sleep is a prerequisite of the job," he mumbled as I climbed from the bed after Hennie. He was in a pair of Harrison's borrowed sweats, and he looked beautiful.

He held out an oversized hoodie I'd stolen from Everett. "Come on, *Liebling*. I'll go start the coffee."

HARRISON'S LAWYER, as well as the agent in charge of our case, had both called by lunchtime, but no one was as efficient as the Dahlonega gossip vine. Harvey, the lawyer, had said all charges were officially dropped and we were free to leave the state again.

The Feds had called to see if I wanted to add

stalking to the list of charges against Paul. Apparently, they'd found information that he'd been hacking my laptop's camera for ages. When Cole had come across that picture of me at the AdEx Awards on his favorite porn site, Paul had seen red. He'd found out the guys' address information from a loose-lipped talent agent who worked for Prince Eric. He'd targeted them, in the hopes that I would run back to Georgia, back to him, like a scared little girl.

The Feds believed that his actions were driven by the fact that I looked like I'd moved on, and therefore, his targeting of our group went beyond criminal mischief into something else.

I just wanted it to be over, really. I didn't want to have to go and testify against him, or give a statement, or any of that shit. I wanted to leave my old life behind, especially when I was sitting in the California sun, a man behind me kissing my shoulder as we sunbathed on deck chairs around a stupidly pretty pool.

Despite the absolute turmoil he'd created in my life, Paul had also set me free. Free from the person I'd forced myself to be for so long. Free from the expectations of my parents and my hometown.

For that, I'd give him more grace than he'd ever given me.

Everett had grumbled, and Hennie had said something about running him over with the food truck—

which at the very least seemed like it should be a food safety problem—but Harrison understood. He'd held me tightly as I spoke to the Feds, his solid warmth around me the bolstering I needed.

Hennie had taken the day off again, which made me feel bad once more, but now that all my open wounds had been exposed to the light of day, hopefully this would be the last day I dragged him away from work. Tomorrow, the rest of us would get back to work again too. This was a last calm moment before life returned to normal.

Darwin had insisted that it was unseasonably warm for November, and we needed to celebrate by lying in the sun and swimming in the pool before we covered it up for the winter. So that's where we were, living the dream. Hennie was lying in the pool, floating like a golden god, his face tilted to the sun.

Harrison sat on the edge, sunglasses on as he tilted his face to the sun. "I'm going to say it—this place definitely appeals to my artistic nature more than the last one." Everett hummed his agreement from where he stood at a small wet bar making cocktails.

"I'm going to say that it feels nicer, because Blake is here. And Hennie. New friends and new lovers make everything better," Darwin added from where he was sprawled behind me in the world's tightest swim trunks. Honestly, I could actually see the piercings down his dick—that's how tight they were. He may as well have been naked.

Everett came and sat on the lounger opposite me, handing me a cocktail that was more vodka than pineapple juice. Sipping it, I sighed happily. He leaned close to me, kissing my jaw. "Think we can convince Hennie into having an orgy to christen the pool?"

My whole body clenched with pleasure, but I shook my head. "He's not ready for your perversion yet," I whispered back, but that didn't stop my brain from filling in the gaps. My body pressed between all four of them. Everett and Harrison kissing behind me as I rode Hennie's face and sucked Darwin's cock. My whole body broke out in goosebumps of pleasure, making Everett chuckle darkly.

"You're right. We've just sold him on the idea of us being together. But soon, Sunshine."

That was one promise I was going to hold him to. I curled my free hand in his beard. "You make me so fucking happy." *I think I might love you.* "Thank you for pushing me out of my comfort zone. Thank you for being an absolute prick and pushing me to my limits."

He turned his face so he could kiss my wrist. "Anytime, baby. Hopefully for the rest of our lives."

He meant it too. *How the fuck did I get to be so damn lucky?*

If I ever saw the director of Baldessari School of Art again, I might actually thank him. He'd changed the course of my life. Showed me that there was more to life than my small hometown. Some of it was good, and some of it was bad, but at least I felt like I was alive. I had a chance to really know how amazing love could be. So I'd say thank you.

But I'd still kick him fair in the dick.

EPILOGUE

BLAKE

"This is a terrible idea, D."

Darwin groaned, biting his fist, though I could barely see it through the mask. "Not from my angle, it isn't."

"We were legitimately just at your mother's house for dinner. This feels sacrilegious."

"You aren't dressed as Mary, *Muñeca*. We aren't about to get smited." He sighed happily. "Consider this my Christmas present, because baby, you look like a gift."

"Christmas isn't for six months, dork." I ran a hand down his face, feeling the gentle scrape of his beard on my palm. "Are you sure about this?" I asked once more, and he laughed.

"I'm more than sure, *Amorcito*." He stepped closer

to me, lifting my mask and kissing me gently. "Are you sure you want to do this?"

I nodded, because the idea still excited me. I was just worried about his career. "This seems like a really weird way to announce you're in a relationship, is all."

"It's perfect. Now peg me, Mouseboy."

I laughed and kissed him hard. My fake dick nudged against his stomach, and I groaned. My hard plastic mask only went halfway down my face, enough to conceal my identity, but not enough that when I pushed him back on the bed, I couldn't take his hard cock in my mouth. I gave it a long stroke, and he groaned. I mean, I could only take a third of it into my mouth, but I stroked my hand up and down the rest, nudging over his piercings.

"Fuck, *Muñeca*, your mouth feels so good. Are you ready?"

"Am I ready to peg you on camera dressed as a mouse from the happiest place on earth?" I shook my head in disbelief. If I'd tried to convince the woman I'd been last year that this was what I'd be doing on a Sunday night, I would have committed myself to an insane asylum, because this was nuts. "You bet your ass I am."

"Going live in three, two..." I lowered my face over his cock. "One," he moaned as I deep-throated his cock down as far as he could go.

I sucked his cock, meeting my lips with my stroking

fist. The thought that there was a live camera here, watching me fuck my boyfriend, was a heady experience. I was in lingerie that made me feel sexy and powerful, the cock strapped to my hips looking particularly impressive.

"*Amorcito,* please. I'm going to come down that delicious little throat."

"Not yet, you aren't. On your hands and knees, Deemon." It was so weird to use his handle name. "Face the mirror, baby. I want to see your face as you come."

"Holy fuck," he breathed, too softly for the audio to pick up, but he scrambled to his hands and knees. He was in front of me, and suddenly, I felt like the most powerful person in the world. Was this how men felt all the time?

Then I caught the reflection of my matte black mouse mask in the mirror. I felt like someone else. I lubed up both his ass and the dildo attached to my harness, sliding my thumb into his ass. I'd gotten all the tips I could from Harrison and Everett, who took turns at being top. I wanted this to be more than a gimmick for Darwin. I wanted him to love it. I wanted this to be something that he enjoyed so much, he'd beg me to do it again.

I slid a finger in, then another, spreading him gently, but the noise he made was one of desperation. "Eyes on me, D. Watch me as I fuck you."

He did as I asked, smirking as he hit the red button on the remote in his hand. The little bullet vibrator against my G-spot buzzed in earnest, making my thighs clench and a moan spill from my lips.

I grinned at him, breathing heavily. "You're such a fucking brat." I pulled back, then slowly pushed my lubed-up fake dick inside him, making him gasp. "Mmm, that's right, baby." My hips butted up to his ass, and I dragged myself back out. His whole body quaked as I pushed back in. *Fuck me.* I hadn't been prepared for how this would make me feel. I choked down my pleasure to stroke a hand down the tensed muscles of his back. "Okay, D?"

"Fuck, yes. More, *Amorcito.* Give me more."

I gripped his hips, trying not to grin. "Watch me work," I moaned, and he lifted his head from the pillow, the look he gave me stopping the air in my lungs. Love and lust poured between us, and more than anything in that moment, I wanted to bring him pleasure.

"Stroke your cock, baby. I want you to paint the bed with your cum."

Then I pushed him further down into the bed, spreading his thighs a little wider since I was short as hell. We'd pushed pillows to support his hips so I had permission to fuck him like I'd always dreamed.

Snapping my hips in a rhythm that I'd like, I held his hips tightly. I looked over my shoulder at the camera and smirked, because I wanted the women, and maybe men, watching this to know how fucking amazing it was. How empowering it was.

Girls, peg your boyfriends because you'll feel like a damn goddess.

Whatever I was doing was driving him hard, because he upped the intensity of my bullet vibe to light speed. I lifted one leg for more leverage and pounded him harder. My abs ached, because this really was a workout.

The sounds coming from both of us were straight-up pornographic. Darwin was cursing in Spanish, lost in the sensations. "*Amorcito*, fuck, I'm going to come." I pulled at his shoulders a little, lifting him up until I could wrap an arm around his waist, putting my hand over his fist wrapped around his dick, as I was buried deep, deep inside him. I wanted to see as he came all over his chest and abs, my hand rubbing his seed all over his stomach.

I pulled back until I slid out of him, and he collapsed onto the bed. Thankfully, he shut off the bullet too.

Standing, I swaggered over to the camera. I smirked down at it as I pressed the red button to end the recording. Then I threw off my mask and shuffled out of the harness so I could crawl into the bed beside my lover. Wrapping him in my arms felt like a weird shift in our dynamic.

"You were such a good boy, D," I murmured in his ear, and he shuddered.

"Don't say those things, *Muñeca,* or I'll be hard again. I'm still trying to wrap my head around how fucking amazing that was."

My grin threatened to crack my face in half. "I love you, Darwin. I've loved you for months."

He kissed me softly. "I know, Blake. I've known for just as long. I fell in love with you that first day—I knew there and then you were the one for me. I still know it, right down in my soul."

There was a thumping knock on the door, and I sighed. Darwin just pulled me tighter into his arms. "The joys of being in a group relationship, baby." He turned toward the door. "Come in."

I wasn't surprised to see all the guys, even Hennie. He'd moved in last month, and he seemed really fucking happy. His parents were less than impressed—and way less accepting than Darwin's mama—but they didn't disown him, and whenever we saw each other, they were polite at least.

It was hard to argue when Hennie seemed so fucking happy, and I knew I'd done that. I made that big man happy. It was an accomplishment I was proud of.

"Holy hell, you guys had 300k viewers during your little live escapade. Which was hot as fuck, by the way. We streamed it to the living roomTV," Harrison said in a rush. "Can I be next?" he teased, and Darwin gave him the finger.

They pushed into the room. We called this the workroom, because the bed was so fucking huge, and it was all set up for Darwin's lives. They all climbed under the covers beside me, spread around the bed.

"Seriously, D, it was the push you needed. You're now the most followed male artist on ClickHeart. Congrats," Everett told him, pride in his voice.

We celebrated each other's successes, and supported each other during the hard times. What we'd created between us was unconventional, sure, but I thought it was perfect.

I laughed, kissing Darwin's cheek. These weren't the accomplishments I thought I would be celebrating with the loves of my life, but then, this wasn't what I thought my normal would look like at all.

But I wouldn't change a thing.

ABOUT THE AUTHOR

Grace McGinty is eclectic. She has worked as a chocolatier, a librarian, a forensic accountant and finally a writer. Like her professional career, the genres she writes are also eclectic. She writes romance, reverse harem romance, fantasy, contemporary young adult and new adult books.

She lives in rural Australia with her crazy family, an entire menagerie of pets, and will one day be crushed by the giant piles of books that litter every room.

Head over to www.gracemcginty.com and join my mailing list for sneak previews into what she is working on and to stay up-to-date with new releases and giveaways!

Turn the page for a sneak peek at Sticks And Stone : An Ice Hockey Romance, available now!

STICKS AND STONE
NOVA

It had taken me three months not to have an anxiety attack every time the front doorbell rang. I'd tried everything: therapy, deep breathing—hell, I'd even changed the doorbell tone, and later took it away altogether. My friends knew not to ring it; they just called when they were out the front. Even the food delivery guys didn't ring anymore.

Maybe I should have tried desensitizing myself to the doorbell instead, because apparently, someone knocking had roughly the same effect anyway.

Breathing in and out, I walked toward the front door.

It hadn't always been this way, obviously. No one is born with an aversion to doorbells. No, my brain—the wonderful and complex piece of equipment that it was

—now associated the doorbell with the worst day of my life.

Even as I walked toward it now, the present was overlaid with memories of three months ago. Opening the door, smiling. Feeling the expression fall from my face as I took in the two policemen in front of me, their faces solemn. Collapsing on the ground, wailing, as they told me that my parents had crashed on the freeway and died instantly. Continuing to wail until one of the officers stood me up, holding me in his arms until the neighbors appeared.

Then Rita, my neighbor and one of my mother's best friends, held me as I cried for the next six hours. Her daughter Chloe—my best friend—arrived hours later and took over, so her mother could properly grieve without trying to hold me together too.

Rita took care of the funeral arrangements. Oscar, her husband, ensured I ate, using that Dad tone that I'd never again hear from my own father to make sure I swallowed every single bite.

Since then, it'd been the worst twelve weeks of my life, but I was moving through life, existing. It was getting easier. Not better, but easier.

Except for the fucking front door.

Sucking deep breaths in through my nose and out through my mouth, I dragged myself back to the present. *Open the door. It's okay. It's probably just Mormons or something.*

My stomach dropped when I saw it wasn't Mormons. I definitely would have preferred that to the sight of my father's lawyer and an unknown woman.

"Miss Stone. It's good to see you." Mr. Lief, my dad's lawyer, didn't say I looked well, because I really didn't. I looked tired, exhausted both physically and emotionally.

"It's nice to see you too, Mr. Lief. I'm surprised, though?"

We'd done the reading of my parents' wills. They'd left me everything, but as their only child, it was pretty standard. I'd sold my father's partnership in his chiropractic firm back to his business partners. My mom had been a customer service clerk at the DMV. They didn't have much except this house and their 401(k)s, so the whole process had been reasonably simple, especially as we didn't have any close extended family. All my grandparents were gone, as well as my Uncle Jerry. My dad had been an only child.

"Not as surprised as I am. May I introduce Mrs. Janette Fischer? She's from Child Protective Services."

Well, now I was super confused.

Mrs. Fischer leaned forward and shook my hand. "Nice to meet you, Miss Stone."

Smiling tightly, I returned the gesture. "Please, call me Nova."

She nodded, the shadow of a smile passing over her face. "May we come in?"

I frowned but nodded, standing to the side as they stepped through the doorway. I was kind of glad I'd just been floating through life like a ghost, because the house was still clean from the last time Chloe had come over and baked me cookies, hovering like a mother hen as she tidied my house for me.

Janette Fischer looked around my childhood home, still filled with my mother's knick-knacks and family pictures, as if my parents were just going to walk back in the door again. It screamed *undealt with grief,* but screw it.

I'd be ready when I was ready.

"I'm not sure what this visit is for, but I promise you, despite the baby face, I'm actually twenty-four," I joked weakly.

Mr. Lief gives me a tight smile. "Sorry for the intrusion, but after Mrs. Fischer reached out, I thought it would be best if I sat in on this meeting. A familiar face, and all that."

Mr. Lief had been my father's golfing buddy since I was ten. If he wasn't here in an official lawyer capacity...

"I'll get straight to the point, Miss Stone."

"Nova," I corrected weakly, because I could already feel my heart beginning to pound too hard in my chest.

"Nova. I'm not sure if you're aware of this, but a child has recently come into the care of the emergency foster system. An infant. His mother, unfortunately, died suddenly of a postpartum brain aneurysm two nights ago. We haven't been able to get hold of her emergency contacts." She swallowed hard. "The child's birth certificate lists your father as his parent, making you the infant's half-sister. From what we can ascertain, you're also his only living relative."

White noise rushed into my ears. Just one long, loud buzz as she continued to speak slowly, but I couldn't hear her over the sound any longer.

My father had a baby. Another child? Jesus, he was like fifty, and he'd been having an affair with someone? Having babies with them?

"Nova?" It was Mr. Lief's voice that snapped me back to the conversation.

"I'm sorry. I had no idea..." I had no idea, what? I had no idea that my dad, who'd just died, was a cheater? I had no idea who this woman was? That I had a baby something?

Mrs. Fischer's face was understanding. "I fully comprehend that this is a shock, Nova. Mr. Lief reacted much the same way when the Department reached out to him."

Mr. Lief was shaking his head, like he was still in shock. *That makes two of us, buddy.*

Mrs. Fischer, with her gray and brown hair, sucked in a deep breath. "The Department always prefers children to go with a family member. The ties of blood and belonging are important. You're the only blood family he has."

My heart felt like it was going to explode in my chest.

"But I want you to know that you aren't obligated to take him in. I understand this is a shock, especially on the heels of your parents' deaths, so take some time to think about it."

"If I don't take him, what happens?" The words tasted like poison on my tongue, but I had to know.

She nodded her head gently. "He's only six weeks old, Nova. He'll stay in foster placement and will probably—most likely—be adopted. Babies have an easier time of it than older children. Although, he does have a congenital heart defect that may make it more difficult—"

"He's sick?" I was going to throw up.

"He has a congenital heart defect, called an atrial septal defect. It's nothing to be worried about just yet, but he may need surgery in the future if it doesn't close on its own."

"And people won't want to adopt him because he's what, bruised fruit?"

Mrs. Fischer shook her head. "I don't think that will be the case at all, but adoption itself is a costly process, and most families can't take on the added burden of a medically unwell child."

I flopped back into the couch cushions, my brain

reeling with the intrusive thoughts that were hammering me from all sides.

My dad had a six-week-old son.

My half-brother had a heart defect and was an orphan.

My parents were dead. Hell, *I* was an orphan.

Was this what my parents had been talking about when they'd crashed their car into a guardrail on the freeway? The police had said they'd lost control, but had it been because my parents were fighting over his affair?

An affair with someone young enough to have a baby?

I'd thought my parents had been happy. They'd loved each other for as long as I could remember, like a true kind of love. They'd often danced together in the kitchen. My dad still used to slap my mother on the ass when she gave him coffee in the mornings.

They'd *loved* each other. But this baby was proof that maybe they hadn't, really. Maybe it had all been a lie.

"I understand this is a lot for you to take in, Nova. You don't have to give me an answer now."

I was mad at my father, which was odd, because fifteen minutes ago, I would've never thought I could picture his face without feeling grief. But now I thought about him and this orphaned baby, and I felt *angry*.

But not angry enough that I would give up a remaining piece of him. That I would set someone else adrift in the world when I could give them a past, a history. Not so mad that I'd forsake the last person in the world who shared my bloodline, let him go to a family who might not be able to pay for his heart problems, or let him sit in foster care because surgeries were too expensive and no one wanted him.

I shook my head at Janette Fischer. "I don't need to think about it. Tell me what I need to do to adopt him."